SUMMER
ON
LILAC ISLAND

ALSO BY LINDSAY MACMILLAN

The Heart of the Deal

Double Decker Dreams

SUMMER

ON

LILAC ISLAND

A Novel

Lindsay MacMillan

HARPER MUSE

Summer on Lilac Island

Published by Harper Muse, an imprint of HarperCollins Focus LLC.

This book is a work of fiction. The characters, incidents, and dialogue are drawn from the author's imagination and are not to be construed as real. Any resemblance to actual events or persons, living or dead, is entirely coincidental.

Any internet addresses (websites, blogs, etc.) in this book are offered as a resource. They are not intended in any way to be or imply an endorsement by HarperCollins Focus LLC, nor does HarperCollins Focus LLC vouch for the content of these sites for the life of this book.

Library of Congress Cataloging-in-Publication Data

Names: MacMillan, Lindsay, author.
Title: Summer on Lilac Island: a novel / Lindsay MacMillan.
Description: [Nashville]: Harper Muse, 2025. | Summary: "A heart-warming escape about mother-daughter relationships, small-town dating, and all that guides us home"—Provided by publisher.
Identifiers: LCCN 2025000220 (print) | LCCN 2025000221 (ebook) | ISBN 9781400348077 (trade paperback) | ISBN 9781400348091 | ISBN 9781400348084 (epub)
Subjects: LCGFT: Novels.
Classification: LCC PS3613.A2758 S86 2025 (print) | LCC PS3613.A2758 (ebook)
LC record available at https://lccn.loc.gov/2025000220
LC ebook record available at https://lccn.loc.gov/2025000221

Printed in the United States of America

25 26 27 28 29 LBC 5 4 3 2 1

For Alyssa and Addison—
Your mother-daughter love shines so brightly.
May you always hold the magic of "Macaroni"
Island close to your hearts.

Mackinac

If there was one thing locals agreed on, it was that Mackinac Island had a split personality.

Winter months found the island a barren tundra. Snow spitting across empty streets, winds careening in from Canada, tangling on the knob of land between Michigan's lower and upper peninsulas. "Closed for the Season" signs dangling from boarded-up windows of Main Street shops. The Grand Hotel dormant, encrusted with icicles.

Along the perimeter, the eight-mile lakeshore path buried by the latest blizzard. The island's iconic horses (no automobiles allowed) wintering on farms downstate, only a handful of mares left to deliver mail and transport workers. Scarcely five hundred residents in total, sequestering behind curtains, quilts, and coffee mugs. Venturing outside only to shovel driveways, haul groceries home on snowmobiles, or traipse to the Mustang Lounge, the island's only year-round bar, for oatmeal stouts and human contact.

But summer was a different story, had a different narrator altogether.

Unadulterated views of the Great Lakes, thawed and tamed and Caribbean blue. Sailboats bobbing happily on the harbor to the beat of an old acoustic hit, the kind of tune that finds revival each generation. Fresh paint gleaming from gingerbread trims of cozy Victorian abodes. Horses clogging the streets with boisterous traffic jams. Ferry boats depositing up to fifteen thousand visitors each day.

Long queues for freshly made fudge, carriage tours, and bicycle rentals. Tourists mispronouncing the island's name. Other tourists loudly correcting them. "The *c* is silent, didn't you know? Mackinac Island is pronounced like Mackinaw City across the bay—the French and English versions of the Native American name Mitchimakinak, meaning 'Great Turtle,' for the island's shape."

More history (or some loose descendant of it) atop the hill at Fort Holmes, peppered with reenactment actors. The Grand Hotel's preppy guests slurping down the sunset from the nation's longest front porch. Children walloping croquet mallets on the hotel's flawless lawns. Seasonal workers passing joints around an illegal beach bonfire, enraging locals once more, twice more. Off the coast, the Mackinac Bridge connecting Michigan's lower and upper peninsulas, draping over the horizon like an heirloom necklace.

The high season was when Mackinac Island came alive. Shimmering and showing off, shrugging off its loner status like an unruly illusionist, exhausting herself with her own excess. The island reeled people in, hooking them with her old-world charm, only to release all but the heartiest hearts in November, when Mackinac again retreated into her shell, hunkering down for the off-season.

Yes, in a place like this, summer and winter were as different as night and day, as oil and water. Or in the case of the Jenkins family, as far apart as mother and daughter.

Chapter 1

Gigi

Georgiana Jenkins, or Gigi as everyone but her mother and grandmother called her, had managed to avoid Mackinac Island for ten consecutive summers.

She was not so fortunate for the eleventh. Here she was, seated atop the upper deck of a Shepler's ferry, skirting back across the Straits.

Fresh water spritzed her face and cast a film over her eyes. Gigi found herself missing the harrowing snowmobile rides across the ice bridge during her winter trips when the lake froze over. The five-mile path was marked by a line of Christmas trees dug into the ice to guide travelers and keep them from plummeting to their death. Then at least there was some danger to distract from the dullness.

She hadn't yet managed to cleanse herself of enough daughterly guilt to boycott coming back for Christmas. That level of liberation was something she aspired to. Perhaps after this summer was over she would have overdosed on the island enough to strengthen her resolve to decline all future visits. Not that she had exactly been invited this time—it was a bit of the reverse, technically speaking—but the principle held.

On her lap, her journal was open. The pages were largely blank, with a two-year gap from when she'd last flung words down, at that time venting about how everyone in LA spent more on skincare than she could afford on rent. This was before she had tried her first microcurrent sculpt facial and promptly become addicted herself, thus blowing through her meager paychecks and winding up destitute, with no choice but to move back in with her mother.

There may have been some contributing factors that led to her current predicament beyond the facials. The inconsistency of the gig economy, the egregious cost of rent, the criminally high tax rate. Summer back on Mackinac Island would be a time to reset, to take a breather and figure out where to go from here. In no way was it a permanent return. Gigi would never settle for such a dull, insular life. Not like her mother had.

She was writing in the journal again at the recommendation of her therapist, Renata. Renata wasn't technically a therapist (Gigi couldn't afford anyone with real qualifications), but she'd completed a course on energy healing so Gigi figured she was close enough.

She usually preferred to treat her emotions like she treated her socks—stashing them messily into a drawer and telling herself she would fold them later.

But she had seen Renata several times in LA, not because of her tense relationship with her mother and sister, nor any unresolved trauma caused by her absentee father. No, far more pressing was the problem of Gigi's crash-and-burn romances that had been trailing her like a cloud of bad karma. She'd hoped therapy might be a quick fix, a way to have someone else validate that her exes were the problem, not her. It hadn't turned out to be quite so affirming.

Gigi was now making a list of her exes, part of the homework. Upon completion, she counted the names by twos, then threes. The total came to thirty-four. Gigi had thirty-four ex-boyfriends. Thirty-five if she included Benjamin Hall, the rascally towhead who'd been Gigi's first high school boyfriend before he swiftly exchanged her for Lillian Tong. Gigi did not, in fact, include Benjamin. It seemed like a suitable, if petty, form of vengeance for a teenage snub, and the list was already too long.

Eyeing the roster, she looked for other exes to cross out.

Her handwriting was sloshy, thanks to the jostling ferry returning her to her horse-and-buggy hometown. Everyone said Mackinac Island was a step back in time. Gigi preferred moving forward, not backward, and tensed up as the shoreline sharpened into view.

She'd hoped the gusty air might settle her stomach, which was coiling terribly, whether due to the rocking waves or the prospect of spending an entire summer in a place she'd thought she'd escaped, she couldn't be sure.

Even the late-middle-aged man seated next to her seemed to notice her discomfort. "You all right there?" he asked Gigi in a thick Scottish accent, offering up a crinkled paper bag. It reeked of bananas and peanut butter.

Gigi declined but changed her mind moments later when necessity struck. Snatching the bag, she ejected the iceberg lettuce salad she'd purchased at the dinky airport in Alpena. She managed to avoid splattering her boho outfit. Her journal was not so kindly spared.

This, too, the Scotsman seemed to notice. Gigi got the sense he was trying to read what she'd written. She clamped the journal shut.

"Sorry," the man said. "Didn't mean to snoop." There was a youthful bounce about him despite the fact that he was about Gigi's mother's age. "What were you working on, if you don't mind my asking?"

Gigi stared him down. His cornflower-blue eyes were bright, the whites remarkably clear. "Nothing."

"'Nothing' is always the best content," the man said confidently. "Most of my books have started from scribbling about 'nothing.'"

"You're a writer?" Gigi asked. It checked out. The argyle sweater vest, the chaotic tufts of white hair jutting out from under a lopsided bowler hat, the loafers tapping on the ferry floorboards, as if to some bagpipe beat. Gigi had pegged him as a professor type, but author fit the bill.

"We're all writers, aren't we?" A cheeky smile revealed tilted, teastained teeth. "But that's right, I've managed to make a living from inventing stories." He gave a booming laugh.

In spite of herself, Gigi was liking the man and the way he seemed to be gaming the system of life.

No one had ever mistaken her for an author before. It was quite flattering. She had the creativity for it, no doubt, but the discipline was another beast. As evidenced by her inventory of failed relationships, she was as good at starting things as she was bad at finishing them.

"I've done an audit of all my ex-boyfriends," Gigi said. She tended to be a fairly honest person, not motivated by morality so much as the fact that the truth was the surest way to shock people. "I'm going back through past relationships to look for patterns."

This part of the assignment had taken so long that Gigi was not inclined to dive into the second and more intensive portion: analyzing them.

Pattern = duds, she'd scrawled on the bottom of the page, circling the phrase a few times, as if after deep cogitation she'd produced a most profound insight.

The Scotsman seemed to find this all highly amusing, a reaction Gigi enjoyed. She couldn't stand people who took life too seriously.

"Quite prolific you've been," he chuckled.

"It's not as scandalous as it sounds," Gigi said. "I had my first real boyfriend at eighteen. Right when I fled the island."

The Scotsman's bushy eyebrows raised quizzically, but Gigi swept past the inquiry. "I'm twenty-nine now," she carried on. "So over eleven years, I've had an average of three point four boyfriends per year. Hardly an outlandish figure."

"Three point four boyfriends per year," the Scotsman repeated, as if tucking away the nugget of dialogue for a future book. Gigi didn't mind that he might plagiarize her. The prospect of seeing her cleverness in print was exhilarating.

"Want to know what I've learned about love?" Gigi asked, hoping he might be inspired twice over. She told him about how since leaving Mackinac, she'd lived in New York, Miami, Austin, Phoenix, New Orleans, Seattle, and most recently, Los Angeles. "But men are the same everywhere," she fumed with a blubbery sigh. "They all make you feel like a crazy person for expecting them to put in an ounce of effort."

The Scotsman clucked sympathetically, though he didn't appear to find her analysis as impressive as Gigi had hoped.

"There's nothing wrong with having high standards," the Scotsman said. "But if I could offer a bit of fatherly advice . . ."

Gigi flinched involuntarily at the word *fatherly*.

"Don't hold someone else to a standard you wouldn't hold yourself to," he continued. "Or you just might end up alone, with no one to miss you when you vanish across the ocean. Like this old gadgie here." He was smiling, but there was an undertone of sadness. Regret, even.

Gigi checked his left hand. There were sunspots, moles, and wispy white hairs, but no wedding ring. She wondered about his own roster of relationships and where things may have gone wrong. Ordinarily she wouldn't hold back from prying, but she'd become too fond of him to put him on the spot, so she led in with a softer opener. "What're you doing on the island?"

He informed her that he was here to gain inspiration for his next book, which he hadn't started writing yet, thanks to an extended episode of writer's block. When Gigi inquired why he didn't post up on a Scottish island instead, he told her he preferred the novelty of places he'd never been and people he'd never met. Gigi empathized greatly.

"And when I heard there was an island in America with no cars allowed—only horses, buggies, and bicycles—I knew that was my spot," the Scotsman went on. "What a romantic quirk for a story!"

"It's less romantic in real life," Gigi cautioned. "Trust me."

"Have you been before?" he asked.

"I grew up here," Gigi said. "Now I'm back spending the summer with my mom." She tried to make it sound like she was being a solicitous daughter rather than using her mother for free housing and laundry.

Gigi had nearly as many ex-jobs as ex-boyfriends. Most recently she'd quit her gig as a cycling instructor out in LA. She delighted in yelling at people to work harder but despised having to wake up early to do it. Upon assigning her all the 6:00 a.m. classes, her manager told Gigi it was an opportunity to demonstrate her commitment. As if Gigi had any of that to a company that didn't even provide health insurance.

Returning to Mackinac Island had been a last resort, but when her mother offered up free rent for the summer—with the flight and ferry included—she hadn't exactly been in a position to refuse. Gigi's credit card was declined when she'd made a late-night pizza order last week, and she was living off the last of the cash her sister had sent for her birthday (a nice wad, Gigi must admit, though that was only fair, given the whole incident of Rebecca choosing her college roommate as her maid of honor over her own sister).

"Any guidance for scrounging up stories on the island?" the Scotsman asked as the ferry turned into the dock. "I write fiction, but it's often inspired by real people. They're the oddest characters of all, aren't they?"

Gigi suspected that she herself starred in the island's most interesting tales but didn't volunteer that information. There were some things she'd prefer not to dig up, no matter how assuredly they would shock.

"You'll want to look into the witch trials of the 1800s," she told him. "Women were drowned in a lagoon." She grimaced. "It's still there, between Mission Point and downtown."

"Is it haunted?" he asked excitedly.

"Allegedly, but it's a tourist trap. The real stories are with Deirdre Moore, president of the euchre club and rumor mill," Gigi said. "You can find her and the other ladies at the Lucky Bean most mornings. And the tennis courts have been taken over by the pickleballers; they're worth checking out. My grandmother plays in a league; it's all nice and petty."

Gigi's smile twitched at the thought of seventy-seven-year-old

Nonni slamming the yellow pickleball at her opponents' faces, letting out a primal roar when she won, refusing to make eye contact with her opponents when she lost.

"Loiter at Doud's too, right on Main Street," Gigi went on. "America's oldest family-owned grocery store. Everyone circles through. You'll get the scoop on the latest tension between the islanders and fudgies."

"Fudgies?" The Scotsman was eagerly scribbling notes on the parchment-like pages of a thick leatherbound notebook.

"It's what locals call the tourists and seasonal residents," Gigi explained. "Because they buy so much of Mackinac's famous fudge. There's plenty of summer drama with fudgies partying and disrupting the peace. But the real villain is the mayor, Camille Welsh. Stuck in the Dark Ages with an ego that stretches longer than the Mackinac Bridge."

"Excellent." Clyde appeared elated to have such promising leads. "If there's ever anything I can do for you, do give a ring to the Grand Hotel and ask for Clyde MacDougal."

"You're staying at the Grand Hotel?" The luxurious hotel was the island's most renowned landmark and very expensive. Her new acquaintance must be an unusually successful author. Gigi found herself filled with more admiration than envy, which was not particularly like her.

"Just for the summer," Clyde said. "As I conduct my research." He let out another titter, seemingly pleased that "research" entailed vacationing at a posh island resort and ingratiating himself in small-town gossip.

"One more question," he said. "You wouldn't happen to know of any eligible women around my age, would you? Someone I might take out to dinner . . . purely for literary purposes, of course." His mouth folded bashfully and his cheeks took on a ruddy hue.

Gigi thought about volunteering her mother, but that would be pointless. Eloise Jenkins didn't date. "Everyone is pretty much coupled up," Gigi said. "The locals, at least. You could find a fudgie, but I can't recommend them in good conscience."

"I see." Clyde's expression sank but sprang back quickly. His broad nose sniffed. "What's that smell?"

Gigi, too, caught a whiff of Mackinac Island's signature scent. "The horses," she said. "Twenty-first-century transportation at its finest."

She expected Clyde to plug his nose as the other tourists on the ferry were doing. Instead, he broke into a boyish grin. "How charming." He inhaled deeply as if to commit the aroma to memory so he might accurately reproduce it on the page.

Gigi grimaced. "Charming indeed," she deadpanned as the familiar manure scent welcomed her home. Or at least to the place that had once been home and now felt the furthest thing from it.

Chapter 2

Eloise

Do you think I'm setting myself up for failure?" Eloise said earlier that day as she and Deirdre took their usual 7:00 a.m. walk along M-185, the lakeshore road circling the island.

It was the nation's only highway prohibiting automobiles—a ban that began in 1898 when townspeople complained that the sounds from the engines were disturbing their horses. Only in a place like Mackinac would that kind of law stick all these years.

The sun was already up, soft morning rays kneading knots out of the water like a set of supple hands.

"Having Georgiana and me in the same house all summer, I mean," Eloise clarified.

It had sounded fine in the abstract. Very nice even, the idea of her drifter daughter home again. How many times over the past decade had Eloise wished that Georgiana might return to the island for more than a fleeting visit? But as the arrival approached, Eloise had become increasingly tense. Sweat formed now on the rim of her visor.

"It'll be terrific," Deirdre assured. "Nothing like some quality mother-daughter bonding time."

"Says the woman with two sons," Eloise muttered, making Deirdre scowl. "Georgiana and I could still bond from separate houses. Lord knows that's been the secret to keeping the peace with my own mother."

Since the passing of Eloise's father seven years ago, Eloise had offered for her mother, Alice, to move in with her. She lived just down the road, after all. But her mother refused, which was a blessing for them both. Alice insisted on remaining in the cabin Eloise's father had built with his own two hands, or so the legend went. Alice continued brewing coffee the way he liked it every morning—very black, very strong—pouring it in his favorite Detroit Lions mug, the colors long faded, then drinking it herself, though she preferred tea.

"It'll be an adventure," Deirdre said, pumping her arms vigorously, clutching two-pound dumbbells as weapons to defend against osteoporosis, the latest menopausal calamity coming their way. "Adventures keep the mind young, ward off dementia. Fred says so."

Fred was Deirdre's husband and the island's general practitioner, meaning Deirdre was too versed on medical ailments. Eloise usually took her friend's warnings with a grain of salt, but the bone density lecture had scared her enough that she had started to increase her milk intake and switch to decaf a few days a week. No dumbbells, though. Eloise got enough weight-bearing exercise from the tasks associated with keeping up a house. Lugging salt bags to the water softener. Hauling groceries, rearranging furniture, changing lightbulbs, then doing those tasks again for her mother. Deirdre was always offering up Fred, as if he were a carton of eggs or a library book—something useful to borrow—but Eloise's pride was a hard wall to fell. She managed on her own, and until recently she'd had Rebecca helping her.

"It's perfect timing that Georgiana is coming home," Deirdre went on. "You've been in a slump since Rebecca's betrayal. Understandably, of course."

Eloise jutted out her pointy chin, becoming one with the cliffside. "I'm not in a slump, and it wasn't a betrayal," she said, though it did feel that way. "Rebecca got married and moved a couple hours away. It's the circle of life."

They passed beneath Arch Rock, the island's most famous sandstone formation, perched up on the bluffs. The story went that when the Ottawa tribe lived here, their Master of Life was angered by the actions of one of the chiefs and in retaliation sent a blazing red sun toward the island. It burned a hole in the rock, forming an arch. Eloise didn't believe in those sorts of myths, but she liked their familiarity nonetheless, their timeworn texture.

Lake Huron stretched before them. No land in sight on the horizon, just the endless lull of the lake. Even after living here her whole life, Eloise sometimes still forgot it wasn't an ocean.

"Rebecca promised she'd always stay on the island, though," Deirdre reminded, as if Eloise might have forgotten. As if she hadn't cradled Rebecca's words, rocked them against her chest as proof that her family hadn't shattered just because her husband had left and her father had died and Georgiana had gone flitting about the country.

"That was before she met Tom," Eloise said. "He's doing well at his financial firm in Traverse City. It makes more sense for them to live there. It's nothing personal." Though it did feel personal, the abrupt uprooting of the daughter she'd thought would always stay close.

"Nothing personal," Deirdre repeated, huffing. "That's what Kimberly said when she told me I had to start calling before coming over to see my own grandsons." She put on a voice, something high and shrill, to imitate her daughter-in-law. "'It's nothing personal—we just like to be able to plan our family time around your visits,'" Deirdre quoted. "As if *I'm* not family. As if *I'm* somehow an intruder. It's an abomination, that's what." She punched her weights, punctuating the rant.

Deirdre was petite, not much above five feet tall, her edges soft and fleshy. But what she lacked in physical stature she made up for in presence. No one walked away from an encounter with Deirdre Moore thinking her a small woman.

"At least you *have* grandchildren," Eloise said. "Rebecca and Tom just got a dog, did I tell you? This ugly little thing, looks like a giant rat. Rebecca tried to tell me it was my 'grand-dog-ter.' Can you believe it?"

"After all we've done for our children," Deirdre fumed. "I knew Mikey was a lost cause, down in Grand Rapids, caught up in that crowd of *bachelors*." She said it as if she were talking about drug dealers.

"But I didn't expect this from Joshua. Kimberly corrupted him, getting them to move to the north side of the island, three whole miles from me."

"Very unfair," Eloise said, thinking how she would kill to have Rebecca so close.

The two lanes of M-185 became Main Street near Mission Point Resort. Formerly Mackinac College, it was now a smaller, more affordable alternative to the Grand Hotel. White Adirondack chairs dotted the lakeside lawn. Guests were breakfasting at the farm-to-ferry restaurant. Eloise rarely went out to eat—it was a waste of money—but something about seeing the diners this morning made her crave a change of pace. She was growing tired of her practiced routine, growing lonely at her kitchen table set for one.

Georgiana's presence this summer would certainly shake things up, and Eloise was looking forward to it on the whole.

Bicycles whizzed by. It was Mayor Welsh and her overly competitive posse. "Morning, girls!" Camille called out. "I would stop and talk, but we're training for our charity ride. One hundred miles!"

"I had no idea she was training for something," Deirdre said to Eloise once the group had passed, Pastor Kevin bringing up the rear. It was all the mayor had been talking about for months.

"First I've heard of it," Eloise replied dryly. "Five miles, did she say?"

Farther down, the heart of town unfurled slowly with quaint bed-and-breakfasts, lakeside condos, and the public marina at Haldimand Bay. Across the street, Marquette Park sprawled at the base of Fort Mackinac, with Doud's Market on the corner, the unofficial gateway into the Main Street hubbub. Old Mr. Doud was directing delivery boys on how to stack milk crates.

"Hi there, Mr. Doud," Eloise called out. He waved back.

"Hilarious, isn't it?" Deirdre commented after they passed. "How we qualify for the senior discount at his store and we're still calling him Mr. Doud."

"I prefer it," Eloise said. "Makes me feel like adults are in control."
They snickered.

The first ferry of the day was dumping tourists into scraps of early-morning scenes. Dockhands setting up for the day. Fudge shop workers stirring silky batches, treacly scents seeping into the streets. Horses getting hitched to buggies, hooves scraping the pavement.

Early morning was the only time of day that Eloise tolerated coming downtown in the summer months.

"There's Georgiana's competition," Deirdre hissed. She pointed across the street to the Chippewa Hotel. The popular Pink Pony restaurant, owned by the Tongs, was located inside, with the gift shop next door. "You would think Lillian might take some time before diving back into dating, but her sights seem set on Dr. Kentwood."

Lillian was the Tongs' only child, Georgiana's age. She was beautiful and brilliant, universally liked. "Lillian isn't competition," Eloise said. "This isn't middle school."

"Exactly. The stakes are higher now," Deirdre said. "They're not just vying for dates to school dances anymore. They're contending for a husband. Hold these, will you?" Deirdre passed her dumbbells to Eloise. "My arms are giving out on me. My whole body is, really. If it weren't for the marriage plot we're hatching, I'd need Fred to prescribe some antidepressants."

Eloise's conscience prickled. "Can we not call it that?" she asked. "It's not really a plot."

Deirdre's honeycomb eyes were bright beneath a thick coat of mascara. Deirdre always applied a full face of makeup before leaving the house, no exceptions. It had long been a marvel to Eloise, a habit she'd aspired to imitate since they were teenagers. Upon turning fifty, she'd finally relinquished the goal, sticking to her trusty sunscreen and Chapstick routine, making peace with the fact that she'd never be a beauty icon. There was a great relief to it, surrendering to the idea of what might be, what could be. And a sadness too, collecting like sediment.

"You're right, *plot* is too boring a word, isn't it?" Deirdre said. "This isn't a book club. A ploy, shall we call it? A ruse? A machination?"

Eloise didn't like where this was going. The horror, the disgust that would be on Georgiana's face if she heard them now. She'd cancel her plans to stay for the summer and go join her father on his latest motorcycle trip instead. "None of that," Eloise said. "It's an introduction, that's all."

"Scheme!" Deirdre exclaimed. "A suitor scheme. Yes, that's it. The alliteration rolls off the tongue. I have to say, if Dr. Kentwood were a few years older, I'd keep him for myself. I have Fred, of course," she added dutifully. "You know men like older women now. I read about it in one of the magazines in the checkout aisle. I wasn't trying to read that tabloid trash; it's just that the fudgies were clogging up Doud's, so I had to keep myself occupied in line. Dr. Kentwood has the most divine shoulders, by the way. So broad, so brown. I get glimpses of him through the guesthouse window. Only from the waist up, nothing scandalous." She sounded disappointed. "I'm not spying—he just doesn't close the blinds."

Deirdre and Fred were housing Dr. Kentwood at their guesthouse, given its proximity to the medical clinic.

"You act like I don't know your ways," Eloise said. "We've been best friends for half a century." Eloise and Deirdre were both born and raised on the island. Their fathers were drinking buddies, their mothers euchre partners (euchre was a wilder, simpler version of bridge and very popular on Mackinac). "You intentionally broke the blinds before he moved in."

Deirdre colored. "I didn't break them. I just didn't have Fred fix them. There's a difference. So when does Georgiana get in? I'll assemble the troops to greet her at the ferry."

"Sometime tomorrow," Eloise said. "I asked for her flight itinerary but she hasn't sent it yet. She knows how nervous I get when she's flying. And all the way from California."

The only time she herself had stepped onto a plane was for her honeymoon in the Florida Keys. It was all the turbulence she'd needed for a lifetime. Never had she prayed so fiercely, just about crushing the bones in Gus's hands with her grip.

"Planes are safer than cars, though," Deirdre said. "I'm a wreck when Joshua and Kimberly drive down to see her parents in Grosse Pointe. Especially with the twins now. It's a relief not to have to deal with lunatic drivers here. Though we do have that infestation of motorized scooters, thanks to the fudgies. The mayor's not enforcing the law; it's an accident waiting to happen. Someone's going to die one of these days." She sounded as eager as she did irate.

"I have a bad feeling Georgiana will get her hands on one of those scooters," Eloise said. "Given how she inherited Gus's adrenaline junkie genes."

"You've got some rebel in you too," Deirdre said. "Remember when you played hooky senior year to go jet-skiing with Gus?"

"Yes, and I turned myself in the next day and begged for detention." Eloise recalled the perplexed look on Principal Anderson's face when she'd told him why she deserved to be punished. "I've never been good at breaking the rules."

They slipped off Main and headed up to Market Street. City Hall, the police department, and the courthouse were all within a stone's throw. The island had one police car, two fire trucks, and an ambulance as the only exceptions to the "no motor vehicles" law. The medical center and Deirdre's house were on Market Street too, along with the Lucky Bean, where Eloise and Deirdre always ended their walks. Their salted caramel lattes were Eloise's one vice—not including Gus, that is.

"Well, you're breaking the rules now," Deirdre said. "It's heresy to set up your child on a blind date. Remember how angry you were when Alice tried to fix you up with that visiting pastor? The conniver doesn't fall far from the tree."

"That was different," Eloise said. "I'm not interested in dating. My mother knows that. Georgiana is interested; she just has abysmal taste. This intervention is for her own good."

"Of course it is," Deirdre agreed. "We don't want her running off to Australia with some vegan yogi astrologist, do we?"

Eloise winced. Deirdre's scenario didn't seem too far-fetched. "This plan might push Georgiana further away from me," Eloise said. "But I can't sit by and watch the train wreck that has become her life."

Eloise felt very firmly that it was her motherly duty to help Georgiana get her life back on track. Georgiana was clearly burned out from the string of shoddy jobs. For all her flaws, her work ethic was deceptively strong. She'd been supporting herself since she was eighteen. Gus told Eloise he chipped in here or there, but Eloise believed her daughter's reports that the help had been minimal.

What Georgiana needed was to rest and reset. That was why Eloise had offered to let her stay rent-free for the summer. Give her a break from work, a breather from the toxic influences of urban life. Remind her that there were other ways to live than scrounging by in danger-ous, overpopulated cities.

Eloise had been surprised when Georgiana agreed to the offer. That, more than anything, was how Eloise knew how bad things must have been for her daughter. Georgiana had no tolerance for Mackinac Island. The feeling had been so strong that Georgiana had run away at eighteen and never looked back. The Great Scandal of Mackinac Island. Though Eloise wondered if Georgiana had been run-ning away from Eloise or the island . . . Probably some combination of the two.

Either way, coming home for the summer felt like a cry for help, and therefore Eloise felt justified to intervene. Part of that intervention was showing Georgiana that other types of men existed beyond the slick-talking, moral-bereft, commitment-phobic boys whom big cities wrongly labeled men. Not that Eloise really knew much about Geor-giana's past relationships, if they could even be called that. Georgiana offered only scraps when Eloise asked.

Their less-than-close relationship wasn't for lack of effort on Eloise's part. She called every Sunday, but it nearly always went to voicemail—

except that Georgiana didn't believe in voicemails ("Why wouldn't people just text?"), so the line promptly disconnected and Eloise had to make do with a lone thumbs-up or smiley face emoji when she texted to check in. Eloise detested emojis and was looking forward to a summer free of them. A summer when, for the first time in a decade, she would get to spend quality time with her daughter.

Assuming Georgiana didn't bolt off the island the moment she found out about the matchmaking.

"The suitor scheme will be good for us too," Deirdre said, plucking Eloise from her inner world. "Splash a bit of vicarious romance into our lives."

It was true enough but made Eloise feel old and shriveled. Gus hadn't visited in two years, though he said he was planning to come for a while this summer. Eloise knew she shouldn't still want the man who left her, but she did. They had history together; they had children together. And besides, it wasn't like she was going to meet anyone else on the island. Mackinac kept her safe that way. Though there were some days that the safety felt a little stifling. Eloise had to concede that Georgiana had a point with that critique, not that she would admit it to her daughter.

"Now believe me when I say I'm not rooting for Georgiana to murder you for what you're about to do," Deirdre went on. "But if she does, we just might get one of those true crime shows to come here. The island is such an idyllic setting for the cameras."

Eloise opened the coffee shop door, mocha aromas wafting out. She tried to keep some humor as her nerves churned. "Try to get my corpse a cameo, won't you?"

Chapter 3

Gigi

Though it was mostly desperation that had brought Gigi back, it wasn't *all* desperation.

A few ounces of nostalgia were sprinkled in there too. On some deep, dusty level, Gigi had missed the island. The slower pace of life, the lack of responsibility, the powdery lakeside beaches. She hadn't had a full Mackinac Island summer since high school. Three months here during the prime high season wouldn't be so bad. She could press pause on real life, catch her breath, and then figure out where to go from here.

It might be tolerable enough if she didn't have to share a roof with her mother. She had no idea how she was going to survive cohabitating after so many years of independence.

Still, she was glad to be off the ferry and found herself imbibing the island with fresh eyes, sipping it like a summer shandy.

Nudging up against the fishing-boat-filled docks, Main Street was in top form. A flurry of horses and cyclists and shoppers who rifled through artsy tote bags, pine-scented candles, and pastel crewnecks at quirky boutiques. The fudge shops had lines out the door, as did Sadie's Ice Cream Parlor and Great Turtle Brewery. Gigi felt a prick of respect for how the island spruced itself up to rake in enough money to keep the economy running, or at least shuffling, in the long off-season. And the crowds made it easy to blend in. The last thing she wanted was to be ambushed by Deirdre or one of her old teachers.

Hopefully her new hairstyle—bleached, in a shag—would serve as an adequate disguise.

Lugging her oversized suitcase behind her on the paved but heavily potholed roads, she ascended the steep hill toward Fort Holmes, a former military outpost dating back to the Revolutionary War. Panting before she reached the top, Gigi continued inland, oak and sassafras trees thickening. She welcomed the peace and quiet after a full day of travel, though the *clop, clop, clop* of hooves disturbed her tranquility. Horse-drawn carriage tours squeezed Gigi off the narrow path until she was forced to haul her suitcase through scraggly weeds and wildflowers.

Gigi felt like a bad cliché from one of those cheesy rom-com movies she couldn't stand. The wayward daughter returning home with no money, no partner, no prospects. This would be the opening scene where the ruggedly handsome carriage driver lost control of his horses and hit her, then professed his undying love within the week—perhaps even the day, depending on how quickly he was overcome by her urban allure.

But, thankfully, no flannel-shirted lumberjack appeared. She was alone, and things became even more secluded as she approached Harrisonville, the tiny village where the island's year-round residents lived. Life up here was less performance, more practicality. A uniform row of two-story homes with pitched roofs and economical siding. Their plain appearance insulated them from tourists.

The sight triggered that old, awful sensation of being ordinary. It was Gigi's greatest fear, really. Everyone assumed her greatest fear was probably being abandoned, given her dad left when she was young. But Gigi understood why he had to go. He was terrified of the same thing she was: to live a mediocre, predictable, forgettable life.

And so her dad had gotten off the island before it caged him forever. He hadn't abandoned them, not really. He'd wanted Eloise and the girls to come with him, but Eloise had refused in her typical risk-averse, self-sabotaging way. So Gigi had grown up with both a mother and a hometown she could hardly look at without seeing the reasons she didn't have a dad to ride bikes with or take to the father-daughter dance down in the school gym.

Gigi had ultimately made her own escape and tried very hard to live a big life, an interesting life. She'd avoided getting stuck on the island and avoided going to college, where she would be told what to think. She'd also avoided working a corporate job that would force her to conform.

She'd lived in many different places and held many different jobs and gotten in with many types of friends. She'd successfully carved an uncommon path for herself. Yet that life, too, proved unfulfilling. Like she was just another face trying too hard to be seen in the city crowd.

Gigi had a nagging fear that the problem might not be where she lived or what she did for work. It might not have to do so much with her boyfriends or her bosses or her friends. The problem might be herself, that she was an inherently unimportant person, the kind of person who makes a splash wherever they are but never leaves a lasting impact.

Gigi pushed the thought aside, already hating how Mackinac brought up so much from her past. How the quiet of the island magnified the voices in her head.

Eloise's half acre came into view. Aloud, Gigi referred to her as "Mother." There was a certain defiance in the formality. It was a reminder that they were both adults and that Eloise did not have the power to micromanage her anymore.

Gigi's trust fund friends back in New York would refer to Eloise's abode as a cottage, but when it was a year-round residence, it was simply called a house. Thistle Dew was its name. Thistle Castle was what Gigi had called it growing up, trying to give it some glitz in name, if not appearance.

Perched up on a rise with a view out over the lake, the house was buttermilk yellow with a peach-colored door. It had a double gable roof, a deep front porch, and carefully pruned landscaping—hedges hearty enough to survive the thrashing winters, plus seasonal flowers. The island's iconic lilacs were nearing their early-summer bloom.

An American flag fluttered in the afternoon breeze. Gigi nearly expected to see it at half-mast, so in mourning was Eloise about Rebecca's move. But the flag was raised to its full height, as was Eloise as she watered hanging baskets of geraniums that brought pops of pink to the porch.

Eloise had a tall, elegant frame that she tended to hide in shapeless empire-waisted dresses, always with a cardigan over. A proud resister of youth-glorification trends, she was aging naturally. Her strawberry-blonde hair was streaked with silver, and crow's-feet continued to deepen around her upturned seafoam-green eyes.

Growing up, Gigi had often been told she was the spitting image of her mother. She'd hated the comparisons at the time but found herself missing them over the years now that they rarely came. Eloise might be puritanical, but she was a great beauty by any standard.

It was good to see how well Eloise looked. Gigi took it as validation that she had been right not to spend much time worrying about her or replying to all those missed calls. She didn't want to be one of those overly solicitous daughters who prioritized her mother above herself. That was Rebecca's place. Rebecca, the younger sister who had always assumed the role of the older sister because she just couldn't help herself. Not that Gigi minded—it let her off the hook. Though now that Rebecca had moved off the island, Gigi felt the sensation of a tilted seesaw, as if the balance had shifted and Gigi was going to be holding more than she wanted.

"Hello, Mother." Gigi announced herself, trekking up the gravel driveway.

Eloise whipped her head around, tossing aside the watering can. "Georgiana!" she shrieked. "What have you done to your hair?"

"Lovely to see you too." It was going to be a long summer, Gigi thought as she lugged her suitcase up the creaky porch stairs. She gave Eloise a quick hug.

Eloise was all out of sorts just as Gigi had anticipated. "You told me you weren't arriving until tomorrow."

"You know I'm no good at communication." It was one of the narratives Eloise liked to reinforce about Gigi. Though the real reason she hadn't told Eloise the correct day was to ensure Eloise wouldn't assemble a welcome committee. Gigi detested welcome committees.

"I haven't gotten anything ready for you yet," Eloise said. Scurrying inside through the side door (the front door was reserved strictly for guests), Eloise set to work.

But it seemed like everything was already prepared. Up in the second-story loft, which Gigi used to share with Rebecca, her twin bed was freshly made up, daisy bedspread pulled taut. Tammy the Turtle, her oldest Beanie Baby, more gray than green these days, sat atop the plumped pillows. Fresh towels and toiletries filled the bathroom. Downstairs in the kitchen, Eloise's renowned homemade peanut brittle cooled on the stove.

"It hasn't set long enough," Eloise chided as Gigi broke off a large chunk of the brittle.

"Tastes amazing." Mouth full, Gigi handed a piece to Eloise, who nibbled cautiously.

Gigi felt a tender twinge as she pictured Eloise running around the house to make things special for her return. Perhaps they'd get along better than expected.

"I suppose it's not the worst thing that you've come today," Eloise said with similar optimism. "You'll have more time to get ready for Thursday."

"What's Thursday?" Gigi broke off another piece of brittle and took a seat at the circular kitchen table. It was adorned with a crochet tablecloth and matching doilies, handmade by Eloise, the expert crafter. Arched bay windows gave a view down to the lake. Eloise's

Ragdoll cat, named Pluto for how he always seemed worlds away, slinked into the kitchen and straight out again, maintaining his typical aloofness.

"I've secured you a date with the island's new doctor," Eloise said.

Gigi didn't react right away. Perhaps it was the jet lag making her head fuzzy, but she'd thought Eloise had said the phrase *secured you a date*. Surely she'd misheard.

"What's that?" Gigi said, trying to keep her voice even, trying to give Eloise the benefit of the doubt that the situation was not, in fact, what it appeared.

"Dr. Kentwood is supporting Dr. Moore at the clinic this summer, what with the influx of fudgies and all their antics." Eloise paused to frown but resumed her prior perkiness as she dove into Dr. Kentwood's descriptors. "Early thirties, devilishly handsome, and single as a slice of Kraft cheese. Now, he's not an islander," she went on, like this was one strike against him, "but he's of wholesome Midwestern stock, rest assured."

Gigi immediately rescinded any hopes of a harmonious summer. She felt even more infuriated with herself than with Eloise. She should have known there was no such thing as free rent.

"What a relief," Gigi deadpanned. "And why is he here?" It didn't check out that any young, single doctor would choose to be isolated out on Mackinac Island.

"Because he values the close-knit community and plethora of opportunities the island offers," Eloise said, as if reciting from a tourist pamphlet. "He's only been here two weeks and the islanders are swooping in to set him up. It's something of a wife hunt, all very exciting. We're hoping meeting a good woman will persuade him to put down roots here."

Gigi found the term *wife hunt* as gruesome as *witch hunt*. "Is he *looking* for a wife?" she asked.

"Seems that way," Eloise said. "Not everyone enjoys frolicking from fling to fling, you know."

This was something, Gigi thought, given Eloise knew almost nothing about her dating life and how the breakups were never—or at least very rarely—Gigi's fault. Any decent mother would be commending her daughter for knowing her worth, for refusing to settle, but here Gigi was getting attacked the moment she arrived.

"I don't frolic," Gigi said, thinking about her long list of exes. "I'm just not going to marry the first person I date and wind up divorced." She almost added *like you did* but caught herself just in time.

"Well, I don't think even you will have much to critique in Dr. Kentwood," Eloise said. "He's a veritable catch and he's picking you up on Thursday at half past six. I know it's a bit soon after your arrival, but it was the only night he was free. He's very popular, like I said, and such a devoted doctor."

"Unbelievable." Gigi was torn between competing desires to laugh and scream. The result was a strained cackle. "I've been here five minutes and you're already meddling."

"I'm not meddling. I'm looking out for you."

"You're auctioning me off to the highest bidder."

"Dr. Kentwood isn't bidding for you, Georgiana. I had to lobby him, if you must know."

Gigi couldn't help but choke on the missed humor of it all.

"Lillian Tong's been spotted with him twice this past week," Eloise added. "*Twice.*"

This piqued Gigi's interest. "I thought Lillian was married." She clearly remembered Eloise telling Gigi about the engagement, with the implication that Gigi was falling behind.

"Jilted, two weeks before the wedding. He was from Boston," Eloise added, as if this explained it. East Coasters—and West Coasters—were all depraved in her eyes. "She came back to the island a few weeks ago to recover from the distress of it all and help her parents with the Pink Pony. There's such a labor crunch, no surprise given how the president has been ballooning the deficit, doling out handouts like there's no tomorrow. But maybe you and Lillian can reconnect. I'm sure she could use a friend right now."

"So you're telling me who I should date *and* be friends with?" Gigi said. "This just gets better and better."

"You and Lillian used to be so close," Eloise noted, in that sad way mothers did when they recalled how their cargo-pants-wearing daughters used to love frilly pink dresses. "I'm just saying maybe this summer could be a fresh start."

"I don't want a fresh start." Gigi rarely thought about Lillian anymore. They hadn't been close since middle school. Lillian hogged the spotlight as they got older, with all her talents in clarinet and tennis and academics, and then the boyfriend-stealing incident senior year had added insult to injury.

"And no offense, Mother," Gigi replied now, "but I don't exactly think you're qualified to be my matchmaker. Given you have the dating life of a nun."

Gigi watched the words sting Eloise and tried to tell herself she was glad for it.

Eloise recovered swiftly. "My judgment can't possibly be worse than those dating app things," she said.

Privately, Gigi conceded that Eloise might have a point. Given the impossibility of dating on Mackinac, Gigi had deleted her apps on the flight from LA and felt a weight lift.

"You're living under my roof now, rent-free, I might remind you," Eloise went on. "Dinner with the doctor seems like the very least you can do to express your thanks."

Gigi groaned, anticipating all the ways Eloise would continue to use this as leverage. "I'll move in with Nonni," Gigi said. Enduring flavorless porridge and conservative radio talk shows (Gigi's grandmother made Eloise look like a moderate) would be nothing compared to this.

"Nonni helped arrange the date," Eloise said. "She played pickleball with the doctor, primed him with compliments about you."

Gigi groaned. The whole plot felt like satirical fiction—marrying off the prodigal daughter to the town doctor. Gigi would have to tip off Clyde on the story lead.

As she thought of Clyde, an idea dropped into her mind. It promised trouble, so she held on to it.

"All right," Gigi said. "I'll go."

"You will?" Eloise had clearly anticipated more of a fight.

"Under one condition." Gigi's lips curled. She was beginning to enjoy herself, knowing Eloise would never agree to it. She'd get so flustered that she'd call off the whole thing and never dare to interfere again. It would teach her a much-needed lesson. "You agree to go on a date with someone I set you up with."

"Don't be ridiculous, Georgiana."

"*I'm* ridiculous? You're the one orchestrating an arranged marriage. And besides," Gigi said, voice softening, "it's about time you come out of hibernation. Have you even been on one date in the *twenty years* since Dad left?"

Eloise blanched. "I enjoy the company of many friends."

It was playing out just as Gigi had thought it would.

"All right, I guess the deal is off then." Gigi feigned disappointment. "And to think I was going to brush my hair out of my eyes and wear my most modest turtleneck for the occasion . . ."

Vexation flashed across Eloise's face. She busied herself at the sink, though there were no dishes to wash. "Who?" she finally asked over the running water. "Who would the date be with?"

Gigi was surprised Eloise even asked. Unless it was Gus, Eloise had no interest in men. She clearly just couldn't keep from prying.

"A Mr. Clyde MacDougal." Gigi presented his name slowly, for effect. "Hailing from across the Atlantic."

Eloise stole a glance back at Gigi. "The Scottish author?"

"You've read his books?" Gigi hadn't yet gotten around to googling to see how famous Clyde was, and she felt a lurch of excitement that he might be a household name.

"No, but Deirdre called about him before you arrived. Told me she'd just met the most amiable fellow who was staying at the Grand Hotel for the summer, working on his next novel. She was in quite a tizzy, frankly."

Gigi decided now was not the opportune time to point out that being in a tizzy was Deirdre's natural state. She was too eager to trap Eloise in her own snare.

"That's correct," Gigi said. "So, what do you say? You go on a date with Clyde and I'll go on a date with the doctor."

Gigi waited for Eloise to decline and lecture her on how daughters should stay out of their mothers' personal matters. But Eloise just fiddled with the lavender in the kitchen table vase, turning the sprigs this way and that until they were back in their original position.

A rap came at the side door. It swung open and Nonni bustled in, bringing with her a bundle of warmth. As someone who declared it treason to pass up a piece of pie, her figure was more filled out than Eloise's but she still moved athletically, a walking advertisement for hip replacement surgery. No matter the temperature, she always wore high-waisted trousers and a tucked-in sweater. That, or a bright floral pickleball dress, one of which she was donning now. Lines crisscrossed her velvety skin, telling of both good times and grief. Her eyes were starting to deteriorate, and she was constantly snacking on carrots. She was holding a Ziploc bag of them now.

"I'm terribly sorry," Nonni said to Gigi. "My memory is going. I had your arrival on the calendar for tomorrow. Liam Townsend just called to say he thought he saw you walking by but you had green hair so he wasn't sure."

"Georgiana told me the wrong date," Eloise said.

Gigi gave her grandmother a hug, letting herself sink into her shoulders the way she didn't with Eloise. "My hair is blonde," she said. "Not green."

"It does look lime-ish in the light," Nonni said, stepping back to appraise. "Though you could shave your head and still be the prettiest thing on this island."

"Don't give her any ideas," Eloise said.

Nonni dropped a kiss on Gigi's cheek. Her lipstick stuck, the texture of something several years expired.

"Nonni, you'll be on my side here," Gigi said, slipping her hand into Nonni's. Her skin wasn't as cold as she remembered. Maybe because she'd only held her grandmother's hand in winter for many years. "I'm proposing an amendment to my mother's matchmaking scheme that she's recruited you into."

"Don't you gang up on me," Eloise said. But Gigi could tell Eloise was happy about the fact that her family might be large enough, united enough, to hold a line.

Gigi explained the deal to Nonni, including how she'd confirmed Clyde was unmarried and looking to date. The only thing Nonni hated more than liberals were homewreckers.

"I like it but your mother won't agree to it," Nonni said. "Not a chance."

They looked at Eloise, who was now sorting the already sorted mail. "Okay," she said. "I'm in."

Gigi frowned, then glanced at Nonni, who was wearing a similar look of confusion.

"Okay?" Gigi repeated. The Eloise she knew would never agree to this. Could it be Eloise had been wanting to reenter the dating scene but needed a nudge? Was she trying to prove Nonni wrong? Or was she just so overinvested in Gigi's love life that she was willing to do anything in order to get Gigi to go out with someone she approved of?

The fact that Gigi didn't know the answer to this spoke to how close she and Eloise were these days.

"You're quite the negotiator, Georgiana," Nonni said. "I should have you call my home insurance agency. Premiums went up twenty-one dollars a month. David used to handle all of that . . ."

"You don't have to go through with this, Mother," Gigi said, appalled by the prospect of having to suffer through a date with such a schmoozing, pompous bore as this Dr. Kentwood figure would no doubt be. "Let's just forget about the whole thing."

"You want to back out, do you?" Eloise said. The delivery made Gigi feel like she was a little kid again, begging to quit clarinet lessons.

"No," Gigi said, refusing to be the one to fold. "I'm just giving you an out."

"I don't want an out," Eloise said, her expression inscrutable. "I told you, I'm in."

Something about the way she said it made Gigi think about how Rebecca had mentioned several times that she thought their mother was lonely. Gigi had pushed the comments away as nothing more than the flawed observations of a chronic worrier. But now she wondered if there might be some truth to them.

Gigi felt a jab of anger toward her dad and how he still kept stringing Eloise along after all this time. She understood why he had left, but she didn't understand why he couldn't stay gone. Eloise refused to move on in case one day he came back for good.

There was something so infuriating about a mother wound that always seemed to trace back to a father wound.

Perhaps this absurd matchmaking scheme would be good for Eloise. Get her out of her shell and on an actual date. Gigi should be awarded a special medal for getting such an improbable feat to happen. And in return she could tolerate a couple hours with the doctor. He couldn't possibly be the *worst* person she'd ever gone out with, given the bar was set in hell.

Besides, the dates would serve as a decent distraction from all that had happened here in the past. And what better reason was there to do something than the promise of stirring up new waves in old lakes?

"You've got yourself a deal, Mother," Gigi said, offering up a freckled hand.

Eloise shook it firmly, a feistiness in her own gaze. "May the best matchmaker win."

———— ≈ ————

Gigi pitched Clyde on the date the next day. While doing some beach yoga so Eloise wouldn't eavesdrop, she called the Grand Hotel and asked to be transferred to Clyde MacDougal's room. He picked up promptly.

"It's Gigi from the ferry yesterday," she said. "The serial dater who nearly vomited on you."

"How could I forget?" Clyde said with a chuckle. "It's good to hear from you."

"I have another story lead for you," Gigi said. "My mom is setting me up with the new town doctor. Everyone is obsessing over him. But in return for going on a date with him, I'm setting up my mom with someone. We're playing matchmaker for each other."

"Your mother is single?" Clyde asked, intrigued. "You didn't mention that yesterday."

"Because she doesn't date," Gigi said. "This is very out of character for her."

"It's quite the hook for a book, isn't it?" Clyde said. "Family saga and romance, set against the backdrop of a characterful island town."

Gigi kicked the sand under her bare feet. She liked how it stuck between her toes. "It's not just that," she said. "I want you to be the man she goes out with. What do you say?"

It took a moment for Clyde to answer. "You're asking me to date your mother?"

"Go on *a* date with her," Gigi said. "Singular. I think you'll get along. Her name is Eloise. She's fifty-five years old, very pretty, very smart, and much better mannered than me."

"Is she open to a real relationship?" Clyde asked. "Or does she just see this date as a means to an end so you'll go out with the gentleman of her choosing?"

"Your guess is as good as mine." Gigi stretched, feeling strong in warrior two as she listened through her earbuds. "But either way you'll get a good story out of it."

"I wouldn't want her to think I'm using her for that," Clyde said.

"It's not like she's innocent," Gigi said. "Given how she's been scheming. Both of you have tainted intentions. It's as promising a starting point as any."

Clyde paused. "I'd like to speak with her and take it from there. May I have her phone number?"

Gigi thought that sounded fair and gave it to him. "Call before 5:00 p.m. Eloise finds it rude when people call too late."

"I'll call right this moment," Clyde said.

"Talk slowly," Gigi advised. "She's not a fan of accents; she hasn't left the island much. And ask her to dinner, not drinks. She thinks drinks are tacky."

"I appreciate the tips, but I think I'll be all right. I do have my fair share of experience asking women out."

"Everything works a little differently on Mackinac, though," Gigi cautioned.

"Love is universal, lassie."

Gigi transitioned into a wobbly tree pose. "Maybe, but we're not talking about love. We're talking about dating."

"Shouldn't those two things be linked?"

"Theoretically. But it rarely plays out like that, does it?"

"Perhaps it will this time."

Gigi was taken aback by how excited Clyde sounded. This was the problem with creative types, how their imagination tumbled ahead of them. It was all right. Eloise would bring him back to earth.

Clyde thanked Gigi once more, then hung up. Gigi hurried back to Thistle Dew, hoping to listen in on the call. She wouldn't believe Eloise had accepted the date unless she heard it with her own two ears.

Chapter 4

Rebecca

Rebecca Wood, formerly Jenkins, talked to her mother three times a day.

Two of those calls she made herself. First on her morning walk, then again as she was preparing dinner. Eloise called the third time before bed. A quick good night, a question about a crossword clue, a Gigi-related vent, or an update on Nonni. That sort of thing.

Yes, Rebecca and her mother talked often. They weren't best friends or anything (Eloise had hammered this into her girls since birth: "I'm your parent, not your friend"), but they were very close. Never before, though, had they had to rely on phone calls to keep in touch. Rebecca didn't like it. Words were not what she enjoyed about conversations. She liked the expressions, the security of being in someone's presence. Eloise sounded older on the phone too. It exacerbated Rebecca's guilt that she had abandoned her mother.

Even though distance made it harder to connect, Rebecca could still tell when something was wrong. The way Eloise's voice pinched, the staccato between words. It was more than a small comfort to know she was still able to discern her mother's mood.

Rebecca had always been an old soul, or so adults liked to tell her when she was growing up. It had never felt like a choice, just an uneven allotment of genetics. Gigi had been granted the free-spirited traits, leaving Rebecca with the leftovers, the neurotic residual.

She wasn't sure if she would have been a different type of little sister if Gigi were more responsible, but she didn't care to speculate. Rebecca liked being the protector in the family. It was the natural order of things, in personality if not birth order.

Rebecca had been the kind of kid who was happiest curled up in the shade with paperback books stacked on her beach towel, sunscreen slathered as she read at an awkward angle to avoid breaking the book's spine. She was the child who loved helping her mother in the kitchen and who diligently scraped the measuring spoon with the flat side of a butter knife, internalizing the importance of having the amount of baking soda be precise. She corrected her older sister's grammar and quizzed Gigi for tests, memorizing flash cards for lessons three grades above her own. She reminded her dad to fill up his canteen with water every morning before he headed off to work and checked it when he got home to ensure he was staying hydrated.

These last memories were truncated. Embryonic, really. Rebecca was only five years old when Gus left for the motorcycle trip from which he'd decided never to return, at least not in any meaningful way. In the cobbled-together years that followed, Rebecca tried to compensate for her father's absence and her sister's insurgence but always felt like she was coming up short.

"You're the child, not the parent," Eloise told her often. "Try not to worry so much."

For example, when eleven-year-old Rebecca insisted on accompanying her mother as Eloise had blood drawn for stomach pains, Rebecca stayed up late catastrophizing while Gigi slept soundly in the twin bed beside her. She sobbed privately with relief when the results came back clear.

The worrying had perks too, though. It was sticky, gummy, reliable. Binding together nebulous matter, keeping atoms from flinging too far out of their electrical field. Eloise understood this too.

When Pop died seven years ago and Nonni's grief yanked her under like a riptide, Rebecca and Eloise managed her appointments, her finances, her cooking, cleaning, and gardening.

The only one worrying didn't seem to help was Gigi, who mistook involvement for intrusion. Most notably when then-fourteen-year-old Rebecca had flown down to Florida to (attempt to) retrieve Gigi after The Scandal. They never talked about it anymore. It was all so long ago.

Now Rebecca's life had a different rhythm to it, one she was still learning, each day like stepping into a pair of new boots that were cushioned but still gave her blisters. The beep of Tom's alarm clock at five thirty in the morning as he rose for an early gym session before work. The silence of a house to herself as she pored over philosophy texts and poetry and researched PhD programs. The lyrical swoosh of Lake Michigan as she ambled along the Traverse City beaches, exotic car traffic humming in the background, horns occasionally splitting the air like gunshots. The clench of her own fists gripping the steering wheel as she adjusted to driving.

Rebecca was only twenty-five. She had expected to live with her mother into middle age. The idea of becoming a spinster had appealed: crocheting, reading, baking loaves and loaves of pumpkin bread. Leaving Mackinac wasn't on her radar screen, nor was being a bride. Romantic pursuits never held much allure. They weren't safe, weren't consistent. So as much as it caught her family off guard when she met Tom at a friend's bachelorette party in Traverse City and got engaged within the year, she surprised herself more. But once love dunked her, there was no going back to her old ways, her old walls.

Moving to Traverse City to be with Tom was the first time Rebecca had really chosen herself. It wasn't as liberating as she'd hoped. Letting herself down, as it turned out, was much easier than letting her mother down.

There were perks too, though. Tom was so loving, so loyal, and their lifestyle was one Rebecca had never known. He made a good salary as a financial advisor, and they had a four-bedroom suburban house with modern appliances and air-conditioning and automatic sprinklers. It was strange to adapt to a life with money, though not as strange as it might have been if Rebecca didn't still live frugally, clip-ping coupons, turning off every light, and cleaning her house as her mother and grandmother had taught her. She wanted to share some of their wealth with her family—something Tom was supportive of—but neither Eloise nor Nonni would accept a handout. Gigi would and did through the cash Rebecca had stashed in Gigi's last birthday card.

Rebecca was sometimes envious of Gigi and often embarrassed by her (she hated when people brought up her sister's past scandals in conversation), but she loved her big sister ferociously and always tried her best to be there when Gigi needed her. But all of those good deeds seemed forgotten. Rebecca had only talked to Gigi a handful of times since the wedding six months ago, and she always sensed an artificial brightness from her sister.

Her mother, on the other hand, was someone she could rely on.

But Eloise didn't answer when Rebecca called home this evening, nor when she tried again fifteen minutes later. This was out of character. Eloise usually picked up on the first ring.

It was probably just because Gigi had come home. Eloise would be busy. Still, Rebecca couldn't quell the nagging sensation that it might be something more. Just to be sure, she texted her sister.

———— ≈ ————

"What do you mean Mom is going on a date?" Rebecca shrieked through the phone. She was equal parts excited and suspicious. "You're pranking me."

Gigi never called, only texted, so Rebecca had braced for bad news when she saw her sister's name flash on her screen. Hands powdered with turmeric, she'd picked up in the middle of cooking. Chicken tikka masala tonight, something new so she and Tom wouldn't fall into a rut. They'd only been married half a year, but Rebecca had a looming fear that he would realize how boring she was and leave her for someone more exciting. Someone more like her sister.

Gigi had a way of entrancing men with her tall, limber figure, her free-spirited aura, her sarcastic quips. Rebecca used to feel like a plain Jane next to Gigi, the safety hose putting out the bonfire that no one wanted to see extinguished. Tom had helped her overcome this insecurity—he truly seemed to love Rebecca—but she still had flashes of doubt that his devotion could really last.

"I'm dead serious," Gigi said. "It's all set up. Friday dinner at the Grand Hotel. I just have to hold up my end of the bargain first."

Rebecca was enthralled, yet envious too. It had been Rebecca, not Gigi, who had been with their mother year after year, sowing the seeds to help her open up again. And now Gigi was swooping in to steal the glory.

It shouldn't matter who got the credit as long as their mother was healing and happy, or so Rebecca told herself.

"Tell me more about this Clyde character," Rebecca said, already deciding he couldn't possibly be worthy of their mother. "Does he seem like a good guy?"

Sadie, Rebecca and Tom's ten-week-old English bull terrier named after Mackinac's ice cream parlor, yapped at Rebecca's feet, begging for scraps. Rebecca fed her a treat, then fretted over it. These indulgent habits were sure to carry over into raising children.

"I think so, but that probably means he isn't," Gigi said, and Rebecca noted the rare moment of self-awareness. The overlap between men Gigi approved of and genuinely upstanding humans was about zero. A Venn diagram with only the slimmest of intersections.

Still, when Gigi told Rebecca more about Clyde, she couldn't help but think it sounded rather promising. An esteemed Scottish novelist summering at the Grand Hotel! Well, their mother could do worse . . .

"Clyde does have an ulterior motive, though," Gigi went on. "He's looking for material for his next novel."

"Oh no." Rebecca's hopes nose-dived.

This was exactly why Rebecca hadn't asked Gigi to be her maid of honor. It would have been inviting calamity into the wedding. As if

Gigi would have actually enjoyed the role of maid of honor—wearing a long ball gown, holding Rebecca's train, having to stick to a schedule. No, she would have hated it. Rebecca had done her a favor really, though remorse had been gnawing. There was already enough drama with her dad not coming. How could he have thought that Rebecca would ask him to walk her down the aisle? After all he had done, or more aptly, all he *hadn't* done. And then to have him be so outraged over the perceived slight that he skipped the wedding altogether . . . Well, it was his loss, though it felt like hers too.

From the time she was a little girl, or at least a teenager, Rebecca had made peace with the fact that her dad wasn't going to be there for her in the ways a father should. She didn't have the same expectations of him that Gigi did. Rebecca wondered if that was why she'd been able to let a man into her life and marry him, whereas Gigi still seemed unable to commit to anyone for more than three months.

Still, Rebecca couldn't help but feel hurt at how Gus favored Gigi. It made sense, she supposed, given how Gigi had gone easy on him after he'd bailed, whereas Rebecca had actually held him responsible for his actions. But the logic didn't make the letdown any better.

Rebecca had called Gus several times to catch up since the wedding, but it always went to voicemail. He'd texted a couple times, as if that were the same.

"Eloise has a motive too, though," Gigi carried on over the phone. "She's only going out with him so I will meet the esteemed Dr. Kentwood."

Rebecca didn't like it. It was one thing for Gigi to be an inept pyro in her own love life, another when their mother might bear the burn scars. "I don't want Mom getting hurt."

She gave the sauce a stir. It was lumpy and brown, nothing like the smooth, gingery sauce in the pictures. For being such a rule abider, she struggled with even the simplest recipes. It depressed her more than it should.

"Eloise isn't going to get hurt from one date," Gigi said. "You're the one who's always saying she needs to get out more."

"Because I lived on the island with her for twenty-five years," Rebecca said. "Including the years when you were gallivanting across the country."

When Gigi absconded, Rebecca was left behind to be the responsible, devoted daughter. The daughter who'd commuted two hours each way to college, sacrificing her social life to live at home. The daughter who'd gotten a remote digital marketing job after graduation so she wouldn't have to move. Eloise had never explicitly asked her to stay, but she'd made enough comments about how she wouldn't know what she'd do if Rebecca left. They had stuck, the adhesive of a thousand flimsy sticky notes fusing into a potent glue.

"There you go again, thinking you know Eloise better than I do," Gigi said.

"Stop calling her Eloise." Gigi had a way of corroding Rebecca's composure. "I do know Mom better; it's just a fact. And her going out with this random guy is a bad idea. It could go very wrong."

"Or it could go very right. What if Clyde ends up being the man of her dreams? What if she gets her second chance at happily ever after?"

"You don't actually believe that," Rebecca said. "You're just being the contrarian."

"Maybe you're right," Gigi allowed. "But Eloise—*Mom*—is old enough to make her own decisions. It's really none of our business."

"Mom also decides to let Dad stay in her bedroom whenever he visits." Rebecca felt her blood pressure rising. "Is that a good decision too? None of our business?"

"That's just more proof of why we should encourage her to date. She needs to get over Dad once and for all."

This was something they both agreed on. "I know that," Rebecca said quietly. "I'm sorry."

"No, I'm in the wrong. I always am." Gigi wasn't bad at apologizing so long as someone else went first.

"Maybe I'm just jealous." Rebecca added yogurt to the sauce, folding it all together. "You managed to get Mom to go on a date within one day of being back, when I've been dropping hints for years and she's always shut me down."

"Don't worry, you'll always be the golden child," Gigi said cheerily. "I just might as well put my problematic personality to good use while I'm here. Shake things up."

"I'll be expecting live updates," Rebecca said. "Follow them around and video chat me so I can see."

"I'd be grounded for eternity."

"Since when has the threat of punishment ever stopped you?" Rebecca asked, a smile forming. She felt closer to Gigi than she had in a while, like she could feel the lessening of their physical distance. California was a foreign country as far as Rebecca was concerned, and she was glad to have Gigi back in Michigan for a little while, even with the complications it brought. It was nice to know their mother and grandmother had Gigi around to help. Perhaps Rebecca wouldn't have to be the adult quite so much. It was a strange prospect more than a good one.

"Make sure Mom wears something attractive," Rebecca added. "Not one of those hideous potato-sack dresses she's had since the eighties."

"I'll see what I can do. She doesn't listen to me like she listens to you."

Rebecca couldn't deny it and didn't want to. "Let me know about your date too. With the doctor."

"I'll grit my teeth and bear it. Like a root canal or a personal finance lecture."

"I thought you liked first dates," Rebecca said. "The free meal, the ability to lie about yourself without being fact-checked . . ."

"Not on Mackinac with the whole island watching. The euchre ladies will blow it all out of proportion, you know they will."

"They care about you. And you can't rule out Dr. Kentwood before you've even met him."

"Of course I can. If Eloise approves of him, that's all I need to know."

"Just keep an open mind," Rebecca said. "When I met Tom, I didn't think it was going anywhere."

Rebecca had been standing off to the side at a rooftop bar at the end of the bachelorette party, tired of her friends' boozy games. A cute guy had come up and asked to buy her a drink. Rebecca told him she didn't drink. She'd expected him to make her feel lame for it, but he'd smiled and said she seemed like a responsible woman, that he was looking for one of those.

Everyone had bet Gigi would be the one to marry young, given her teenage promiscuity. Rebecca had slipped under the radar.

"I know the story," Gigi cut in. "I would've made a very nice speech about it at the wedding if you'd asked me, but that's right, you asked Maggie. Your best friend forever."

Gigi's words hit a nerve. The truth was that Maggie had moved to North Carolina with her husband and had been so wrapped up in her new life that Rebecca felt like the bottom of Maggie's priority list. Even before the wedding Rebecca had felt them drifting apart, but she couldn't demote Maggie once she'd already asked her. Rebecca respected convention, unlike her sister.

"Gigi," Rebecca said. "I thought we decided to put that behind us."

"We did," Gigi said, though the phrase felt loaded. "So long as you're not offended when I don't ask you to be in my wedding to the doctor. It'll probably be next month, what with the speed of Mom's scheming."

"I'll look out for a save-the-date," Rebecca said, glad they could at least joke about it now. It was progress from the silent treatment phase, which had lasted several months. Perhaps this was the summer they would grow closer again, find their stride as adult sisters.

"I'm going to order Clyde's books," Rebecca said, googling them on her phone while keeping an eye on the stove. "It'll be good to see what worldviews he espouses."

"Don't get ahead of yourself," Gigi cautioned. "They're just getting dinner."

"I know that." Rebecca quickly scanned the book reviews. They were highly polarized, a good sign. She'd always felt that the best books caused the biggest splits in opinion. "Tom's home from work," Rebecca said as the hum of the garage door signaled his arrival. "I have to go."

"You're not still cooking for him, are you?" Gigi asked, vitriol in her voice.

"So what if I am?"

"It's so traditional."

"*I'm* traditional."

"No, Mom is traditional and shoved it on you," Gigi said. "Like Nonni did to her."

"For the last time, I took Tom's last name because I wanted to." Rebecca was tired of having to defend her choice. "Not because anyone pressured me to *abandon myself*." The only pressure she'd felt was from Gigi.

"It's your conditioning," Gigi said, taking on that patronizing tone. "You think you have a choice, but you really don't. That's how the patriarchy survives, through caged women who think they're free. It's good you moved away. You'll have space to figure out who you are."

"I already know who I am," Rebecca said, though the words hung in the kitchen like fog. Not heavy enough to drop, not light enough to rise. More than her name had changed since getting married. "And I'm not always the victim." *Not like you*, she wanted to add but didn't, just hung up and turned the stove down to a simmer as she went to greet her husband at the door.

Chapter 5

Eloise

T he doctor is coming, the doctor is coming!" Eloise exclaimed the next day, peering out through the damask drapes. "He's turning into the driveway now."

Eloise left her window perch to continue tidying up the house that Georgiana had spent the last forty-eight hours sullying with mis-matched socks, crumpled napkins, and nearly empty Diet Coke cans. The worst of it had been dealt with but a general sense of disorder remained. Eloise refolded the blankets on the couch and straightened picture frames on the mantel.

"Why do you still have so many photos of Dad around?" Georgiana asked, footsteps plodding down from the loft. "You always say you're going to get rid of them."

Eloise bristled, staring fondly at the images of the four of them: her, Gus, and the girls. Gus's hand slipped around her waist like it was his favorite habit. She was meticulous about turning the photos away from the sunlight, so they hadn't faded much. "I don't want to erase the past."

"You can't pretend it's the present either."

The words scraped. "I'm not pretending." Eloise turned away from the mantel to face her daughter. Georgiana bore the air of someone who, after a long and arduous trial, had come to terms with her fate in the gallows. She was dressed in a crop top and frayed jean shorts that barely skimmed the tops of her thighs, if that could be called being dressed at all. Eloise didn't think so. "Tell me that's not what you're wearing."

Eloise could practically hear what the islanders would say when they saw Georgiana out like this. She wanted to save her daughter from the criticisms, and herself too.

"There was no time to steam my ball gown, I'm afraid," Georgiana bemoaned.

"Don't be smart with me." Eloise reached for the heap that was Georgiana's hair, tucking the bangs behind her ears. Too short to stay, they flopped back down into her eyes.

"I'm not being smart," Georgiana said. "I'm being stupid. You've made that very clear."

Not for the first time, Eloise wondered if this setup was a mistake. But Dr. Kentwood was already here. There was no backing out now.

Tugging at Georgiana's shirt, Eloise tried to bring it down to cover her belly but to no effect. The scrunched fabric immediately recoiled to its prior position.

That's when Eloise saw it. Dark ink spilling out from under her daughter's shirt. "What's that?" Eloise asked.

Gigi pulled her shirt up above her rib cage, revealing a flower tattoo the size of a palm, defiling her smooth skin. Eloise yelped.

"It's a tattoo," Gigi said, clearly enjoying the reaction. "Do you like it?"

Eloise wanted to give Gigi a good lecture, but James might hear from outside. She shoved one of her cardigans into her daughter's hand. "Put this on. Please."

The clopping of hooves came from the gravel driveway.

"You've got to be kidding," Georgiana muttered, stealing her own glance out the window. "What's he doing showing up on a fucking horse?"

"Georgiana," Eloise said sternly.

"Can't you ever just call me Gigi?"

Eloise winced. She resented how her daughter's name had been defiled. It was Gus's fault, really. Toddler Rebecca had come up with *Gigi* when she could only babble her sister's name. Gus had adopted it. Eloise had not.

"Georgiana is a beautiful name," Eloise said. "And there will be no swearing in my house." She never had to scold Rebecca like this. "You're always complaining about how you wish guys would put more effort into dates."

"Not this kind of effort. Why didn't he ride his bike or walk like a normal person?"

"I thought you didn't want someone normal," Eloise said. "Being escorted on horseback would be many girls' dream."

"And other girls' nightmare."

"Then don't go." Eloise knew Georgiana was too intrigued by Eloise's upcoming date with Mr. MacDougal to renege, and Eloise found she was relieved that the plans were still on track. She had enjoyed the author's vibrant demeanor over the phone, and after consulting with Deirdre, she'd called back to accept the invitation for tomorrow night.

"I can't cancel now," Gigi said. "It's not a good look. I've got my reputation to worry about."

"Because that's always been your primary concern around here." The residue from Georgiana's high school days lingered like a greasy film. The way she had run off with that scoundrel and worried Eloise sick. The way she'd never apologized, even to this day.

Focus on rebuilding from the present, not rehashing the past, Eloise reminded herself. It was a line from one of Pastor Kevin's sermons that had resonated, so she'd written it down and tacked it on the refrigerator.

Georgiana made to exit the side door, reaching for the handle.

"Don't you dare go out there," Eloise warned.

"Why not? Is it an open-fire zone?" Georgiana said dryly.

"The gentleman always comes inside to collect you," Eloise said. "Did you forget everything I taught you?"

"Tried to." Georgiana slouched onto the floral slipcover couch. "And here I await collection from my suitor. How modern."

"Not everything old-fashioned is evil," Eloise said.

"Arranged marriages are."

"It's not an arranged marriage," Eloise said, exasperated. "It's just one date."

After all she had done for her daughter over the years, this seemed like a very small ask. But of course Georgiana didn't see it that way. Eloise was the villain in the story Georgiana had written about their family. The stick-in-the-mud mother who needed to control everything and everyone. And to make matters worse, Gus was the hero, the misunderstood good guy. He did play the part quite convincingly. Eloise should know, given how frequently she, too, cast him in this role. How difficult it was for her to release him completely.

The doorbell chimed. After waiting a moment to preserve the illusion that she hadn't been spying, Eloise opened the front door.

The doctor was there, dapper as a daydream. Tall, dark, and handsome, with a jawline strong enough to cut granite. Which it would have to, Eloise knew, given the composition of Georgiana's heart, or at least its outer casing.

"Dr. Kentwood!" Eloise ushered him inside, embarrassed the house wasn't much to see. He'd grown up in a ritzy Detroit suburb, she'd heard from Deirdre. But he had that humble way about him, like he was familiar with taking out the garbage and weeding the yard. "So lovely of you to stop by."

"Because this is such a coincidence," Georgiana said under her breath. "Not a premeditated scheme at all."

Blood boiling, Eloise shot her a firm behave-yourself-young-lady glare behind the doctor's back. "I'd like to introduce you to my elder daughter, Georgiana."

Dr. Kentwood wiped his riding boots on the doormat. "Pleasure to meet you." His voice was deep and melodious.

"The pleasure is all mine, Dr. Kentwood," Georgiana said. She dropped into a deep curtsy.

Eloise winced, eager to get them on their way before Georgiana had a chance to ruin things more. "Be back by ten," she said, shooing them out the door. "Have fun."

"Oh, we will, Mother."

All Eloise wanted was for her daughter to get some normal, small-town dating experience and to get to know a good man who might actually treat her as she deserved. But apparently these ambitions were too lofty, as Georgiana seemed set on turning the whole date into a parody.

Despite her misgivings, Eloise's spirits ascended as she watched them go. She was reminded of her first time out riding with Gus, back when they were fifteen. He'd been trying to tout his maturity (he was two years older) and win over her parents, only to bring Eloise back with a sprained wrist after his horse, Bucky, had lived up to his name. But it had still been one of the best days of her life. Gus and Georgiana were natural-born firebrands. Like Eloise, Dr. Kentwood seemed like more of a stickler for rules.

Perhaps the match might have some hope yet.

Chapter 6

Gigi

G igi followed the doctor outside.

The word *debonaire* popped into her mind, varnished in sarcasm. It was clear why Eloise endorsed him. Like Mackinac itself, Dr. Kentwood was a relic of a prior generation.

He was dressed in breeches and a double-breasted blazer with big silver buttons. His tall, lean frame gave him the look of someone too finnicky about his protein intake. Cropped dark hair was matted from his riding helmet, and he was very clean-shaven, as if he'd just come from the barber. Wide-set gray eyes cooled his otherwise warm features.

If his hair were grown out and his body draped over a surfboard, Gigi might say he had potential. As it stood now, he certainly did not. His formality felt like a personal affront.

Gigi never would have swiped on him on a dating app, and not just because she tried to avoid people with self-important jobs like "doctor." He was objectively very handsome but had no edge to him, no glint in his eyes, no strut to his step. It was apparent from the first introduction that Gigi's personality would have to dazzle for the both of them.

She was mostly glad for this. It would have been highly unfortunate if she actually liked the doctor. She could never live that down with Eloise. Besides, the last thing she wanted was for anything or anyone to tether her to the island. Come Labor Day, she was gone. Where she was going was yet to be determined, but the departure date was set.

The goal for tonight was just to uphold her end of the deal so the real fun could begin with Eloise and Clyde. She still couldn't believe her notoriously single mother was going on an actual date. Rebecca was thrilled too, and jealous, which made Gigi feel good. It had been a long time since Rebecca had been jealous of her, and it felt like a sign that their relationship might be returning to homeostasis. Gigi was already tired of holding the grudge about the wedding. The truth was she missed her little sister. Mackinac wasn't the same without her, and it felt good to have something to bond over with Rebecca, even something as unlikely as their mother's dating life.

Tonight Gigi would enjoy a free meal and perform as if she were the leading lady in a film from the forties. Pretending she was on a movie set was a trick she used to dispel any awkward intimacy. She'd only dated a few people long enough for her to drop the act, and none long enough to call it love, though one had tried three years back and Gigi had been forced to correct him.

Gigi knew her big love was out there, but it seemed increasingly unlikely that she was going to stumble upon it in the continental United States. She'd started browsing through job openings at Swiss ski resorts, as she adored the idea of the Alps and how exotic people would find her over there, but small hurdles like visas and finances stood in her way.

For now, she was stuck with Mackinac.

"Would you prefer to ride double since it's just a short distance to the restaurant?" the doctor asked. "Or you could ride alongside."

"I don't have a horse," Gigi answered.

Too much mess and stench, Eloise always said, though Gigi had begged for one as a child. Her dad had promised a pony for her tenth birthday. Perhaps he'd known all along he wouldn't be there to follow through. Gigi preferred to think that he'd meant it at the time. Either way, she'd grieved not getting a pony even more than she'd grieved when her dad moved out. She clumped the messy ten-year-old emotions together, throwing tantrums for weeks, for months, wailing to Eloise about how unfair it all was. Her mother should follow through on the promise her dad had made. Eloise didn't see it that way. As she grew older, Gigi could see Eloise's side more. That after Gus breached their marriage vows, keeping his pledge about the pony probably wasn't important to her. But it was important to Gigi. She'd tried not to believe in promises or make them after that.

"Double is fine," Gigi said to the doctor. She could ride her bike but figured she might as well commit to the bit. Besides, traveling by horseback would be a nice change from gridlocked LA traffic, and she did love riding. Her first job had been mucking stalls at the Grand Hotel stables.

"Will you be okay with bare legs?" The doctor's eyes rested on Gigi's frayed shorts. He seemed to be trying not to stare, and Gigi felt a stab of triumph.

"I'll be fine," Gigi said. "Contrary to popular belief, horseback riding doesn't actually require you to dress like an eighteenth-century British nobleman."

He flinched but didn't miss a beat. "I was going more for a nineteenth-century polo player."

Gigi laughed in spite of herself. "Mission accomplished."

It was a nice night, warm by Mackinac standards, but Gigi was grateful for Eloise's cardigan, which she put on now. Her time in Southern California had weakened her tolerance for anything below seventy-five degrees.

"I overdid it a little, didn't I?" he went on, gesturing to his breeches and boots. "I'm new to riding. Didn't grow up with it downstate."

Gigi found his self-effacing posture more endearing than she wanted to. "You're from modern civilization then," she said. "Consider yourself lucky."

His jawline squared off even more as his lips pulled together. "Depends on perspective, I guess. I was ready to get out of the city, somewhere quieter."

"Well, you certainly got your wish."

His eyes met hers and twisted in like a key or a knife, Gigi wasn't sure which. "Guess I did."

The gray of his gaze felt very cold but in a way that made Gigi sweat through her deodorant. Breaking eye contact, she turned to his horse, a gorgeous Friesian with a chocolate coat and thick black mane and bristly eyelashes. Gigi gave the horse's withers a friendly pat.

"This is Willow," Dr. Kentwood said. "Dr. and Mrs. Moore adopted her last year. I'm staying at their guesthouse for the summer, so they're letting me ride her." He scratched behind Willow's ears in the spot horses enjoy only if they really trust you. Willow neighed happily. "Willow, meet Miss Georgiana."

"Gigi," she corrected. Declining the doctor's outstretched hand, she hoisted herself up onto the saddle. "What's your first name? Or would you prefer we wait until our betrothment before revealing such personal intimacies?"

He nearly smiled. "I'm James."

Gigi already knew this from Eloise, and she'd learned other things, too, from her internet sleuthing, like which fancy schools James had attended and that he'd gone to a medical volunteer camp in Haiti two summers back. He had the sort of "good guy" internet search results that made Gigi think he was either plain vanilla or hiding something. She hoped it was the latter but sensed it was the former.

Somewhat clumsily, James joined Gigi on the saddle, sitting in front. Gigi scooched back so they wouldn't touch, though she felt a strange pull to move closer. She put it down to her hormones rebelling against her dating drought. She hadn't gone out with anyone in a couple months. She'd been trying to raise her standards, not that it had gotten her anywhere except curled up in bed alone watching the trashiest reality TV she could find, her own brand of comfort food.

James gently tugged the reins. Gigi turned back to the house and gave a hearty wave for Eloise, who was sure to be spying.

"So, good doctor," Gigi said as Willow carried them toward town, "where are you taking us to dine on this glorious summer eve?"

Though it was approaching seven o'clock, the sun was still high and blithe. Being so far north and on the western edge of the eastern time zone meant June nights stretched extra-long on the island.

"The Carriage House," James said. "If that's okay?"

The waterfront restaurant had the most heavenly tin roof sundae with homemade hot fudge and salted skin-on peanuts. Growing up, Gigi and Rebecca often chose the Carriage House for their birthday dinners. It was always a splurge. Eloise was a stay-at-home mom and part-time crafter until Gigi's dad left, at which point she'd become the church bookkeeper, a not-quite-full-time job she was still doing now.

"A suitable establishment indeed," Gigi said. Bored of her own antics, she abandoned the Regency-era act. "So how much is Eloise paying you to take me out tonight?"

James's already rigid body tensed. "Your mother didn't pay me."

"Well, I'm sure she will. She finds me impossible," Gigi said. "You've probably heard the stories about me . . ."

James didn't answer right away, all the confirmation Gigi needed. Shame flashed. Sometimes it took a moment to remember she didn't care what other people thought.

"Rumors don't interest me," he said.

"Rumors interest everyone." She was trying to solve the puzzle of why he'd agreed to the date. Gigi's reputation was as tattered as they came. A family doctor didn't seem the type to crave association with someone like her. "I suppose this is a savvy PR move for you," she said. "Take me out for dinner and show everyone how charitable you are. Or perhaps you just didn't know how to say no to Eloise. You wouldn't be the first victim of her persuasion."

"What flattering theories," James quipped. "Any others to add to the mix?"

Gigi loved the feeling of excavating his sarcasm.

"Taking me out could also be a self-esteem booster," Gigi said. "You can flaunt your college and med school credentials, knowing I dropped out of high school the week before graduation. Finding

yourself stuck on a rural island for the summer, not exactly a prestigious appointment, you can feel better about yourself by comparing
your career to mine."

James didn't say anything.

"Well?" Gigi rapped him on the shoulder, accidentally taking note
of how muscular it felt. "Am I right?"

"Yes, you really nailed it. You'd make an admirable Sherlock. For
your information, Miss Georgiana," he went on, seeming to intuit that
this formal address would be the most effective way to rile Gigi further,
"I wanted to get dinner because I'm new to the island and don't have
many friends. Your mom said you were coming home for the summer,
so I was hoping we'd get along. Apparently," he added, rolling back
his broad shoulders, "that was very idealistic of me."

Gigi respected how he stood up for himself, even if she didn't believe him.

"Don't pretend this isn't a date," she said.

"I never said it wasn't," James conceded. "But we don't have to
go if you don't want. I can turn Willow around and take you home."

"No, no, we have to finish what we started." It wasn't on brand, of
course, with how quick she was to forsake things partway through,
but she liked projecting an image of commitment, if only because it
was something new to try. Besides, things were just getting interesting, and Gigi wasn't going to give Eloise any reason to back out of
the date with Clyde.

They skidded into silence. Gigi scooched up closer to James on the
saddle, just so she wouldn't jostle so much. He gave no sign that he was
even aware of her breath, let alone her body. It had been a while since
she'd met someone so immune to her charms. Usually guys ate up the
harsh-humored ice queen act. She was annoyed he wasn't more into her.

"I'm sorry we got off on the wrong foot," James said. "How about
we start over?"

There was a puzzling calmness to him that was nearly contagious.
Gigi wanted to stay upset but couldn't get her temper flaring like it

usually did. She put it down to boredom and how she didn't care enough for him to make it worth the effort. Still, she was glad to find he wasn't one of those overly stubborn types like her last dozen or so exes.

"I'm the one who should be apologizing," Gigi said. "I'm kind of an asshole, especially around guys I'm trying to impress." She was alarmed the words tumbled out of her, but she liked it too. The feeling of stripping away all the performance art, even if only for a moment.

James swiveled his neck so he could access his peripheral vision. "You're trying to impress me, are you?"

"Only to please my mother," Gigi said quickly. "I'm a very dutiful daughter, you know."

He laughed. The sound was springier than Gigi expected. "Of course."

James was warming up, coming out of his shell. Gigi couldn't blame him for being nervous at the start. She did have that effect on people. And he was from Michigan, after all, so he was biologically hardwired to hide his feelings under ten layers of winter coats.

Mackinac's wooded interior was giving way to clear views over the Straits and into town. The mere sight of Gigi riding on horseback with Dr. Kentwood would pour gasoline on the gossip fire. Deirdre was probably snatching up her binoculars right now.

Gigi wanted to lean into it and spoon-feed new rumors to usurp the old tales that seemed to swirl and shape-shift but never die. She draped herself around James, resting her head on his shoulder. It felt better than she wanted to admit. He smelled subtly of leathery cologne with just a touch of hay. The scents paired well.

She stood by her assessment that she wouldn't have swiped right on him on a dating app, but if she'd met him at a coffee shop, she might've given him a chance. Especially if he offered to pay for her extra-large iced caramel latte with whipped cream.

"You all right back there?" James asked. He seemed taken aback by her sudden burst of affection.

"Never better." Gigi was glad to have an excuse to hide behind. "Just giving the islanders something to talk about."

——————— ≈ ———————

"I never should've agreed to meet up with this fudgie," Eloise fretted the next day.

She rifled through her color-coded closet in search of something elegant enough for dinner at the Grand Hotel. "Kitty says she saw Mr. MacDougal buying seven jars of peanut butter at Doud's. *Seven.*"

"Well, it's scientifically proven that a person's integrity and peanut butter consumption are directly correlated." Gigi was lounging on Eloise's four-poster bed, adding creases to the crisp and tidy comforter. "And besides," Gigi carried on, tossing pillows into the air like juggling pins, "Clyde is something of a public figure in Scotland. He's bound to have a few celebrity quirks." The search results had yielded pages upon pages about Clyde and his internationally acclaimed novels.

Eloise tugged at her low bun. "You're a scheming weasel, you know that?"

"Learned from the best." Slyness sliced Gigi's smile. "But I held up my side of the deal. It's only fair that you hold up yours."

The remainder of the date with James had been a success, or at least that was the external consensus. By the time Gigi arrived home from dinner, Eloise had received multiple phone calls reporting how "besotted" and "intimate" Gigi and James had looked.

James had asked her a lot about herself, a nice trait, and told her about how he'd felt burned out from city life and the grind of being a general practitioner in Detroit. He'd requested the Mackinac post. "I needed a break. A small town to recharge and focus on my patients without any of the noise or bureaucracy." He seemed like someone who held himself to ridiculously high standards. Getting him to break free of his conventional path would probably be a difficult task. But if anyone could help him do it, Gigi knew it would be her.

"I'm confident we'll see each other again," Gigi had told Eloise when asked if there would be a second date. It was true. A run-in was inevitable on an island this size.

He hadn't asked for her number at the end of the night. It wasn't surprising, given Lillian was in the picture. Gigi was used to losing out to her, not that experience lessened the blow. James was probably looking for someone who was better "wife material." As if that phrase weren't synonymous with the world's dullest traits. Gigi had felt him cringing when she told him about how she'd lived with six surf instructors in Venice Beach and they took turns stealing beer and ice cream from the corner market. But if someone wasn't able to embrace all of her, he didn't deserve any of her.

An ignorant and ebullient Eloise had been basking in the success of her matchmaking until she had to turn her attention to her own predicament. "I don't even know how to do this," she now lamented, throwing up her hands. "My last first date was when I was a high school freshman."

Like Eloise, Gigi's dad grew up on Mackinac. He and Eloise were high school sweethearts, marrying at nineteen. All had seemed well until Gigi turned eight and her dad decided he couldn't waste another moment on this suffocating island. He took off traveling the globe on his motorcycle, leaving Eloise to raise their two daughters alone.

Growing up, Gigi blamed Eloise for the divorce more than her dad. She reasoned that if Eloise had been the type to enjoy exploring, perhaps they all could have gone with him. Instead, her dad went solo, only popping back to Mackinac every couple years or so, avoiding any consistent pattern. He was absent enough that Gigi had a hard time remembering him but present enough that she couldn't forget him. Nor could Eloise, who'd remained doggedly loyal to the man who'd left her.

Now that Gigi was in her late twenties, she was able to look back and see that the divorce was both of their faults and that Gus had been far from the perfect husband or father. But she still felt like Eloise should've been more open to moving off the island with Gus. Mackinac seemed to have this grip on Eloise, this spell. From the start, Gigi had been determined not to fall into the same trap.

"Everyone knows you're the best conversationalist on the island," Gigi said, thumbing through Eloise's closet, casting aside the heaps of formless dresses and saggy mom jeans. "Wear this." Gigi plucked a jade-green calico dress. With puffed sleeves and an elegant A-line cut, the dress was conservative but would show off Eloise's slim waist and draw out her eyes. "Rebecca suggested it," she said.

"You didn't tell Rebecca about Clyde, did you?"

"Of course not," Gigi lied. "I just said we were going out for a fancy dinner."

Eloise reached for the dress, though not without grumbling about how she was too old for it.

"You could borrow my crop top," Gigi offered. "If you want a more youthful vibe."

"What a thoughtful offer, but I think I'll pass."

Once ready, Eloise collected her nicest satchel, triple-checked that she wasn't forgetting anything, and made for the door. "Wish me luck." She had a jumpy energy that Gigi couldn't place. "I'm off to meet Mr. MacDougal."

"What happened to your rule about the man always coming to the house?" Gigi had been looking forward to seeing Clyde again and observing how he and Eloise interacted.

"Conventional dating rules don't apply after age fifty," Eloise said. "And besides, I don't want him to know where we live. He might be a thief, for all I know."

"He's staying at the Grand Hotel all summer. Something tells me Grandma Jenkins's old teacups wouldn't merit a heist."

"You never know with fudgies." Eloise's ski-slope nose tilted upward. "One must always be on guard."

"Want me to chaperone?" Gigi offered.

"Enough, Georgiana. Now, don't forget to run the dishwasher and sweep the floor while I'm gone. You've hardly been home a day and this place is already a pigsty."

"Yeah, it almost looks as if people actually live here now."

Eloise headed out the side door, muttering something about never making deals with the devil.

"Don't forget to be home by curfew, Mother!" Gigi called out from the front porch. It was a nice change to have the roles reversed and dole out instructions. Though she had to admit it was an odd feeling watching Eloise walk away. She found herself genuinely invested, even nervous, on Eloise's behalf.

"What do you think, Nonni?" Gigi asked when her grandmother popped over to check in soon after. "Will the date be a success?"

Nonni camped out in an Adirondack chair on the porch, unfolding her daily crossword and holding it at arm's length, squinting one eye and then the other so she could make out the words. "My bet is she'll be home within the hour," she said. "With a silver platter to serve your head on."

Gigi checked her phone, just in case James had figured out a way to get her number. He might have asked Deirdre or one of the islanders.

But there was nothing from James, just a sloppy string of texts and memes on the group chat with her former roommates in LA. They were taking tequila shots on Venice Beach, by the sounds of it. Not one of them had texted Gigi individually to check in since she'd left. It was as if her presence in their lives had been nothing more than a blip.

"We'll have to see," Gigi said to Nonni. "But I certainly picked a much better match for her than she did for me."

Chapter 7

The Grand Hotel

The Grand Hotel didn't consider herself a narcissist by any means, but she did like to show off. There was nothing wrong with that, as she saw it. It would be a crime, really, to hide from the world when she'd been endowed with a beauty like hers.

With Victorian architecture, maximalist décor, and a 660-foot-long front porch lined with teeming flowers and American flags, she was a symbol of Gilded Age excess.

No two rooms were furnished the same. The suites were designed by seven former First Ladies. Legend had it that skeletons were unearthed during the hotel's construction due to the island's shallow, limestone-riddled soil. Year after year, guests claimed the hotel was haunted.

Since opening her doors in 1887 for wealthy families who traveled by steamboat from Chicago and Detroit for the summer, the Grand had seen many romances. The front porch earned its nickname "Flirtation Walk," Michigan's version of the Italian *passeggiata*. Infamous "Resort Girls" chatted up young gents. Thanks to the remote beach setting, teenagers could disappear for trysts, free of the chaperoning endured back home.

The Grand had secured a spot on the celebrity summer circuit and hosted her share of couples over the decades. Politicians and partners, actors and costars, musicians and groupies. But she had never had a couple quite like the one sitting there tonight at the dining room's farthest window table.

It wasn't the way the couple was dressed (though his style certainly stood out), nor the flutter of nerves (though she kept bobbing forward and backward, as if being tugged on a marionette string), nor how they were sharing the calamari appetizer while swapping stories, swapping glances. It was more the underlying fizz of it all. It was a common enough quality among young lovers but a novelty among guests so . . . seasoned.

It was a delight, the hotel felt, to have them here tonight. The Grand and her army of ghosts (yes, the ghosts were real, just too intelligent to let themselves be detected) would be doing all they could do to ensure the date went well. Because it certainly was a date—just look at them. The smiles so giddy, so gooey!

The Grand wouldn't intervene so much that the gentleman would invite the lady back to the Betty Ford suite with him. She would never accept, and they had the whole summer before them. Best to let things unfold slowly. But a little nudge, a complimentary top-up of their drinks. Well, it wouldn't hurt.

Chapter 8

Eloise

Three sips into her wine, Eloise felt nearly drunk.

It wasn't the sluggish effect of a hefty pour of red on a dragging winter night. It was the bright buzz of something summery, a morning mimosa, as if she were the kind of person to mix orange juice with anything other than vitamins.

Eloise's senses were dialed up. The Grand Hotel's gilded trappings, the syrupy rays of sun dripping through the window, the quirky charisma of the man across the table from her. She might not be tipsy, but she was certainly tipp*ing*. Forward, as if her chair were perched on a hill, trying to topple her toward Clyde.

"You all right?" Clyde asked as Eloise worked to zip her spine to the back of the green-and-white-striped chair. "Are you not comfortable?"

"It's nothing. I just have to be careful about my posture," she explained away. "Lower back pain."

Clyde asked the server for a pillow for lumbar support. One was provided straightaway. Eloise tucked it behind the small of her back and pretended that solved the problem.

Coming into the evening, Eloise had prepared exit options. It was the only helpful tip Georgiana had offered. If the date wasn't going well, she would tell Clyde she felt a migraine coming on or that her mother had taken a fall and Eloise needed to go home.

Now an hour into the date, Eloise hadn't needed to give an excuse.

On the contrary, she found herself scrounging for reasons to elongate the night.

Clyde talked a lot and told long, arching stories. Eloise was glad for this. It meant she didn't have to carry or steer the conversation. She could listen, she could follow.

"My last book was a sci-fi thriller set on Despina, one of Neptune's moons," Clyde told Eloise as they cut into their entrées. The island salmon for Clyde, whitefish for Eloise. A welcome change from her home-cooked meals for one. "Humans were colonizing and accidentally brought an extinct alien population back to life that had been frozen within the core," Clyde went on, eyes aglow. "And the natives weren't exactly pacifists, were they?" He tossed his head back and laughed heartily.

As a rule, Eloise disliked when people enjoyed their own humor too much. But it was endearing in Clyde. The stylish setting helped too. They were in the Grand Hotel's main dining room. At a window table, no less, overlooking the porch, down onto the Straits of Mackinac. The evening sun struck the water with the softness of a snare drum brush.

"In the end, I wasn't able to do a research trip to Despina, sadly," Clyde said as if he had seriously investigated it. "But the book before that one was a murder mystery on the Amalfi Coast. My favorite place I'd visited before Mackinac." His grooved lips split into a smile as he sipped a Hummer, a Michigan-famous cocktail made with white rum, Kahlua, and ice cream. Clyde had been thrilled to read about it on the menu, determined to immerse himself in the local culture.

"Do you ever run out of ideas?" Eloise asked.

Clyde waited until he set down his glass to answer, wiping his hands on the cloth napkin in his lap. His manners were crisp. He'd gone to boarding school in Scotland, Eloise had learned, but slowly wiggled out of the "golden cage," thwarting his parents' hopes that he would carry on the MacDougal lineage of lawyers.

"Can't say I do, but I have my share of other problems," Clyde said. "I go a bit nutty from all the things swirling around up here." He tapped his temple.

"I can imagine. Not that you seem crazy," Eloise clarified. "Just the notion of inventing stories from nothing, writing book after book. It feels insurmountable. I'm better with numbers than words." *Clearly*, she nearly added but didn't want to draw attention to her bumbling.

When they'd met in the lobby earlier, Eloise's first thought was, *I'm glad I wore this dress.* He was handsome, with such clear blue eyes and that warm, twinkly smile. Not to mention the accent. She had thought herself sensible enough not to swoon over the rhotic lilt of a Scotsman's voice, but this assessment had proved delightfully untrue. He had a peculiar sense of style, though; a bit too avant-garde—a billowy black pinstripe suit with a polka-dot bowtie, brown moccasins, and high tartan socks.

"I always wear two pairs of socks on each foot," he'd told her. "One layer for comfort, one layer for flair."

Combined with his feather-adorned fedora, the outfit was quite peculiar. But the confidence with which Clyde donned the eclectic ensemble had made Eloise reconsider. Perhaps it was in vogue over in Europe.

"You have a beautiful way with words," Clyde protested now. "That accent of yours is captivating. And I'm not just saying that so you might agree to a second date. Though I'm hopeful about that too."

Eloise's nerves sloshed again. Her stomach had been roiling on the walk over. She'd nearly turned around, but the prospect of having to go back and face Georgiana had been enough of a catalyst for her to see this through. She was glad she had.

The dining room was packed. All tourists, which negated the risk of being spotted. Even if someone did see Eloise, they would assume she was just being neighborly, welcoming the newcomer. She could lean over and kiss Clyde right now and no islander would believe it when they heard it. Not that she was thinking about kissing him, of course.

Farther down the dining room, a live orchestra played. The volume was tasteful. Eloise didn't have to raise her voice to be heard over the music.

Eloise fiddled with the topaz ring on her left middle finger, twisting it like a bottle cap. She had started wearing it some years ago. It made her hand feel less naked after she'd finally removed her wedding band.

"But I'm ruining my chances by talking too much, aren't I?" Clyde carried on. "Verbosity is one of my faults. Not my only one nor the wickedest, but the most vexing, or so I've been told. I must know more about your story. How long have you lived on the island?"

"I was born here." She was aware of how dull, how provincial this made her sound, especially to someone as worldly as Clyde. But with age came confidence in who she was and who she wasn't. She felt no tug to embellish. "My grandfather started a construction company here, and my father took it over. The island is in my blood, I guess you could say."

"Fascinating." He looked like he meant it. "Are you involved with the business yourself?"

"No, my father didn't think it was a woman's industry," Eloise said. "And I wasn't particularly eager, though my then-husband was involved for a while." She tended to refer to Gus as her *then-husband* rather than her *ex-husband*. It was softer on the ears and the emotions. "My dad eventually sold the business when he retired. It took him a while to come around to the idea. He wanted to find the right buyer, someone who wouldn't overdevelop the island. Many old-timers feel Mackinac has become too modern. My mother included."

"Too modern?" Clyde said. "Really?"

Eloise smiled, giving Clyde permission to laugh along. She was protective of her island the way she was of her daughters, never allowing anyone to take the first dig.

"But she's stayed," Clyde said. "Your mother."

Eloise squeezed lemon over the fish fillet. "Mackinac is our home."

The way Clyde nodded made Eloise want to tell him more about Gus. About how his departure had made her determined to remain on the island, give her daughters a stable home. But there was no need to bring that up. *"Keep it light,"* Deirdre had coached before the date. *"Like lemonade."*

"Eloise!" Voices called from the window, making them both flinch.

Paula and Kitty, the other two of Eloise and Deirdre's euchre foursome. They were standing on the porch, just on the other side of the window.

Paula was part of the original trio from elementary school, the much-needed hypotenuse to Eloise's and Deirdre's right angles. Kitty moved to the island fifteen years ago. Eloise had been skeptical at first; Kitty was an East Coaster, among other things. But now Eloise couldn't imagine Mackinac without her.

"How serendipitous to run into you here!" Paula exclaimed.

Eloise was half amused, half embarrassed. "Serendipitous indeed," she remarked, knowing Deirdre must have alerted them. Paula and Kitty never dined at the Grand Hotel, disapproving of the paycheck to portion-size ratio.

Eloise briefly introduced Clyde.

"Delighted to meet you both," Clyde said, sticking his arm out the open window and wringing the hands of both women, as if this were a perfectly natural meeting.

"We're practically Eloise's sisters," Paula told Clyde. "So you'll have to win us over too."

"We can be bribed," Kitty added. "With Hummers and chocolate."

"Ladies," Eloise scolded, trying to laugh it off.

They finally trotted off, turning to give Eloise the thumbs-up as they went.

"I'm so sorry." Eloise massaged her palms. "If it were Georgiana, I would have expected it, but grown women . . ." She shook her head, though gratitude for her friends surged too.

"Why let age ruin us by making us sensible?"

It was something Gus might have said. "Very true," Eloise replied, though sensibility was something on which she prided herself.

The bellmen began taking down the flags from the porch. "It's a sunset tradition," she explained. "They do it every night."

"Lovely." He turned his eyes back to hers. "You have beautiful posture, by the way. Very regal."

Eloise felt herself redden. "Georgiana tells me I look ridiculous, like a wax figure."

"Well, your beauty does deserve to be in a museum," Clyde said. "But for now, I'm glad I get to enjoy it all to myself."

"I see why you're a writer." Eloise took another sip of wine. "Good lines."

"I don't write romance, though," Clyde said. "I'm not trying to get a story out of you, if that's a concern. I just found Georgiana so delightful, I couldn't wait to meet the woman who raised her."

She appreciated that he addressed his reasons for coming tonight, as it had been nagging. His words about Georgiana landed well too, though Eloise still felt like a subpar mother.

"Are you saying you have pure intentions?" Eloise asked, coiling a strand of hair that had come loose from her bun.

"I wouldn't exactly call them *pure*." Clyde's blue eyes danced. "Sorry, that was cheeky of me."

Eloise became all too aware of the fact that he had a hotel room waiting for him upstairs. "I don't mind cheeky."

"Don't mind it, or like it?" Clyde said. "I'm insufferable about syntax, you'll learn."

Eloise dabbed her napkin to her mouth, covering her smile. "Like it."

The server came by to refill her wine. She declined, trying to ward off accidental flirting. Though intentional flirting was worse, which was what she seemed to be doing now. It was disgraceful, really.

And she loved it.

Chapter 9

Gigi

When nine o'clock came around, Gigi was pleased there was not yet any sign of Eloise. It must mean the date was going well.

But as night skulked later and the sun finally set after ten, flickers of unease appeared. Gigi really didn't know Clyde. It now seemed hasty to have forced them together so quickly.

Everything all right? she texted Eloise, then gave her a call. There was no reply. Eloise likely had her phone off. Cell phones, in her view, were "brain cell assassins."

Rebecca was texting for updates too. Not wanting to worry her, Gigi told her all was well. Her sister had the type of personality where she assumed someone had gone into a coma if they didn't reply within thirty minutes. Nonni would be the best person to talk to, but she'd gone to bed once she'd finished the crossword. Gigi had helped, googling the answers on her phone, then presenting them as if they'd appeared from her own genius. "Eloise either likes him or she's too polite to extricate herself," had been Nonni's assessment. "Most likely the latter."

Gigi perused the notepad next to the bulky landline. Eloise had written down everything from bank passwords to friends' birthdays to Rebecca's and Gigi's addresses (each of Gigi's now-defunct addresses crossed out firmly, as if Eloise had struck her pen multiple times to express frustration at yet another move). Locating Deirdre's number, Gigi gave her a call.

"Paula and Kitty saw them at dinner, said they were getting on quite well," Deirdre told her. "I wouldn't worry about that, dear."

Gigi was only mildly reassured. It wasn't like Eloise to stay out so late. She was always in bed by nine thirty sharp. "What should I worry about then?"

"I saw Dr. Kentwood this afternoon," Deirdre said. "I've been having a bad spell of migraines, and I can't go to my husband about that sort of thing. He doesn't give me the same attention as his other patients, tells me I'm overreacting. Anyway, I told Dr. Kentwood that it looked like you two hit it off. And oh, I'm sorry to say it, but he has some reservations. Said you have a severe personality, I'm afraid."

The words burned. Gigi had pegged James as a lot of things, but a gossipmonger wasn't one of them.

"I hate to be the one to break the news to you, dear," Deirdre prattled on. "But I thought it was kinder you heard it from me directly."

"The doctor was probably just smarting that I rebuffed his good-night kiss," Gigi said. James hadn't tried anything when he'd walked her to the door, but Deirdre didn't need to know that.

Deirdre latched onto this twist. "I did think there must be more to the story, given how enraptured you both looked riding to dinner."

Gigi reverted to the topic of Eloise's whereabouts.

"Not to worry, dear," Deirdre assured. "I'll initiate the phone tree and see if anyone's spotted her."

Gigi thanked her, then headed outside. The first stars were beginning to drop into the sky like clusters of quartz. The stars were so vibrant on the island, free from light pollution. She allowed herself one glance before locating her retro penny-farthing in the shed. The tires were flat. She had no patience to inflate them so she opted for her old Razor scooter. Well worn, the wheels were more square than circular now, making for a bumpy ride. She pushed along, headlamp lighting the way. After several minutes of hearing only the static of crickets and tree frogs, a pattering of feet approached.

"Mom?" Gigi was aware of the quiver in her voice and how she dropped the formality of *Mother*.

But it was not Eloise. It was James, out for an evening jog. An evening sprint, more like it. His athletic shirt and shorts were drenched in sweat and his face shone. The look was far more casual than his one last night. It suited him better. Gigi's first thought was that she had missed him. Her second thought was that that made no sense. Her third was that she detested him.

She braked on her scooter, screeching to a halt. "What're you doing here?"

"Just getting in a bit of cardio." James stopped too. He wasn't even out of breath. "Everything okay?"

"I think something might've happened to Eloise," Gigi said. "And it's my fault."

"How is it your fault?"

If James was going to bad-mouth Gigi, she was going to clap back. "Because I told her I'd only go out with you if she let me set her up on a date too," she said. "And now she's on the date and hasn't returned."

James digested the information. "That makes me feel better."

"Why would that make you feel better? I was using you."

"That much was clear. But you did it to help your mother find love. Very altruistic of you, really." His face was impossible to read. Gigi had the sense he was teasing her.

"It wasn't altruistic." She was aggravated that he was pinning such praise on her, however sardonically.

A cry spilled out from farther down the path. Gigi recognized it as Eloise's.

Leaving her scooter, she tore toward the sound.

The cry came again, only this time Gigi realized it was a laugh. Eloise was ambling up the path, arm looped through Clyde's. "Georgiana!" Eloise called out. "What're you doing out?" Spotting James a little ways back, she cast a knowing look. "Well, well, if this hasn't just turned into a double date."

"It's not a double date," Gigi snapped as she breathed a massive sigh of relief. "It's a search party. It's late and I hadn't heard from you. Honestly, Mother, you could have been dead, for all I knew."

Eloise was obviously pleased with the fuss. "Looks like my daughter does care about me after all." She mussed Gigi's shaggy hair, even planting a kiss on top.

"You should've checked your texts," Gigi said, never so glad to be embarrassed. "It was highly irresponsible of you."

"It's all my fault, I'm afraid," Clyde jumped in. He was dressed like a Mary Poppins character and seemed even bouncier than when Gigi had met him on the ferry. "I was boring your mam with a few too many stories."

"Not boring me in the least," Eloise said. "Clyde is a fascinating addition to the island. It's fortunate you've connected us, Georgiana."

"Most fortunate." Clyde tipped his fedora at Gigi. "Though I do think I would've found you anyway, my bonny Eloise." His eyes lingered on Eloise's. They both blushed in the stark light of Gigi's headlamp.

Gigi didn't like how quickly this was all moving. She had hoped Eloise would realize dating wasn't so bad, not drool all over the man. "I'll take it from here." She stepped in to take Eloise off Clyde's arm.

"Nonsense," Eloise said. "Clyde will show me home." And she continued up the path with him.

Gigi watched in disbelief. Middle-aged mothers weren't supposed to star in summer romances; their twentysomething daughters were. Something had been switched in the cosmos, the signals crossed, and Gigi didn't like it.

"Is she demonstrating symptoms of a concussion?" Gigi asked James as she doubled back to him and her scooter. "Or maybe something was in her drink . . ."

"Not everyone needs to have a brain injury or be drugged to enjoy their dates," James said.

"Only those of us with severe personalities, I suppose," Gigi quipped.

She expected him to deny it. He didn't.

"I believe I used the word *angular*," he said.

"So much better. Thanks for clarifying." She glared at him. His eyes looked nearly green tonight. She wanted to keep staring but looked down at her shoes instead. The laces were coming loose.

"I'm sorry," James said. "Deirdre's questions caught me off guard; she just kept going. But it's no excuse."

"No, it's not. Especially when I'd recounted to Eloise how well you and I had hit it off."

"Gigi." His voice was soft in texture, firm in meaning. "Our date was a little strange, and you know it."

She felt it as the rejection that it was. She wished she could start over, never even go out with him in the first place.

"How dare you say such a thing?" She stepped into the outrageous character she'd played when she'd first met him, before she'd been foolish enough to let the act drop. "I, for one, was up all night updating my Pinterest wedding board and writing 'Mrs. Dr. Kentwood' in my journal in my finest cursive, quill and all. And now all my grand hopes . . . they're shattered at my feet." She let out a wounded sniff. "How will I ever recover?"

"Your acting talent is top-notch," James said. "Surprised you didn't go the Hollywood route."

"I'm far too original for the commercialism of the entertainment industry." In truth, Gigi had put together a reel from an acting class she'd dropped into a few times, but she hadn't liked it enough to send it out to agents. It wasn't her acting that was the problem. It was the editing of the clips, the shoddy work of a grad student who'd done it for free. "Now, if you'll excuse me," she said to James. "My severe personality and I must get home."

With a forceful kick of her foot, she started off on her scooter to follow Eloise and Clyde. She found herself oddly winded before even reaching the hill.

Chapter 10

Eloise

Eloise was not one to snooze her alarm. It was one of those things she didn't believe in, along with Botox and government welfare programs. But she snoozed it the next morning not once but three times before switching it off altogether.

Rising to confront the day was simply too much to bear after how she'd acted last night. So coquettish, so rash. She was mortified.

She stayed in bed long after she should have headed off to her bookkeeping job at the church. They wouldn't miss her. It was a small parish. She only needed to go in once or twice a week, though she kept a five-day schedule. She enjoyed the order of a routine, the tidy delineation between weekends and weekdays. And it helped her feel justified in her salary, which, although slim, was listed as full-time on the payroll, meaning it came with benefits.

Eloise missed Gus more than she had in a long time. She missed the way he would sprawl out on the bed, reach over, and cup her toward him in the middle of the night. No scent of his cologne lingered from his most recent visit last summer, but the indent of him remained. Even after everything, she still felt safest in his arms. She was too old to start over, too tired for it.

Her bedroom door creaked open. "Why are you still asleep?" Georgiana called out.

Eloise answered from under her mound of pillows. "I'll be up soon."

Georgiana took a seat on the edge of the bed. "What's wrong? Are you sick?"

Eloise lifted her head. She felt older first thing in the morning, with the puffiness and fresh creases of sleep, but younger, too, just now, plagued by the green angst of an ingenue. "Nothing's wrong," she said. "Everything's wrong. What was I thinking?"

"What do you mean?" Georgiana asked. "I thought you had a good time with Clyde."

Eloise was talking to herself as much as her daughter. "Sharing my life stories with a complete stranger, staying out too late, letting him kiss me good night . . ." She winced.

"But that's what happens when a first date goes well," Georgiana said.

"I'm a fool," Eloise said. "A fiftysomething fool. How could you have let me do such a thing?"

"Me? You're blaming this on me? You're the adult here."

"We're both adults." Eloise exhaled. "But you're right, it's my fault. I should've known better than to agree to your squirrely deal."

"You were the one originally conspiring. What happened? Did Clyde tell you he wasn't interested?"

"If only." Reaching for her cell phone next to the bed, Eloise handed it to Georgiana. "He *texted*." Eloise felt strongly that phone calls, letters, and in-person communication were the only acceptable channels when it came to relationships. And yet at 4:17 a.m., Clyde had texted to say he was having trouble sleeping because of what a good time he'd had. He asked if he could take her out again soon.

"Blasphemy," Georgiana said, reading the text. "How dare he follow up so promptly? Believe me, no guy ever communicates this well. I've gotten my share of middle-of-the-night texts, but they're always of the 'U up?' or 'Yo, wanna hang?' variety."

Eloise felt ill, the way she often did when Georgiana elaborated on her dating life. It was one of the reasons Eloise had stopped (or at least cut back on) prying into her daughter's dating life over the years. Georgiana hated telling and Eloise hated hearing.

"I'm not ready to date," Eloise said. "I know that sounds ridiculous given how long it's been since your father left. It's just . . ." She glanced at the bedside table, where another family photo was framed. The four of them on the beach at British Landing, foliage spotted with autumn's peak. "It's never really felt like it's over between us."

Having lived at home, Rebecca knew about the episodic rekindling with Gus, but Eloise had tried to shield Georgiana from it. Though the girls talked; of course they did.

"But it *is* over," Georgiana said. "He's never coming back, not for good."

Eloise's first impulse was to deny it. But her instincts couldn't be trusted; she'd learned that much. "Probably not."

"*Definitely* not. And Clyde is here and he's into you. Give him a chance."

This was how Georgiana worked. Whenever Eloise opposed something, Georgiana was suddenly all for it. "I thought you didn't like him," Eloise said.

"I don't really know him. I just think it's good to start opening yourself up."

"Opening means closing."

"Or maybe closing means opening," Georgiana countered. "What's the worst thing that could happen if you see him again?"

The answer, though near, took a while to emerge. "He could hurt me."

Georgiana nodded. "But he doesn't have the power to break your heart after a date or two. So long as you disentangle expectations from imagination, as my therapist says."

"You see a shrink?" Alarmed, Eloise sat up.

"She's not technically licensed, if that makes you feel better," Georgiana said with a smile Eloise did not return.

Eloise peered into her daughter's face, looking for signs she'd missed. "Georgiana, why didn't you tell me you were struggling?"

"I'm not struggling; it's just part of general health maintenance. Everyone in California does it."

Eloise was anything but reassured. "Have you been having bad thoughts?" Eloise pulled her daughter toward her. She cradled the back of her neck, the fuzzy scruff of her hairline. No matter how old the girls got, they would still always be her babies, her creations to protect. She had failed as a mother. She'd known it for a while, but this was the cold, hard proof. Was that why Georgiana had come home? Not because of her monetary situation but her mental one?

"Stop it, Mother." But Georgiana didn't try to wiggle out of the hug. "I'm fine. I'm just trying to figure out where to go next in life. That's all." The explanation echoed in the dell of the indefinite.

"Me too," Eloise whispered. She felt something between the two of them that hadn't been there for a very long time, if ever. The threading of a fine-spun fiber, the treading on a footpath that looped back together after a fork.

Georgiana got to her feet. "I'll make pancakes," she told Eloise. "Join when you can."

By the time Eloise appeared in the kitchen in a loose-fitting frock, she was feeling more like herself. She took over at the griddle, wanting to do something nice for her daughter, however small. "You always undercook them," Eloise said.

"The batter is the best part."

"For those who like salmonella, perhaps."

"What's life without a little risk?" Georgiana said. "How about this? I'll go on a second date with the doctor if you do with Clyde."

"You don't have to go on a second date," Eloise said. "I know you don't like the doctor. I just didn't want to see it."

Her hopes of opposites attracting had dwindled down to nothing. Georgiana liked guys with ponytails who went to music festivals and reeked of marijuana—or at least that's how Eloise pictured them, from the vague descriptions and rare photos. But Eloise couldn't force Georgiana into anything. She wanted her daughter to be happy and healthy. Nothing more, nothing less.

"James isn't *that* bad," Georgiana said. "We just didn't have any sparks. Not like you and Clyde."

Clyde. There he was, back in Eloise's thoughts. "Sparks aren't always good," Eloise said. "They burn things down."

"And they light things up." Georgiana set the table, even folding the cloth napkins in the triangular way Eloise preferred. It touched Eloise to see her daughter trying. "You'll get back to him at least, won't you?" Georgiana asked.

"Of course I will. I don't subscribe to the ghouling antics of your generation."

"Ghosting," Georgiana corrected with a grin. "And let me know if you want help drafting the text. Breakup texts are my specialty. It's an art form, really."

"I'll be giving Mr. MacDougal a call," Eloise said, heat rising at the thought. "Just not quite yet."

Georgiana snitched pancake batter from the bowl, licking it from her finger. "No rush. It's good to keep guys waiting a bit. Play the game." She winked.

"I'm not playing a game." Eloise pressed the spatula down on the sizzling pancakes to ensure they cooked thoroughly. "I'm just relearning how to date."

"Yeah, well." Georgiana gave a knowing shrug. "Those two things are one and the same, really."

Chapter 11

Gigi

"There she is!" Deirdre ambushed Gigi after Sunday service.

The Union Congregational Church, known locally as the Little Stone Church, was a Mackinac landmark. A Gothic-style building with a bell-tower steeple and stained glass windows, it was tucked behind the west crook of Main Street, halfway up the hill.

"We knew you'd come back eventually," Deirdre added.

Gigi, who quit church cold turkey the moment she moved off the island, was disappointed in herself for allowing Eloise to drag her along today. But it had been too early in the morning to formulate a cogent argument, and this summer would be about picking her battles. Wasting her bargaining chips to get out of church the first weekend didn't seem wise. Though she was starting to reconsider as the euchre ladies—Deirdre, Kitty, and Paula—descended upon her with perfume-poisoned hugs during the coffee-and-donut hour on the church's grassy lawn.

"Only a matter of time," Kitty agreed, stacked bracelets clanking as she clapped her hands. Her fingers were elongated by fake nails—talons, really. A couple of them seemed to have fallen off, likely due to their excessive weight.

"Our Mackinac charm wins over even the hardest hearts." Paula reminded Gigi of a vintage teacup, in shape and ambience. Having lost her husband to cancer, she now lived with Kitty, who had never married, in an old Victorian by Mission Point.

"I'm not back," Gigi said. "It's just temporary, for the summer."

Deirdre clucked. "That's what Dr. Kentwood says too, but all signs point to him staying longer."

As if rehearsing choreography for a talent show routine, the ladies turned in unison to stare at James. He was speaking with Lillian. She was even glossier than Gigi remembered. Silky black hair draped down her back, long past the length where Gigi's hair frayed into split ends. Hourglass curves gave shape to a salmon-colored sheath dress, toned calves accentuated by nude stilettos.

"Lillian walking on grass in those shoes is more impressive than Jesus walking on water," Kitty marveled.

"Kitty," Deirdre scolded as Eloise and Paula stifled their laughter.

Even with the heels, Lillian was quite a bit shorter than James. Gigi was a gawky giant by comparison. They were sipping from cardboard coffee cups, likely bonding over their shared interest in running marathons and avoiding sugar. The scene inspired Gigi to take an extra-greedy bite of her glazed donut, not that anyone would appreciate the symbolism.

"Don't worry, dear," Paula said, patting Gigi's shoulder. "You'll find someone soon." The other ladies joined in. It didn't seem as if Gigi's story of turning the doctor down had gained much traction.

"Thank you so much." Gigi pasted on a saccharine smile. "But I'm not looking."

"That's when it always happens," Kitty gushed. Paula quickly agreed.

"All right, girls, let's not scare her away from joining us for euchre," Deirdre said. "Though I do have a favor to ask . . ." She batted her lashes, clumped with too much mascara. "As you know, the Lilac Festival is coming up."

The Lilac Festival and the Fudge Festival were Mackinac Island's two staples, bookends to the heart and heat of summer.

"Every year it seems it's up to me to pull the whole event together," Deirdre complained, though it was obviously a source of great pride.

"We're short on participants for the cornhole tournament. Everyone's defecting for pickleball." She huffed, making it clear just what *she* thought of the pickleballers and their tactless thwacking.

"Georgiana will be happy to play cornhole," Eloise volunteered. "I'll be busy running the lilac resin jewelry workshop. Perhaps you can ask Clyde to be your partner," she said to Gigi.

The comment made Kitty bounce on her orthopedically friendly, ocularly gruesome sandals. "So you and Mr. MacDougal are . . . ," she prompted Eloise.

"Acquainted as friends. Nothing more and nothing less." The composure in Eloise's voice was offset by the flush of her cheeks. Since having the "just friends" conversation with Clyde last night, Eloise had been talking nonstop with Gigi about how she'd done the right thing, which was how Gigi knew she was wondering if she'd done the wrong thing.

"Well, who knows how it might evolve," Paula noted.

"I didn't see him at church today," Deirdre said critically.

Gigi's skin itched. Being on church grounds triggered flashbacks to being the island's black sheep. Singing in the church choir while hungover, parishioners gossiping about Gigi as they sang hymns of unconditional love.

"I'm not feeling great," Gigi told the ladies. "Think I'd better head out."

"It's the fudgies' fault," Deirdre said. "All those germs they bring over on the ferry. The clinic has been packed, though everyone's requesting Dr. Kentwood. I fear it's hurting Fred's confidence."

"In that case, you might switch away from Dr. Kentwood yourself," Kitty said. "How many appointments did you have with him this week?"

"That wouldn't do anything," Deirdre snapped. "Fred would think I was pitying him. It's emasculating."

Gigi tried to catch James's eye on her way out, but he was too absorbed by Lillian to notice. It was less like being rejected and more like being invisible. But wasn't that what she'd wanted from this summer? To blend in, lie low, and then beeline out of here again. Was it just her incessant need to cause a scene that made her want James to notice her? Or was there something more troubling to it?

A few raindrops landed on her face, despite a mostly clear sky. Gigi felt it was Mackinac Island herself taunting Gigi, laying down the law about who held the power this summer.

Stop it, she told the island. *I've had enough of you.*

More raindrops spritzed her, though the sun continued to shine brightly.

———— ≈ ————

Before circling back to Thistle Dew after church, Gigi called her sister.

Rebecca picked up on the second ring. "Mom friend-zoned Clyde," Gigi told her.

Rebecca groaned. "Why is she sabotaging this? I've already finished Clyde's first book. It's unconventional but very well written, with a strong moral compass."

The image of Rebecca poring over a stack of his novels produced a squirt of sadness. "I told you not to get your hopes up."

"Too late," Rebecca said. "I'm the optimist so you don't have to be. Is Dad visiting this summer? Is that why Mom is being weird?"

"How would I know?"

"You talk with him more than I do."

"Not much more," Gigi said. It was pathetic parenting, cruel even, how he reached out to Gigi more than Rebecca. But Gigi was glad for it. She wanted to be his favorite. "He's still in South America, last I heard." He texted her some photos a few weeks ago—mountains, motorcycles, a low-res campsite selfie. Gigi had messaged back asking if he was coming to Mackinac this summer and which dates. He hadn't replied yet.

"I swear, if he waltzes back in again . . . ," Rebecca said.

Gigi didn't want to admit that she was hoping for a visit from him. She hadn't seen him in a couple years now, not since he dropped into LA for a weekend during a trip down the coast. "I'm not trying to talk about Mom and Dad," she said. "I'm trying to talk about me."

Rebecca was quiet as if Gigi had pinched her, leaving nail marks like she used to during their childhood fights. "What about you?"

"This whole thing is a failed experiment," Gigi said, walking toward Main Street. "Coming back for the summer."

Returning was supposed to give her some time to rest and recharge, but she was exhausted by the small-town happenings and how everyone was in each other's business.

Instead of being recentered and full of clarity, she felt more astray than ever. And instead of enjoying the rush of exploring new places, she felt suffocated drifting through old ones. Stuck here, stunted by her past life.

"It's only been a week," Rebecca said. "You're readjusting."

"I don't want to readjust," Gigi said. "That's my point. My LA roommates won't take me back. They filled my room two days before I even left, very kind of them. But I could find another apartment or move somewhere new. Get a job waiting tables. Lots of places are hiring; it wouldn't be hard."

"You hate waiting tables," Rebecca said.

"I hate all work," Gigi said. "Except bossing people around. But I can't be a boss until I'm a good employee, and I can't be a good employee until I'm a boss. It's a vicious cycle, completely rigged."

"Now you understand why I married Tom," Rebecca said. "I never have to work again. Just kidding," she added quickly, though Gigi wasn't sure she was. Rebecca had always been attracted to security, and Tom certainly brought that with his money.

Gigi wasn't sure how to feel about her sister suddenly being upper middle class, but she was grateful at least that Rebecca and Tom had been generous with her so far. They'd chipped in far more this year than Gus had when Gigi had asked him for help. Gigi had not approached Eloise. Eloise would have said no, and Gigi's pride wouldn't have allowed the ask in the first place. It was a promise she'd made herself at eighteen: Never again be dependent on her mother.

Yet another reason why living with her this summer felt like such a blow.

"We have the spare room for you whenever you want it," Rebecca went on. "I got that fancy organic soap for the bathroom. The lemongrass one you like."

It was Gigi's favorite and very expensive. She wanted to say thank you but the words were far away, tucked up on a top shelf. "Traverse City wouldn't be any better," Gigi said. "It's still the insufferable tedium of Midwestern life."

"It was just an offer."

Gigi strode down the middle of Main Street, forcing buggy drivers and cyclists to move for her. She passed Ryba's and Murdick's, two of the fudge shop staples, and carried on toward May's, the most liberal with free samples. She hardly noticed the manure stench, a bad sign of assimilation. More potent now was the grisly smell of grease and meat pouring out from the Chuckwagon, a counter-service-only restaurant crammed between the Mackinac Inn and the Haunted Theater.

"Why don't you reach out to Lillian?" Rebecca asked. "Isn't she back too?"

"Great idea," Gigi said. "Let me become besties with my ex-best-friend-turned-archrival who's now dating the guy Eloise tried to give my dowry to. Why didn't I think of that sooner?"

"Lillian is dating James? That's a good-looking couple."

Gigi fanned her neck with the church bulletin, which she was accidentally still holding. "How do you know what James looks like?"

"I did my online research. Couldn't find much. It's always a good sign when guys aren't active on social media." This was a dig at Gigi's exes, a smattering of whom had sizable online followings, posting multiple times a day, often shirtless. "But the picture in James's professional bio is divine," Rebecca said. "That jawline. You're sure you're not interested?"

"He has the personality of stale wheat bran," Gigi said, feeling it perfectly justifiable to slander him when he had done it to her first. "The kind that Eloise used to force-feed us for breakfast."

"It wasn't so bad if you added chocolate milk. And some people take a little while to warm up."

"James and Lillian are a good match," Gigi said. "Both equally bland. It's just infuriating how everyone thinks he picked her over me. I could get James to forget about Lillian in a second if I actually tried."

"Sounds like you might like him," Rebecca said.

"Definitely not," Gigi said, a little too forcefully. "I just like the idea of getting back at Lillian."

"You're going to hold the grudge against her forever, aren't you?"

"Like a trophy."

"Remember in elementary school when you stole Mom's eyeliner because you wanted your eyes to be like Lillian's?" Rebecca asked.

"I was a young racist," Gigi said. "I'm not proud of it. All the unlearning I've had to do. Enlightenment is very lonely."

"That wasn't my point," Rebecca said. "My point was that before you hated Lillian, you were obsessed with her. Wanted to be her, even. Can't you try to find that friendship again?"

Gigi felt it flaring up once more—nostalgia for what she'd lost, what she'd deliberately broken. Because as much as she liked to remember their friendship fallout as Lillian's fault, Gigi knew underneath the stacks of stories she'd edited over the past decade, she was responsible. Being back on this island reminded her of that so rudely.

"I never wanted to be her," Gigi said, trying to push away the thoughts and feelings. "I only ever wanted to beat her."

Gigi had a craving for something sweet to counteract the bitterness. She entered May's beneath its striped awning. The rich aroma of melting chocolate greeted her. A fourth-generation family business, May's gained fame during World War II. Sugar was rationed and islanders had to wait in long lines. Harold May was a local hero, making fudge through it all, though he'd had to close the store at noon every day. Long after the war ended, people kept flocking through the doors.

Today a pimply-faced college-aged worker stirred cauldron-sized kettles with an oak paddle. It kept the fudge from sticking over the gas stovetop. Another employee poured a boiling batch onto a marble cooling table. With a nimble flick of her wrist, she folded the fudge with a wide spatula.

"Are you at May's?" Rebecca asked. "I can hear Mrs. May's voice. Tell her I say hello."

"Will do." But Gigi darted out and went to Joann's Fudge across the street, where she had less of a chance of being roped into conversation. After sampling peanut butter, cookies and cream, butterscotch, and mint chocolate chip, she put in the order she knew she would from the start: two slices of dark chocolate espresso fudge. The only thing better than pure sugar was pure sugar with caffeine.

"I thought you were vegan," Rebecca said, overhearing the order. "Doesn't fudge have dairy?"

"Every rule needs an exception or it loses its originality."

"Get some turtle fudge for Mom," Rebecca said. "She loves the nuts and caramel."

"Don't boss me around." But Gigi added a slice of turtle to her order. She paid at the counter with a crumpled twenty-dollar bill she'd found in her bedroom desk. Babysitting money from high school, most likely. "But maybe you're right and I did give up on James a little too fast."

"You're twisting my words," Rebecca said. "Don't use him to get back at Lillian. You're better than that."

"Am I?" Gigi mused. She had a strong craving for a joint. "I know you're making that face. The one where your nostrils get all snakelike."

Rebecca's voice dipped, the way it did when she got caught. "I'm not making any face."

Gigi left the store, unwrapping the fudge as she went. She bit into one of the slabs like a granola bar. Chocolate dribbled onto the not-quite-knee-length sundress she'd put on for church. There was something gratifying about an outer mess aligning with an inner one, though mismatched things were more her style.

"Go ahead and judge," she told Rebecca. "But I've got to find some way to keep from physically decaying from boredom this summer. And this just might be it."

"Isn't there something more productive you could do with your time?" Rebecca said. "Like get a part-time job or give some thought to what you want to do after the summer? We could make a list together."

This was just like Rebecca, thinking a new list was the solution. "I do have an idea for a business I could start," Gigi said, her smile curling up like smoke.

"Oh?" Rebecca said. "I could see you as an entrepreneur. You have the personality for it."

"Meaning I'm unhinged?"

Rebecca sidestepped the question. "What's the business idea?"

"A marijuana dispensary on the island." Gigi loved how she could feel Rebecca's exasperation through the phone. "There's definitely a market for it with the fudgies."

There was a pause. Gigi wondered if the call had dropped.

"That's really not what I meant," Rebecca said. "Aren't there any other kinds of businesses that pique your interest?"

"Not really."

After hanging up with Rebecca, Gigi knew what she had to do. It didn't have to do with the dispensary, though she did think it was a decent idea. It had to do with James.

She needed to go on a second date with him to determine if she actually liked him or if she was just thinking about him because there were no other options. In doing so, she could persuade Eloise to give Clyde a second date as well. One for one, two for two.

Gigi would keep things simple and old-fashioned, as James seemed to prefer. She would simply walk up to the medical clinic, knock on the door, and ask him to lunch.

He would say yes, Gigi was nearly sure of it. Not because he wanted to, perhaps, but because he was too well mannered to decline.

Mackinac had plenty of conflict, but it was the quiet, passive-aggressive kind. No one rejected someone to their face. It simply wasn't how things were done. James would know that by now and wouldn't want to ruffle feathers in the town he relied on for his employment.

Gigi saw her opening. She was going to take it.

—————≈—————

Gigi went down to the medical clinic the next afternoon. She wore board shorts and an oversized T-shirt. Dressing down always made her feel up for more. Like no one expected anything of her, so she could only over-deliver.

The small waiting room was packed with patients. Most were women. None seemed very sick.

"I'd like to see James," Gigi told Helen, the receptionist. Helen had never been Gigi's biggest fan, not since Gigi had babysat for her kids many years ago and let them watch an R-rated movie. Little Charlie had nightmares for months afterward, or so Helen had hyperbolized to the whole town.

"Dr. Kentwood has a long wait." Helen nodded toward the roomful of women. Some were touching up their makeup. Others were sizing up Gigi. "But Dr. Moore can see you now."

"It has to be James," Gigi said. "I don't need an appointment, just five minutes."

"You'll need to wait in line like the rest of the patients."

"Could you just tell him I'm here? He'll want to see me." She hoped that was true.

One of the office doors swung open. James stood there in a white lab coat and khakis. He looked like a doctor on a TV show but without the pomp and circumstance. There was a confidence about him that hadn't been there in his horseback riding attire or even his track suit.

"Gigi," James said. "Thought I heard your voice."

Gigi was glad he found her so recognizable. "I need to talk with you about something—"

Helen interjected, "She doesn't have an appointment."

"It'll only take a minute." Gigi was chewing too hard on the piece of gum in her mouth.

"It's okay, Helen," James said. "I've got time." He gestured for Gigi to join him in his office.

The office was a tight cube, the walls bare. A single window with the blinds down, fluorescent ceiling lights humming. Orderly folders and a lone potted succulent on the mahogany desk. It felt very sterile, like the office environment Gigi had always feared.

"Very uplifting, this place," Gigi said.

"Thank you," James said, scooping up the sarcasm and serving it right back. "But I'm only here for the summer. No point getting too comfortable."

The reminder poked Gigi like a thorn. Not that she herself was sticking around beyond August. "Right."

"So. What did you want to talk about?" James took a sip of water from the thermos on his desk. She hoped she'd made his throat go dry.

"I wanted to say that I think you're right," she said.

"Right about what?"

"I can be a bit severe."

James shifted on his feet. He was standing close to her, not tucked behind his desk. "Angular," he corrected. "I said 'angular.' And I really didn't mean it as a negative."

"Well, it's true. I *am* angular. I've had to develop some sharp edges." Gigi could launch into her "child of divorce" story but didn't. It tended to scare guys off. "But the angles come with upsides too," she went on. "I bargain for cheaper rent; I persuade managers to hire me; I put creepy men in their place. And I get guys I like to go out with me."

James's eyes flickered. Their gray felt brighter today, the color of the lake right before the sun came up. "I'm sure you do."

"So, are you in for lunch tomorrow?" Gigi asked.

"What's that?"

"Lunch tomorrow," Gigi repeated, affecting the bravado she didn't quite feel. "You and me."

"You're asking me out?"

"You're very intelligent, James. I see why you're a doctor."

He smiled, teeth poking through. But his posture stiffened. "I'll have to get back to you."

"Because of Lillian?"

He didn't say anything.

"I see." Gigi made for the door and was already outside on the clinic's front steps when James caught up with her.

"Did your mom put you up to this?" he asked.

"No," Gigi said. "She doesn't know I'm here."

"And it's not a dare or something?"

"I don't give in to peer pressure."

James nodded. He looked like he believed her. "Can I let you know later today?" he said. "About lunch?"

"If you have to think about whether you want to go out with me again, I think that's your answer," Gigi said. "I may not have a college degree, but I can read the signs."

"I'm not unsure," James said. "It's just a little complicated. Can I have your number?"

Gigi tried hard not to let him see how happy that made her. He passed over his phone. She punched in her digits and saved her name with a red heart.

She hadn't even made it back to Thistle Dew when her phone rang.

"Hello?" she answered.

"Gigi. It's James Kentwood."

She usually hated when people called instead of texted, but her insides soared without permission. "Ah, as opposed to the other James I was waiting to hear from. Thank you for clarifying."

"I'm in for lunch tomorrow. How's noon at the Pink Pony?"

Gigi had to work to keep from sounding too happy about it. "That works," she said. "See you then."

She hung up quickly, before James could change his mind.

Chapter 12

Lillian

Tables at the Pink Pony filled up fast. The restaurant and bar were first come, first served, no reservations allowed.

Juxtaposing the Grand Hotel, the Pink Pony was Mackinac's go-to spot for casual diners. Bachelor and bachelorette parties, families who didn't trust their kids to behave, tired tourists needing revival in the form of funky cocktails and burgers. Located at the end of Main Street, with an outdoor patio overhanging the lake and a music podium where up-and-comers strummed country and indie rock covers, the Pink Pony was the place to kick back and relax.

Except for Lillian Tong, who stood sweating in the restaurant's sweltering kitchen waiting for another batch of orders.

"What is Gigi Jenkins doing here with Dr. Kentwood?" Lillian's mother hissed.

Trina Tong's petite frame quaked beneath her general manager uniform: a loose-fitting skirt that fell below the knee, swallowing her legs, along with a tailored blazer stitched with a pony logo, the galloping emblem of her American dream. The lunch-rush ruckus was in full swing—chefs barking, pans clanking, timers dinging. "Does that girl have no shame?"

"It's okay, Mom." Lillian wiped her clammy palms on the black apron she wore over the bubblegum-pink server shirt. She'd slipped back into her waitress role as if she'd never left for college, even braiding her hair in the fishtail pigtails that used to be her signature. "Men and women are allowed to have lunch together."

"Don't let your grandmother hear you saying that," Trina said. Lillian's parents immigrated from Vietnam decades before for her dad to study hospitality at Michigan State. That Trina had also earned a degree of her own and now comanaged the Pink Pony were secrets they sheltered from Lillian's grandparents. Along with the fact that she went by Trina, instead of her given name, Tuyen. "Gigi has always been jealous of you, ever since you beat her out for first chair on the clarinet."

"I don't think clarinet auditions had anything to do with it," Lillian said. "And I've only known James a few weeks. He's not my boyfriend."

James had told Lillian that Gigi asked him out to lunch. He'd asked Lillian's opinion on what to do. "Go ahead with it," she'd said. "It's not like we're exclusive."

"He's not your boyfriend because he's practically your fiancé," Trina said. "He's besotted. The whole island is saying so."

Lillian tried not to smile, sewing the edges of her mouth to keep them from untying. "I just got out of one engagement. I'm not looking to jump into another."

She'd only meant to stay a week or two with her parents while Alex was moving out of their Chicago apartment and Lillian was canceling the wedding vendors, recouping as much of the deposits as she could. But it had already been a month. Her parents needed her. They were short on staff. For better or for worse, Lillian was not wired to forgo family duty in pursuit of her own dreams. Not that her dreams felt much like dreams anymore. They were shells of their past selves, dusty relics.

"Now is the best time to do it, though," Trina said. "You were already preparing for marriage. You just have to switch out the groom." Her dimples pleated.

"Oh, is that all?" Lillian checked on the orders for her tables.

"Dr. Kentwood is probably scared of Eloise," Trina said. "I heard she paid him to take Gigi out. Only way that girl could get a respectable date. The scandals she has to her name."

Gigi, who had run away with the governor's son the week before high school graduation. Gigi, who had worried her family and the whole town sick before they found her. Gigi, who had once been Lillian's best friend and then turned on her the summer before ninth grade. Lillian still didn't know exactly why. She thought it might have had something to do with the turmoil of Gigi's father coming and going that summer, but mostly Lillian figured Gigi had gotten sick of her the same as she'd gotten sick of soccer and clarinet and choir.

Or maybe it was because Lillian had been too intense with friendship bracelets and sleepovers and the secret forts they'd built in the woods. She had suffocated Gigi, just like the island had. So Gigi had left both of them in the dust.

The governor's son hadn't even been that good-looking or charming. The glamorous lifestyle had turned her head. Or maybe she'd just been determined to make her escape and he'd been the closest accomplice, the getaway car.

"Mom," Lillian said with a spasm of longing. "Gigi isn't a threat. Believe me."

"Of course she's not. You're in a different league—tennis state champion, valedictorian, prestigious Chicago lawyer." Reciting Lillian's résumé worked like lotion in Trina's worry lines. Lillian needed it too, still clinging to her parents' pride.

"*Former* Chicago lawyer," Lillian said, her body flinching with failure.

Trina smoothed her skirt. "They'll take you back whenever you're ready. You said so yourself."

Lillian had, but only so her parents wouldn't worry. Her decision to stay longer on Mackinac wasn't just to help out at the restaurant. The island swaddled her in the woolliness of youth. Someone else making the decisions, folding the laundry. A hood had been pulled back over her head. She liked it more than she should for how it narrowed the scope of her vision. With abdication of responsibility came ease, or some look-alike.

The thought of plunging back into the shark-filled waters of her corporate law firm, toiling away in that skyscraper on deal terms for mergers and acquisitions when her relationship, her entire life path, had veered off course, was enough to scare the fear of quitting right out of her. She'd put in her notice last week. The same day Gigi returned, her presence complicating things like always.

Lillian scooped up baskets of onion rings and smoked whitefish dip to bring out to one of her booths. "I'll cover James and Gigi's table."

Trina nodded. "Keep a close eye."

Lillian found them out on the patio, overlooking the harbor where a small cruise ship was docked. The tables' pink umbrellas rippled, wooden poles rocking in the wind. Gigi had moved her chair into the sun, her body long and bendy like a question mark. James sat up straighter, sliced by shade.

Lillian fought the impulse to tug her braids, pull them like a fire alarm. "Hey there," she said.

Gigi flicked the bangs out of her eyes, revealing the drops of green beneath. "Look who it is," she said. Her creamy lips curled. Nearly a smile, almost a sneer. "It's been a while."

Ten years. It had been ten years since they'd seen each other. "Yes, it has been," Lillian said.

Gigi had always been confident, but there was a flippancy to it now, like she couldn't be bothered with showing off. A stud on her freckled nose, bold with its subtlety. Short hair suited her, edgy and free, falling just below her chin, the skin of her swan neck exposed. The bleach didn't do her any favors, washing her out. But she pulled it off, just as she did with her overalls. No shirt underneath, just the skim of cleavage and sunburn, clavicle bones jutting like jewelry.

"I hope it's not awkward that we're here," Gigi said. "We can go somewhere else."

"No, it's all good," Lillian said. She'd suggested that James bring Gigi to the Pink Pony so she could observe the date. Removing her notepad from her apron, Lillian clicked open the pen. "What can I get you to drink?"

Gigi ordered a frozen rum runner. James opted for an Arnold Palmer.

"Let's go in the hot tub," Gigi was saying when Lillian returned with the beverages.

The Pink Pony had a large jacuzzi next to the patio, open to guests. Lillian's parents had tried closing it several times, but the attempt was met with too much pushback. But in the privacy of their own home they ranted about the skimpy bikinis, the sloppiness of the clientele.

James perused the menu. "I didn't bring my bathing suit."

"We could get some from the gift shop," Gigi said. She laid a hand on James's forearm. He didn't pull away. "Though on second thought, not with the mayor in there."

Camille Welsh was in the hot tub, sipping a Mackinac mule and loudly introducing herself to tourists. She had been mayor since Lillian was little. No one ever ran against her, and term limits hadn't made their way to the island. It wasn't the kind of community to disturb the status quo.

"I'm the mayor for the last sixteen years, you know," Camille was boasting now. "You wouldn't have even heard of our island before I took office. And no, I wasn't elected as a teenager, I know what you're thinking," she told a fudgie. "I'm older than I look! It's all the fish I eat from the Great Lakes. The oils are very good for the skin."

"We wouldn't fit in there with the size of her head," Gigi commented.

"It's become part of her post-cycling workout routine," Lillian said. "A hot tub town hall, people are calling it." She felt guilty gossiping, but something about Gigi brought it out in her.

Gigi smiled, her canines flashing something feral. "What a dedicated city government we have."

Lillian wasn't a fan of the mayor either. "At least our doctors work hard," she said, meeting James's eyes, their warm hues holding the line like allies.

"Trying to," James said. "This is the first lunch break I've taken in weeks. Appointments have been booked solid. Something's going around."

His modesty was adorable, not an ounce of it affected. "Yes, I wonder why everyone's flocking to see you," Lillian mused. "The great mystery of Mackinac Island."

Gigi pointed at all the tropical cocktail picks crammed into her glass. "What's with all the umbrellas? It's a waste of paper."

When the Tongs first moved to the island when Lillian was in fourth grade, Gigi was entranced by the Pink Pony. She loved those little paper umbrellas, begging Lillian to bring them to school so Gigi could prop them in cafeteria milk cartons, wave them around like flags, like swords, like wands. Lillian had gifted a whole bag of them for Gigi's pony-themed tenth birthday party. Gigi had been sure her dad was getting her a real pony, but he had only sent a Beanie Baby pony instead. That was back when they'd been inseparable, before everything was severed.

Lillian's feet ached. She was tired of standing, suddenly desperate for the sedentary luxury of her Chicago life. Sitting in an air-conditioned office, the plush back seat of a cab, a chic restaurant booth where someone else was serving her. "You used to like the umbrellas," she told Gigi.

Gigi's expression smudged. A remembering or a forgetting? The smear of it looked the same from this angle.

"I can throw them away." Lillian offered her hand, aware of its bareness since she'd given back the ring. The way skin rubbed against skin, no golden barrier.

"No, it's fine," Gigi said. "I'll give some to James."

"I'm good," James said, casting Lillian an apologetic look. But he let Gigi put three umbrellas in his iced tea anyway.

Chapter 13

Rebecca

Rebecca liked collecting Petoskey stones, the fossilized corals native to Northern Michigan. It was something she and her mother did on Mackinac. Ever since Rebecca was little, they'd go down to Windermere Point or British Landing and sift through the sand and water. Gigi never had the patience for it. She stomped shells with her bare feet instead, using the broken bits to write her name in the sand. Large block letters so propeller planes dipping by might see her name, remember it.

Tom wasn't fond of the activity either, preferring to nap on the beach or livestream a sports game. Rebecca had overcome her fear of driving and started taking solo beach trips during the week while he was holed up at the office doing whatever it was that financial advisors did. "Playing therapist to rich people," was how he described it.

Petoskey stones were easier to find when wet. The distinctive "rising sun" pattern of rays popped on the surface. Today Rebecca waded into Lake Michigan up to her shins. She reached down and scooped a handful of lake-floor debris, then filtered it through her fingers.

As she searched, she called her mother, hoping she might reveal something about Clyde to her. Gigi's updates were infuriatingly sparse. Rebecca missed her place as Eloise's first confidante. So much already seemed to be changing since her sister had gotten back.

"I look like a madwoman talking to myself," Eloise told Rebecca over the phone. She was hiss-whispering, the rasp sounding like static. "Everyone in Doud's is staring."

Rebecca had gifted her mother wireless earbuds after Eloise had lamented that they wouldn't be able to go on their walks anymore. She'd only just figured them out, likely because Gigi was there to manage the technology.

"They're probably just staring because of your radiant beauty," Rebecca said. Her eyes were on Sadie, who was off leash and testing the water.

Lake Michigan bunched in turquoise clumps near the shoreline, then dispersed into deeper blue. Windblown dunes and scraggly shrubs gave dimension to the landscape. The panoramic views reminded Rebecca enough of Mackinac that she couldn't help but compare. Her eyes searched for the bridge that wasn't there.

Traverse City still didn't feel like home. Their next-door neighbors hosted a barbecue last night and didn't invite Rebecca and Tom. Tom didn't think it was a big deal, said they should just go over and join in. But Rebecca had haunted from their window instead. The sting was still there today, not that she was going to tell her mother about it. Eloise would use it as an opportunity to bring up why she and Tom should move to Mackinac, why it was a criminal act to live more than fifty miles away.

"Or maybe they're staring because they've heard you're the island's most sought-after bachelorette," Rebecca carried on, getting quite the thrill over using the word *bachelorette* to describe her mother. She'd thought of her as a divorcée for so long that this was an exciting change indeed.

"Don't tease me, Rebecca," Eloise said. "It's one thing when your sister does it, but you're supposed to be on my side."

"I'm always on your side." Rebecca hoped her mother knew how true that was. She bent down to unearth a mussel shell lodged in the sand. It wasn't just the stones she liked. Shells were good too. She and Eloise would use a hot glue gun to merge shards from multiple shells and then fashion them into necklaces, earrings, trinkets. A mosaic of brokenness made whole. "I just think you're also on Clyde's side," Rebecca said. "Even if you're not letting yourself admit it."

"What's that supposed to mean?" Eloise said.

"You're doing that thing where you mentally rattle off all the ways it could go wrong." Rebecca caught up with Sadie, who was digging a hole, sand spraying. "Believe me, I know the trick."

This was perhaps the most daunting thing about becoming a parent. Rebecca felt reasonably equipped for the tasks of keeping a little human alive, sacrificing her time and money. Harder to face was the prospect that the child might know her in ways she didn't know herself. These thoughts had been percolating since she'd been reading family planning books. She and Tom had just started trying. It might take years, so better to get going. Rebecca had never been naturally good at things the way Gigi had. Her success came from hard work and persistence.

"I appreciate your input," Eloise said. "But I have enough to worry about with Georgiana going around playing these games with the doctor. Did she tell you she's suddenly interested in him? Or at least claiming to be?"

If she were face-to-face with her mother, Rebecca would have shared what Gigi told her about wanting to steal James from Lillian. But through the phone came a level of distance, and Rebecca felt a sisterly devotion kick in. Besides, Rebecca wasn't even sure she bought Gigi's shallow explanation.

"I thought you wanted her to date him," was all Rebecca said to her mom.

She rinsed off more stones in the lake. The water washed over her feet, creeping up to her ankles. Even in summer, the Great Lakes remained cold. Surfers swathed in wet suits paddled out into the low waves, trying to catch their patchy foam.

"Date him, yes. *Pretend* to date him to aggravate Lillian, no." Eloise dropped her voice even lower. It was hardly audible. "Trina Tong is over in the dairy aisle and won't even look at me."

"You and Mrs. Tong have never been close," Rebecca reminded. "Doesn't that trace back to how you didn't invite her to your euchre group when she moved here?"

"Euchre is a four-person game," Eloise whispered. "Kitty had just joined; we were already full. It was nothing personal. I told her that."

Rebecca suspected her new neighbors might say something similar about their barbecue last night.

"My point is that I'm walking on eggshells in my own town," Eloise went on. "Though I daresay I should have seen it coming. My own naivete for thinking Georgiana might have matured by age twenty-nine . . ."

Rebecca set a Petoskey stone in her tote bag. It rattled against the other fossils and shells. The clanking of nature's coins. She continued on, scanning the lake floor. "Gigi takes after Dad that way."

It sounded worse out loud than it had in her head, and Rebecca regretted the comment. She was going to apologize for it but then realized her mother hadn't taken it as much of a dig. Eloise tended to see comparisons to Gus as net positive.

"Your father was married with two children by the time he was Georgiana's age," Eloise reminded her.

It wouldn't be productive for Rebecca to point out that a mere five years later, he had all but tossed aside both titles. Eloise's rose-colored glasses could only be removed by Gus himself, cracked by the pressure of his own palms, his empty promises. Whenever his Mackinac stopovers ended, Eloise spent weeks denouncing him— his fickleness, his lack of responsibility, his abysmal communication. Never, she insisted, would she open her doors for him again.

"He's not coming to the island this summer, is he?" Rebecca asked.

"I don't think so. Why do you ask?"

"Just curious." Rebecca kept her voice casual, knowing how the topic would wind up her mother like a clock, a countdown with no end.

"You know your father," Eloise said, though it wasn't really true. Rebecca used to wish she knew him better. She used to wish it so much, on every dandelion seed she blew across the island. Nowadays she didn't wish on anything. Not dandelions, not stars, not even birthday candles. She focused on what she had, not what she lacked, and that was that.

Rebecca dropped the topic. "Just think of it this way. Gigi could be getting into trouble with drugs again or those violent protests. Be glad she's keeping things tame."

"For now," Eloise said. "I'll need to train Pluto to be a marijuana-sniffing cat. Georgiana's been complaining that we don't have a dispensary on the island. Said she might get a permit and open one herself. Spent all day researching it. The only burst of work ethic I've seen applied toward becoming a drug dealer."

Rebecca didn't dare confess that she may have inadvertently planted the seed. "An abomination, as Deirdre says."

"I miss you, Rebecca," Eloise said. "You always keep things in balance. The family fulcrum."

The words felt delicious to hear. Validation that Gigi wasn't usurping Rebecca's place.

"We'll be up for the Fourth," Rebecca said, brightening at the thought. "And don't let Gigi steal all the main character energy this summer. You deserve some too."

"Supporting character fits me better. I'm a mother, after all."

"But you're not *just* a mother," Rebecca said. It was something she had started thinking about a great deal for herself. How she could gain an identity as a mother but not lose all those other identities: woman, daughter, wife, friend, sister.

"My world begins and ends with my girls," Eloise said. "I wouldn't have it any other way. You'll understand someday."

Rebecca didn't dare mention that she hoped that day would come very soon. Eloise would obsess over it, then feel let down each month that nothing happened. Rebecca was doing everything she could not to let it consume her. Her mind kept going to all the potential things that could go wrong.

"I'm just saying, it's good to look out for your own needs too," Rebecca said.

"Now you're sounding like your sister. You two are conspiring about Clyde, I know it."

"Gigi is always conspiring. I'm just an innocent observer."

"Sure you are," Eloise said. "Hold on just a moment."

Her voice came through muffled. There seemed to be some kind of squabble.

"I'm back," Eloise said, coming in clearer again. "The fudgie working the checkout told me they raised the senior citizen age from fifty-five to sixty. Tried to swindle me out of my savings."

It was just like her mother to win a fight based on principle. The only time she initiated conflict was when someone overcharged her or cheated in euchre.

"Congratulations," Rebecca said. "You're no longer a senior citizen."

"I'm not ashamed of my age," Eloise said. "I won't be injecting my face with fillers and poison like some people around here." Mayor Welsh, Rebecca knew she meant, not daring to utter an insult in public. "But I'll talk to Mr. Doud about the policy change. It's his son's doing, no doubt. He's been making some terrible changes. Only stocking organic produce now. Red peppers are seventy-five cents more apiece. Not per pound, per *pepper*."

"Organic is good, though," Rebecca said. "Protects against cancer."

Eloise harrumphed. "Of all the horrors in this world," she said, "nuclear weapons, liberal politics, deranged gunmen . . . pesticides are the least of my concerns."

What Rebecca would give to see Gigi's reaction to hearing *liberal politics* lumped in with that list of atrocities.

"The lilacs have finally popped, at least," Eloise said. "I'm walking home now, and everything is bursting purple."

Rebecca could picture the island draped in its majestic floral robes. She missed it terribly.

"Deirdre keeps going on about how line dancing at the Lilac Festival won't be the same without you leading it," Eloise carried on. "But you'll be back soon enough, I suppose. Georgiana will sleep on the couch, of course, so you and Tom will get the loft. We can push the beds together."

Rebecca twisted her feet deeper into the sand. "We actually booked the Main Street Inn," she said. "Just so we're not crowding you and Gigi."

Silence sprawled. "You're not staying with me?" Eloise's voice was high and tight.

Tom had been sure that Eloise would understand and see that this was a very reasonable thing. Rebecca should have trusted her instincts, planned the delivery better. "I'm sorry," she said, feeling tactless. "I just think Tom might be more comfortable having our own space."

"Tom can stay at the inn then," Eloise said. "You're my daughter, Rebecca. I'm not letting you stay in a hotel."

"Mom." Rebecca traced the diamond ring on her left hand. "Tom is my husband now."

"Of course," Eloise said after a moment. "I'm sorry." She sounded so dejected, like her windpipe had a leak. Rebecca felt awful, though she was proud of herself for standing up to her mother. She hadn't had much practice at it until recently.

"I'll still spend the whole weekend with you, obviously," Rebecca said. "It's really just for sleeping and showering. And I'll bring my Petoskey stones with me," she hurried on. "I've found a lot of good ones. We can do some crafting."

"How about we collect new ones when you're here?" Eloise said. "Mackinac has a far better variety than Traverse City. Something about the wind patterns."

Rebecca didn't ask for her citation. She just dunked another fossilized rock into the ocean-like lake, cleaning the sand, the dirt, the gobs of duckweed until it shone like a gemstone. "I'd like that."

Chapter 14

Alice

Even after all these years, the Lilac Festival still entranced Alice Klein—or Nonni, as her granddaughters called her.

It was where she had first met David, back in the summer of 1965, when seventeen-year-old Alice was crowned the Lilac Festival Queen. David, visiting from downstate, watched. "Every man on the island was drooling," he would say, retelling the story. "But I was the only one stupid enough to think I might stand a chance with her." He'd found her line dancing and asked if she'd be his partner for the next song. "All right," she'd said, taken with his confidence, his all-American features. "Let's see what you've got."

They'd kept dancing their whole lives. Whether in the ballroom or the kitchen, they never ceased keeping a beat.

After the cancer got him, people remarked how lucky Alice was to miss someone as much as she missed David. To have experienced that kind of marriage. Alice knew she had been lucky once but didn't feel that way after she lost him. It was incredible she didn't have a limp, so lopsided did she feel without her husband of fifty-one years.

Then there was the gnawing guilt that this was her fault, that it had been her infidelity that had poisoned David, not the fumes from the construction sites like the doctors said. The shame was too searing to be shared. Eloise would never look at her the same if she knew. Neither would Alice's granddaughters.

For a long time after David's death, Alice didn't go anywhere, except outside to the generator, just behind the garage. David had said that if he was able to communicate from the other side, he would meet her at the generator at 3:00 p.m. on Wednesdays when it ran its weekly test. He'd been like that—romantic but in a practical, Midwest way. So every Wednesday, rain, snow, or sleet, Alice had huddled by the generator, ears and eyes perked for a noise, a vapor, any sign at all. She never found anything. Stray seagulls and monarchs didn't count. It was supposed to be clearer.

Ultimately it was the Lilac Festival that rescued Alice, that first year without David. She hadn't wanted to go, but Eloise and Rebecca were set on it. Alice decided she could muster the strength to leave the house for a couple of hours, even if it was only in her track suit and tennis shoes, her stringy hair hidden beneath a baseball cap.

She watched the crowning of the Lilac Festival Queen, for old times' sake. That was when the pennies appeared. Three of them, right at her feet, all facing heads-up. She and David had a habit of scooping up spare change and adding it to the piggy bank in their bedroom. "*We'll buy a boat one day,*" David would say each time they plunked the coins in. It always made Alice laugh with the wooziness of what *might be*, especially during the early years, when buying fresh fruit rather than frozen was a once-a-month luxury.

Of the three pennies Alice found, the first was dated from David's birth year. The second from her own. The third from their wedding anniversary.

It was enough for Alice. Here it was, proof that David was looking out for her from beyond. There must be a constraint on the generator, or perhaps this was one of his jokes. But the point was that he loved her, he forgave her (because heaven had no secrets; surely he knew everything by now), and he wanted her to keep going. She hurried home, fluffed her hair, and reentered the world of the living.

Even now, seven years later, Alice still looked for pennies and kept finding them. In the garden, the church, the pickleball court. She didn't tell anyone about her obsession. She liked keeping it between her and David. Something that was just theirs.

She no longer stood beside the generator on Wednesdays at 3:00 p.m. But she still listened to its hum and peeked through the window, just in case.

———— ≈ ————

Alice pulled up to Thistle Dew in her golf cart. David's golf cart, really, but she drove it now.

Golf carts were allowed on Mackinac, though frowned upon except for the injured or elderly. Alice was happy to use her age to her advantage. There was no room for pride on an island this size.

"Nature's perfume," Alice said, taking a whiff of lilacs as Georgiana emerged onto the porch. She was dressed in itty-bitty shorts and a tank top with perilously thin straps, her lovely face hidden beneath a droopy bucket hat and bug-eyed sunglasses. "Can't complain about the smell of the island now."

"The mix of flowers and excrement is almost worse," Georgiana said. "Like spraying cheap perfume in a bathroom after getting the wrong end of a baked-bean casserole."

"There's nothing cheap about these lilacs," Alice cut in. She thought about the lilac flower crown she'd been wearing the day she met David. She wished she'd kept it, preserved it.

"I didn't mean to offend you, Nonni," Georgiana said quickly. "Just the island."

Georgiana had been such a sweet child, always over at their house, pushing her tiny toy mower alongside David's big one, aglow at the thought that she was helping. But her teens and twenties had been hard. A rough, scaly exterior had formed. By the time she was in high school, Georgiana had stopped popping by to see David and Alice after school, stopped coming over for Sunday brunch, stopped sharing much at all about her life. And then of course there had been the terrible way she'd absconded from the island, exposing the family to such emotional and reputational damage.

One would have thought that leaving for college might have been a good enough ticket off the island. But not for Georgiana. It was forever a tangled web with her. Not like the clean lines of her little sister. Though Rebecca had nuance too, more than Eloise often wanted to admit.

Alice had remained very close to Rebecca over the years and was privately glad that Rebecca had moved off the island. It was time for her to come into her own as a woman. Perspective was important, though she herself had lived her whole life on Mackinac.

Eloise had never gotten quite enough perspective, as far as Alice was concerned. Though Alice was partially to blame for that. She and David had schemed to keep Eloise and Gus from leaving. They'd even given Gus a good job working for David, thereby eliminating any reason to look elsewhere. It had been selfish, Alice could see now.

Georgiana, on the other hand, had gotten too much perspective, trying on places like purses, hardly deigning to keep in touch with the plebeians back home. She was always warm to Alice but hadn't exactly gone out of her way in recent years. When David died, she came back for the funeral and flew out again the next day. She seemed to think she was above the island, above the people who lived here.

Though maybe that observation wasn't entirely fair. Alice didn't feel she knew her granddaughter well enough for an accurate characterization. She spoke on the phone with Georgiana very rarely and saw her once a year at Christmas. She'd even stooped to googling pictures of California—that liberal inferno!—so she might know a little more about her granddaughter's life.

The way Georgiana treated Eloise was particularly difficult to watch. She rebelled against her mother because she didn't feel secure enough to rebel against her father. Or at least that was how it looked to Alice. Eloise wasn't going anywhere, and Georgiana knew that and exploited it. The lack of gratitude, the endless sarcasm, the cold-shoulder treatment.

It was one thing for an adolescent, but now that Georgiana was in her late twenties, Alice felt time was running out for a true course correction.

This summer offered the chance for a reset.

Perhaps this might be when Gigi came back to them, not as the little girl she'd been, but as a woman who was softer and less combative, easier to love.

"You sure I can't tempt you to play, Georgiana?" Alice asked, thinking it might be a nice way for them to bond, hacking balls at other people's faces. "I'd be happy to replace Mr. Townsend. An upgrade, I'm sure."

Alice had never been an athlete growing up—what girl was in her generation?—but she'd been bitten by the pickleball bug a few years ago. She was the strongest she'd ever felt, physically at least. Having Liam Townsend as her partner didn't hurt, she supposed.

"Can't," Georgiana said. "Mother is having me do her dirty work for her. Play cornhole with Clyde so she doesn't have to, though she's clearly dying to see him again."

Alice did find it sweet that Georgiana was so invested in Eloise's budding "acquaintanceship," as Eloise called it. She'd expected Georgiana to be resistant, given how loyal she was to Gus, but perhaps she'd misjudged.

"Ah, the proxy strategy." Alice nodded. "She did that with your father in the beginning. Convinced me to tutor him in math at our house, then spied the whole time."

"You're a couple of conspiracy theorists," Eloise said, coming out onto the porch. "I'm needed at the jewelry workshop, I told you."

Alice hadn't seen Eloise this worked up over a man since Gus. "You act like I didn't raise you," Alice said. "Georgiana, what's the latest with you and the doctor?"

"No update," Georgiana said. "We got lunch, that's all. But my mom now has to go on a second date with Clyde. That's how the rules work."

"You hate rules," Eloise said. "And I'm not going to be pressured into another date just to go tit for tat with you. You agreed to see Dr. Kentwood again by your own volition. I didn't force you."

"You guilted me," Georgiana said. "But Lillian was there third-wheeling our date. She and James are clearly into each other."

"He'll be bored by Lillian," Alice said, hoping this would perk up her granddaughter.

"Well, he'd be infuriated with me. What's worse—being bored or angry?"

"Bored," Alice said, meaning it. "At least anger has real emotion in it. Flip it around, rearrange it, and it just might become love."

"Interesting perspective," Georgiana said. "But I'm focused on finding my inner happiness before I find a partner."

"I'm not sure that's the right order." Alice couldn't stand those modern mantras. "I was miserable before meeting your grandfather."

"I thought you were in love with Liam Townsend," Georgiana said. "And then gave him the heartbreak of the century."

"Being in love doesn't mean you're happy," Alice said. "My relationship with Liam was a tumultuous teenage mess, to say the least." So much passion, so little patience.

She'd toppled right over and David had caught her, held her, loved her. Even when she'd foolishly fooled around with Liam, Alice never doubted that David was the one for her. Life with him had forever buoyed her, steadied her. There might not have been as much raw chemistry, but a foundation of friendship was the most important ingredient for marriage. Today's generation had lost sight of that.

"Pop brought happiness the way yeast made bread rise," Alice told Georgiana. "Slowly and reliably, always smelling like home."

"Thanks for searing the image of my grandparents making love into my brain," Georgiana said.

"Don't distort my words," Alice said. "The metaphor was about bread rising, not lovemaking."

"But you said so yourself—it was a metaphor."

Alice was flustered. "I won't apologize for talking about how well your pop loved me."

"Well," Georgiana said, looking from Alice to Eloise. "At least one of the three of us knows what true love feels like."

Eloise looked like she wanted to object and say she knew about true love too. But she just disappeared into the flower beds to carry on with her gardening.

Alice revved the golf cart engine. "Want a ride into town?" she asked, hoping Georgiana might take the offer so they could have some one-on-one time.

"I'll take my bike," Georgiana said. "There's a better chance I'll collide with a fudgie that way. Need to teach them some lessons."

"I don't disagree," Alice said, knowing better than to tell her to be careful, lest it result in the opposite.

"Looks like you have a taker, though," Georgiana said, nodding to Liam, who was walking up the drive, bouncing a pickleball on his paddle as he went.

———— ≈ ————

It had happened six years into their marriage.

Bow season had just opened and David was off on a hunting trip. His parents were watching Eloise (age two) for the weekend, down in Charlevoix. Liam had stopped by the house with a case of bourbon.

"Thought you might be lonely with David out of town," he'd said, standing there on the front steps.

"I'm not lonely," Alice had responded. "But come on in. It's cold outside and I've just baked a poached pear pie."

She knew it was a bad idea but figured she had enough sense not to let anything happen. She had figured wrong.

"Do you ever wonder about it?" Liam had asked after they'd drunk too much. "You and me . . . what could have been?"

"I can't say I do. It all worked out the way it was supposed to." Alice felt bad saying it given that Liam still hadn't married, still hadn't gotten the family he wanted.

"Did it?" He touched her forearm. It felt like a patched-up promise.

"Yes," she said, but then held out her glass for a refill.

She was surprised by how easy it was to stray from her moral compass. With Liam there had been no hardships endured. They hadn't lost a baby together or nearly lost a house. She hadn't picked up after him for years or cleaned his vomit from the toilet. She had broken up with him in high school, clean and swiftly.

And then she ended things a second time, ended them before they really started. Nothing had ever passed between them again. Alice had always been cordial to him since their tryst, never wanting to give the impression that she might have a reason not to be. That her three nights with him back in the autumn of 1982 might have fractured her marriage, her whole life. But they hadn't been caught, and as far as she knew no one was the wiser. She certainly hadn't told anyone and assumed Liam hadn't either. Nothing had imploded. Miraculously, it had all turned out all right.

Liam recouped just fine, and for the last decade he'd devoted himself to none other than the delightful creature that was Camille Welsh. They'd never married but had been together for over a decade. But just a few months ago, Camille ditched him for a Yooper (what Michiganders called someone from the Upper Peninsula) she'd met through cycling. "Chuck is a man who knows what he wants," Camille had told Paula who had told Deirdre who had told Alice. "He's moving to Mackinac for me. I could never leave, not with how attached the islanders are to me." Since the split, Liam once again seemed to be noticing Alice.

Alice had been hesitant to rekindle anything, even friendship. It felt unfair to David. But she did have history with Liam and there was a comfort in that, especially at her age. His irreverent humor made her laugh like she hadn't in years, and he brought out flecks of youth in Alice that she thought she'd buried with David.

She'd made it clear to Liam that all she had to offer was friendship. Her loyalty would always be to David. But Liam accepted her friendship gladly, and they enjoyed their pickleball and euchre together.

She had to admit her life was richer with Liam back in it. Though she made sure to sprinkle in a rotation of other male friends so no one got the wrong idea. Liam or Eloise most of all.

And if Eloise ever found out about the affair . . . Well, Alice would be too disgraced to ever be seen with Liam again. She'd probably have to leave the island altogether.

"Mind if I hop in?" Liam said now, approaching the golf cart. "Need to conserve my energy so we can take the trophy from Pastor Kevin and that cheating line-caller wife of his."

"Very charitable," Alice said, holding back an uncouth giggle. Liam greeted her with a quick kiss on the cheek. It felt strange to have a man kiss her in front of her daughter and granddaughter, however chaste and chummy it might be. Georgiana was watching them curiously. "Hop in," Alice said to Liam.

Before he was even settled in the passenger seat, Alice floored it out of the driveway, partially to impress Georgiana and partially to escape before she made any sly comments about how there might be something between her and Liam when there absolutely, certainly was not.

Chapter 15

Eloiѕe

Since when has Nonni had a boyfriend?" Georgiana asked Eloise as Nonni zoomed out of the driveway at Thistle Dew.

"That's just Liam Townsend," Eloise said, yanking up weeds from the garden bed. The sun was getting hot. "They grew up together."

"Wasn't that Nonni's high school boyfriend? The one who was dating Camille before she left him for the Yooper?"

"Correct," Eloise said. "But they're only friends."

Eloise found comfort in how her mother had men to spend time with, and even more comfort in how her mother assured she had no interest in ever dating again. Eloise's dad was her one and only.

"And he's okay with that?" Georgiana prodded.

Eloise didn't like the way Georgiana was trying to stir up trouble. "Of course he is. Why do you ask?"

"Because I know how to tell if a guy is interested," Georgiana said. "And that Liam . . . he's smitten."

"No, he's not." The observation rattled Eloise, not that she put much stock in it. Georgiana was biased by her twentysomething lens, through which every friendship seemed to have some sexual undertone to it. "They're just good friends."

"Like you and Clyde?"

Eloise ducked her head deeper in the flower bed, tending to the shasta daisies to make sure no weeds were strangling the flowers. "No, nothing like us," she said, feeling dizzy—just from the constant up and down of gardening, she told herself. "We're mere acquaintances and have only known each other a couple of weeks. Your Nonni and Liam have known each other their whole lives."

"That's a lot of history," Georgiana said, spinning Eloise's words against her yet again. "And now they're both single and spend lots of time together, but there's nothing going on between them?"

"They're at a different life stage than you, Georgiana," Eloise said. "As am I. Your grandmother and I seek platonic companionship, not romance."

"And Nonni has told you this?"

"Well, not verbatim." Eloise couldn't imagine talking with her mother about this kind of thing. Even broaching the topic felt like it would be an insult to Eloise's father, whom her mother had loved—and still did—so dearly and loyally. "But I know my mother, and she's happy with Liam's friendship."

"I'm not denying that," Georgiana said, getting her bicycle from the garage. "I'm just saying she might be happier with some tongue on that kiss."

"Georgiana!" Eloise felt queasy. "Watch your mouth."

Georgiana sped off on her bicycle, dinging that annoying bell as she went. "Watch your eyes."

Chapter 16

Gigi

Gigi bicycled over to the cornhole tournament.

She wore a helmet but didn't strap it. Eloise wasn't able to yell at her for riding without one, yet her chin wasn't pinched by the strap. Loopholes like these were Gigi's sweet spot.

The lilac bushes were in the surge of bloom. Petals padding the streets, the island's rendering of a royal carpet. Gigi enjoyed the skid as she approached Main Street.

It was flooded with fudgies. An onslaught of buggies dashing this way and that. Police officers patrolling on horseback, as if anything worse than shoplifting or bicycle theft ever happened here.

Gigi was not thinking about James as she pedaled. Or rather, she was thinking about how she was not thinking about him.

She had enjoyed herself at lunch with James, more than she'd intended to. There was definitely something between them. Not in-your-face fireworks but little tugs of temptation. The kind of thing made sexier by how understated it was. James had felt it too; she knew he had.

But Gigi had yet to hear from him.

Lillian probably got upset and forced a label on their relationship, told him not to talk to Gigi. It was all so childish. Gigi felt that old craving to swipe through hundreds of dating app profiles to distract her. If only Mackinac had such high-quantity, low-quality men as LA did.

She tried not to let James put her in a bad mood. She tried instead to focus on the riveting new development that it wasn't just her mother who had a suitor. Her grandmother seemed to as well. It was a plot twist Gigi hadn't seen coming, though Eloise was clearly in denial.

Caught up in her thoughts, she nearly took out a cluster of oblivious pedestrians.

"Someone's on a mission," one of the officers called out, catching up to Gigi on his horse.

Gigi glanced over. The officer was attractive in an unruly sort of way. Tousled blond hair gave the impression of sleeping through five alarm clocks after a night of tequila shots. Gigi knew the look well.

Gigi slowed her pace. "If I don't bring back the gold in the cornhole tournament, my mother will deem me a blot on the family name," she said. "As if she hasn't already."

The officer's caramel eyes flickered, amused. "Would your mom be Eloise?"

"How'd you guess?"

"You look alike," he said. "And I heard her daughter was back in town."

"Here I am. The notorious rebel."

"I think I've got you beat there," he said. "Got driven out of my own hometown; that's why I'm here."

Gigi couldn't tell if he was lying or not. She liked that quality. "Well, do yourself a favor and try to get kicked off the island too," she said. "There's nothing to do here."

"Nothing?" His eyes glimmered like he was enjoying an inside joke. "Cruiser and me get up to some fun, don't we, boy?" He patted his horse, a handsome chestnut Clydesdale.

Cruiser was a good name for a police horse, Gigi decided. It might not have the elegance of Willow but brought more levity.

"I should give you a speeding ticket," the officer said. "But I'll let you off with a warning this time."

"Very generous of you," Gigi said. "Now, if you'll excuse me, I have a trophy to win."

Gigi accelerated again, whizzing down Main Street with the authority of Moses parting the Red Sea.

"I'm Ronny," the officer called out after her. "Thanks for asking."

Gigi felt a smile sneak onto her face. She dismounted at Windermere Point, the pebbly stretch of beach where the cornhole competition was taking place. The Doghouse Food Shack—Mackinac's go-to spot for hot dogs and root beer floats—was located on the point, with picnic tables for seating. In the distance, the Round Island Point Lighthouse was visible in the Straits, adding a dash of barn red to the blue horizon.

Clyde appeared at Gigi's shoulder. He was wielding a professional camera, snapping photos of contestants warming up, tossing bean bags at boards. "What a fascinating sport."

"Please don't call it a sport," Gigi said. "It's a redneck lawn game. But we've got to win." She wanted something to brag to Ronny about next time she saw him. Not to mention that she'd found out James and Lillian were competing as a team.

"Can I ask you something before we start?" Clyde said. "It's about your mother. I'm sure you know she told me she just wants to be friends." He fiddled with the camera. "Do you think I might change her mind?"

Gigi doubted Clyde would be able to make it very far with Eloise. She was so set in her ways. The way she answered the questions about Nonni showed that Eloise saw romance as a young person's affliction. But he was a kind, unconventional man, and Gigi felt a genuine desire to help him.

"You're not going to change her mind," she said. Clyde's face crinkled in resignation. "But," Gigi went on, "maybe you can change her heart."

"Change her heart, not her head," Clyde repeated. "Yes, that's it. That's just what I'll have to do!"

The pep was back in Clyde's step and beginner's luck was on his side. He sank four bean bags, advancing them to the second round.

They secured that game and the following against Camille and her boyfriend.

"It wouldn't be right for the mayor to steal the show," Camille said as she grudgingly conceded her loss.

"Yeah, having a mayor who actually led would be quite unseemly," Gigi muttered.

Camille didn't seem to hear, but James did. He cracked a smile and Gigi felt that confusion again—he *did* seem to have a decent sense of humor; he just kept it buried. She wanted to know him better but now felt she'd lost the chance to Lillian.

Soon they were in the finals against James and Lillian, who were dressed in color-coordinated Wimbledon whites and were definitely giving couple vibes. Gigi felt a sweaty flashback to senior prom, seeing Lillian and Benjamin slow dancing together. Except this time felt much worse, with actual adult feelings involved.

Gigi and James lined up next to each other across from their partners. "Hope you enjoyed your winning streak," she said.

"We are enjoying it, yes," James said. "Though I've got to say, you're pretty solid," he added as Gigi looped another bean bag through the hole.

"It's all about my follow-through," Gigi said. "When I start something, I finish it. I don't leave the other person hanging."

James shot her a sheepish look.

"Your girlfriend is carrying your team," Gigi said. Lillian had sunk two bean bags through the hole in the time it took for James to land one on the board.

"She's not my girlfriend." He kept his voice low.

Gigi was pleased to hear that things might not be moving at the lightning speed that the euchre ladies were predicting.

"Just a piece of helpful advice then," Gigi told him. "Don't step foot anywhere near Dali's Jewelry or the islanders will start congratulating you on your engagement."

"This whole thing is getting ridiculous," James said, more impatiently now. "Half the patients who show up at the clinic have no ailments whatsoever. They're just trying to pitch their nieces or granddaughters at me, like they think this is *The Bachelor* or something."

Gigi cringed thinking about how Eloise had been one of these women persuading James to take out her daughter.

"The joys of small-town life," Gigi said. "Although," she went on, trying to get under his skin, "you could always pay me to be your fake girlfriend. So people stop trying to set you up."

"I'm not going to pay you to be my girlfriend," James said. "That would just raise another set of issues."

Gigi felt out of sorts. Picking up a bean bag, she arced it into the hole, giving her and Clyde the winning twenty-one points to secure the championship. She faced James, enjoying the range of emotions tiled across his face. "Your loss then," she said.

Chapter 17

Eloise

The lilac earrings Eloise wore during the jewelry workshop felt bulky.

Back at Thistle Dew afterward, she took them off, but the heaviness remained. The workshop had gone well—forty-seven attendees, many of whom tipped generously—but Eloise hadn't felt her usual spark for it. She'd been distracted. Everything felt a bit frizzy.

"Turn that down, please," she said to Georgiana, who was sprawled on the couch, bare feet propped on the glass coffee table, computer blaring some trashy reality show. "And move your feet off the table. You're smudging the glass."

"I'm giving it some character," Georgiana said, reluctantly rearranging herself. "Aren't you going to compliment me on being the cornhole champion? I'm sure our house will be named a historical monument for it."

"I heard you did very well." Eloise used the sleeve of her cardigan to rub the coffee table clean. "How was Clyde?"

"Pretty decent for his first time playing."

Eloise wasn't inquiring about how competent a cornhole player he was. She was asking how he was, in light of recent events. And she was certain Georgiana knew good and well that was what she meant. But Eloise wouldn't beg for information, wouldn't grovel. She made a pot of peppermint tea and brought two steaming mugs out to the couch.

"I asked for Diet Coke," Georgiana said.

"Go help yourself then."

Georgiana dissolved back into her computer screen. "What do you know about Ronny?"

It took Eloise a moment to register the question. She was deep into rehashing her phone call with Clyde, dissecting her word choice, criticizing her tone. Had she been too hasty in suggesting they keep things platonic?

"Do you mean Officer Ronny?" she asked.

"Yeah, that one." Georgiana said it casually. Too casually, like she had something to hide.

Eloise's headache mounted. A scraping, a grating. But expressing her disapproval would just make Georgiana want him more. She'd learned that lesson the hard way.

"I don't know him personally," Eloise said.

"I heard there was a petition to get him removed," Georgiana said.

There had been two petitions, actually, but nothing had come of them. Islanders liked to collect signatures for everything, from banning cruise ships to hiking the ferry tax to banning political yard signs. None had yet been successful. "He's rubbed a few people the wrong way, I suppose."

"Don't worry, I'm not going to run away with him, Mother," Georgiana said, clearly sensing Eloise's apprehension. "I'm just . . . lonely here, I guess. No Rebecca, no friends. James choosing Lillian over me. All that happy stuff." Her eyes widened, dewy and doleful. It was a trick she'd mastered as a toddler to get sympathy. Eloise felt herself softening.

"Did James tell you he wasn't interested?" Eloise asked.

"He won't say it outright, but I can take the hint."

Eloise was disappointed in James. She'd thought he'd at least be the type to communicate clearly. It had been a mistake setting them up in the first place. The odds of it working had been so slim, and now Georgiana would lash out, throw herself at someone new.

"So what's Ronny done that's so bad?" Georgiana pressed.

"What *hasn't* he done?" Eloise said. "Giving private tours after dark to tourists. Only the young female ones, I should add. Drinking on duty, taking that horse of his out racing through the trails. No one's been this unpopular on the island since . . ."

"Since me?" Georgiana finished for her.

She couldn't pretend otherwise, though it upset her how much pride Georgiana seemed to take in her infamy. Eloise sipped her tea. It singed her tongue.

"You've changed, though." Eloise heard the vacillation in her own voice.

"Have I?" Georgiana said, and she sounded like she might actually want Eloise to answer.

"Sure you have," Eloise said. "You've seen so much of the country. You've gotten a diverse array of work experiences." She tried to put a positive spin on it for both of them. "And you cared enough about how I might be faring after Rebecca moved away to come visit for the whole summer."

"You know that wasn't the reason," Gigi said. Eloise wished she would just take the bone sometimes. "I had no other options."

Eloise had to take a cooling breath. She reminded herself her daughter was not mentally well. These were the sick parts talking, the scared parts.

"The thing about you, Georgiana," she went on. "*Gigi*," she said, wanting to show that she was really trying, even as the truncated name scuffed her lips, "is that you have always created opportunities for yourself, and you always will. It's a very good trait."

Gigi turned down the volume on her show just a little. She seemed to be listening.

"How about being my date for the cruise tomorrow?" Eloise suggested. The Lilac Festival always ended with a big sunset cruise, the kind of thing islanders grumbled was a waste of taxpayer money but no one would ever hear of canceling.

Georgiana made a face. "I'd rather swim across the Straits of Mackinac without a wet suit than be stuck on a boat with the islanders and all of their nosy interrogations."

Eloise ordinarily would have chastised Georgiana for speaking this way about their neighbors. She would have told her she wasn't invited after all. But this summer was showing Eloise that she needed to meet her daughter where she was. She had to try from multiple angles, crack open the back doors and the windows and the chimneys too.

"I heard Ronny is DJing," Eloise said.

Georgiana pushed the hair out of her eyes to better assess Eloise. "You're lying."

"I'm not. Kitty is organizing it and said Ronny offered to DJ for free. Wants to get exposure, whatever that means." Eloise's face pinched. She didn't approve of DJs. They were so loud, so unrefined. But maybe Georgiana needed a night out of the house. It might be good for them both.

"I'll think about it," Georgiana said.

Eloise took it as the small win that it was. Perhaps now was the right time to probe again about Clyde. Those nonanswers Georgiana gave earlier simply wouldn't do.

Eloise blew on her mug to stall for time. "Did Clyde mention if he was going on the cruise?"

"It didn't come up," Georgiana said. "But I'm sure he will be."

"Why do you say that?"

"He's dying for another chance with you."

Eloise's insides released. Errant darts at a dangerous target. "He's not."

Georgiana closed her laptop. The shrill voices from the reality show ceased mid-sentence. "He told me today."

It was too much for Eloise. The way Georgiana disclosed this information so calmly, so clinically, as if stating that the electric bill had arrived in the mail. "And you're just now telling me this?"

"What was I supposed to do?" Georgiana said, tea sloshing on her shirt. "Bring it up right when you walked in? You get so agitated when Clyde comes up."

"I'm not agitated." Eloise's body tingled. "I'm perfectly fine."

"Right." Georgiana opened her laptop again. The voices resumed. "My mistake."

Eloise's only prior experience with a man making her agitated was Gus. She could make the sentence shorter. Her only prior experience with a man was Gus.

Gus had riled her up, it was true. Gloriously so.

He'd been two grades above Eloise. A colossal gulf in elementary school, but they knew each other loosely. (The Mackinac Island schoolhouse was so small back then, divided into just two rooms: younger students and older students.)

It was Deirdre who had fixated on him first. Ever since fourth grade, doodling hearts with Gus's initials in her notebooks, magicking up his name on the Ouija board they used in Paula's parents' basement. Eloise agreed he was charming and funny and dreamy and all the superlatives but saw no point in getting attached to someone she could never have. He always had a girl next to him in the hallway. Someone older, someone prettier.

Ninth grade came. High school. Though still in the same building they'd been in since kindergarten, it was a big moment. Especially to Deirdre, who was adamant that *this would be the year* Gus Jenkins fell for her. How could he not with her grown-out bangs and braces-free smile? It was only a matter of time, Eloise and Paula assured Deirdre.

The week before school started, the girls went on a much-anticipated shopping trip to the mall in Mackinaw City. Their mothers accompanied them but opted to linger at the hair salon, entrusting them each with a crisp twenty-dollar bill, reminding them to bring back the change, that God was watching.

Eloise and Paula had to weigh in on every outfit that Deirdre tried on through the lens of *What will Gus say?* It was tiresome and shallow, not that Eloise should judge. She worshipped false idols too, growing fond of her reflection in the mirror, the subtle curves that had started to appear. Her knees were no longer so knobby. In a moment of impulse, she spent her wad on a pleated miniskirt that Alice would purge from her wardrobe as soon as it was discovered. But the thought of wearing it even once was enough.

Yanked along by Deirdre's influence, Eloise and Paula took Epsom salt baths, tended obsessively to zits with toothpaste and apple cider vinegar, and slathered oily lotions onto freshly shaved legs. (Alice still restricted Eloise to only three razor widths on each shin. Paula was allowed to shave her calves but not her kneecaps. Deirdre, without permission, sheared her entire legs, from toes to upper thighs.)

"Don't complain," Deirdre told Eloise. "Your hairs are blonde and peachy. Mine are jet black and coarse like a horse's tail. Not fair."

Also *not fair* in Deirdre's eyes was the fact that several months into ninth grade, Gus still hadn't made a move.

"Why don't you just ask him out yourself?" Paula asked. "Girls don't always need to wait for guys."

"Of course they do," Deirdre said. "It's called romance."

Romance also apparently meant laying booby traps for Gus. The first attempt came in the form of Deirdre's fifteenth birthday party, mid-December. The main event was a toboggan ride on the hill down from Arch Rock. Guests would draw their partner's name from a hat. It would be rigged, naturally, so Gus would select Deirdre. Cozied up on the sled as the toboggan shot downhill, their bond would be cemented for life. This plan was foiled when Gus declined the invitation, citing basketball practice, though two other boys on the team attended. (Gus was quite the jock; he would have played football and soccer too, but the school was too small to field the teams.)

Deirdre enlisted help with plan B. And so Eloise found herself asking Alice, who was a substitute teacher, to tutor Gus. Everyone at school knew Principal Anderson had told Gus he'd be suspended from the basketball team if he didn't get his math scores up. It was the only threat that might work on Gus, and work it did. He began meeting with Alice every Wednesday after school, at Eloise's house.

Deirdre would invite herself over and sit in on the sessions, pretending she, too, struggled with calculating the volume of a sphere.

"He's almost in love," Deirdre told Eloise and Paula repeatedly, emphatically. "I can see it in his eyes."

Eloise wanted it to be true so Deirdre might start acting halfway sane again, but Gus seemed in a bad mood whenever Deirdre appeared. Eloise supposed that was what boys did when they liked you. Pretended not to.

Then one day near the end of the school year, Gus showed up at Eloise's house on a Thursday, not a Wednesday. Alice was at church setting up for a Bible retreat.

"My mom's not home today," Eloise told Gus, standing before him in the doorway.

"That's okay." Gus ran a hand through his dark curls, which were already growing out for summer.

"Deirdre's not here either."

"Good," he said. "I came for you."

That was the moment, Eloise would note afterward. The moment it all shifted.

"You can't come in," Eloise said.

"I didn't ask to." His smile was the tangy sort of thing that made her think of orange soda and how she wasn't allowed to have it. "Let's go to the bluffs," he said. "There's good cliff jumping."

Eloise had never been cliff jumping. Her parents had never forbidden it, probably because they'd known Eloise wouldn't be tempted by it.

Eloise always did the right thing. Being an only child was a weight she carried, stowed dutifully in her pocket. It was made heavier by the fact that Eloise was supposed to enter the world with a companion. Her twin sister, Penelope. A stillborn. For the past fifteen years, they'd visited the cemetery every Sunday after church, laying fresh sunflowers and lilies at the little grave. The loss was alive the way her sister never would be. Eloise tried to compensate by being doubly good, doubly lovable. But she was tired. Tired of trying to make her parents happy, Deirdre happy. She wanted to do something just for her. She wanted to go cliff jumping with Gus Jenkins.

"The water's too cold," she told him, her rule-abiding habits making her resist.

"I'll buy you coffee after. Or hot chocolate. I work at the dock, you know. They pay real good."

"My dad gets home at six."

"We'll be back by five forty-five. Promise."

She didn't come home till six twenty, but Eloise's father wasn't fazed. He was sipping whiskey after a long day on the construction site, watching a staticky game on the antenna TV.

"We went in the lake." Eloise didn't explain the *we* and he didn't ask. Lying terrified Eloise, but it turned out omitting the truth wasn't so bad.

"You're not allowed in the water without me," Alice scolded later when she saw Eloise's one-piece hanging on the drying rack. "You know that."

"I'm sorry," Eloise said, but she was actually the opposite of sorry. She carried her family's record player into her bedroom and twirled to a Fleetwood Mac album long after she was supposed to be asleep, turning it over and resetting the needle once it finished.

Gus hadn't kissed her or asked her to be his girlfriend. He'd just held her hand as they jumped from the rock, then took it once more as they scrambled back up to jump again.

The entropy of it, the ecstasy of it! Even then, Eloise knew she'd never be able to quit him.

Skull Cave became their meeting place. Eloise would dash there breathless after whizzing through homework and chores.

"Like this wasn't your plan all along," Deirdre said after Eloise confessed the budding relationship. "Pretending like you cared about me, just trying to get Gus for yourself."

Deirdre didn't speak to Eloise again for four months and twenty-three days. She finally broke the silence to ask Eloise if Gus's basketball teammate Howie might ask Deirdre to the homecoming dance.

———————≈———————

Eloise stood in front of her closet, once again searching for something date-worthy to wear. Not that the cruise was a date with Clyde—certainly not.

Her closet was where she felt closest to Gus. A few scraps of his clothes were still there, though they'd long lost his outdoorsy scent. When he moved out the first time, he didn't take his clothes with him and Eloise didn't mail them. (Where should she send them? He was always on the move.) Not long after he left, she bagged them up, intending to add everything to the church's donation pile. Then Gus called saying he missed her, that he was coming to visit. She'd carefully returned all the items to the correct hangers and shelves so he'd never suspect how close she'd been to throwing them out, throwing him out.

Over the years Gus wore the clothes when he visited and Eloise had liked knowing having them there meant he could swing by spontaneously. He didn't need to pack anything except a toothbrush. She had spares of those too, in case he forgot.

Eloise had never been good at holding on to anger. It hit her hard but crumbled quickly. Soft like limestone, not the granite of other people's grudges. What could she say? She was a Mackinac Island girl through and through.

Gus's side of the closet had become sparser over the years. Bit by bit, he'd taken anything he actually wanted. The rejects remained. A few pairs of frayed jeans, button-downs that he complained choked his neck, winter boots and scuffed belts. The skeleton of the life they'd had together. But that was all it was anymore. A skeleton. Bones didn't keep her warm. Eloise was tired of rubbing against them as if they might.

————————

It had been a few months since Eloise had heard from Gus. He'd told her he'd give her a call to "plot out the summer" when he was back in the country. Probably mid-May, he'd said. It was now late June.

He was out traversing the globe while she was here, reserving space for him. Space he didn't want. Space that still felt mostly empty even when he occupied it. The loneliness of one-sided devotion.

From her closet, Eloise plucked a red polka-dot sundress. The dress she'd worn the day Gus proposed. He'd prepared a beach picnic shortly after high school graduation. Barbecue chips, Hershey's Bars, and a six-pack of Coors, all pilfered from his parents' pantry. When he'd dropped to his knee with his grandmother's ring, Eloise had never been so surprised.

"But I'm leaving for college," she'd said.

She'd been accepted into Northern Michigan University in the Upper Peninsula. They would do long-distance while Gus worked for Eloise's father's construction company, then marry afterward. They'd talked about it, mapped it all out.

"I know you've been down in the dumps about moving," Gus said. "Now you don't have to."

It was true that Eloise was sad about leaving the island, leaving Gus, leaving her parents. But the prospect thrilled her too. Stepping outside of herself, into herself. It was just that she'd been trying to hide the excitement from Gus since he wasn't coming too.

"What's wrong?" Gus asked. "Aren't you happy?"

"Of course I am." And she meant it. She accepted the ring. It was slightly loose but not enough to pay to have it adjusted. Fingers swelled with age. She would grow into it.

Girls went to college to find husbands, Eloise reminded herself. She had already found hers. It was a small compromise to make for a life with the man of her dreams.

Eloise's parents were overjoyed with the match, relieved Eloise was no longer venturing off the island. And they now had an heir—an islander from a reputable family, no less—to the construction business. Eloise felt embarrassed to admit it, but she would have married Gus even if her parents didn't approve. She would have eloped. Gone with him to Indiana or Iceland, wherever he wanted.

That was the saddest part, she often thought later. How ready she was to move for him, mold to him. She would have followed Gus anywhere then, if only he'd asked. And by the time he did, they had other factors to consider: the girls, their aging parents, income stability, retirement funds.

Gus resented Eloise's sense of duty. She resented his shortage of it.

Things worsened when Gus's father passed. A heart attack in the shower. Only fifty-four years old. Gus coped by drinking and riding his Harley on the mainland. "I need to live," he kept saying.

When he announced he wanted to go on a weeklong ride through the Rockies, Eloise encouraged him. He would work out his grief, his existential crisis, then come back refreshed and ready to hunker down for the winter. Play backgammon with the girls and put on those little puppet shows he did so well.

Instead, he'd called from fuzzy pay phone after fuzzy pay phone to tell her the trip was extending a few days, then a few more. In the end, he'd made her be the one to say it.

"You're not coming back, are you?"

There was a pause long enough for Eloise to wonder if the line had disconnected. "Not yet, Ellie. I'm sorry."

Even the way he'd broken her heart had been exquisite. Doling out the pain in increments, giving her only the portion she could handle one day, then more the next once she'd acclimated.

"What should I tell the girls?" she'd asked, as if he might provide a sufficient script.

"Tell them I'll be back to take them trick-or-treating."

He hadn't been, but when he came at Christmas, he brought a whole bag of Beanie Babies, toting them in a sack like Santa. Five-year-old Rebecca was uninterested; eight-year-old Georgiana was infatuated. She slept with the stuffed animals every night and took turns toting them along with her to school, telling her classmates they were from her dad, that he was a professional race car driver.

Eloise should have hated Gus. She should have punished him. Yet she was glad she hadn't, grateful she wasn't stronger. A life with Gus in it, in whatever capacity, was so much better than one without him. And the girls needed their father. So she'd let up on the pressure, the questions, and allowed him to ebb and flow in his own tide. And when Eloise broke down, she was the only witness, her cries muffled by the mattress they used to share.

It had never felt like she was giving anything up by letting Gus come in and out of her life. There was no opportunity lost, no one else she wanted to be with.

At least there hadn't been.

There was something about Clyde. It wasn't altogether dissimilar from how Gus made her feel when they'd first started dating. But Eloise didn't have the excuse of youth or raging hormones to explain this . . . this what, exactly? This crush? It was such a juvenile word.

"Closing means opening." She heard Georgiana's words, turned them over like Petoskey stones.

Eloise removed the red sundress from its hanger and laid it on the bed. She prided herself on still fitting into her high school clothes. Her wallet thanked her for it too.

This was the dress for the Lilac Festival cruise. She would iron it and spritz it with a new scent. See if there might be some life left in it.

Chapter 18

Gigi

D o you plan on going swimming?" Eloise asked. She was waiting for Gigi by the door. They were heading over to the cruise together.

"Obviously not," Gigi said. "The water's freezing."

"Then why are you dressed like that?" Eloise's eyes swept Gigi like a bristly broom. "It's see-through."

Gigi was wearing a bikini with a sheer cover-up. She was old enough now that she didn't throw teenage tantrums or sneak out her bedroom window. More obvious forms of insurgence had become rather mundane, but she still got joy from the smaller things that sent Eloise spinning without giving her enough reason to actually reprimand Gigi.

"It's fashion," Gigi countered. "I consider it part of my civic duty to bring twenty-first-century trends to Mackinac. Otherwise they won't arrive for another decade, at least."

Eloise seemed to be trying hard not to take the bait. Gigi had to admit she was getting a little better at it. She draped a beach towel over Gigi's shoulders. Gigi let it stay. She would shed it on the boat, make a statement.

They walked over to the dock. Eloise kept an aggressive pace. Gigi lagged, kicking pebbles with her rubbery flip-flops.

Gigi was looking forward to getting out on the open water. She was feeling trapped from spending so much time in Thistle Dew, sink-ing into that old couch, sleeping in that tiny twin bed. It was nice of Eloise to take her as her plus-one for the cruise, though since she'd shut down Clyde, it wasn't like there was anyone else she would've invited. The euchre ladies all helped organize the event, and Nonni won her own ticket for winning the senior bracket of the pickleball tournament with Liam. She was already on board so she could load up on freebies before the food was picked over. The Great Depression lived on in Nonni's rapacious approach to buffets and open bars.

Gigi thought about what Eloise had said to her yesterday, about how she created options for herself. It was true, she reflected, and nice to have her mother see it. The issue was Gigi didn't know which option she wanted to create next. No matter where she lived or what she did for work, it would feel like a new version of an old life. Gigi had never thought before that change could become repetitive, but it seemed like that was exactly what was happening.

The evening air wasn't warm or cool. The neutrality of it all held a comfort that disagreed with Gigi, who craved more polarity. Clouds blotted the sky like bandages.

Gigi stalled for photos on the walk over. She posed against the most iconic backdrops (horses, fudge shops, the lake), all filtered to perfection so her friends in LA might be jealous when they saw the pictures on social media. Perhaps they'd text her to check in, maybe even ask to visit.

"We're late," Eloise chided.

"This is why I need an electric scooter," Gigi said.

"Or it's why we should ban cell phones."

Gigi had been hoping for a yacht, but it was the same shoddy vessel as always, decorated with crêpe paper streamers and droopy helium balloons. They showed their tickets and walked on.

The cruise boat was packed with both islanders and fudgies. Tourists delighted in meeting locals, inquiring about their lifestyle as if they were a primitive species ("What do you do for food in the winter?" "Do you get vaccines for the germs that horse excrement carries?" "Do cousins marry each other, given the size of the gene pool?").

The boat smelled like charred barbecue. James and Lillian were seated at a table alongside Lillian's parents. They seemed to be getting along well, Gigi noted with displeasure. She'd entertained a fantasy of a nasty split, both of them blaming each other for the cornhole loss.

Gigi thought again about how frustrated James had seemed by all the talk about him and Lillian, and yet here he was, feeding into the rumors himself. He lacked a spine, that was all there was to it. He desired Lillian's attention yet wanted to keep his options open. Gigi had seen this film before.

Even Lillian deserved better.

Nonni was at the bar sipping a dirty martini, not with Liam but with Mr. Murdick, one of the fudge shop owners. Liam was watching at a distance, looking dispirited. Good for Nonni, Gigi thought, keeping Liam wanting more, making him jealous. Nonni might as well go for it with Liam. It wasn't like it was cheating when your husband had been in the grave seven years. But Nonni didn't see it like that.

Gigi had half expected Eloise's Ronny reports to be a ruse, but sure enough, he was behind the DJ board. He was still in his officer uniform and wore polarized aviators.

"There he is," Eloise said. But she wasn't looking at Ronny or Mr. Townsend. Her gaze was on Clyde, who was talking with Kitty and Paula by the buffet. "He's getting the ladies on his side, I'm sure of it."

"There are no sides," Gigi said. "It was a first date, not a divorce."

Eloise pulled her shawl around her shoulders, covering the pretty red dress underneath. Gigi had never seen the dress before, but when she'd asked if it was new, Eloise had frowned and said, "Anything but."

Gigi loaded her plate with beer-battered curly fries, artichoke dip, and soggy pickles. "Such great vegetarian options," she commented wryly.

"Are you getting enough protein?" Eloise asked, half concerned, half distracted. She was staring at the back of Clyde's top hat. "He's flirting with everyone on this boat."

"He's not flirting," Gigi said. "That's just his personality."

"Well, it certainly doesn't make me feel very special, does it?"

Eloise was a walking contradiction. Gigi should try to listen better, but she didn't have the capacity to hold the stress of both her mother's life and her own. She chose her own, as every survivalist did. Gigi was not Rebecca, after all.

"I thought you didn't want to feel special," Gigi said. "I thought you wanted to just be friends."

"Not now, Georgiana."

Gigi went to the bar for an IPA. By the time she returned, Eloise and Nonni had sat down at Lillian and James's table. Gigi thought about taking her plate to another table just to make a point. Instead, she sat down next to James and thought about how even if James had liked her, they would have been doomed since they were both leaving at the end of summer. It made her feel a little better.

"Curly fries and pickles," James said, glancing at her plate. "Quite a victory dinner."

Gigi crunched on the fries. "Glad to get a doctor's approval." She would give him nothing except proof that she was not pining for him. Pointing her chair away from him slightly, she tried to cut the connection between them. It didn't work. Her body was still fidgety. She bounced her knee.

From across the way, Clyde was stealing surreptitious glances over at Eloise.

"He's looking at you again," Gigi muttered to Eloise.

"Who are you talking about?" Nonni asked. She'd assembled a tower of oatmeal raisin cookies from the dessert bar and was wrapping them in napkins, packing them in her bulging purse.

Eloise looked down at her plate. She cut up her pulled pork into even smaller shreds. "Nothing," she said. "We're talking about nothing."

Chapter 19

Alice

The girls were acting strangely, Alice noted as she sat between them at dinner.

This wasn't out of character for Georgiana, but Eloise's behavior alarmed her. She was jumpy and tense, accidentally salting her coffee instead of her food.

It had to do with Clyde, Alice was sure of it. Eloise must be feeling awkward since she'd turned him down. But she'd done the right thing. There was something a bit much about the Scottish author. He was charming, he was successful, but he certainly wasn't an islander. Alice suspected he was going to exploit the island with his novel, clog it up with his cultish readers. The media would publish articles about what a hero he was, how he'd stimulated economic growth. As if growth was always a good thing. As if things hadn't been better before, back when no one outside of a hundred-mile radius had ever heard of Mackinac.

Besides, the last thing Eloise needed was to fall for someone who was leaving. She put forth an image of strength, of durability, but Alice wasn't fooled. Her daughter was vulnerable. She always had been, ever since she'd been born. Only four pounds and eleven ounces. Eloise had shared the womb with Penelope, then lost her twin that very first day. It impacted Eloise, even as an infant. She didn't do well when Alice left the nursery for more than a couple of minutes, shrieking and shrieking, tiring out her tiny lungs. Some called it colic. Alice called it coping.

"Look at them," Georgiana pouted, watching James and Lillian on the dance floor.

She was clearly smitten with the doctor but wouldn't admit it, lest she gratify her mother. Georgiana was more stubborn than any mule Alice had met, and she'd met quite a few. She and David used to have a whole barnful to haul the construction equipment.

"How anyone can dance to this music is beyond me," Eloise said.

"It's not even music," Alice said. "It's a synthetic explosion. I should have brought earplugs."

"I'll go request something more your style." Georgiana bounded over to the DJ booth. As she walked, she dropped her beach towel.

Alice heard the shudder of her own gasp. Georgiana was wearing a string bikini beneath a barely there cover-up. She'd never seen a less appropriate outfit.

"Here we go," Eloise said grimly. "She's got her sights on Ronny."

Alice prayed it wasn't true. "She's just trying to make someone jealous."

"Perhaps." Eloise was unfocused. She kept glancing over at Clyde.

"He's not staying," Alice said gently. "Just remember that."

"I'm aware."

Alice blamed herself for what happened with Gus. She and David were so quick to give their blessing. (Well, David was quick; Alice hadn't been consulted, but that hadn't bothered her at the time.) She should have asked questions, should have given Gus a lecture when he'd run off. She couldn't go back and change it now. All she could do was make sure she didn't take her eye off the ball again.

A big band tune from the fifties came on. "Finally, a song that doesn't feel like a jackhammer grinding into my skull," Alice said.

It was one of David's favorites. What she would give to be able to dance with him one more time. Excusing herself from the table, she went to the bar and ordered an old-fashioned, David's favorite.

Liam Townsend appeared at her shoulder. He was bald with a beer belly, but Alice still saw the boy in him, the strapping teenage heartthrob who'd won her over with Glenn Miller serenades and wildflower bouquets. His ebony eyes landed on Alice's and stuck. "How about joining me for a jitterbug?" he asked. His voice had gotten huskier with age. Alice couldn't help but note how it suited him.

"You don't dance," Alice said. Liam had always been a curmudgeon on the dance floor. Silly as it seemed, it had been one of the things early on that had made seventeen-year-old Alice confident in her decision to ditch Liam for David. She'd found a metaphor in choosing a partner you didn't need to teach to dance, someone who already knew the steps.

"Well, our taste buds change every seven years," Liam said. "Perhaps the same might be true for my ability to dance. Shall we find out?"

Alice was tempted to take him up on the offer, but it felt too intimate, especially with all the islanders looking on. "Not tonight, I'm afraid," she said, taking a sip of her old-fashioned and wincing as it chafed her throat. She hated whiskey, always had. But drinking it reminded her of her husband.

"Worried your granddaughter is onto us?" Liam said, nodding in Georgiana's direction.

Alice wanted to blame Liam's brazenness on the alcohol, but he was speaking coherently, his eye contact firm and sober.

"There is no *us* to be onto," Alice whispered. "I do wish you would stop talking like that."

She wasn't trying to be rude, but really, what was Liam doing? They'd had such a good thing going recently.

"You don't think about it?" Liam asked. "What we could be now, after all these years wondering."

Guilt reared up in Alice again. "There have been no years spent wondering," she said, and she felt good about how true that was. Alice had not even lost hours, let alone years, wondering if she should have left David for Liam. She had known back then she had made the right choice and she knew that now.

"You are a good friend, Liam," Alice said. "A very good friend."

Liam shook his head. "I'm not," he said. "I never was. I've always wanted more, Alice, from the time we were kids. I never figured out how to stop. But I can see your heart is still with David."

Alice wanted to get out of her own way. She wanted to lead Liam out on the dance floor and see if he surprised her. But she couldn't do that, not when David had been her forever dance partner. She didn't want to stop wishing for him in the vaults of her brain, the veins of her body. It was how she kept him alive.

And also how she absolved her own sin.

"Yes," Alice said, unable to look Liam in the eye as she said it. "It is."

Chapter 20

Lillian

L illian stared longingly out the window.

The boat was passing the Round Island Lighthouse, jutting out on an isthmus, rocky and remote. Seagulls swooped and circled.

What would it be like to live in that lighthouse? Lillian wondered. All alone, logging the weather, operating the lights. Subsisting on weekly groceries and the warmth of a crackling fire. Hosting someone for the night or a lifetime. No parents to judge, no neighbors to gossip.

Lillian was tempted to jump off the top deck now and swim to shore. Roll in the sand and stones, feel the grainy texture scrape her skin. Release the conditioning of what it meant to be clean.

"You okay?" James asked as they swayed to a ballad. The dance floor had filled and the space felt muggy and cramped.

"I'm fine," Lillian said.

James was not a good dancer. No rhythm. But Lillian kept her hands on his chest, aware of her parents looking on. She couldn't be upset with James. This was her fault, really. She was ashamed of herself. Yet it was a different kind of shame that had spurred her to suggest the idea in the first place.

She should be trying harder to sell her affection. But her parents found PDA gauche, so her platonic-level physical affection with James was another point won in their book. And if Lillian looked morose, they would put it down to the fact that she wasn't over the broken engagement. That she was still pining after Alex.

Lillian did miss Alex, very much so, but it was in the way she might miss a brother if she had one. She missed the comfort he brought, the consistency. It had been the right thing to break off the engagement. Lillian wasn't questioning that. What she was questioning was if she was actually going to be that much happier on the other side. More than anything she'd wanted freedom, and now that she had it, it felt overwhelming, like a stormy current she couldn't swim in.

"Looks like they're hitting it off," James said, looking over at Gigi and Ronny. Lillian followed his gaze.

Gigi was dancing behind the DJ booth, arms flailing, head bobbing. Beneath her see-through dress, her bikini clung like lingerie. The outline of her nipples showed. Ronny's hands were wrapped around her waist.

"Good for them," Lillian said. Both of their eyes kept sliding back to Gigi. James didn't even try to hide it.

Lillian did.

Chapter 21

Gigi

It felt like one big game of euchre. Everyone had a partner. But instead of playing cards, they were playing hearts. Gigi and Ronny. James and Lillian. Eloise and Clyde.

Gigi hadn't seen when Eloise and Clyde started dancing, but something must have happened to change Eloise's mind about keeping her distance. They'd been inseparable for the last six songs, even clowning around as Ronny switched to EDM. It was odd seeing Eloise with a man. Childhood images burbled like the coffee her dad used to make.

Evenings in the family room with James Taylor records playing. Gigi and Rebecca inventing plots for their doll families (Rebecca dreamed up weddings, babies, and new houses; Gigi contributed deaths, illnesses, and tornados). Their parents waltzing from the kitchen to the family room and back again.

Eloise was looking at Clyde like she used to look at Gigi's dad. Except the expression had a new texture to it—enchantment, innocence.

Gigi wasn't sure anymore if she was rooting for Clyde. Some harmless flirting was one thing, but seeing them cozied up like lovers made Gigi's stomach flip.

She snapped a few pictures of them on her phone to send to Rebecca. She wanted to text her dad, too, and ask when he was going to visit this summer. But he still hadn't replied to her last text, and she refused to double-text any guy, including her father.

"Want to get out of here?" Gigi asked Ronny.

"We're on a boat," Ronny said. His features were glazed from the gummies they'd both had. "Where would we go?"

"There are places." Gigi felt the high move from her chest to her hips. "But on second thought, maybe it's more fun to stay here, out in the open."

She was into Ronny as much as she was into the guys she usually hooked up with. No more, no less. He was too arrogant, too vapid, for her to actually fall for, but that was just as well. Gigi had a hard time liking people if she was worried about loving them.

All she wanted right now was an escape.

Coming back to the island had made her confront old memories, old versions of herself. The fifth grader who strutted around telling made-up stories about her dad, as if he were some superhero flying all around the world, not just a regular guy who left because he got bored. The eighth grader who became jealous of her best friend because Lillian had two parents who attended every single sports match and band concert and awards ceremony and never stopped bragging about her. The twelfth grader who never even graduated, just threw herself at the governor's son and begged for him to take her away like she was some damsel in distress.

Gigi hated who she'd been on this island. She hated the desperate, powerless sides that Mackinac magnified in her. It was impossible to re-create herself, not in one summer.

And subverting expectations felt too heavy tonight, too hard. She might as well slip back into her old caricature.

She slid right up to Ronny, right into him.

The kiss was sloppy and rough, the kind of thing Gigi associated with college, though she'd never been. She poured herself into it, knowing it would draw the attention of James, of Eloise, of all the islanders. Knowing it would show them all that she didn't give a damn what they thought. If she was going to go up in flames this time, it was going to be because she was the one lighting the torch, swallowing it whole.

———— ≈ ————

"Honestly, Georgiana. Causing a scene in front of all those people. You'd never know you were nearly thirty." It was later that night and Gigi was just arriving home. Eloise was waiting up to corner Gigi for the lecture she'd known was coming.

After the cruise docked, Gigi and Ronny had made a getaway on the back of an electric scooter he'd confiscated from a fudgie. They'd done laps around Main Street, then ridden over to the beach at British Landing. He'd invited her back to his place, but Gigi headed home, using Eloise as the scapegoat. She'd told Ronny how completely miserable it was to be in her twenties and living back under her mother's dictatorship, all the while being glad to have such an easy out. Ronny bequeathed the scooter to her, under the condition she use it to sneak out to see him.

"Thank you, Mother." Gigi kicked off her shoes, refusing to line them up with the others on the doormat. "It must be the new eye cream I'm using."

"This isn't LA."

"I'm aware."

"You can't come back and wreak havoc again. I thought we were doing things differently this time."

"And what exactly is the crime in question? Two adults kissing?"

"It was more than kissing," Eloise said. "And in front of all those people."

Gigi tried to distract herself from the part of her that already regretted the spectacle. James must have thought she was cheap, if he hadn't already. She went to the kitchen for a Diet Coke. She had the munchies and ripped open an old pack of M&M's, stale from how long Eloise kept things in the pantry. "Most of the people on the boat were tourists anyway," Gigi said. "They'll be gone soon enough."

"The euchre ladies saw."

"Good. Now they'll cut it out with the whole Dr. Kentwood nonsense."

"Don't tell me that's what this is about."

"Kissing Ronny should hardly be a scandal. Even for prudes like you."

"I'm not a prude; I'm prudent. Ronny's trouble, and you know it."

"We're a good match then. Two wrongs make a right and all that." Gigi offered an M&M to Eloise, who frowned and pushed it away. "I think this is a diversion tactic. To avoid talking about what happened between you and Clyde tonight."

Eloise's nostrils flared, the same way Rebecca's did. "Nothing happened. We danced, that's all."

"You like him."

"You're inebriated," Eloise said. But her eyes shone, almost like she was glad that Gigi called her out on her feelings so she wouldn't have to keep them a secret. Gigi felt disoriented again, like she had while watching Clyde and Eloise together. The kitchen floor seemed to be swaying, as if she were still on the boat.

"Please wipe down the counter and let's go to bed." Eloise handed Gigi a rag to mop up the crumbs. "We have to get up early for church."

"*You* have to get up early," Gigi said. "I'm sleeping in."

At least when she was asleep she didn't have to face the shit show that was life back on this claustrophobia-inducing island.

"Good night, Georgiana," Eloise said, looking like she wished she could say more but knew it was too dangerous.

There was something satisfying about knowing her mother was scared of her. There was something sad about it too, but she wasn't in the mood to go there.

Gigi swiped a box of granola from the pantry and stomped up the stairs. "Good night, Mother."

"No eating upstairs," Eloise called after her.

Gigi ignored her.

Chapter 22

Rebecca

Rebecca had taken five pregnancy tests so far, all negative. That was okay, she kept telling herself. It was a numbers game.

For the first two tests, Tom stood in the bathroom with her, eyes glued to the little stick. When only one pink line appeared, disappointment spiked his face. Rebecca shut her eyes.

"No big deal," Tom said, hand on her shoulder like a coach strategizing after a narrow loss. "We'll get it next time."

Rebecca appreciated how invested he was. He made her feel like they were a team, a unit. Though she was the one having to nourish her body with organic foods and supplements, taking notes on all the parenting podcasts, grimacing through planks and leg lifts because one isolated study showed a loose potential link between Pilates and fertility. Tom, meanwhile, was carrying on, business as usual. Wolfing down bacon for breakfast, talking taxes with his clients, playing rough-and-tumble basketball with his colleagues. Rebecca didn't fault him. It was just the reality. Before it even started, parenthood wasn't truly equal.

She was also the one who kept bleeding.

This time she decided to take the pregnancy test without Tom, before he got home from work. It would give her time to compose herself once it came back negative. She would do a fifteen-minute meditation, go for a walk with Sadie, and then be fine to tell Tom about it over dinner. They would move on to discussing their upcoming Fourth of July visit to Mackinac and all the things Rebecca wanted to show him: the stone-skipping competition, the carnival at the Grand Hotel, the patriotic finery at the fort. It was good, it was necessary, to have tangible things to look forward to.

On the toilet, Rebecca saturated the little stick. She drew long inhales to calm her nervous system, silently repeating a mantra that one of the podcasts had recommended. *I am not attached to the outcome. I am not attached to the outcome.*

And there it was. Not one pink line but two.

Rebecca was pregnant.

Emotion gushed from her eyes, her nose, her hands. It became obvious how she had never, not for one millisecond, been detached from this outcome. And thank God she hadn't been.

The happiness was so big, so billowy, that she didn't believe it. Trusting the bad had always been more natural for Rebecca than trusting the good.

Maybe that started after her dad left, maybe before. She'd been so young that she didn't recall if her behavior changed after he left or if she'd always been the type to floss twice a day, check her answers three times before submitting a test, and cover her nose and mouth to protect herself from secondhand smoke when Paula pulled out a cigarette. She avoided monkey bars because she was sure she'd fall and break an arm like her classmate Hilary Porter had. And when Eloise left them with babysitters, Rebecca never relaxed. Once Eloise said she'd be back from euchre by nine, and at 9:01 p.m., Rebecca was standing by the door, face glued to the windowpane as she watched anxiously for the familiar orb of her mother's flashlight. Eloise might have had a heart attack or taken a fall on her way home. She might be lying there unconscious, stampeded by horses. This was how Rebecca's mind worked.

She wouldn't tell Tom yet. She needed to be sure. Tomorrow she would go to the OB-GYN and take another test. Maybe two.

The doctor confirmed the pregnancy. Rebecca was only a couple weeks along but already had a due date: March 28. It was immediately the most sacred square on the calendar.

"How was your day?" Tom asked when he came home that night, sweaty from his intramural basketball league.

Magical! she wanted to sing but couldn't spoil the surprise.

"Good," Rebecca said. She was snacking on carrot sticks, hummus, and cherry-bacon jam (a Traverse City specialty). It was probably too soon for pregnancy cravings, but the placebo effect had kicked in.

"Everything okay?" Tom asked, setting down his bag. "You seem a little off."

Rebecca liked that Tom knew her well enough to notice her mood shift. "It's probably just the hormones," she said, trying to keep a straight face.

Tom's face fell. "You got your period?"

"No," Rebecca said, breaking into the biggest smile of her life. "That's what I'm trying to tell you."

She showed him both test results. She had never seen him so excited, even when Michigan State beat Michigan on a last-second interception returned for a touchdown. He punched his fists in the air, roared something primal and guttural. "Let's go! Let's frickin' go!"

Rebecca was more convinced than ever that she had married the right person. This was the kind of excitement that a father should have for his child. Seeing them as a blessing, not a burden. A reason to step up, not step out.

"Should we call our parents?" Tom asked once the hooting had subsided.

Rebecca shook her head, though she, too, wanted to share the good news, shout it from the rooftops. Even the thought of calling her dad brought her joy. Motherhood was already changing her.

"We're not telling anyone until three months," Rebecca said. "Miscarriage odds are too high." She felt her cortisol spike as she said it.

"Okay," Tom said. He put a palm on Rebecca's stomach and her breathing started to calm. "I think I felt something. A kick."

"That's just my stomach growling. The baby's only as big as a peppercorn right now."

But Rebecca put her hands on her stomach too, overlapping his. They stood there in the kitchen like that for a while, feeling nothing, feeling everything.

Chapter 23

Eloise

H ave you heard from your sister?" Eloise said to Georgiana, who was guzzling coffee in the kitchen.

It was the morning after the cruise. Rebecca wasn't answering Eloise's calls. She did text once to say she had a scratchy throat, but it still wasn't like Rebecca to be so quiet. Eloise's motherly antenna was up. Perhaps she and Tom had gotten into a fight. Well, the honeymoon period was bound to end sometime. They would be okay. If anyone could handle marital conflict maturely, it was Rebecca.

"She replied to the photo I sent of you and Clyde dancing last night," Georgiana said. "But nothing else."

Eloise blinked. "You took a *picture?*"

"A few. Want to see? They're very cute."

"Please delete them. Now."

Eloise wondered if this was why Rebecca wasn't replying. Perhaps the photo had upset her. Eloise felt guilty, like she had let her daughters down. Like she had let Gus down too, though she was aware that part made much less sense.

Georgiana poured a refill of coffee, using up the last of the pot. "Only if you turn on the air-conditioning."

"It's a waste of energy," Eloise said, because she knew Georgiana would accept that answer more than *It's a waste of money.* "Put ice cubes in your coffee."

"That waters it down," Georgiana said. "I need mine as strong as I can get it."

"You wouldn't if you didn't drink so much."

"I only had four beers," Georgiana said, as if that would make Eloise feel better. "And one gummy."

Eloise wrinkled her nose. She smelled something other than Georgiana's hangover. "Is that a candle? Georgiana, you know the house rules about candles."

"One little candle isn't going to burn the house down," Georgiana said.

"It happens all the time." Eloise hurried up to the loft to blow it out since Georgiana clearly wasn't going to. "I see it on the news."

"So, just to be clear, you're all for the American populace having guns in their homes, but candles are off-limits?"

Eloise returned from the loft with the confiscated candle in hand. "You're the one asking for the air-conditioning and you're putting more heat in the house."

"I wasn't lighting the candle for warmth. I was lighting it for aroma. This house smells old."

"The house *is* old. It has character. And I thought I raised a daughter with some of that too."

"So sorry to disappoint."

Georgiana started eating cereal straight from the box, reaching in with her bare hands. Eloise clunked a bowl and spoon in front of her, but she didn't take the hint.

Eloise massaged her temples. "How about you go down to the shops on Main Street today? Reintroduce yourself, see who's hiring."

"Why would I do that?"

"Making a little money wouldn't be the worst thing," Eloise said. "I know I said free rent, but it would be nice if you could chip in for groceries and that sort of thing." It wasn't about the money. It was about the sense of purpose a job would bring.

"I thought the whole point of this summer was to give me a break," Georgiana said. "Even you said you could tell I was burned out from working too much."

It was true, but now that Eloise saw just how counterproductive resting seemed to be for her daughter, she was reevaluating. "I didn't say it was *just* from working too much. There were many factors."

"Like my friends who you say are a terrible influence even though you've never met them?"

"The same friends who kicked you out of their apartment?"

"They didn't kick me out," Georgiana said, though Eloise could tell she'd touched a nerve. "They knew I had to go take care of my mom for the summer."

"And how are you finding it to be going?" Eloise asked. "Taking care of me, I mean."

"It looks like I'm not needed after all. You've found someone else to do the job."

Eloise wanted to tell Georgiana that she would always need her. She wanted to tell her that no one could ever replace her, a man least of all. Even Gus was never in the same sphere as her daughters. Georgiana and Rebecca came first; they always would. But Eloise felt like she was walking on eggshells, like saying one wrong thing would make Georgiana attack her further. And she wasn't sure she could take that, not this morning.

"I hope you don't mean Clyde," Eloise said. She tried to get the conversation back on track. "Just think about getting a summer job? Maybe one of the fudge shops or the Pink Pony. It could be fun."

"No point starting something I'd have to stop in a couple months," Georgiana said.

Eloise went quiet at that, thinking of Clyde and how he'd told her his return trip to Scotland was booked for the first week of September.

"Let me know if you hear from Rebecca." Eloise trailed her daughter to the door.

"She's probably busy calling venues for your wedding to Clyde," Georgiana said. "You know how she likes to plan."

"You enjoy making my blood pressure spike, don't you?"

"Stress tests are good for your heart," Georgiana said. "They keep you healthy."

Eloise tried to calm herself. "Just please try calling your sister? Maybe it's just me she's ignoring."

"Or maybe not everything is about you."

Chapter 24

Gigi

Gigi couldn't stand how slowly the line was moving at Sadie's Ice Cream Parlor. She was tempted to apply for a job there, just to show them what competency looked like. Eloise would be pleased.

"Long line," a voice said, joining the queue behind Gigi.

It was Lillian, standing there in a pleated white skirt, tanned legs bearing all the shape that Gigi's gangly ones lacked. The Pink Pony's logo was embroidered into the fabric of her collared tank top, and she had a pickleball paddle in hand. Sweat glistened from beneath Lillian's visor, just enough to look like skillfully applied highlighter.

"I was just playing pickleball with James," Lillian carried on when Gigi didn't say anything. "You should join us sometime. I only picked it up this summer. Thought my athletic career peaked in high school, but pickleball is something I can still get better at."

The statement reeked of an existential crisis. Gigi had heard Lillian had quit her fancy lawyer job but wasn't going to ask. The last thing she needed was Lillian trying to bond with her over the real world spitting them out and depositing them back here, on Mackinac's sad little shores.

Gigi scrolled on her phone, pretending to be tending to messages. The truth was that she hadn't heard from her so-called friends at all. They seemed to be living their best lives without her.

Eloise hadn't been entirely wrong about how they'd kicked her out of the apartment when she'd fallen behind on rent. They could've at least given her a couple more months to come up with the money. She'd chipped in to help out when they'd fallen short before. That was the problem with new friends—they could turn on you quickly without any remorse. There was nothing tying them together. That was the fun part too, how you could reshape your identity so quickly, but the lack of loyalty didn't sit well with Gigi.

"Happy for you," Gigi said to Lillian. "Your parents must be proud."

Much of Lillian's insufferableness could be traced back to her parents. In high school they'd framed every newspaper article about Lillian and donated her trophies to the town hall, under the sham of "sharing wins with the whole community." The trophies were probably still there, expertly polished, not that Gigi was going to check.

A jingling came from down the street. It was Mayor Welsh, riding her Belgian draft named Rowan, shaking the bells she'd fastened to the reins so no one would miss their arrival.

Camille brought Rowan to a halt in front of Gigi and Lillian. "How are you two ladies enjoying your time back home?"

Gigi thought she felt Lillian wince at the word *home*, but maybe it was just the reverberation of her own shudder.

"Hello, Mayor Welsh," Lillian said, voice smooth and treacly.

"Camille," Gigi said.

"Look at all this hubbub. It's just superb." Camille gestured down Main Street as if she were single-handedly responsible for the vibrant tourist season. There was a rasp in her voice from tobacco. "Well, I've got to be going. Need to get my training in for the race, and the governor invited me over for a barbecue later." She leaned toward Gigi. "Don't worry, we won't bring up *you know what*."

"Bring up what?" Gigi asked coolly.

"That trouble you got into with the prior governor's son." Camille laughed. It sounded more like a belch. "Quite a scandal you brought us into. But we moved on from it, didn't we?"

"I sure did." Gigi waved, a dismissal. Camille took it, only because tourists were asking to take photos with Rowan. This made Camille happier than taking digs at Gigi.

"I can't stand that woman," Lillian said once Camille had jingled away.

The critique surprised Gigi. Lillian was one of those annoying types who never breathed a bad word about anyone.

"Is she that bad?" Gigi wasn't inclined to agree with Lillian, even over something as blatant as this.

Lillian made a face, her well-defined Cupid's bow pinching. "She's not very progressive."

"It's Mackinac," Gigi pointed out. "No one's progressive."

"Some people are. Camille just silences anyone other than her sycophants."

Perhaps Lillian's years living in Chicago had done some good to chip away at the conservative cage they'd been raised in.

"If you ever want to stage a rebellion, I'm in," Gigi said. The idea appealed far more than she'd expected.

Lillian's phone chimed. From the way Lillian smiled when she read the text, Gigi guessed it was James.

Gigi checked her own phone. She still had no reply from her dad.

"Just one of my Chicago friends," Lillian explained as she stashed her phone in her pocket. "She sent me a funny meme about lawyers."

"I'm sure," Gigi said, not buying it.

They finally reached the front of the line. The scrunched inside of Sadie's smelled like toasted marshmallows and the malt-and-vanilla scent of freshly baked waffle cones.

"Oh, good, they still have some lilac left from the festival," Lillian said, scoping out the ice cream flavors. "My favorite."

Gigi had planned to go with chocolate mocha and grasshopper but now changed her mind. "I'll have lilac," she ordered at the counter, before Lillian. "Two triple-scoop waffle cones."

It cleared the container clean, and her wallet.

"Sorry," Gigi said to Lillian. "I said I'd take one back to the house for my mom."

Lillian didn't point out that it would melt before making it that far. "That's okay," she said, smiling. "Enjoy."

Exiting the shop, Gigi took a lick of the ice cream. It tasted even more like detergent than she remembered. She spit it out onto the asphalt. Across the street, she spotted Clyde scribbling in his moleskin journal.

"Here you go," Gigi greeted, shoving the extra waffle cone at Clyde. "I got you an ice cream."

Clyde looked confused, then accepted. "Is this a bribe to stay away from your mam?"

"Maybe," Gigi said. "You'll have to answer to me, you know. If you break her heart."

"If anyone gets hurt, I have a feeling it'll be me," Clyde said. "I care for your mam very much. All I want is a chance to get to know her more. What do you say to that?"

"It doesn't really matter what I say, does it?" Gigi said, feeling at least a little reassured. "It's my mother's decision."

"She obviously values your input."

Gigi wished it were true. "What makes you say that?"

"Well, she talks about you nonstop, doesn't she?"

"If by talking about me, you mean complaining about me," Gigi said.

"Your mam brags about you, Gigi."

Gigi liked how he called her Gigi without her having to ask.

"She showed me on a map all the places you've lived," he went on. "Even pitched me a story about a brave, spirited woman who leaves her little hometown and makes friends wherever she goes."

It didn't seem like Clyde was lying, but she couldn't be sure. His job, after all, was to make up fictional plots. "Sounds like a boring story."

"There's no such thing as a boring story," Clyde said. "Only boring writing."

Gigi wondered if it was true.

Clyde thanked her for the ice cream and took his first lick. "Like soap for the spirit," he declared happily, and Gigi couldn't help but smile at how everything about Mackinac seemed to delight him.

It was quite the contrast to Gus.

As Gigi carried on with her walk, she couldn't help but feel the fondness returning for Clyde. If Eloise wanted to keep spending time with him, Gigi wasn't going to stand in their way. Or, at least she would try not to. There was always the chance she might cause trouble spur of the moment, but she wouldn't *plan* any trouble, and that was something.

Cruiser was walking Main Street, Ronny in the saddle. Gigi hadn't seen him since the cruise.

"Well, look who it is," Ronny said, catching sight of her. "Little Miss Ghoster."

Gigi had gotten three texts from Ronny, all of them lacking punctuation and all sent after 9:00 p.m. She hadn't replied to any yet.

"I wasn't ghosting you," Gigi said. "I've been busy."

"Baking sourdough bread with your mom?" Ronny's lopsided smile told her he didn't mind. "Or watching rom-coms while giving each other manicures?"

"Don't forget the matching pajama sets," Gigi said, feeling a certain pull toward Ronny. Or a push, but what was the difference? "It's been quite a full schedule."

"So no time for me, then?" Ronny said it lightly, just as Gigi would if she were in his shoes.

It was a welcome change from James's cowardly silence. Gigi might as well go for Ronny. She knew what to do with someone like him. How to play the game, how to pour on the charm. It wasn't like she was looking to meet her next boyfriend on Mackinac anyway. A fling was all she wanted.

"Let's meet up at the fort tonight," she said.

He grinned. "How're you going to sneak past Mommy?"

"I'll find a way," Gigi said. "I always have."

Chapter 25

Mackinac

Locals either loved the governor's summer residence on the island or hated it.

A white mansion perched on a bluff on the east side, it couldn't be missed. People complained that the house was an eyesore, that it wasn't built within the zoning regulations, that the governor's private plane was deafening, an environmental stain. There were criticisms, too, that the governor used the estate as a backdrop for photos—grilling burgers for neighbors, playing cornhole with kids, wading ankle-deep into the lake while discussing climate change. It was a prop, some felt, to create a narrative of being in touch with constituents, everyday folk, when the reality was the house sat empty ten months a year. And governor after governor, no matter which side of the party line, seemed to quickly forget Mackinac once they were back at the Lansing capitol.

Islanders liked to speculate on who would be invited to the governor's famous "spur-of-the-moment" barbecues (read: the staff planned them for months, then sent out last-minute invites to preserve an air of spontaneity, as it polled well with voters). Many insisted they wouldn't attend even if they were invited, that they would boycott to send a message about whatever controversial political policy was currently in the spotlight. But no one ever turned down an invite, except for old Mrs. Neely, who had just broken both her hips in an unfortunate tumble down the fort steps. Even then, the governor stopped by to visit her at the medical clinic, bringing her flowers and chili mac and cheese. The photos were a big hit.

But it was the kidnapping attempt that brought the most notoriety. Several years ago, there was a plot to kidnap the governor while she was on Mackinac. The whole thing failed spectacularly—FBI agents had the crooks in cuffs before they even got off the ferry—but the lore lingered, sweetening with age. Islanders were starting to place bets on when the next kidnapping might occur. They didn't want anyone to get hurt, of course, but the news coverage was exhilarating.

Before the kidnapping story, the governor's residence was known for the tale surrounding Alexander Vanderhosen III. The prior governor's son, he ran away with Mackinac Island high schooler Georgiana Jenkins.

It was a privileged getaway if ever there was one. They took the governor's private plane.

It might have ruined Alexander, but it didn't. The governor was able to control the angle of the story, clear her son's name so he could carry on with his Ivy League to Wall Street path. The reporters framed it on Georgiana, a troublemaker, shoplifter, clout chaser.

In the years since, it had become one of the few things islanders agreed upon, and fudgies too. The governor's son had been taken advantage of. It was the girl's fault.

Mackinac didn't agree, but what could she do? She was only an island, after all. She could spit waves onto the shore, but no matter how hard she tried, she couldn't speak.

Chapter 26

Gigi

G igi first met Alexander on the beach at British Landing.
It was a rainy April day during her senior year of high school.
She'd left the house to evade the lecture Eloise was giving about Gigi's
lack of college plans.

"College just cages you in conformity," Gigi said.

"Is that what you think?" Eloise asked. "Or what your dad thinks?"

"What I think." It was true that those were Gus's words, but Gigi
agreed with him of her own free will. She'd originally planned to
go to college as the most expedient way off the island, but the more
she'd talked about it with her dad on his latest visit, the more she'd
started questioning it. She'd have to take out so many student loans
that she'd be forced into some high-paying corporate job after grad-
uating just to get out of debt, and she'd be stripped of whatever
independent thinking she had left. She might as well get a job straight
out of high school and save up some money while figuring out for
herself what she actually wanted to do.

"Besides, *you* didn't go to college," Gigi said to Eloise.

"Because I got married," Eloise replied.

Eloise was trying to control her again, live out her own dashed
dreams through her daughter. Gigi wouldn't stand for it.

"I'll get married too, then," Gigi said. "That'll solve everything."
Then she fled the house, heading down to British Landing for some
alone time.

The beach was damp and shrouded in clouds. It was spitting rain. Gigi preferred the gloom. It was easier to imagine she might be someplace interesting when she couldn't see the horizon.

A young man was sitting in the sand. He looked like he'd come from the golf course or a job interview, maybe both. A bottle of wine and a book lay beside him.

Gigi guessed it was the governor's son, the one who was just a few years older than her. Alexander Vanderhosen III. He went to Cornell or Columbia; Gigi couldn't recall and didn't care.

Gigi walked up to him, curious to see what he was like. "Shitty day, huh?"

Alexander looked up. His eyes were inky, the color of midnight. "Pretty shitty."

Gigi took this as an invitation to sit down. Wet sand clumped to the backs of her legs. She was glad she'd shaved.

His book was a collection of poems by Edgar Allan Poe. Gigi had paid attention to the lessons on Poe in school because he wrote a lot about death. Gigi figured that if you were going to be a poet, you might as well be a depressing one.

"Can I have some?" Gigi asked, eyeing the wine.

"How old are you?" he asked.

"Ah, you're one of those."

"One of what?"

"Rule abiders."

This bothered him. It was obvious in how he kicked the sand, like he was trying to leave a divot. "No, I'm not. That's why I'm here. I'm rebelling."

"Oh?" Gigi said. "Against what?"

"My parents. Oppression. The whole fucked-up capitalistic world."

"All topics worthy of an uprising." Gigi sifted through the sand, searching for shells. Eloise and Rebecca always liked to collect them. Gigi liked to crunch them up and scatter them.

Alexander looked at her, really *looked* this time. "Who are you?"

"One of the ghosts who haunts the island."

His lips, full and pouty, nearly folded into a smile. "An evil ghost or a friendly ghost?"

"Evil," Gigi said.

He laughed nervously. "You still haven't told me your name."

"Gigi. And you're Alexander."

"Xander," he said. "Alexander is too pretentious."

"Only when you include the three Roman numerals afterward."

"Are you mocking me?"

"Solid deductive reasoning skills. Putting your fancy college education to good use."

He looked glad to be called out like this. "What're you doing on the beach?"

"I was going to go skinny-dipping," Gigi lied. "Care to join?"

His face shifted. His legs did too. "How about we go to the hot tub back at my house? My parents are at some fundraising event at the Grand."

Gigi noted even then how he seemed fond of the privilege he professed to resent, but she didn't point out the hypocrisy. She wanted to see the house. She'd always loved the governor's mansion, envied what it represented. An entire world that existed without her. Here was her chance in, her chance out.

"We'll go skinny-dipping another time," Xander said as they stood up. "But the water has to be warm."

"Mexico," Gigi said. "We'll go to Mexico."

———— ≈ ————

They didn't make it to Mexico, but they went to Florida two months later.

The plans came together quickly. Long nights, short fuses. Applauding each other's genius. Ranting about society's archaic template for success, how it trapped everyone in a zombie-like existence. College, marriage, kids, retirement, death. One manic sprint to the grave.

Musings morphed into planning over edibles on the beach. Marijuana wasn't legal yet. Xander had gotten them from a fraternity brother, stocking up at the end of last term.

"Let's run away," he said. "Let's just fucking go."

Gigi popped another gummy. "I'm in."

Their romance always felt like a race. For Gigi, a race to start a new life, far away from Mackinac. For Xander, a race to end an old life, the one where he had to get straight A's, network with politicians at holiday parties, and evaluate every life decision in the context of how it would strengthen or smear his résumé.

It wasn't like she thought Xander was her forever guy. She didn't want to get married until she was much, much older, if at all. Her parents were proof that young love didn't last. But this didn't need to last. It just needed to get her off this island.

Gigi didn't have a passport. This limited their options, though the governor's private plane only flew domestically anyway. The plane was a key part of the plan.

"It'll be ironic," Xander said when Gigi asked why he wanted to make their getaway on the jet when it stood for everything they were rebelling against. "And my parents will freak."

"It just seems a bit excessive," Gigi said. "Stealing the plane. We could find another way. A motorcycle, maybe."

"You're thinking too small," Xander said, and Gigi thought he might be right. "If you really want your parents to respect you, you have to show them that you're capable of big things."

"This doesn't have anything to do with my parents," Gigi said, though she was already thinking about what they would do when they found her missing. She would be teaching them a lesson. Her mother a lesson about what happens when you're overly involved in your child's life. And her father a lesson about what happens when you're absent from it.

"Okay," Xander said. "But we're still taking the plane."

"Fine," Gigi said. "But you're bailing me out if we get in trouble."

"We're not going to get in trouble."

Gigi should have known that what he meant was he was not going to get in trouble because of his last name and connections and all the things Gigi didn't have.

Xander forged a note from the governor saying he and Gigi needed to be taken down to Florida for a college function. The pilot didn't question it.

Gigi packed in the night while Rebecca slept. She could have packed in the day, but doing it in the dark felt more scandalous.

The day of their departure, Gigi headed off to school, then slipped back to the house to collect her suitcase after Eloise was at work. She thought Xander might back out, but he was waiting for her at the airfield. Ten minutes later, they were taking off. It was Gigi's first time flying. She didn't tell Xander that. She just drank the mini wine bottles from the fridge and stared out at the cotton-candy clouds.

This is living, she thought. She felt very close to her dad in that moment, though she hadn't seen him in a while.

She hoped he would be proud of her getaway. Worried too, of course, but once he tracked her down, he would be proud. Maybe he'd even offer her a job at the repair shop he was working at down in Asheville. They could go on trips together on the weekends, that sort of thing. She would have proved to him that she wasn't a kid anymore, that she could handle real adventure, even danger. Sometimes it felt like he still saw her as the eight-year-old she'd been when he'd moved out. This would remind him that she was almost eighteen now, a real adult.

The plane touched down in Tampa. They would drive to Miami to throw off the authorities (a search party would surely commence shortly). Gigi assumed they would rent a car, but Xander had a driver pick them up in a black Lexus.

"Here we go," Xander said, squeezing Gigi's hand as they sat in the plush back seat. "We're on our own now."

The hotel in Miami looked like a spaceship. Glitzy and modern, mood lights blinking. Three infinity pools, six hot tubs, and a jungle spa. Xander handed over his credit card, paid by his parents.

"Won't they notice the charge?" Gigi asked in the elevator up to their suite.

"They never check the bill," he said.

Gigi thought they would be making it on their own, Bonnie and Clyde style. But maybe Xander was right. The best way to oppose privilege was to abuse it. And didn't she deserve this after being shuttered away on Mackinac her whole life?

The first night was a thrill. Room service and robes and sex and tequila shots in the hot tub (Xander tipped well enough that no one carded them). They slept in until noon, had a couple's massage in a private cabana, and guzzled frozen margaritas to cure the hangovers.

"Do you think they're looking for us yet?" Xander asked.

"Probably." Eloise would have pieced together that Gigi was with Xander. Gigi pictured her walking up to the governor's mansion, rapping the brass knocker. Rebecca would probably be drafting a speech for Gigi's funeral.

The third day was when the cracks started appearing, fissures on thin ice.

"I don't know what's taking them so long," Xander said from a poolside lounge chair. "To find us."

Gigi, too, was feeling disconcerted. She'd expected her parents to work faster than this. Perhaps they weren't that worried after all.

"We don't want to be found," Gigi said, flipping onto her back to even out her tan. "That's the whole point."

"I know, but it would still be nice to know they were looking."

"Maybe we should switch hotels. Throw them off." She liked the idea of trying to tangle their tracks so it would make sense if no one located them.

"Maybe." Xander flagged down the server for another tequila sunrise. "Not so much cranberry this time. And more salt on the rim."

The fourth day was the end of the line.

"Who are you texting?" Gigi asked. It was late but they were still in bed, both of them listless and grumpy, heads pounding.

"My brother," Xander said.

"I thought we said no phones. They can be tracked." Gigi didn't yet own a cell phone. Eloise didn't believe in them and Gigi didn't have the money to buy one herself. Still, she liked picturing hypothetical texts and voicemails she might have received by now. The teary pleas from her mother, the raspy "I love yous" from her father.

"Relax," Xander said. "It's fine."

Gigi peered over at the texts. They were talking football, sharing YouTube videos about NFL preseason trades.

"Apparently my parents know where I am," Xander said. "They're just too selfish to come get me. Classic."

Gigi absorbed this. "They know where we are?"

"Yup."

"Does that mean my parents know too?"

"Dunno," he said. "Probably."

"But no one's coming to get us?"

"Nope."

Gigi felt furious. How dare they let her rot away with the governor's son? How dare they not come and look for her?

The runaway plot had lost its fizz, its freshness. A bottle of cheap champagne gone flat.

"I think I'll probably head out in a few days," Xander said. "My buddy Colton is having our whole fraternity to his parents' place in Nantucket."

"We're going to Nantucket?"

"*I'm* going to Nantucket."

Gigi was starting to despise Xander.

"And what am I doing exactly?" she asked, sitting up on the pillows, tugging the sheets to her side.

"Whatever you want," Xander said, still texting his brother. "That's the point of freedom, right? You can go back to Mackinac if you want. You're clearly homesick."

"No, I'm not." Though Gigi did ache for the lakes, the trees, the horses. The scent of Eloise's peanut brittle, the sound of Rebecca flipping the pages of her books.

The phone in their room rang. Xander answered but Gigi could hear the voice on the other end. Xander's credit card was no longer valid, the hotel had been notified. They would have to put down a new payment method.

"They cut me off," Xander said, slamming down the phone. "Fuckers."

He started chucking things into his suitcase. Their room looked as if a small bomb had detonated in it. Bathing suits and boxers, condom wrappers and room service trays. They'd kept the "Do Not Disturb" sign on so they could sleep as late as they wanted.

"I'll buy you a plane ticket back to Michigan," Xander said when Gigi told him he was only thinking about himself.

"You don't have any money," she said.

"I still have my emergency credit card," he said. "My brother said our parents put a five-thousand-dollar limit on it, but it'll get me to Nantucket at least."

Five thousand dollars was more than Eloise earned in a month. Gigi knew this from watching Eloise budget at the kitchen table, filling in her spreadsheets by hand. There was a shift in Gigi, a shake.

"I'm not leaving," Gigi said.

She was starting to feel ashamed of herself. There was no way she could face Eloise after this.

"You're putting your credit card down?" Xander said. He knew Gigi didn't have a card.

"No, I'm getting a job down here. I'm staying in Florida."

She was homesick but she couldn't return to Mackinac. It wasn't just that she didn't think Eloise would take her back. She hadn't come all this way only to quit when her partner in crime bailed.

Radical change was what she'd wanted, and this was just accelerating the goal. Taking the training wheels off the bike that her dad had taught her to ride and then left her to career down the big hill alone. The bike that her mother had deemed too dangerous to ride alone, so she'd locked it in the garage with a key that she kept out of Gigi's reach.

Gigi was done with her past . . . all of it.

"Why would you stay in this place?" Xander said with the implication that this had been the worst four days of his life, a harsh test of his survival skills.

"Because, unlike you, I actually want a new type of life."

"Don't call me to bail you out of jail," were the last words Xander spoke as he hustled out of the room, nearly sprinting to the elevator.

Soon after, there was a rap at the door. Gigi didn't answer, expecting it to be the cleaning staff telling her she had to leave.

"Gigi? Are you in there?"

Gigi knew that voice. She opened the door. It was Rebecca, looking like a total wreck. "You're okay," Rebecca said, flinging her arms around Gigi. "You're okay."

"Of course I am." She had never been the hugging type, but Gigi returned the embrace. "No need to cry," Gigi said, delighted to discover she had the ability to produce such emotions in her sister. "Is Mom with you?"

The answer was no.

"She didn't want me to come either," Rebecca said. "Even when the governor told us where you were. I had to sneak out, get Dad to sign a form to let me fly as an unaccompanied minor."

"You talked to Dad?"

"Of course I did. You were *missing*. Dad made me feel better, actually. He wasn't worried at all."

Gigi tried to take comfort in this but found it difficult. It had been so much nicer to pretend that her parents really cared about her than to test the hypothesis and watch it fail.

But Rebecca was here. Her little sister who was so terrified of airplanes, so terrified of going against their mother's will. But she had overcome all of that to come and find Gigi. She vowed never again to take Rebecca for granted. It didn't matter that Rebecca was Eloise's favorite. Gigi didn't care anymore about being her mother's favorite or her father's. She wanted to be her own favorite, and she was going to figure out what that looked like.

"Look at us," Gigi said to Rebecca as they stood there in the chandelier-lit hallway. "A couple of fugitives."

Rebecca tried to smile but still looked close to tears. "Yes, you know me. The wild child."

"I'd say sneaking off the island and getting on an airplane qualifies as rebel territory."

"The flight was awful," Rebecca said, looking woozy. "But I needed to make sure you were okay."

"I'm fine," Gigi said. "Perfectly fine."

———— ≈ ————

Her sister flew back the next day, without Gigi. Rebecca begged her to come too and assured her that she would help manage Eloise. But Gigi was steadfast, flaring up with anger at Rebecca for coming at all.

"I didn't need to be saved," Gigi said. "I needed to escape."

Gigi wasn't proud of how she treated her little sister, but she really couldn't help it. She was hardwired to metabolize softness into concrete after twenty-four hours.

Gigi found a hostel in a gritty slice of Miami. She negotiated a rate of fourteen dollars a night (down from the forty-five advertised). Then she walked into twenty-two restaurants and bars to see if they were hiring. Some asked for her résumé. She didn't have one and didn't feel like typing one out at a library computer. It would all be forged anyway.

Finally she got a place to take a chance on her. An Irish pub called the Brazen Head. It smelled like Guinness and beef stew. Gigi walked by it one day and saw a line of people waiting to get seated. The staff was nowhere to be found. Sensing an opportunity, Gigi stepped in and stood behind the host stand.

She wrote down customers' names on the notepad and spewed out estimated wait times (ten minutes for friendly customers; two hours for hostile ones). The real hostess finally returned. A girl not much older than Gigi, with an aura of stress. She was doubling as waitress too. "Who are you?" she asked Gigi.

"I'm the new hostess," Gigi said.

"Joe didn't say anything about a new person."

"Do you want the help or not?"

The girl nodded. "You stay here; I'll do the food."

The next day they went to Joe together and pitched Gigi for the job. He hired her on the spot. She made six dollars and twenty-five cents an hour and could work her way up to a waitress, which she did a few months later, when she turned eighteen. She liked it at first, the way she could charm customers and get them drunk enough to tip too much. But it came with a cost. The fake smiles, the niceties, the men ogling her, the women screaming at her for not putting the salad dressing on the side like they'd asked.

"Why are you ordering a salad at an Irish pub anyway?" she said once, then regretted it when the customer left no tip.

The problem with waitressing was that it made her be somebody she wasn't. She'd fled one conformist environment just to be shoved into another.

She quit after six months and got a job at a bike shop. She knew a bit about bicycles from Mackinac, and the things she didn't know she winged with such bravado that even the mechanics at the shop started wondering if they'd been doing it wrong all along.

Chapter 27

Deidre

Deirdre Moore was a bad friend.

She first had inklings of this back in elementary school when she changed an answer on Eloise's math test after it was submitted to keep Eloise from receiving a perfect score yet again. She didn't want Eloise to fail, but she wasn't thrilled about her success either. Having her somewhere in the middle with Deirdre would be nice.

She sensed she was a bad friend again when Eloise told her she was dating Gus and Deirdre responded as if Eloise had been carrying on an affair with her husband. On an intellectual level, Deirdre knew she didn't have any claim over Gus Jenkins, but she'd been in love with him for so long. And he'd given so many signs that he was interested in her too—that eye contact, how it lingered! Ultimately he must have realized that Deirdre would put him in his place too much. He wanted someone who would let him reign and wander. That was Eloise.

When Gus walked out on the marriage, Deirdre felt one terrible jab of satisfaction. Gus had chosen Eloise over Deirdre, and she'd had to watch them together for so many years. She'd had to stand up at their wedding as maid of honor, see the births of their beautiful girls (it was deeply triggering for Deirdre; she'd always wanted a girl but found herself raising boys instead). When Gus left, Deirdre felt redeemed. She hadn't missed out on the most magnificent man ever to grace the shores of Mackinac. She had dodged a bullet.

She had also been a bad friend in how she kept Eloise holding on to hope that Gus might come back. At first, Deirdre had told Eloise that Gus was gone for good, that Eloise needed to move on. But Eloise had taken it so badly that Deirdre figured it was kinder to help her keep the faith alive. There was no such thing as false hope, after all. Fred was always saying that to his patients. And it wasn't like Deirdre was lying to Eloise. She *did* know that Gus would come back. She just also knew he wouldn't stay.

Deirdre felt for Eloise and her . . . predicament, as she supposed it could be called. Though it did thrill her how she was the only person Eloise confided in. Deirdre hoped the secret never came out. She didn't want to have to share it.

There was one secret about herself that she wished she could share with Eloise. It pertained to why Deirdre had been so bad at keeping in touch when she went off to college and Eloise stayed on the island to get married. It wasn't just jealousy that had made her go dark. But whenever Deirdre came close to confessing, something stopped her. She wasn't scared of Eloise's judgment. She just knew Eloise wouldn't be able to fix anything.

Then there was the secret Deirdre was holding about Eloise's parents. One night many years ago over a bottle of brandy, her uncle Liam told Deirdre about his affair with Alice Jenkins, formerly Klein, back in the autumn of 1982. Liam made Deirdre swear on the Bible not to tell anyone. Deirdre had upheld the oath to this day. To tell Eloise the truth would be to shatter the way she viewed her parents, the way she viewed the world. There was no need for such disillusionment, not at this stage, with David gone and Alice getting on in years. Still, Deirdre felt like a bad friend for withholding the truth.

The worst thing about being a bad friend was that Eloise thought Deirdre a very good friend. She had a way of making Deirdre feel as if she were in contention for sainthood.

Deirdre never confessed her sins to anyone, except God, who wouldn't tattle, and Fred, who wouldn't listen. After being married so long, she often felt invisible around Fred, like she was no more exciting than the toaster. Deirdre often felt Fred still didn't know her as much as he should after three decades together. Though she supposed she was to blame there, given the big piece of information she had kept from him all these years. She and Fred got along well enough, but the romance was dead. Though wasn't that inevitable? It happened to everyone.

Except Eloise. Gus had left before the boring stage of marriage kicked in, and now Eloise was getting a second chance at love with Clyde. It felt like Eloise was being rewarded for her marriage having failed—which was completely unfair as far as Deirdre was concerned.

This was the latest reason she was a bad friend. She was jealous.

Vickie at the florist shop told Deirdre that Clyde sent Eloise two dozen gladiolus. Gladiolus were Deirdre's favorite. They were Eloise's favorite too, but only because Eloise tended to copy Deirdre. Take Gus, for example.

———— ≈ ————

Deirdre strode down Trillium Drive toward Thistle Dew. She wanted to fact-check the news about the gladiolus. She let herself in, no need to knock. Eloise was in the kitchen, tending to a trumpet vase. The gladiolus were even more stunning than Deirdre had feared.

Fred used to buy Deirdre flowers. Mostly carnations or already-wilting roses. He had the funds for nicer things but thought it a waste of money. "I'd rather be frugal and then take a fancy trip to Europe," he always said.

But they never went to Europe.

"Look at those," Deirdre said to Eloise. "Did Gigi buy them as a thank-you for hosting her?"

"That would be the day," Eloise said. "They're from Clyde. He had a bouquet delivered for Georgiana too. She took them up to her room and said it was the first time a man had ever given her flowers. She didn't even sound sarcastic." Eloise looked quite overcome.

Deirdre feigned surprise. "So you're giving him another chance?"

They *had* looked good together on the dance floor. Part of Deirdre, the decent part, was rooting for them.

"I might have been a little hasty in cutting things off, that's all," Eloise said. "There's no harm in getting to know each other. It's not like . . ." She trailed of, trimming the stems so they fit better in the vase.

"It's not like Gus is around?" Deirdre finished.

Eloise took a whiff of the gladiolus. "I didn't mean that."

"It's okay if you did. We never really get over our first love, do we?" Deirdre let the question hang there. "Point is, you deserve to be happy." Deirdre felt that she, too, deserved to be happy, and though she was *content*, that wasn't quite the same, was it? "Gus isn't here and Clyde is. It's not a difficult equation to solve. Though of course there's still the fact that you and Gus—"

"—I'm playing golf with Clyde tomorrow," Eloise cut in. "A safe daytime activity."

"You don't play golf," Deirdre said.

"He's going to teach me."

Eloise was not one to learn new things. She liked her routines, her habits.

"Don't look at me like that," Eloise said. "It's not like I'm caving to pickleball and polluting the island with those obnoxiously loud balls."

"What about the balls?" Deirdre said, enjoying the effect she was having.

"Deirdre Moore!"

"I'm just jealous," Deirdre said with a wink. This was the only way she was able to admit the truth, under the guise of a joke. "Fred and I don't have exciting dates anymore."

"Well, you have loyalty. Stability. Trust. Those things are worth their weight in gold."

"I suppose so," Deirdre said, though she couldn't help but think about the one thing they would never have. The reason Deirdre still needed to take melatonin every night even after all these years.

Eloise changed the topic. "Georgiana is going to see Ronny again."

Deirdre thumbed the gladiolus petals. "What gives you that idea?"

"She was smiling while texting someone today," Eloise said. "And she washed her hair, even blow-dried it."

"Oh dear," Deirdre said. "Not good."

"Of all people she could go for. *Ronny*."

"It's like she's trying to take years off your life expectancy," Deirdre said.

"Feels that way sometimes," Eloise said, exasperated. "I know you always used to wish for girls, Deirdre, but let me say, I think God may have protected you by giving you sons. Daughters can cause so much hurt."

Deirdre knew Eloise didn't really mean that. She was just saying it because she felt guilty that she'd gotten so many things Deirdre wanted. But the words still throbbed.

"Mmm," Deirdre said, plucking one of the gladiolus from the bouquet to take home for herself. "I can only imagine."

Chapter 28

Gigi

G igi approached the fort on the confiscated scooter. It was after 10:00 p.m., the designated meeting time. She liked the feeling of keeping Ronny waiting.

Of all the spots on the island, the fort was most associated with paranormal activity. People swore they saw ghosts of soldiers clad in war-torn uniforms, heard their strangled cries. Gigi didn't buy it. As a kid, she'd always been on the lookout for spirits, but nothing good ever turned up. A rogue creak of a door or a burned-out lamppost didn't satisfy.

Beyond ghost hunting, the fort was popular for stargazing. Located at Mackinac's highest point, its views of the skies were sweeping. Down below, the last ferry had long departed. Off the coast, the lighthouse blinked, illuminating the water just enough to make Gigi aware of how little of it she could see.

"Look who showed after all."

Ronny, in a T-shirt and cargo shorts, was seated on the ruins of an old stone wall. A beer in his hand, a six-pack at his feet. There was no Cruiser. Ronny appeared to have walked.

"Told you I would," Gigi said.

Ronny had a speaker blaring nineties punk rock. Loud enough to make people raise their eyebrows, quiet enough that they wouldn't file a noise complaint. Gigi knew the volume well.

"Let the games begin," she said, taking a seat next to him. She was wearing safari shorts and an oversized sweatshirt.

Ronny ran his hands through his long, lemony hair. "That's all this is to you, huh?" he said. "A game?"

Gigi shrugged. "That's all life is to me."

"Truth." He reached for another beer and offered Gigi one.

She accepted, cracking it open on the rock wall rather than the bottle opener Ronny was using. The awed look on his face triggered Gigi's endorphins.

There was something so familiar about Ronny, something homey, even. She thought about what her therapist in LA had said. *"When you have a traumatic childhood, someone who feels like home might not be a good thing. It can mean they feel like instability and anxiety. You can easily mistake anxiety for excitement. The bodily reaction is nearly identical. What you really want is someone who makes you feel something new. Something more like peace."*

As Gigi played back the words, she couldn't help but think of James and how he brought a strange calmness over her. Or maybe it was just boredom. She wasn't really sure of the difference.

She sipped her beer to wash away the bad taste.

"I'm off duty tonight," Ronny said, though Gigi hadn't asked. "And we deserve something for surviving this hellhole for the summer, don't we?"

"Tell me about it."

"What are you doing back here anyway?" Ronny asked. "A free spirit like you doesn't belong. Did your mom guilt you into visiting?"

"Something like that."

Ronny guzzled his beer. "You're a better kid than I am. My parents have to come visit me if they want to see me."

Gigi envied the boundaries he'd set. She would like to give her parents the same ultimatum, but she was worried they simply wouldn't come see her at all. "Do they?" she asked. "Visit you?"

"Every once in a blue moon. Still way too often, if you ask me." He laughed but it lacked resonance. Gigi detected pebbles of melancholy, sidestepped by humor. She wondered if he was happy being so independent or if he'd found it lonely like she had.

"Why were you kicked out of your hometown?" she asked.

Ronny's jaw twitched. "I don't ask about your past, you don't ask about mine. Deal?"

Gigi felt it, that compulsion to be liked. Not to be loved or cherished, just to be approved of as the chill girl, the one who wouldn't cause a scene when he didn't text her tomorrow. "Deal."

His hand rested on her bare thigh. "All the tourists are high on fudge and think this is some fucking fairy kingdom," he said. "You get it, though."

"Being high on weed always beats being high on fudge." She took a joint and a lighter from her pocket. After taking a drag, she handed it to Ronny.

"Why can't every girl be a troublemaker like you?" he said.

"*My little troublemaker*," Gigi's dad used to call her, a proud lilt to the phrase. Gigi knew that on some level her rebellious streak had always been a plea for love from the one man she'd needed most. That was the thing about being in her late twenties now. She had more self-awareness. But she still kept choosing the same actions, the same patterns. Maybe it was habit or maybe it was just that she found life more fun this way— luring people in, letting them go.

Gigi took the joint back, gave it another puff. "Yeah," she said, "I'm pretty great."

"Modest too." Ronny wanted her, she could tell.

It was enough for Gigi to want him, too, or at least to be curious about where their relationship might go next.

Clouds were rolling in quickly from the coast, obscuring the stars. The wind was picking up, the air humid. A storm seemed to be coming. Gigi liked the thought.

She stood up and tugged down her shorts so they didn't ride up her ass. "You promised me a tour of the fort."

Ronny grinned. He'd either never had braces or had stopped wearing his retainers years ago. Gigi liked the lack of perfection.

"I did, didn't I?" He slung his free arm around Gigi's shoulder.

Something about the motion drizzled déjà vu over Gigi. She'd been on this date before. Not with Ronny but with one of the other guys from her past she'd put on a performance for to impress.

She thought back to what James had said about how she should have been an actress. In many ways she had become one. The thought had a sour flavor.

Ronny led her over to the cannons, aimed at the water. "This is where the Americans fired the cannons at the British," he said, putting on the air of a tour guide. "During the Battle of Mackinac."

"Nope," Gigi said. "The British won the fort in the war of 1812. The Americans tried and failed to retake it in 1814—that was the Battle of Mackinac. The fort was returned to the US at the end of the war and stayed active until 1895. During that time, the island transitioned from a fur trade hub to a tourist destination." She recited the words swiftly, no pauses.

"Who invited the nerd?" Ronny said.

"It was ingrained in us in school like the ABC's." Gigi pointed to a white stone building built into the hill, its shingled roof refurbished in the style of the 1700s. "Those are the officers' stone quarters, originally barracks for the British during the Revolutionary War. The oldest building in Michigan."

Ronny yawned. "Enough with the history lesson," he said. "Let's get to anatomy class."

Gigi wondered if Ronny was really so vacuous or just pretending to be. She would give him one more chance to impress her.

Leaning against the door of the barracks, she faced Ronny, challenging him to move first.

He tossed his beer can on the ground, crunched it under his boot, then closed the gap between them. His breath tasted like beer and weed and barbecue sauce. The kiss was less restrained than on the boat. His hands found the back of her shorts, then the front.

The first clap of thunder echoed from off the coast.

"Let's get out of here," he said.

"I'll take you back to my mom's," Gigi said dryly.

"I wouldn't make it out alive."

"I thought you were an adrenaline junkie."

"And I thought you liked me, but you're setting me up to be murdered."

"To be fair, my mom would probably execute both of us."

The thought made Gigi smile. She felt a strange splash of gratitude for Eloise. Her mother could go too far sometimes, but it was nice to know she cared and was there.

"What a comfort," Ronny said. "Let's go back to mine."

With Gigi on the back of the electric scooter, Ronny drove full-speed to his apartment. Gigi whooped as they careened down the hill. As a kid, she used to ride her old manual scooter up and down the hill at the fort for hours at a time. Every Christmas she'd asked for an electric scooter, once she stopped asking for a pony. In the end, she'd gotten neither.

They flew past the medical clinic just in time to see James locking up for the night.

Ronny didn't slow down, just called out to him, "'Sup, Doc!"

If James replied, his words were swallowed by the night. He'd seen them, though—Gigi knew he had. She was glad. He would know she wasn't waiting around for him, wasn't pining.

They lurched into the gravel driveway of Ronny's place. As Ronny switched off the scooter, Gigi thought about driving herself home or taking a solo lap around the island.

If they hadn't passed by James, she might have done that. But something about seeing him locking up at the clinic for his important job as a doctor made Gigi aware of how little she had to show for nearly thirty years on the planet. How far away she was from her dreams and, worse than that, how she didn't even know what they were anymore. She'd spent the past decade not running toward anything, just running away.

The idea of figuring any of that out tonight was too daunting. She felt newly drawn to Ronny as a distraction, so she followed him inside, enjoying the shape of her shadow under the porch light. Long and distorted like she might be somebody else, perhaps already was.

The apartment was sparse and messy, a true bachelor pad. Before she could even kick off her shoes, her phone chimed. Gigi would have guessed it was Eloise, unleashing her wrath that Gigi was out so late, except that Eloise would call, not text.

It was Gus.

After many weeks of silence, here he was, suddenly back in her orbit. Excitement rose. Anxiety too, since they were different sides of the same coin.

> Gigi!! Sorry I missed ur last text . . . r u surviving the island and ur mom?! Unfortunately looking like I won't get back there this summer . . . my South America trip got extended a few weeks. Will keep u posted 😊   😊   😊

As soon as Gigi finished reading the text, she wished she had waited longer to look at it. This was all her dad had for her after being off the grid for so long? One flimsy text to tell her he wouldn't be coming back to Mackinac to see her? The emojis especially infuriated her.

Feeling a new punch of that old pain, she made to leave Ronny's apartment.

"Where're you going?" Ronny said from the stairwell.

"It's past my bedtime," Gigi said.

Ronny scoffed. "You're a grown-ass adult."

"That makes one of us." Gigi opened the front door.

"You scared your mom's gonna yell at you?"

"I'm really not," Gigi said. "I'm just tired."

Gigi was not looking for a boy. She was looking for a man. A man to be her father and a man to be her partner. She didn't have control over the first. But she sure as hell did over the second.

"Good night, Ronny," Gigi said, setting out into the dark, the flashlight from her phone illuminating her way. It was starting to rain. "And goodbye."

"You're a fucking tease," Ronny called out after her. "No wonder no one on this island can stand you."

There was a violent clap of thunder. Gigi liked to think it was Mackinac coming to her defense. More likely it was a storm she'd created from her own chaos.

Either way, Gigi followed the lightning home.

Chapter 29

Lillian

"Y ou have to tell Gigi how you feel," Lillian said to James as she refilled his iced tea.

Lillian was behind the bar tonight. The Pink Pony's usual bartender had called in sick. It was suspicious timing with the bonfire the fudgies were throwing to kick off the Fourth of July weekend. The island was buzzing with the arrival of summer's biggest holiday.

"Ah, yes, everything is as simple as just telling people the truth," James said, swiveling on a barstool. He'd come straight from the clinic and was still in his scrubs. "I forgot about that." He gave Lillian a warm smile.

"Touché," she said. "I'm going to tell my parents the truth by the end of summer." She grimaced, anticipating their reaction. But she was nearly thirty years old. It was time to grow up and face her parents, even if it might mean losing them. "Hold me accountable?" she said to James.

"Certainly. Though I'll miss being your fake boyfriend, I must say."

"You've played the part well," Lillian said gratefully. "But it's time you upgrade to Gigi." She winked.

James jolted. "I don't even know how I feel about her," he said. "All I know is that I feel. It's highly unpleasant."

"Such is the joy of a new crush."

James frowned, cleft chin pinching. "I don't have a crush."

"Right." Lillian started whipping up rum runners and blueberry moonshine sparklers for the swarming customers. "My mistake."

"Gigi is completely unlike any girl I've ever dated," James went on. "On paper, we'd never work."

"But . . . ," Lillian prodded.

"She just seems so unapologetically herself," James said. "And as someone who's spent his whole life staying on the straight and narrow, it's intriguing, I'll admit."

"I can empathize," Lillian said. "So it's just her strong-willed personality that has caught your eye? Nothing at all about her physical beauty?"

She couldn't help giving him a hard time. His job required him to be so serious that Lillian felt it was her duty to help him lighten up.

James cleared his throat. "She is rather striking."

"She's a total smoke show," Lillian said bluntly.

"Well, it doesn't even matter how I feel because she's with Ronny."

"That won't last," Lillian said. "Believe me, I've seen it play out before."

Gigi entered relationships the same way she entered the Great Lakes. Sprinting barefoot along the rocky beach, plunging headfirst into the water. Bodysurfing on the fiercest wave she could find. Then dashing out again thirty seconds later, shaking herself dry or snatching someone else's towel because she forgot her own.

"And besides," James said, lowering his voice though it wasn't necessary over the acoustic guitarist filling the bar with country ballads, "even if, hypothetically speaking, I did start dating Gigi, where would that leave you?"

Lillian had met James on her second day back on Mackinac this summer. They went on a bike ride at her mother's urging. "It'll be good to have someone close in age to talk with," Trina had said. Lillian couldn't think of a good reason not to go except that she didn't want to, which wasn't good enough. By the time they'd finished the lakeshore lap, James knew more about Lillian's life than anyone else on the island. There was a gentle, nonjudgmental way about him. But she wouldn't keep exploiting his kindness.

"You don't need to cover for me anymore," Lillian said. "Our deal was only supposed to last a couple weeks, not the entire summer."

Lillian hated the pity she'd gotten from the islanders and her parents, who saw her as a victim of her commitment-phobic ex-fiancé. She had been eager to get the attention off her broken engagement and onto a new relationship, even a fake one. She'd wanted to show them she was strong and vibrant and successful. But she'd gone about it the wrong way, she could see now. The fake relationship with James had really just been one elaborate procrastination tool to help her delay the conversation she needed to have with her parents.

"I don't mind it," James said, almost too readily. "I'm happy to help."

"Now you're the one trying to use me," Lillian teased, "as a reason not to go after the girl you like."

James stirred his iced tea with his straw. "I don't like her like that."

"Keep telling yourself that."

Even with all the years that had passed, Lillian still felt a raw yearning for her friendship with Gigi, their expired intimacy.

James looked at her. Those gray eyes reaching, trying to grip. "The cocktail umbrellas you gave her at lunch," he recalled. "Were you and Gigi ever . . ."

Lillian's temperature rose. "No," she said quickly. "Never."

"Got it," James said, and Lillian could have left it at that, but she kept talking, glad to have a reason to bring up the past.

"I was definitely in love with Gigi in high school," Lillian said, keeping her voice low. "But I didn't really come to terms with it until later. She's hated me since we were fourteen."

"You know what they say about the line between love and hate."

Lillian clanked the bar glasses a little too hard. "Gigi Jenkins has never had romantic feelings for me." Part of Lillian perished as she said it. She sometimes wondered how something dead could keep on dying. "That's one of the only things I'm sure about these days."

Lillian still didn't understand exactly what had caused the rupture be-tween her and Gigi. Eighth grade had ended on a high note with a water balloon fight down at the beach. Afterward, over grilled cheese sandwiches, Gigi had gifted Lillian with a new elephant stuffed animal to take with her to her summer camp down in the Lower Peninsula.

"I know we're too old for stuffed animals, but my dad doesn't re-alize that," Gigi said. "He still brings me a new one every time he visits."

She pretended to sound annoyed, but Lillian wasn't fooled. Gigi was overjoyed whenever her dad gave her anything. His time, most of all.

"I like it a lot," Lillian said, patting the trunk of the toy elephant. "What should we call him?"

"Bandit," Gigi said. "Since you're going to band camp."

"Bandit it is." Lillian liked that Gigi was a little bossy. It meant she didn't have to make so many of her own decisions.

While Lillian was at camp, she received a letter from Gigi in the mail. It was handwritten, six pages double-sided. Gigi was abuzz with the news that her dad was visiting and she'd caught her parents kiss-ing when they thought she and Rebecca were asleep. *I think he might be moving back for good this time!* had been Gigi's closing line, before her *Lots of love* sign-off and the huge, loopy signature. She signed all of her letters *Georgiana* because she said it was more fun to write in cursive than *Gigi*.

Lillian had written back but there was no reply. She'd sent a follow-up letter just in case the first one didn't arrive, but still nothing (neither of them had cell phones yet). Upon returning from her six weeks away at camp, Lillian went over to Thistle Dew right away. As she approached the house, she heard Gigi's voice through the open window. Gigi was asking Eloise to tell Lillian that she wasn't home.

"I'm sorry, Georgiana isn't feeling well today," Eloise had said to

Lillian, a regretful look in her eye. "But would you like some peanut brittle? I just made a fresh batch."

When the first day of ninth grade arrived a few days later, Gigi sat with the tenth- and eleventh-grade girls for lunch. They huddled together, excluding Lillian like she'd contracted the black plague.

"Did I do something?" Lillian asked Gigi the next day at her school locker. It took an embarrassing amount of courage to confront her best friend.

"Don't act like you're so naive," Gigi said.

"Is it about your dad?" Lillian asked. She tried to say it gently, having heard from her mother that Gus had left the island right after the Fudge Festival.

Lillian knew how much Gigi's dad meant to her. She had once told Lillian that if she had to choose between her mom and her dad, she would choose her dad. When Gigi asked Lillian who she would choose, Lillian said she couldn't pick, that she loved them both the same. Gigi told her that answer was cheating.

"No, this is not about my dad, Lillian," Gigi said, and Lillian cringed at how her name sounded sharp and weaponized.

"I just wasn't sure, given what you wrote in your letter," Lillian said.

"Haven't you ever heard of creative writing?" Gigi snapped. "It was fiction. I'm going to be a great novelist one day."

"I bet you will be," Lillian said kindly. "So why have you been shutting me out?"

Gigi slammed her locker and started down the hallway. Lillian had to walk quickly to keep up with Gigi's long strides.

"There are seasons for everything, Lillian," Gigi said. "And I just think that our friendship has run its course. Our growth trajectories are not in alignment."

It sounded so strange and so un-Gigi-like that Lillian could only assume that it was repurposed language from a conversation Gigi had overheard between her parents.

"Are those your words?" Lillian asked.

"Of course they are. I might not be as book smart as you, but I'm not stupid."

"I know you're not."

"You're not better than everyone, Lillian."

"I know I'm not."

Gigi offered no more explanation than that, and nothing Lillian did could win her back. Eventually she stopped trying, busying herself with thoughts of college and the big, fancy job she was going to have one day in a tall skyscraper that would make all of this look very small, very insignificant.

Without friendship to bind them together, envy slithered, filling the gaps. Lillian coveted how Gigi had the confidence to crack jokes and brush off a teacher's scolding like it was no big deal. How she had those long legs when Lillian was stuffing old newspapers into her shoes to gain an extra inch of height. How she never studied but still aced every math test.

The envy seared so bright during senior year that Lillian mistook it for desire for Gigi's boyfriend, Benjamin. But when Lillian got with Benjamin, she realized her mistake. She broke up with him on prom night after seeing Gigi in her dress. She was a mermaid, a fairy nymph, a devil, and an angel all in one torturously gorgeous body. The blurry line between being jealous of a guy's girl and wanting her for yourself took Lillian a while to figure out. That was even how she and Alex had met. He'd been dating one of the paralegals at her office, a striking woman named Tamara who now despised her.

———≈———

"One of us might as well get to be with Gigi," Lillian said to James, now at the Pink Pony bar. "It's not going to be me, so might as well be you."

"Now I feel like a jerk." James tugged at the collar of his medical coat.

"Come on, I'm not that fragile. I have enough to worry about with my broken engagement."

James asked how she was feeling about that. Relieved, she said. Yet lost too. "Alex was my best friend. And now, just like that, he's cut me out."

"He knows the reason?"

"Yeah, but he says that makes it worse. That I was deceiving him the whole time. I really did love him. *Do* love him." Lillian missed him, the way he would text her every morning to wish her a good day, how he would cook her breakfast on Sundays, the one day she let herself sleep in. "Just not in the way you should if you're going to commit your life to someone."

"You did the right thing." James had such a reassuring way about him. "Hopefully you can be friends someday."

"Hopefully you and Gigi can be *more* than friends one day," Lillian said, trying to tilt the conversation away from her. "Once I stop hogging you all for myself."

He shook his head. "Gigi thinks I'm the dullest person on the planet. Can't really blame her. You should've seen me on our first date. I was as stiff as a scarecrow."

"I know the feeling," Lillian said. "But Gigi will be obsessed with you once she gets to know you. She loves surprises, loves layers. Just try relaxing around her. And *tell her how you feel*."

"So she can publicly reject me and make a spectacle in front of all my patients?" James said.

"Gigi is a lot of things, but she's not cruel," Lillian said.

"Dumping you as her friend seemed pretty cruel."

She had filled him in on just a little of the backstory. "She was going through a lot," Lillian said. "With her dad and everything. I don't know if she's told you much about him . . ."

"No," James said. "He hasn't come up."

Lillian nodded. "Gigi takes a while to warm up. But she's good at her core." Lillian searched through her memories for an example that would illustrate it better. "Like one time on the playground, these kids had captured turtles in a sand pail. They made it a game, picking up the turtles, dropping them from the top of the playground slide. Gigi couldn't stand it. She snatched the bucket and ran to the lake to release the turtles. She got detention for being late to class. But she saved them. She saved those little turtles."

Lillian's heart compressed. After so much uncertainty since ending her engagement and quitting her job, unrequited love was actually a relief. She knew what to do with it, how to hold it.

"That's a nice story," James said. "It's also from about twenty years ago. I want to know who she is now."

"Then go and find out."

James considered it.

"You should tell her about your mom," Lillian said gently.

James had told Lillian his mom had passed away when he was in college. To cope he'd poured himself into school and his residency and now his practice.

"And scare her away?" James said. "Women tend to see me as damaged goods after I drop that happy little story."

"Nothing softens Gigi quite like sharing traumas." She was smiling but serious too. "Just try to spend more time with her. Drop the doctor persona."

"It's not a persona." He seemed hurt by the insinuation.

"I didn't mean it like that," Lillian said. "I just mean let her get to know your different sides. And I'll set the record straight if the townspeople give you a hard time."

Lillian wanted to think that she could come out in the open with everything, but she knew she'd probably still wiggle around the truth a little while longer.

"Don't let other people's opinions hold you back," Lillian carried on. "We can both learn from Gigi on that one."

Paula and Kitty bustled into the Pink Pony, scouting for seats at the bar.

"Did you hear Georgiana was seen bolting out of Ronny's apartment two minutes after she'd entered the other night?" Paula was saying.

"Good for her," Kitty said. "She can do so much better."

Lillian smirked at James, who looked cheered by this gossip.

James stood up. "Have this stool," he offered to Paula. "I was just heading out."

"No, no, Dr. Kentwood," Paula said. "We don't mind sharing, do we, Kit?"

"Of course not," Kitty said, and they cozied up.

James insisted on giving up his seat anyway, saying he had to get some sleep. "We'll talk tomorrow?" he said to Lillian.

She nodded. The ladies whistled as James departed.

"You're one lucky girl, Lillian," Paula said.

"He's one lucky guy," Kitty corrected.

"We're both lucky," Lillian said, turning away to make their drinks, not that her face would betray much emotion. She'd learned to cover up nearly everything by now. It was one of her greatest skills and also, perhaps, her fatal flaw.

Chapter 30

Rebecca

Frothy lake water leaping, nipping at the ferry boat. White-capped waves curling like frosting shavings. The Grand Hotel gleaming from the hillside, holding itself with more grace than the White House. How had Rebecca ever walked by without gaping?

People always said Mackinac Island was the one place that never changed, but Rebecca knew this wasn't true. Everything looked different when she arrived with Tom for their three-day stay for the Fourth of July. The colors more saturated, the contours more sloping.

Mostly it was the people who had changed, in the best of ways. Six months away had softened her mother's face, sweetened her sister's, and illuminated the sagacity of her grandmother's. The three women were lined up at the dock, along with Deirdre, Paula, and Kitty. All except Gigi were waving American flags, as if welcoming soldiers back from war.

Ordinarily Rebecca would feel guilty they'd all gone to this trouble for her, but today she accepted the reception happily. It was a much-needed change from the curtness of her Traverse City neighbors. (They'd held another barbecue yesterday, and still no invite. It was intentional, Rebecca was sure of it.)

"Hurry, honey," Rebecca called back to Tom, who was carrying their bags. "They're waiting for us."

With Sadie tugging on her leash, eager to explore the island for the very first time, Rebecca raced ahead and fell into her mother's open arms.

"It's you." Eloise took Rebecca's chin in her hands, as if verifying that her daughter wasn't a holographic trick. "And this one," she said, eyeing Sadie. "It's looking a bit more like a dog these days."

"High praise," Gigi said.

"She," Rebecca corrected. "Sadie is a *she*, not an it."

"I've had it with all the pronoun nonsense," Deirdre mumbled as Eloise apologized for her mistake.

Nonni draped a hug over Rebecca like one of her hand-crocheted afghans. It smelled like vinegary perfume, sandalwood candles, and security. "You're radiant," Nonni said. "Just radiant."

"I'm not." Rebecca was on edge that they might detect traces of pregnancy. She knew it was ridiculous to think she'd be showing so early, but she'd packed only loose-fitting sundresses just in case. One was billowing around her now.

"Say hi to the camera!" Mayor Welsh appeared atop Rowan, phone pointed at Rebecca. "This will go viral, I'm sure of it. People love wholesome family content. It's what we're known for, isn't it?"

Before Rebecca could ask her to abstain from posting her image online, the mayor was jingling Rowan's reins and parading away. "Make way, make way. The mayor's coming through!"

"That's how you know you're a big deal," Gigi said wryly. "When you have to announce your own presence and exactly two people move for you."

Nonni sniggered.

"I'm praying to the good Lord that someone runs against her in the next election," Deirdre said, now wielding her flag like a dart, as if contemplating a game of pin the tail on the mayor's horse. "I can't handle another term of this."

"How about you put your name in the hat?" Paula suggested. "You'd be very popular."

"We'd vote for you," Kitty added.

"Politicians dance with the devil," Deirdre said. "I could never be a part of that."

"Then why are you praying for a new mayor?" Gigi asked. "Isn't that basically just asking God to corrupt someone else?"

Deirdre garbled her rebuttal. Rebecca wasn't fazed by the bickering. She felt at home. Even the crowds of fudgies were less annoying. "How magical is it," Rebecca said. "To be able to call this place home, when millions of people flock here for their dream vacation."

"It's madness, not magic," Gigi said. "Wait until you get stampeded by the college idiots. You'll be on the next ferry out."

That was when Rebecca noticed the man standing behind Eloise. His hands were stashed in his pockets, his feet tapping the boardwalk as if he were practicing an Irish jig or in dire need of a restroom—it was difficult to tell. Rebecca recognized him from the photos. He looked younger in person.

It was Clyde MacDougal, Rebecca's new favorite author. She'd finished four of his novels so far. The sci-fi thriller set on Neptune's moon was her favorite. Not her usual type, but he developed the characters so well. It was a universal story of friendship at its core, exploring otherness in a very clever way. It was also his least popular book to date. People left scathing reviews about erroneous scientific details he used to describe the moon. But wasn't that the point of writing fiction? To be able to invent without the constraints of facts? Rebecca loved writing and always had, but she had no desire to publish herself, even articles for academic journals. Too many people weighing in, telling her what she was doing wrong. Her skin was too thin for it, sheer as tissue paper.

Eloise had brought up the topic of Clyde during one of the phone calls Rebecca hadn't managed to shirk off. (She had been avoiding conversations with her mother. Eloise would be able to hear the secret in her voice. It was that maternal instinct. What if Rebecca didn't have that when the baby came? What would she do?)

"I think it's best if you don't meet Clyde, don't you?" was what Eloise had said to Rebecca. "It would intrude on family time. You're only here such a short time as it is."

"It wouldn't be intruding," Rebecca had said. "It would be adding."

She'd had to call back three more times—perfecting her "everything is perfectly normal, I'm not growing a human in my belly" voice—to insist she *wanted* to meet Clyde, that she would be crushed not to, before Eloise finally agreed to it.

"I'll pencil him in for a quick hello at the ferry," Eloise had said. "Perhaps he can drop by the fireworks too. But the rest of the weekend I want my Rebecca all to myself. Tom too, of course," she'd added hastily.

Eloise was always forgetting about Tom. She had since the beginning, when she'd referred to him as Todd for the first two months of their relationship. It bothered Rebecca. He was her husband now, after all. But he did have a way of blending in, answering questions only when asked, always wearing neutrals. He was a vast contrast to Clyde, who was dressed in a banana-yellow linen suit.

"Rebecca," Eloise said now, "this is Mr. MacDougal." The glint in her eye confirmed to Rebecca what Gigi had said: Their mother was falling for him. She had, perhaps, already fallen.

"Call me Clyde," he said. "Your mam has been singing your praises. Your sister has been too," he said, though Rebecca knew he was taking creative liberties here. "It's simply divine to meet you in person."

Simply divine. It was one of those phrases Rebecca would like to incorporate into her daily life but knew she wouldn't be able to pull off.

Clyde was warm and charming, everything Rebecca hoped he would be. She wanted to give him a hug, but her body stiffened like wood.

Rebecca rarely missed her dad anymore. Not actively, at least. There would always be a passive missing, she supposed. The void of something having been emptied before she'd really known what it was like to be full. Rebecca hadn't clung to Gus the way Gigi had after he left. The way Gigi still did. Rebecca had let him go. She would not chase him and she would not miss him. Those were the ground rules. She stuck to them well.

But right now Rebecca missed her dad. She missed him with memories she'd never meant to hold on to. They'd stuck around anyway, the way he had not.

———— ≈ ————

"You're back!" Rebecca greeted her dad from the front porch one summer afternoon. He and Gigi were coming in from sailing. Rebecca was four years old. "And a half!" she always added.

"There's my Becca Bean." Gus lifted Rebecca, flipped her upside down. The sensation made her queasy, but she could tell her dad liked it so she pretended to as well.

"Come with us next time," Gigi said. "We saw a fish that was thirty feet long! Didn't we, Daddy?"

"It was pretty big," Gus said.

"I'm scared of the water," Rebecca said. "Like Mommy is."

"Your mom isn't scared of the water," Gus said. "We used to go cliff diving together. We used to do a lot of things together."

"Cliff diving?" Gigi's eyes were as big as cookies. "Take me, take me!" Eloise joined them on the porch. "Maybe when you're older."

"You can't keep them little forever, Ellie," Gus said. "They're going to grow up one of these days."

He set Rebecca back on the ground. The world took a moment to return to right side up.

"Not this day." Eloise greeted Gus with a quick kiss on the lips.

"Gross," Gigi said, pulling a face.

"Dinner's ready," Eloise said. "Rebecca helped me bake the bread."

"It was fun!" Rebecca twisted her hands in the pouch of her apron, which hung to the floor like a princess dress. "Like playing in the snow."

"Why do you like snow so much?" Gigi said. "It's so cold."

"Because it smells like magic. I love winter."

"Are you sure you're my daughter?" her dad asked.

The question concerned Rebecca. "Why wouldn't I be?"

"Because I can't stand winter. I'm a summer guy."

"Me too," Gigi said. "I'm a summer guy."

"Gal," Eloise corrected. "You're a summer gal."

"Oh," Rebecca said. She really did prefer winter, but summer was clearly the right answer. "I like them both the same."

Gus smiled. "Very diplomatic. Our future politician."

"What's a politician?" Rebecca asked, looking up at him, so tall, so smart.

"They make the rules," Gigi said. "When I'm mayor, I'm going to make it summer year-round. Just watch."

"You've got my vote," Gus said.

Rebecca tried to think of something to say that her dad would like just as much but couldn't. She wiggled into her booster seat at the kitchen table and nibbled on the fresh-out-of-the-oven bread she'd helped her mother bake. "It burned my tongue," she said.

"That's what you get for eating before we say grace," Gigi said, holding out her hands for their daily prayer. Rebecca took her sister's hand on one side, her mother's on the other. She prayed silently that God would make it so her dad loved Rebecca more than Gigi. Not every day, that wouldn't be fair, but just for a week or maybe a month. Time didn't make sense anyway. She just wanted a little more of her dad than what she had now, that was all.

"Thank you, Jesus, for everything," was what Rebecca said when it was her turn. "'Specially summer."

"Nice to meet you," Rebecca said to Clyde now. She simulated a smile. The bend of it, the brightness. Everything felt inverted.

Eloise interjected, perhaps sensing that Rebecca felt a little off. "Why don't you girls go get some fudge?" she said, discreetly slipping a twenty-dollar bill in Gigi's hand. "Tom, we'll show you to the house."

"The inn." Rebecca shot her mother a warning look. "We're staying at the inn."

"The inn," Eloise said, bearing the loss decently. "Yes, that's what I meant."

There was a tug on Rebecca's arm. "Come on, let's go to May's," Gigi said.

"My treat."

"Mom's treat, you mean." Rebecca couldn't remember Gigi ever offering to pay for anything, even birthday gifts for their mother. Gigi would find something online and then text the link to Rebecca so she could buy it. "Team effort," was Gigi's refrain.

"The family hike to the bluffs starts in twenty minutes," Eloise called after them as Rebecca and Gigi started off down Main Street, just the two of them.

"Doesn't get more American than this," Rebecca said, taking in the red, white, and blue. Flags fluttered in front of every storefront and a banjo player plucked "My Country 'Tis of Thee" as a crowd gathered around like it was Carnegie Hall.

"Except for being on a Native American reserve with actual Americans, you mean?" Gigi said. "Or going back to the 1800s on Mackinac when the Odawa tribe lived in peace, before the white people chucked them out and killed them off?"

"Can we please save the tirade for another time?" Rebecca asked. "I just got home."

Rebecca braced herself for the rant to worsen, but Gigi's expression changed.

"Ronny warning," Gigi said, nodding to an officer on a Clydesdale. "Avoid eye contact."

It was easy to see why Gigi had gone for Ronny. Trouble emanated from him like heat waves from scorching asphalt. "What happened with you two?" Rebecca asked.

"He was a dickhead," Gigi said.

"Care to elaborate?"

"No thanks. You tell Eloise everything."

"That's not true." Rebecca fought the impulse to put a hand to her stomach. "I won't say anything, I promise."

"Fine." Gigi seemed relieved to be able to carry on. "I went back to his apartment one night. He wanted me to stay over, but I wasn't feeling it so I left. It seems I shattered his fragile male ego and we haven't spoken since."

Rebecca didn't ask why Gigi had gone over to his place at all or what she'd expected to happen. She just turned and glared at Ronny. He shifted in his saddle when he saw Gigi.

"I told you to ignore him," Gigi said.

"I'm allowed to stare down dickheads," Rebecca said. "It comes with little sister territory."

"Guess it does," Gigi said, and she looked a little happier.

———— ≈ ————

"What do you think would happen if I started busking?" Gigi asked, sitting on the curb when Rebecca exited May's Candy Shop. She'd tired of the line and slipped Rebecca the twenty, then waited outside. "If I paid fifteen people to crowd around and film me as if I were a big deal, everyone else would join the crowd too. I'd have enough tips to buy a Malibu mansion. Artistry is pure emotional manipulation. That's all life is, really."

"Are you high?" Rebecca asked. Gigi had that faraway look in her eye.

"Sadly not," Gigi said. "Though I still think there's a market to open a weed dispensary on the island. But it's legal now, which lessens the appeal."

"And that would require you actually living here, you know."

"True." Gigi made a face and stood up. "It's your fault we're going to be late for the family hike. You were really soaking in your celebrity in there."

"I was not." But Rebecca had been, and she'd loved it.

Mrs. May had squealed so loudly when she'd seen Rebecca that a tourist had been ready to call 911. Principal Reid was there too, loading up on sweets for his family barbecue, which he was quick to invite Rebecca and the entire Jenkins-Wood clan to. And when old Mrs. Doud tottered in, she lassoed Rebecca with her cane for a hug.

"So what's your deal with Clyde?" Gigi asked. "You don't like him?"

"I think he's great," Rebecca said. "I just didn't think it would be so weird seeing Mom with someone else."

Gigi took a big bite of fudge. "He's loaded, at least. He treats Mom to everything. Me too. Did I send you a picture of the flowers he sent me? And he has an open tab for us at the Grand Hotel restaurant."

"Who's the feminist now?" Rebecca asked.

"I'm not the one dating him for his money."

Rebecca felt the attack personally. "That's not why Mom likes him."

"No, but it doesn't hurt, does it? There's got to be a bright side to having your mom act like a lovesick teenager."

They started up the hill toward the fort.

"I thought Dad might come back for the Fourth," Rebecca said.

"We were texting a little the other day," Gigi said. Rebecca could tell she was trying not to make her feel left out, but the exclusion smacked anyway. "His South America trip got extended. Said he'll be on the road another few weeks."

That was just like their dad, the slow chipping away at timelines, at promises. "Has Mom been talking to him?" Rebecca asked.

"Not that I'm aware of."

"Good." The last thing they needed was for Gus to insert himself in the middle of Eloise's new relationship.

"So you're Team Clyde?" Gigi asked.

"I'm Team Mom."

Ceremonial cannons fired from the fort. Children huddled around. Rebecca thought about the new traditions she and Tom would make with the baby. Then she remembered it wasn't safe to imagine those things yet. The eight-week ultrasound was scheduled for next month. Rebecca lived in fear of finding blood on her underwear. *One day at a time*, she told herself and the baby at least fifty times a day.

"Don't tell me you're on a diet," Gigi said, chocolate dribbling from her mouth. "You've barely touched your fudge."

"Just trying to limit my sugar." She'd never be able to forgive herself if her poor eating habits impacted the baby.

"I knew marriage would strip all the fun out of your life," Gigi said. "You don't drink anymore; you don't eat sugar. What's next?"

"I didn't drink even before meeting Tom." Being out of control, however mildly, had never appealed. "Your problem is that you associate toxicity with love. And because Tom and I have a healthy, stable relationship, you assume we must be bored to death."

"Well, are you?" Gigi asked. "Bored?"

Rebecca was hot and sweaty from the climb of the hill, her breath shallow. "Not at all."

"Glad to hear it."

Silence stretched. The cannons filled it.

"I'm being a jerk," Gigi said.

It wasn't an apology, but it was close. Rebecca wondered if this summer was changing her sister.

"It's fine," Rebecca said. "Just between us, I *have* been a little bored. Not with Tom, but with everything else. I have no job, no friends. I sit at home all day and research PhD programs and spy on the neighbors through the curtains. I'm Boo Radley."

"Who's Boo Radley?"

"*To Kill a Mockingbird*," Rebecca said. Gigi's face stayed blank. She'd only ever read summaries for school, never the whole books. "The point is, I don't know how to break into social circles. Not like you."

"It's because you were too popular growing up," Gigi said. "You never had to try to make friends like I did. But it's easy. I'll teach you. Take some edibles to the beach and share them. Instant popularity."

"Such wisdom," Rebecca said. "I'll give it a try."

They closed in on Harrisonville, passing the Grand Hotel stables. Like the rest of the hotel's amenities, they were elegant and pristine. Set back on the property, the barn was painted forest green with a red roof.

"Remember when you worked at the barn?" Rebecca said. "You reeked of horse even after you showered."

"That was probably the best job I've ever had," Gigi said wistfully, and Rebecca found it strange, though nice, to hear Gigi talking about something good that had happened on Mackinac.

"Maybe I should see if I can move into one of the stables," Gigi went on, watching a pair of Hackneys graze in the pasture. "Escape the confinement of Thistle Dew."

"Living with Mom isn't that bad."

"It's not good."

"No one's forcing you to stay," Rebecca said. "Go join Dad for one of his *once-in-a-lifetime* trips."

Rebecca couldn't stand that phrase. It was how Eloise described Gus's absenteeism in the years that followed the split, when he would come back to visit and then vanish again. *"He wanted to stay longer but he had a once-in-a-lifetime trip."* As if marriage wasn't supposed to be once-in-a-lifetime too. As if your family wasn't the main adventure. How many mountains and oceans and deserts did he really need to see? Didn't they all look the same after a while?

"Maybe I will," Gigi said.

She wouldn't, Rebecca knew. Gigi had already tried that once, going with their dad on one of his trips. It hadn't gone well. Two weeks later, Gigi had called Rebecca in a deep meltdown, asking her to wire her three hundred dollars. "Dad is a child," Gigi had screamed over the phone. "An absolute child."

Rebecca still hadn't gotten the full story. It was one of the things Gigi refused to talk about, along with the incident with the governor's son.

"Just don't run away again," Rebecca said now. "Please."

"Is it technically running away if I'm an adult?"

"Yes," Rebecca said. "It is. Just promise you'll tell me before you do anything, okay?"

"I'm not going anywhere," Gigi said glumly. "Not yet, at least."

"The offer for the spare bedroom at our place still stands." Rebecca fought thoughts of how one of the spares would hopefully be converted into a nursery soon.

"You're just saying that because you're lonely," Gigi said.

"Or because I love you."

"Maybe they're the same thing."

Rebecca broke off a piece of fudge and let herself taste it. "Maybe they're not."

Chapter 31

Eloise

It had been a bad idea to invite Clyde to join them for fireworks. Eloise wasn't capable of being a functional mother with him sitting so close.

The armrests of their folding chairs were brushing. It was all she could do not to reach over and take his hand.

Eloise could feel eyes on them. Word might get back to Gus. He kept up with some of the Mackinac guys, texting about college football, or so she heard. Part of her wanted him to know she was seeing someone. But this made her feel terrible, like she was using Clyde. She wasn't. She liked him more than she should. A depth between them was forming over tennis and afternoon tea at the Grand Hotel. Dinners at the Gate House and Woods Restaurant. Sunset strolls along the beach. Evening phone calls just because Clyde wanted to hear her voice before bed. She'd even let him give her a golf lesson and enjoyed it. (This was the most jarring. Her distaste for golf was a core tenet of her personality.)

Another part of her didn't want Gus to find out at all. She wanted Clyde to herself, stashing up private memories to keep her warm through the winter when Clyde would be back in Scotland and Eloise would be alone sipping tea that was never quite hot enough, lighting candles that were never quite bright enough.

"If they don't start these fireworks soon, I'm headed to bed," Deirdre said, furrowing her brows at the dark horizon. "It gets later every year."

"We're not in a rush," Fred said, reaching out for his wife. "It's a nice tradition."

Deirdre reluctantly sat on his lap and looked a bit mollified. "I suppose you're right."

"Yes, what nicer tradition is there than polluting the air with fire when the earth is already burning?" Georgiana chimed in. "So wholesome."

"You could boycott," Rebecca said.

"Wouldn't do any good," Georgiana said. "Mackinac doesn't have a functioning government, as we've established."

"Girls," Eloise chided, though she really meant *Georgiana*.

Fireworks always started around dusk. Two displays launched just off the island's southern coast. Eloise and the others were watching from Marquette Park.

Islanders were flocking over to see Rebecca. Eloise suspected this was partially a cover to snoop on her and Clyde. It had taken a while for the murmurings to start, but after dancing on the cruise, the chemistry had given them away. Or perhaps Deirdre had leaked something.

Clyde was snapping photos, commenting on how everything looked like a postcard. Kids scampering barefoot on the grass, sparklers and rocket popsicles in hand. Parents slurping homemade Hummers from red solo cups. Dogs yapping, overstimulated before the fireworks even started.

Clyde turned the camera on Eloise. She ducked her head. "Please don't. I don't like pictures."

"How about we get one together?" Clyde said.

Rebecca overheard and offered to take one for them. Clyde passed her the camera.

"Very cute," Rebecca said as she took the picture.

Rebecca had told Eloise that she liked Clyde—*adored* him—but Eloise wasn't convinced. What must her daughters think of her dating? She was supposed to be the role model, the responsible one, and here she was introducing her family to a man who would be gone before she knew it, as Eloise's mother so kindly reminded her on a regular basis.

"What do you think of our island?" Eloise asked Tom. She was trying to make more of an effort with him, for both Rebecca's sake and her own. Tom was a necessary ally if she ever wanted her younger daughter to move back to Mackinac.

"It's great," he said with a big smile. "Clyde's right, it feels like a postcard."

"I'm glad you like it," Eloise said. "Perhaps we could have Liam Townsend take you around to show you some properties while you're here. Where is Liam?" She looked at Alice, who was seated next to her, sipping a spritzer.

"How should I know?" Alice said, and Eloise was glad to hear her say it. She'd almost thought Georgiana might have been onto something with all the time they'd been spending together.

"Mom," Rebecca said, a warning in her voice. "We're very happy in Traverse City, I've told you. Tom has all his clients down there."

"People need help with their finances on Mackinac too," Eloise said. "Not such a large clientele perhaps, but very loyal."

"Let them be, Eloise," Alice murmured.

Eloise felt annoyed at her mother, also for how intently she seemed to be watching Eloise and Clyde, as if warding off any funny business. Eloise couldn't believe she was being chaperoned at this age. She felt an ounce or more of empathy for Gigi.

"Remember how your father used to be in charge of the fireworks for the island?" Alice said to Eloise. "So foolish, but I never could stop him. Always something of a pyro, David was."

Eloise recalled the crackle of summer bonfires in their backyard, the leaf piles burning in the autumn, the roaring fireplace heating the cabin in the winter. On an island surrounded by water, fire marked the calendar of Eloise's childhood.

"I like seeing you like this," Clyde said softly when the others were distracted again.

"Like what?" Eloise asked.

"In your mothering element with both your girls home. I'm getting to see a different side of you."

Eloise tensed. The more sides she showed, the more likely he was to dislike one of them, maybe all of them. Gus had preferred Eloise before they had kids, before her worrying side took over in motherhood. She hoped Clyde wouldn't have a similar reaction.

"I know I'm a little uptight today," Eloise said. "I just want Rebecca to enjoy herself."

"You're doing wonderfully." Clyde placed his hand on top of hers on the armrest.

Eloise felt the heat of it. She pulled away, clasped her palms together in her lap. "Not now," she murmured. "I'm sorry."

His forehead indented, but he nodded. "I understand."

The first firework squiggled up over the lighthouse. More followed, the noise building, rattling like popping corn. Soon the sky and Straits were lit up by the kernels of a thousand falling sparks.

Eloise felt her nerves steadying. It was dark. Everyone was watching the show. And even if they saw, what did she really have to be ashamed of?

She reached back out and took Clyde's hand.

Clyde's body shifted under her touch. It made her feel powerful, like a witch. She'd never believed in witchcraft before, but she believed in this. He interlaced his fingers with hers and gave a squeeze.

Once and then twice, Eloise squeezed back.

Chapter 32

Gigi

They look like they're getting serious," Rebecca whispered to Gigi, nodding toward Eloise and Clyde, who were holding hands while watching the fireworks. Rebecca seemed to be having a hard time with it.

Gigi felt strange about it too. She associated her dad with the Fourth of July. It was the holiday he most regularly came back for. And in the earlier years before he left, he used to put Gigi on his shoulders as they watched the fireworks. She always wanted to be as close to the flames as she could be, so she would reach out both hands, trying to touch them. One time she'd been stretching so hard that she'd toppled right off her dad's shoulders. He'd caught her by the ankle before she hit the ground.

"They're not serious," Gigi said to Rebecca now, trying to reassure both of them. "It's only been a few weeks."

"But she's already inviting him to family gatherings," Rebecca said.

"Just let them figure it out themselves. You don't always have to be the adult."

"Actually, I do, given I *am* an adult. As are you."

"Ah, thank you, I hadn't realized," Gigi said coolly. "I just mean be the kid for once. Let Eloise take care of herself."

Rebecca stiffened at that and curled back into Tom on the picnic blanket.

Gigi glanced once more at Eloise and Clyde. Eloise's head was tilted toward Clyde, as if she wanted to rest on his shoulder.

Gigi wondered what Gus would do if he saw. If he would get jealous enough to come visit and try to win Eloise back. Or if he would just wish her well and go busy himself with a new woman, someone who wasn't more attached to an island than she was to him.

The temptation to find out was too strong.

Gigi snapped a subtle selfie with Eloise and Clyde in the background. She sent it to her dad, along with a text she knew would get his attention:

> Happy 4th! We're watching fireworks with Mom and her new boyfriend. Hope all is well. 😊   😊   😊

Then she stashed her phone in her pocket and watched another firework detonate.

Chapter 33

Alice

A lice left the fireworks early.

She couldn't help but dwell on how excited David used to be after he finished the show. They would head over to the Mustang Lounge for a nightcap. He was a local hero. Everyone would clamor to talk with him, tell him how impressive the grand finale was and which shape of firework was their favorite.

Not Alice, though. She was nearly always livid with David after the fireworks, insisting it would be the last time she'd let him put himself in that kind of danger. But her memories had a nice way of editing themselves to make her sound calmer, more supportive.

She drove home slowly in the golf cart now, back to the cabin David had built for them all those years ago. Well, he had help from the rest of his crew, but David had overseen it, that much was true.

At the top of the hill, Alice passed Lillian and James. They dropped their voices when they saw her and gave her a cheery hello, but Alice wasn't fooled. They were arguing about something. It wasn't surprising. They had too much in common. Their similarities would chafe. The reason her relationship with David had worked was because David had been so steady, so predictable. Alice had been the volatile one, the wild child. Nothing close to Gigi's level, of course, but Alice drank, she smoked, and David was not the first man to take her to bed.

Liam had been, not that she was thinking about that given how cold he had been to her tonight. Brushing her off, sitting on the opposite side of the lawn. It was childish, really, how he was taking the rebuff.

The point was that polarity was needed in a relationship. It was why Alice had initially thought Gus and Eloise were such a good fit. He added the spunk, brought it out in Eloise, who had always been too serious of a child, too consumed by the need to be good. The trouble was that Gus's zest for life had gone too far, right out the door.

She took a detour by the cemetery. It was located amid the undulating hills of the island's interior, enclosed by forest. Milky moonlight splashed on the rows of tombstones. Getting out of her golf cart, Alice walked to the two graves side by side. David and their daughter Penelope. Alice always kept fresh flowers there. Lilies and hydrangeas. The petals cushioned the ground like church pew kneelers.

In the distance, Alice heard cheering and clapping. It must be the grand finale.

She found other people's happiness oppressive. Everyone was coupled up, even Eloise (Alice hoped she knew what she was doing). It made Alice all too aware of the hand she no longer had to hold, the body that wasn't next to her in bed.

Georgiana didn't have anyone, but that was different. She had her whole life ahead of her.

There was a melancholy to having your great love behind you. A relief you had found it, when so many never got that chance at all. And a sadness too, that everything from here on out was second-best.

Alice could go back to Liam and tell him she had reconsidered, that she, too, wanted to explore what they might be in this stage, this season. But it would only exacerbate her guilt.

Alice stooped low over the tombstone, head bent. "I'm sorry, David," she said. "I'm so sorry."

She listened hard for an answer. There was nothing, just tree frogs chirping like a metronome, keeping beat to the songs she and David would never dance to again.

Chapter 34

Gigi

Y ou want me to third wheel?" Gigi said the following week when Eloise and Clyde asked if she'd like to join them for dinner at the Grand Hotel. Rebecca and Tom were back in Traverse City.

"I'll be the third wheel," Clyde volunteered.

Gigi considered it. "Okay. So long as I don't need to dress up."

"It's the Grand Hotel," Eloise said. "Of course you'll dress up."

"Wear whatever you're most comfortable in," Clyde said.

This ended up being a striped cotton dress, basically a nightgown. Eloise hardly even insulted it, which was one indicator that she was fully consumed by Clyde these days.

As Gigi sat across from Eloise and Clyde, both dressed to the nines, she wished she'd put in a little more effort. For her sake, not theirs.

Gigi used to dream about being Queen of the Grand Hotel. It was one of the alter egos she conjured up after her dad left, when fantasy was her favorite refuge.

Being princess never appealed. Gigi wanted to be the ruler, the one with the power. Golden-tasseled carpets and chocolate muffins delivered to her turret suite. Beanie Babies and battery-powered toy cars overflowing from the playroom. A four-poster bed with purple curtains. A whole staff waiting on her and townspeople lining up on the streets in hopes of glimpsing even her hat (which would be out-landishly stylish).

A private helicopter featured in the vision too, so Gigi could collect her dad. She'd felt intuitively that a helicopter would be the surest way to bring him back home.

Once in her teens, Gigi started to reject those dreams. No point being tempted by something that could never come true. So she mocked that life instead. Ridiculed it. Especially once she'd started dating Xander.

After he'd bailed, Gigi stayed in Florida for another year. She quit the bicycle shop and got a job at the take-out window of a regional fast-food chain called Swift & Quick. Gigi knew from the start it was doomed (no decent place could have redundant words as its name). The highlight of her day was telling customers they were out of fries when they weren't.

Punching Alexander's name into Google was something Gigi caved to every now and then. He was married to a woman named Marigold. One of those debutante types from Virginia. They had one child named Tabatha and lived in Bloomfield Hills, a wealthy Detroit suburb. Tabloids reported that Alexander was planning a state senate run. Sometimes Gigi hoped he was happy with his life choices. More often she hoped he was miserable.

Pining was not her style. The mush of it didn't suit her. But being here at the Grand, dining with Clyde and Eloise, tuxedo-clad servers bringing out delicacy after delicacy, Gigi felt a few drops of regret land on her shoulder.

"Those mushrooms giving you the boke?" Clyde said, watching Gigi as she picked at her plate.

They were sitting at a table for four, near the ballroom. The double doors were closed, music emanating out. The light from the chandeliers was low but not limp.

"Georgiana's palate has always been particular," Eloise said. She was seated beside Clyde, across from Gigi.

"I'm all for mushrooms," Gigi said. "Just not this kind."

Clyde chortled.

"How about some lamb chops?" Eloise asked, passing a dish toward Gigi.

"I'm vegetarian," Gigi said pointedly. "Remember?"

Clyde proceeded to order an array of meatless options for the table. Most of it wasn't on the menu, but the server didn't bat an eye. Clyde was a natural at this life. Gigi wondered if he would do to Eloise what Xander had done to her. Or worse, would Eloise leave Gigi for him? As much as Gigi wanted Eloise to venture out and explore the world, she didn't like the prospect of her mother being whisked off to Scotland.

"How's the novel coming along, Clyde?" Gigi asked.

Clyde's face lit up. "Very much still in the ideation phase. Collecting stories, absorbing all the sensory details." He steered a cheeky grin toward Eloise. "Then when I'm back home in Edinburgh this fall, I'll start stitching it all together. Good books take years to fashion. I've stopped giving in to my publisher's pressure to churn one out every eighteen months. Nothing kills creativity quite like the conveyor belt of capitalism."

Gigi liked that phrase, committed it to memory. It made her feel better about not having achieved much by conventional standards.

"A book every year or two doesn't sound too bad," Eloise said. "You could make it a whole series set on Mackinac. More excuses to visit." She said it lightly, but Gigi could feel the undertones. "Or stay longer on this trip."

"You know I wish I could, bonny Lou," Clyde said.

Gigi took a sip of her whiskey. Gus always called Eloise "Ellie." It felt premature for Clyde to have his own nickname for her.

Clyde talked about how he had to be back in Scotland for press events in September, explaining he'd coauthored a book that would be published this fall. A time-travel novel set over the span of three thousand years.

"But remember, what's fer ye will not go past ye," Clyde said to Eloise.

The color rose in Eloise's cheeks. "What's meant to be will be," she said.

Gigi couldn't reconcile this girlish, Zen version of her mother with the one who lost her temper when Gigi loaded the silverware the wrong way in the dishwasher.

A slice of apple pie appeared, still warm. Gigi dove into it. On the third bite, her throat started to scratch. "Shit," she said. "Pistachio."

She was allergic. When she'd had to go to the ER a few years ago, the doctor said next time would be worse. Potentially life-threatening.

Gigi turned to Eloise. She looked like her mother again, face pinched with worry, eyes scorched with fear.

———— ≈ ————

"You're lucky your mom got you over here so quickly," James told Gigi at the medical clinic. Gigi's reaction had subsided after James administered an epinephrine injection. He was checking her pulse now. It was still elevated. "You should carry your EpiPen with you everywhere."

Gigi hopped down from the treatment table. "It all worked out."

"The man just saved your life, Georgiana," Eloise hissed while James was inputting data into a computer. "Can't you give him a proper thank-you?"

Gigi did want to thank him. But she'd sooner take another bite of that pie than do it with Eloise standing right next to her.

"I was never in any actual danger," Gigi downplayed. "If anyone deserves credit, it's you. You drove like a maniac. Made Ronny's driving look tame."

Eloise had located the Grand Hotel's nearest golf cart and put the pedal to the metal. "I don't condone speeding," Eloise said. "It was an extenuating circumstance."

Gigi reached for Eloise's hand, then released it just as quickly.

Out in the waiting room, they rejoined Clyde, who'd ridden along in the back of the cart. He'd called the clinic's emergency line, then filled the tense journey with a story about how one of the characters in his third novel—a failing comedian named Felix—had been bested by his peanut allergy. "He would've been fine medically speaking, but I had to kill him off for the pace of the plot," Clyde had said, as if this were reassuring.

"The Grand Hotel should put you up for the summer for what they put you through," Clyde told Gigi now.

"Good idea," Gigi said. "I should threaten to sue."

"A very mature takeaway from tonight," Eloise said. They headed out, James locking up behind them.

Gigi dawdled at the door. Eloise and Clyde went ahead to the golf cart. "Thank you," Gigi said to James, keeping her eyes on her chipped fingernails. "For getting here so fast."

"I live next door." He nodded over to Deirdre and Fred's guesthouse. It was a squished-looking Tudor-style hut, only the size of a two-stall garage.

"That place makes my New York apartment look spacious," Gigi said. "Though I did share it with four roommates. Five if you include the rat that lived under the sink."

"Sounds cozy," James said. "It works for me. I like being close to the clinic. And it's only short term."

"Right." Gigi's throat was still itchy, though the hives had subsided. "Mackinac is just your charity case for the season."

"That's not what I meant," James said. "And aren't you only here for the summer too?"

"That's right," Gigi said, feeling a little frustration and fear as she said it, like she should've already figured out her game plan for what she was going to do next. "But I don't pretend to have a noble profession," she went on. "My presence detracts from the island, everyone agrees. So my charitable act is actually leaving."

"You don't detract." James checked that the door was locked, as if anyone needed a dead bolt around here. "But by that logic, are you saying my presence adds to the island?"

"You're twisting my words. I was just glad someone was on call tonight. It didn't have to be you. But," Gigi went on, feeling the urge to drop him a compliment, a lone raspberry buried among the pricker bushes, "if I had to pick between you and Dr. Moore as far as whose night I'd want to ruin with a medical emergency, it would be yours."

"I'm honored," James said, eye contact lingering. "And you didn't ruin my night. I like helping my patients; it's my passion."

"Hopefully you have a little more passion in your life than *that*," Gigi said without thinking.

A pause stretched, charged with something—chemistry or concern, one of the two. Something about the way James took half a step back told her he felt something too. Or maybe that was just her ego wanting it to be true.

"Just for future reference," James said, "if you were trying to get my attention, there are easier ways."

Gigi realized she was smiling. She didn't try to stop. "Yeah," she said. "That's exactly what I was trying to do."

Then she dashed over to join Eloise and Clyde in the back of the golf cart.

───────── ≋ ─────────

"We'll have to have a do-over dinner with Clyde soon," Eloise said when they got back to Thistle Dew. "So you can get to know him better."

"That's okay," Gigi said, cocooning under blankets on the couch. "I think I have a pretty good sense of him already."

"You don't like him?" Eloise said, face falling. She brought Gigi a Diet Coke from the fridge and cracked one for herself too.

"I do like him," Gigi said. "He'll just have to pass more of my tests first."

Eloise looked touched by this. "I know it must be strange seeing me with someone other than your father."

"Why would it be strange?" Gigi said, trying harder than usual not to make this about herself. The allergy scare had shaken her up, though she was reluctant to admit it, and she wanted to try a little harder to be nice to her mom. "You've been divorced twenty years."

Eloise fiddled with the blankets. "I was worried about you tonight," she said, sitting adjacent to Gigi on the couch. "I know I don't tell you enough, but—"

"Don't, Mother," Gigi cut in. "No need for us to get all sappy just because I nearly died. Let's go back to our normal state."

"Where we judge each other's dating behaviors?"

Gigi grinned. "And you make annoying comments about how great James is and I say he's really nothing special."

"He *is* a pretty amazing doctor," Eloise said. "Pours so much of himself into his job."

"He needs better boundaries. Classic workaholic habits."

"He has plenty of time for Lillian, it seems."

"Good," Gigi said. "They deserve each other."

"You deserve someone too," Eloise said. "Someone special."

"I'm aware of that. But for now I guess I'm stuck with you." Gigi wagged her tongue affectionately.

"Such a sense of humor you have."

"I'm glad you appreciate it."

Gigi turned on a show that neither of them liked but both of them didn't hate. It was the kind of compromise that had once felt too big and now seemed just small enough, like it could fit in the space between their shoulders as they watched from different couch cushions, feet tucked under the same blanket.

Chapter 35

Lillian

L illian was sleeping like a log these days.

Maybe it was the strenuous days on her feet at the Pink Pony or the serenity of the island at night, or just the calm that came from no longer planning a wedding she didn't want to go through with.

Though still captive to many fears, Lillian had at least freed herself from marrying someone with whom the happiest she could ever hope to be was *not too bad*. The most passionate thought she'd ever had about Alex was, *What a good guy. I hope nothing bad ever happens to him.*

Lillian had been the something bad to happen, though she told herself it was good she'd walked out now rather than years down the line with kids and a mortgage to sort out.

She'd been a perpetual insomniac with Alex, working late into the night, rising for early-morning workout classes before returning to the safe bunker of her office. Productivity was her coping mechanism, her distraction from that screaming voice inside. And when she did have a free night to ruminate on the fact that something big and pivotal was missing in her relationship, she tossed and turned.

Alex had suggested they get separate bedrooms so her restlessness didn't keep him up too.

"Is that healthy for us?" Lillian asked.

Alex shrugged. "Better than the alternative."

And that was more or less how Lillian had thought about it too.

Better to be with Alex, married and sleeping in separate rooms, than risk the life that came with following her heart.

Follow your heart was so trite anyway, so removed from reality. The issue was Lillian did believe in love, something titanic and technicolor and far too original to ever be flattened into an aphorism. It was this romantic streak that ruined her and saved her, ruined and saved. A cycle she couldn't break even with all the breaking.

Because here she was, trapped again with James, a new cage of her own making.

For their own reasons, they were both scared to end the charade. So they bickered about how they shouldn't be bickering because they weren't even together.

Even with all this, Lillian had been plunking into a sleep too deep for dreams. When she awoke in the mornings, she felt jet-lagged, her head foggy like after she'd smoked marijuana. She hated being high, the way her judgment felt so slippery, like it might glide away and never come back. She needed the tracks, needed the treads.

———— ≈ ————

"Take the day off," Trina said when Lillian came down to breakfast a week or so after the Fourth of July frenzy. "Go to the Lakeside Spa and book a massage."

"You don't like massages."

"I was raised to think they were a waste of money," Trina said. "But you have money, Lillian. What you don't have is peace. You're carrying so much tension in your shoulders."

Lillian figured she must look very bad for her workaholic mother to be letting her off the hook. "I don't mind. I like keeping busy."

"Is there anything you need to tell me?" Trina's dark eyes circled Lillian's.

Lillian's pulse quickened. Had someone overheard her conversation with James and told Trina? Maybe this wasn't the worst thing. It would be better than having to break the news cold.

"You're not pregnant, are you?" Trina said.

Lillian registered the question and realized her secret was still safe. "No," she said. "I'm not that."

"Good. Then rest today and back to work tomorrow."

Lillian accepted the day off.

She knew how she was going to spend it. A massage wasn't going to fix things. A talk with Gigi might. It was only fair to James.

Lillian put on a fitted tennis dress and a visor. Carrying her racket and a water bottle, she headed over to Thistle Dew. Lillian knew this half-mile walk well. She'd made it many times in elementary school when she and Gigi were "best friends forever," with beaded bracelets to prove it.

Lillian rang the bell twice before the door opened. Gigi was standing there in an oversized T-shirt and boxers. Her hair resembled a haystack. She had clearly just woken.

"What's going on?" Gigi asked.

Lillian tried not to make her voice too bright. "I came to see if you wanted to play tennis."

"I don't play tennis."

"We could just rally. Very casual."

Gigi was squinting, whether from sleep or animosity, Lillian wasn't sure. "Why don't you play with James?"

"He's working. And there's something I wanted to talk to you about."

"What?" Gigi asked.

"I'll tell you when we play."

"You're being cryptic."

"I know."

Gigi contemplated, then gave her answer. "I'll hit with you, but don't try to give me any tips."

"That works."

The tennis courts at the high school were full of pickleballers. Gigi's grandmother was there, trying to recruit them.

"Let's play at the Grand Hotel instead," Gigi told Lillian. "I'll text Clyde to get us a court."

Lillian noted how comfortably Gigi said this. She'd thought Gigi might disapprove of Clyde, given how she had always idolized her dad. Perhaps that dynamic had changed. Lillian knew that Gus still came to Mackinac now and then, still strung Eloise along. As far as Lillian was concerned, Gigi and Eloise were both too good for him.

Clyde met them outside the hotel's tennis facilities. He had water bottles and towels for them and told Gigi to put lunch on his tab afterward, encouraging them both to order whatever they wanted.

The courts were gorgeous, newly resurfaced with the paint still vivid and crisp. Lillian fed Gigi some easy balls. Gigi whacked them hard. She was athletic but inconsistent. Her grip on the racket was terrible. One little tip and she could be so much better. Lillian refrained from saying anything.

"It's too hot out here," Gigi said after a while, but before Lillian had managed to broach the topic of conversation. "Let's go to the pool."

The pool and hot tub were tucked away in the lushness of the grounds. Hotel guests were tanning, reading, and ordering poolside sliders.

Gigi plopped onto a chaise lounge and made herself comfortable, ordering a mimosa and a very posh portobello burger, happily telling the waiter to put it on Clyde's tab. She looked like she was used to this life. It made Lillian wonder about the adventures she'd had since high school, the identities she'd strapped on and then taken off again.

Clyde was sitting nearby, scribbling in his journal while spooning peanut butter straight from the jar. He was sprawled out, wearing only a Speedo.

"Is that really necessary?" Gigi asked Clyde, cringing at the Speedo. "We could get you proper swim trunks from the hotel gift shop."

"But why ruin the view for the hotel guests?" Clyde said with that infectious grin. "Speedos are quite liberating. Americans waste too much time being self-conscious, I must say."

Lillian agreed with him. She could tell Gigi, too, admired his confidence.

"I'm thinking of moving to Europe," Gigi said. It sounded very vague, like she was testing Clyde to see what he might say.

"That could be wonderful," Clyde said. Gigi seemed to like how he took her seriously. "Who would you want to be over there?"

Lillian thought that was a good question—who a person wanted to be, not what they wanted to do.

"Someone who can scam the system and sit at a pool all day and make enough money to live in a fancy hotel," Gigi said, slurping her mimosa.

"You certainly have the creativity for it," Clyde said. "The resourcefulness too."

"Don't forget the charm," Lillian added, and she loved the way it made Gigi smile. It made her feel like they were in this together, both trying to figure out how to shape their lives after this summer.

She thought of the long letters Gigi used to write her and how packed with imagery they were. Lillian still had a few of them in her memory box under her bed.

"Why not write a book of your own?" Lillian suggested.

"I would get bored after five pages," Gigi said. "I can't stick with any one thing too long."

"Every weakness is also a strength," Clyde said. "If you work better in short bursts, perhaps a short story or poetry collection would suit you."

"You could write little vignettes about all the places you've lived over the years," Lillian suggested. "Maybe make it a satire," she added, knowing Gigi's style.

Gigi seemed to be thinking about it. "I'd rather have someone else write a book about me than write one about myself," she decided.

Clyde chuckled. "Fair enough. On that note, I know I promised not to feature your mam in my book," he said. "But the heroine I keep seeing has her same regal posture and silk chiffon laugh. I do hope Eloise isn't upset."

"She shouldn't be offended about being your muse," Gigi said. "Comes with the territory of dating an artist."

Lillian thought back to the art she had once created for Gigi. The art she had never shared with her or anyone else. Music had always been Lillian's first love. Not the strict sheet music for band recitals. The free-flowing lyrics that oozed out of her in the middle of the night. She didn't write songs anymore, but she had once. When she was a teenager, many of them were inspired by Gigi. She'd told herself back then that it was natural to write about your best friend turned nemesis. Only looking back did she see how searingly sapphic it all was.

They changed into their bathing suits. Gigi wore hers so well. The shape of a mannequin, the gait of a woman who would blow such a figurine to smithereens.

Lillian became aware of how she'd put on a few pounds. She'd gotten out of her workout routine this summer and eaten too many of the Pink Pony's chili cheese fries.

"So," Gigi said as they dipped into the pool, bathwater warm. "What did you want to talk about?"

"It's about James," Lillian said.

"I already gave you my blessing."

"It's not that." Lillian moved closer, her voice drowned by the trickle of the pool's waterfall. "We're not together," she went on. "I don't actually like him like that."

"What do you mean?" Gigi said. "He's exactly your type."

A laugh husked out of Lillian. "No," she said. "He's really not. We've been pretending to be a couple, but we're just friends."

Gigi's eyes flashed. "Why would you do that? Just to spite me?"

Lillian hated that this was Gigi's first thought. "No, he's been helping me out so my parents don't exile me." Silence radiated out. "So the whole island doesn't exile me."

Chapter 36

Gigi

Gigi's interest was piqued.

There had always been something a little too waxy about Lillian and James's relationship. Here was the evidence that Gigi hadn't been bitter. She'd been correct.

"Why would the island exile you?" Gigi asked Lillian in the pool.

"My ex-fiancé didn't call off the wedding," Lillian said. "I did."

"Okay?" Gigi was trying to connect the dots. "That's still not some scarlet-letter secret that will turn you into a social pariah. People call off weddings all the time."

"I wasn't in love with him," Lillian went on. "I loved him, yes, but I wasn't *in* love. Not the real thing. I've never actually been in love with a man."

Lillian was evidently very torn up about this. Gigi felt the urge to be kind. It was suddenly much easier to be friendly knowing she wasn't with James. "Honestly, I'm not sure I ever have either," Gigi said.

"Never?" Lillian seemed surprised.

"Not really," Gigi said. "I get swept up in the hormones and honeymoon stage and then go running when it gets tough. Blame it on daddy issues." She laughed, though it didn't taste funny on her tongue. It tasted metallic.

"But you're attracted to men," Lillian said. "Even if they're sometimes the wrong ones."

"They're always the wrong ones," Gigi said, thinking of Ronny and feeling a splash of self-respect for how she'd walked out on him. "What's that got to do with anything?"

Lillian kept her eyes on the bottom of the pool. The tiles shone with refracted light. "It's just a difference," she said. "Between you and me."

The implication seeped into Gigi gently, with the waves their bodies had made.

She felt surprise first and guilt second. She replayed all those years she'd been a menace to Lillian. Their friendship-turned-rivalry looked different in this light. Was that why Lillian had been so obsessed with being the best at everything? Because there was another area where she felt inadequate? Not that this made her inadequate, of course, but she could see how Mackinac would have made her feel like that.

"So you're for the girls," Gigi said, hoping Lillian could feel how much a nonevent this was for her. "That's great. No need to go around putting up smoke screens."

Lillian seemed to breathe more deeply, but that might have just been because Gigi was watching her now. Seeing her now.

"But you're well-traveled and worldly," Lillian said, and Gigi soaked in the praise. "Not like the islanders. They'd drown me in the lagoon if they found out."

Gigi thought Lillian was being a bit dramatic. Though she'd had a lifetime's practice disappointing people, so maybe she was better inured. "Everyone loves you," Gigi said. "They'd be fine with it."

"Not my parents," Lillian said glumly.

Gigi empathized. Lillian's parents were quite conservative, first-generation immigrants who had always liked to remind Lillian how much they had sacrificed to give her a better life. And now they would likely see it as Lillian throwing that better life back in their faces.

Gigi felt newly grateful for her own mother. Though Eloise vocally disapproved of a lot about Gigi's lifestyle, she knew Eloise would always love her, always let her back in the front door (or the side door at least, since only special guests were permitted to enter from the front).

"You can talk to my mom if you want," Gigi offered. "She'd actually be pretty reasonable about it, I think."

Lillian thanked her for the offer. "You're lucky to have her," she said. "And by the way, this is why James hasn't been pursuing you more. I've had him trapped in this PR contract."

Gigi moved into the deep end to tread water. Lillian followed her gracefully.

"Don't blame yourself for that one. He's not interested in me."

"He is," Lillian said. "You just intimidate him."

"That's what my mom and Nonni used to say when boys weren't interested in me. I don't need pity."

"It's not pity; it's true. He cares about you, Gigi."

Gigi couldn't help but hope Lillian might be right. "Then he should be man enough to tell me himself. Not use you as his mediator."

"He thinks if people start seeing you two together, it'll make my life harder. Raise more questions."

"Even if you and James break up, no one's going to think you're into girls," Gigi said. "You and I could make out right now and people still wouldn't get it."

Lillian blinked. "Won't that make it harder, though? That no one has seen it coming?"

"Maybe," Gigi admitted.

"I'll be disowned." Lillian circled back to the start of the same argument she seemed to have had with herself hundreds of times.

"Being disowned by an entire island isn't really so bad," Gigi said. "Take it from me."

Lillian appeared comforted for a brief moment, then confused. She was watching someone over Gigi's shoulder. Gigi turned around to look. A man was walking toward them. Dark-haired and burly, in black leather pants, thick stubble shading most of his face. Gigi's body jolted underneath the water.

"That kind of looks like . . . ," Lillian said.

Gigi opened her mouth. A single word dropped out. "Dad."

———————— ≈ ————————

The wrinkles on his forehead had deepened. His face was stiff and sunburnt. A new scar marked his upper lip. But it was him, with that air of adventure, as if he had seen things that no one on this island could ever understand. Gigi approached cautiously, wary he might disappear like a mirage.

"Kiddo!" Gus said, opening his arms wide.

Gigi let him hug her. She hugged back. It felt like home. He smelled like sweat, bourbon, and worn leather.

"I like the new hair," Gus said. "Almost didn't recognize you."

"That's kind of the point," Gigi said and Gus laughed.

"You didn't tell me you were coming."

"I know how you like surprises," he said, dark eyes twinkling. "After I got that text of yours, I booked my trip right away. Is your mother around?" He scanned the grounds.

Gigi felt powerful that her one little text had spurred him into such action. It was far more than she'd expected. Yet she was hesitant, too, wondering if she'd meddled too close to the sun. "She's at work."

"I heard she's been spending some time at the Grand."

"Her boyfriend lives at the hotel," Gigi said, sticking with the word *boyfriend* that she'd used in her text. "He's from Scotland, very famous."

"That's exciting," Gus said, but he didn't look excited. "Mick Reeves says they're getting real serious," he went on.

Mick was a Harrisonville neighbor, famous for his ferrety mustache and ability to belch the University of Michigan fight song. "I didn't know you kept up with him," Gigi said.

"Just saw him down at the Yankee Rebel. He bought me a drink and we watched the end of the Tigers game."

So Gus had been on the island drinking and watching baseball for some time before he'd thought of going to find his daughter. It didn't surprise Gigi, but it still hurt. The scraping of something old made new once more.

She wondered again if she had made a mistake texting Gus that picture. Though if she was being honest with herself, this was probably what she'd secretly wanted. For Gus to get jealous and come back to the island and fight for Eloise, fight for their family. But it had seemed so unlikely, so impossible, until right now. And now that it actually might be happening, the whole thing seemed like a very bad idea.

Eloise was having a magnificent summer with Clyde, and now Gus was going to ruin it, which meant Gigi was going to ruin it.

"Let's get your mother and take her out to lunch," Gus said. "We'll go to the Chuckwagon. None of this fancy-person shit."

Gigi almost felt guilty for enjoying it here.

Clyde had noticed Gus's presence. He was walking over, still wearing nothing but the Speedo.

"That's him, isn't it?" Gus said. "What's he doing wearing a thong?"

Though Gigi had just critiqued Clyde's Speedo herself, she now felt the urge to defend him. "Speedos are a cultural thing. They're the norm in Europe."

"This isn't Europe," Gus said. "It's America."

Clyde came to a stop in front of them.

"This is my dad," Gigi said to Clyde. She wanted to feel proud of it. She wanted to feel like she was rooting for her father more than a quirky man she'd only met a month ago. But she was having a hard time feeling anything other than guilt for the fire Gus seemed about to start.

"Gus Jenkins." He was not one for handshakes, but he shook Clyde's hand now with what looked to be a death grip. "Eloise's husband."

"Ex-husband," Gigi added quickly. She wanted Clyde to know

that there was nothing still between them. Even as part of her—the part that had sent Gus the text—still hoped that there was, that there might be.

"No." Gus's smile stretched wide. He looked a bit deranged, really. "We never got divorced."

Gigi stood there waiting for the punch line. It never came.

Chapter 37

Eloise

E loise had intended to finalize the divorce, she really had. Maybe not the first year after he left, nor the second, but in the third year she put her foot down. She retained Laurel Summers as her attorney. They drew up the papers and had them delivered to the latest address Gus had given her. The papers bounced back. This happened several more times, the envelopes either returning unopened or disappearing into the void.

"I'll get around to it, Ellie, I will," Gus had said when Eloise confronted him over the phone. "It's just not my biggest priority right now."

"And what is your biggest priority?" Eloise had asked. It was not his wife, nor their daughters, nor the money he swore he would send but never did (he scraped by on odd jobs, so Eloise didn't feel it was fair to push for anything).

"Finding myself," Gus had said. "I need to know who I am before I can be there for anyone else."

This was where he lost Eloise. She did not believe in finding yourself because she didn't believe in losing yourself. "It's not fair to me, Gus," she'd told him, delivering the words she had practiced in front of the bathroom mirror. "You're keeping me from moving on."

"You want to move on?" He'd sounded so hurt by this, so crushed.

"I need to move on."

"I still believe in us, Ellie." There was a whimper in his voice. "I know you're still my forever. Signing the papers would be throwing all that away."

Eloise might have pointed out that moving out had thrown all that away. Instead, she told him they could revisit the subject in a few months. In that time, she'd decided she wasn't so ready to move on after all. So she'd let it drop, liking how it felt to still be linked to him, legally if not physically.

A few years later, it had been Gus requesting that Eloise sign the papers (he'd lost the original documents she'd sent, so he'd had new ones drawn up). Gus was engaged to a twenty-six-year-old surf instructor he'd met in Hawaii. Her name was Honour.

Eloise decided to make him wait. She wasn't going to stall forever, but she didn't see a need to hurry when he'd been dragging his feet so long. It was better for the girls, she told herself, if Gus took his time before bringing another woman into their lives. The idea that Georgiana and Rebecca might have Honour as a stepmother was enough to draw out every last speck of spite that had been balled up inside her.

The engagement crumbled after eight weeks, when Honour told Gus she wanted to explore polygamy and hoped he would be "evolved enough to support an open marriage."

"An open marriage!" Gus vented to Eloise over the phone. "What's even the point?"

"What's the point indeed?" Eloise said. *Not so honorable*, she'd thought happily.

"How about I come see you and the girls next week?" Gus said. "I need to get out of this place."

Eloise thought this might be it, his come-to-Jesus moment. Getting his midlife crisis out of his system, flinging into a failed engagement, then realizing what he had back home. But he only stayed ten days before the itch to leave returned, flaring up like eczema.

"Let's go to Florida," he'd said to Eloise one night when they were on the screened-in porch watching the sun slip down over the lake. "Live by the ocean. I'll run fishing excursions."

"I can't just pick up and move," Eloise had said. "The girls are in school. They have their activities, their friends. And my dad's health . . ."

"The girls will make new friends. Adaptability is good for kids. And we'll come back and visit your parents every summer. A child's job isn't to be their parents' caretaker."

Eloise thought that was exactly what a child's job was. "We're not moving," Eloise had said. Which meant Gus was moving without them.

"Someday my legs will lose their restlessness," he'd told her when he kissed her goodbye that time. "I'm just not there yet."

Neither of them brought up the legal documents again. The islanders assumed they were divorced and Eloise didn't correct them. Only Deirdre knew. She didn't want Rebecca and Georgiana to find out. They would think she was weak. And if Eloise's mother found out . . . well, Eloise would feel like even more of a disappointment.

Eloise had known she would have to pay for her sin at some point. She just hadn't expected it to be one month into a fresh relationship, her new beau showing up at her door and telling her he had just met her husband.

"I'm so sorry," Eloise told Clyde. Her head was cloudy. "I should have told you."

Clyde looked the most somber she had ever seen him. The blue of his irises had darkened three shades. "You should have."

"There's nothing still between us," Eloise said. "Really. He's just swinging by to see Georgiana."

"I might write fiction, but I'm not bad with facts," Clyde said. "You two aren't over."

Eloise hated how her very first reaction was hope. She swatted it away like a horsefly. "Does anyone ever really get over their first love?"

"Yes," Clyde said. "They do. Or at least they make space for some-one new."

"I have space for you, Clyde."

Clyde let his stare linger. "How long is he staying?"

"I'm not sure."

A beat passed, squeezing them both. "You know where to find me if something changes," he said. "But I'm not going to be your backup. I deserve more than that."

"So much more." Eloise felt like she was spinning. Not in a romantic way, but a ruinous way.

Tipping his fedora, Clyde walked down the drive, disappearing over the crest. Eloise drew two shallow breaths and went inside.

———— ≈ ————

"Does Rebecca know?" had been Gigi's first question this afternoon, after verifying it was true that Eloise and Gus were still legally married.

"No," Eloise had said, and Georgiana looked glad about that.

"I mean, it makes sense. Kind of explains a lot, actually."

"Explains what?"

"Why you've never moved on. Why you never changed your name back."

"I didn't go back to my maiden name because I like sharing a name with my daughters."

"Right," Georgiana had said. "Of course."

Now Georgiana cornered Eloise in the kitchen as they cleaned up from a dinner of pork chops and cheesy potatoes. Gus's favorite.

"Where is Dad sleeping?" Georgiana wanted to know.

"On the couch." Eloise told herself the lie was to protect her daughter from any false hopes of a reconciliation. "Won't you join us for a while?" she called after Georgiana. "We could watch a movie."

"I'm pretty tired," she said. "Unemployment is hard work."

Eloise knew Georgiana had been hoping Gus would visit all summer. Now he was here and she was sulking. She wanted Georgiana to enjoy the time with her father, though it was slightly gratifying that her daughter's moods applied to Gus too, not just Eloise.

"It really is," Gus chimed in from the couch where he was watching a game on TV. His plate was on his lap, his bourbon on the coffee table. Place mats and coasters didn't seem so important right now. "Most people just toil away at their little jobs, not picking their head up to think about the world," he went on. "But you and me, Gigi, we're big-picture people."

Eloise felt attacked. She worked hard to put food on the table. Not everyone had the luxury of thinking about the big picture. "It's easier to think on a full stomach," she said, hoping she didn't sound as conflicted as she felt.

Just yesterday she'd been envisioning a potential future with Clyde, and now here she was, reverting to her old ways with her ex. Gus seemed to think he'd won her back, just like that. Eloise's heart wasn't so clear.

Losing Clyde felt like a high price to pay for a momentary reunion with Gus. Because that's all this would be with Gus—momentary. Though that was all it would have been with Clyde too. At least she was a throughline in Gus's life.

But Gus just grinned, that smile of his splashing like the light of a trusty old lantern. "I've missed your cooking, Ellie. Campsite food tastes like bricks compared to this."

Eloise wasn't sure it was much of a compliment.

"There's plenty more," Eloise said and took Gus's plate to the kitchen for a refill.

Chapter 38

Rebecca

H e's back," was all the text from Gigi said.

Rebecca knew immediately. Their dad was the only "he" in their life who didn't require identification.

"He could've visited two weeks ago when we were there," Rebecca told Tom over dinner. An elaborate butter shrimp dish tonight—protein and fat for the baby, who should now be the size of a pea, per Rebecca's research. "But instead he deliberately waited until after we left."

"I doubt it was personal," Tom said, pushing the shrimp around his plate with his fork. "He doesn't seem to put much thought into things."

Rebecca prickled. "It was definitely personal."

Tom assumed the best in people, a great quality until it came to her dad. Tom didn't get it. His parents had been happily married his whole life. For his sake, Rebecca was glad he couldn't relate. But she wanted to feel like he was on her side.

"This is my dad's way of punishing me for not asking him to walk me down the aisle," Rebecca went on. "Well, we'll see if he makes more of an effort when the baby comes. He can't assume he has un-limited access to his grandchild."

Pregnancy was making Rebecca spiteful. Or maybe it was the cu-mulative effect of being an outsider in her new life. She was feeling more and more like Gigi. Surprisingly, she liked the zing of it, the way words launched off her tongue.

"We're not going to use our child as a bargaining chip," Tom said. "Having a good relationship with the grandparents will be important for his development."

"Or hers," Rebecca said. And she didn't need a lecture on the baby's emotional development. She was the one reading all the books and regurgitating them to Tom before bed. "I guess we don't have to decide everything right now." Though deciding things was what she'd been doing lately. Drawing up plans for the nursery, bookmarking baby clothing and strollers, screening potential babysitters to find one she could trust (none yet), investigating preschools, and even getting sucked into a few college prep articles. (She would like their child to be able to go to an Ivy League; it had never felt on the table for Rebecca. She wanted everything to be on the table.)

"How about we drive back up to the island to see your dad this weekend?" Tom suggested. "I could take a half day on Friday."

"No," Rebecca said, though it meant something that he offered. "He'll probably be gone by then anyway."

She wondered what time her dad would sneak into her mom's room tonight. Perhaps Gus would be warier under Gigi's watch than her own.

They sat in silence as they ate, silverware clanking. Music drifted over from next door.

"I think we should host a party," Tom said abruptly.

Rebecca looked up from her plate. Tom was not a party person. He didn't like attending them and despised hosting them—the way people treated your stuff, the inability to kick them out after two hours. It was a rant Rebecca had heard several times.

"Why?" she asked. "Did you get promoted?" Rebecca's excitement rose. They could get a head start on the baby's college fund.

"No, I just think it would be good for you, good for *us*. We can invite the neighbors."

"But no one will come." Rebecca felt her tear ducts activate. "I'm going to be such a lame mom," she said. "I don't *do* anything."

Tom patted her shoulder and told her she was going to be a great mom, the very best. "And that's why I think the party would be good," he said. "Give you something else to focus on other than the baby."

Rebecca had put looking into grad school programs on pause. Her heart wasn't in it. She liked the idea of learning but hated the idea of teaching, which would be the most likely employment on the other side. To put all that time, effort, and money into school when she just wanted to stay at home with the baby, at least for the first year or two, seemed silly. Though so did being "just" a mom. She could practically hear Gigi's judgment. Even Eloise had always advocated for women to have their own source of income. Rebecca felt weak for relying on a man to provide for her. Yet she felt strong with Tom, stronger than she ever had before. It was a paradox she couldn't quite grip.

"What would the theme be?" Rebecca asked. She was a firm believer that all parties must be themed. Nonni was the same way.

"Summer?" Tom suggested.

"That's not a theme. It has to be more creative."

"Ask Gigi. She'll have ideas."

"She'll say Woodstock or Burning Man."

Gigi had gone to several hippie festivals, living off the land, probably walking around naked and high. Rebecca squirmed just thinking about it.

"Burning Man isn't a bad idea," Tom said. "We could light a bonfire, have everyone bring a little something to throw in. A metaphorical catharsis."

Metaphorical catharsis was not a phrase she had expected to leave Tom's lips. She thought she'd married a financial advisor. She liked that she was still learning new parts of him. Though it scared her too, the idea of the unknown.

"People would think we're druggies," Rebecca said.

"Okay," Tom said, slipping back into his usual self. "It was just a suggestion."

"I appreciate it. We just need to consider our reputation. We've clearly gotten off on the wrong foot here."

"I don't think we've gotten off on the wrong foot. I think we've gotten off on no foot," Tom said. "No one knows anything about us."

"No one's tried to get to know us!" Rebecca was so done with the insularity of this place.

"*Don't you have a car?*" Rebecca imagined the neighbors would say if she knocked on their door asking to borrow eggs. "*The grocery store is only ten minutes away.*"

"Maybe we'll have to be the one to make the effort," Tom said.

She shelled her shrimp, chewing slowly. "I'll think about it."

Chapter 39

Deidre

It's unbelievable how Eloise has two men fighting for her," Deirdre told Fred one night from opposite sides of their bed. "It's like a soap opera. And I don't like soap operas," she clarified.

"You sure watch a lot of them," Fred said. He'd gotten in bed early, citing a cold. It was what happened when your whole career was caring for other people. You forgot about yourself. And your wife.

Deirdre was trying to read her beach romance novel but couldn't get past the first paragraph. It was the author's fault, not hers. And with all the events of the past week . . . well, Deirdre wasn't the only one on the island having trouble focusing. Paula and Kitty had seen Clyde down at Mission Point, skipping stones and looking "devastated."

"Clyde is the right choice, obviously," Deirdre told Fred now. "But Eloise just can't quit Gus."

It would be satisfying, after all this time, to see Gus Jenkins get his comeuppance.

"I can't believe they're still married," Fred said. "And that you knew this whole time."

"Friends are allowed to keep each other's confidences." Deirdre was already nostalgic for the time when she'd been the only one in on the secret. She knew her life's purpose should be more than a secret keeper, but she still felt her significance diminished.

"Well, maybe it'll work out this time," Fred said. "Gus seems more mature, more tired of the nomadic life."

"You said that last time," Deirdre pointed out. "It's the same old habits with him. He can't help himself jumping from one thing to the next." Mentally she considered herself one of those things he had jumped from, despite their never being together beyond the plotlines of a teenage journal.

"Don't pick a fight, Dee. It's been a long day." Fred coughed.

"Which is why you should retire," Deirdre said. "Eloise and Clyde go dancing four times a week."

This was a slight exaggeration, but they had gone multiple times, and at the Grand Hotel ballroom, no less.

"All we do is eat dinner at home and talk about the grandkids and watch separate shows on TV and go to bed," Deirdre carried on. She was being a bit harsh but couldn't stop.

Fred switched off the lamp nearest him. "We're getting old. That's what life is."

"It doesn't have to be."

"You're right." Fred's patience snapped. "Life could be more exciting. I could leave you and show up unannounced every couple years. We could have a dramatic battle over divorce papers. I could sleep with other women and use you as my backup. Is that what you're asking for?"

"No," Deirdre said, growing quiet. "That's not what I meant."

"What did you mean then?"

Deirdre wished she could scoot across the bed and lean her head on her husband's chest, fall asleep entwined like they used to. She wished she could apologize. She wished she could thank him for being here, for being hers. She wished she could tell him about the secret that had been beating on her heart, beating down her hopes, for thirty-six years now.

But there seemed to be an invisible barrier keeping her from crawling to his side of the bed.

"I just don't think it would kill you to put in more of an effort, that's all."

"Why is it always on the man to put in the effort?" Fred asked.

"Because," Deirdre said, burrowing her nose back in her book. "That's just how it is."

Chapter 40

Gigi

"How about we go sailing this afternoon?" Gus asked Gigi over beer and burgers at Thistle Dew. It was the third day since his return. He'd grilled out four times already. "Just the two of us while your mom is working."

Gigi agreed. She loved sailing but had never really learned how. Gus had been in the process of teaching her when he'd first left, and he'd never been back long enough for the lessons to continue with any regularity.

They took off from the harbor in Fred Moore's sailboat, a twenty-footer named *Forget-Me-Knot*, which he let Gus borrow whenever he was back. The sails fluttered like the kites Gigi and Gus used to fly together on the beach at British Landing.

"Everything okay with you?" Gus asked, tending to the ropes. "You've seemed kind of down. If it's this doctor guy I keep hearing about . . ."

"It's not James." Gigi hadn't seen him since Lillian had dropped the news about their ruse. Things were in his court as far as she was concerned. "You do see what you're doing, right? With Mom?"

A wave from a wake boat sloshed into them. They rocked, then righted. "What do you mean?" Gus said.

"You're not letting her get over you." Gigi picked at her nail beds.

When he spoke, he sounded curious. "Do you think she wants to get over me?"

"Of course she does," Gigi said, but the words felt rickety.

Gus nodded but didn't look convinced. "Then why did you send me that photo of her and that Irish buffoon?"

"Scottish," Gigi corrected, sidestepping the question. "Clyde is Scottish."

"I know your motive, Gigi. You're my daughter."

She thought she heard some pride in how he said it. Both of them had the same selfish streak.

"Do you want me to leave?" Gus went on. "Is that what you're asking?"

It was not what Gigi was asking. What she was asking was for him to stay, but not because of Eloise . . . because of Gigi.

"I just don't want her getting her hopes up again," Gigi said.

Gus checked the wind indicator, monitoring the direction and speed. "Don't you think I get my hopes up too? Don't you think every time I come back here, I wonder if maybe this will be the time it works?"

Gigi assumed Gus always knew he wouldn't stay when he came back to visit. He never brought more than a backpack. But could it be that his departures were as unplanned as his arrivals?

"So many times I've asked your mom to come away with me," Gus said. "And so many times I've been close to moving back here. I don't want to give up on us. We're meant to be together, your mom and me."

His face held the pain of a thousand goodbyes and a thousand and one hellos, or maybe that was just Gigi's own expression bouncing off his sunglasses.

"Then be together." Gigi hated how close she sounded to begging. "Just make it work. You're adults. Make it work."

Gigi liked Clyde, but he wasn't her dad. They wouldn't have the same family unit. Clyde would never know Eloise like Gus did. He'd never know Gigi like that either.

"I'm trying this time, kiddo," Gus said. "I'm really trying."

They made their way out to the open water, the island shifting into the background. With its limestone bluffs rising from the water, it was clear why the Native Americans named it Great Turtle. It really did look like a shell emerging from the water. Something living, something breathing.

"So what did you hear about the new doctor?" Gigi asked. She couldn't resist revisiting the topic, not when he'd dangled it like that.

Gus laughed. "That you and Lillian are in a head-to-head battle to make him your husband. So I'm guessing you don't actually like the guy, you're just trying to win?"

Gigi briefly considered letting him in on the latest development but decided against it. It wasn't fair to Lillian, and Gigi didn't trust that Gus would keep it confidential. "Something like that."

"Your mom mentioned you've spent some time with that new officer, Ronny. I like him. Seems like a fun guy."

Gigi cringed. "James is the better person," she said, thinking how she'd like to spend more time with him now that she knew the backstory with Lillian. "But there's no point. We're both just here for the summer."

What once would have been her ideal setup—something with an expiration date already set—now felt too hollow, too tinny.

"Probably better that way," Gus said. "Your twenties are for exploring."

"I'll be thirty next year," Gigi said.

Gus looked taken aback by that. "Thirties are for that too. Your whole life is. But sometime you might reach a point where you just want to hunker down with the person you love and stay put awhile."

It felt like the breeze had picked up. The island was far away now. It was just Gigi and Gus out here, unfenced.

"Are you at that point?" Gigi asked, trying to understand how her dad had changed. *If* he had changed.

"I'm closer than I've been in a long time."

Gigi wanted to ask a lot of follow-up questions. She didn't.

"So where's my adventurous daughter off to next?" Gus asked. "After summer wraps."

"Not sure yet," Gigi said. She didn't want him to know that she was starting to find his model of hopping from place to place very unfulfilling. She worried that would drive a wedge between them further. "Wherever the wind takes me."

"You're always welcome to tag along with your old man," Gus said, which was all the confirmation Gigi needed that he didn't intend to stay on Mackinac much longer. "Don't forget that."

Gigi hadn't forgotten. She'd taken him up on that offer once, six years ago, when she was leaving New York and in need of a place to go. She'd joined up with Gus for a ride along the Eastern Seaboard. It had been fun for the first week, then a complete trainwreck.

"That didn't exactly go so well last time," Gigi said. They had never really talked about it. She could see now how she'd inherited a lot of her avoidant traits from Gus.

"It was all right, wasn't it?" Gus said. "We had fun."

"The trip ended with me sleeping on a park bench," Gigi reminded him. "Because you were taking that girl back to your hotel room." Gigi said *girl* instead of *woman* because she'd been closer to Gigi's age than to her mother's.

"I said you could get your own room," Gus said.

"But you didn't offer to pay for it."

Gigi had called Rebecca asking for money so she could leave. Rebecca came through for her, though she asked too many questions, like always.

"Why're you bringing this up?" Gus asked, getting defensive. "We're having a perfectly nice day."

"It's not bad to bring up the past," Gigi said. "Sometimes you need to go backward to go forward."

Gus was looking at her like he didn't really know her. "Who brought the shrink on board?"

The fact that Gigi nearly took this as a compliment showed how far she had come since the days of wadding up her emotions and stashing them into a drawer like socks.

"I'm sorry you didn't have a great time on that trip," Gus went on. "But you were pretty difficult at that stage." He seemed to think this was a decent apology.

"Yeah," Gigi said, thinking back to that younger, flailing self with some embarrassment, but some compassion too. "I guess I was."

Awkwardness rubbed between Gigi and her dad. She wasn't sure he felt it. She wasn't sure he felt much at all.

Gus's eyes dropped to Gigi's rib cage. "Is that a new tattoo?"

Gigi traced the ink with her fingers. "If five years old is new."

"Love it," Gus said. "Any meaning to it or just a cool design?"

Dandelions symbolized defiance to Gigi. Misunderstood flowers demonized as weeds, boldly spreading their seeds, refusing to succumb to toxic pesticides.

"Just a cool design," she said.

"A tattoo is on my bucket list," Gus said. "Maybe we could get one together sometime. A father-daughter thing."

"I don't think Rebecca would want one," Gigi said.

"We could get one just the two of us," Gus said, in a way that implied he hadn't really thought Rebecca would be part of it.

The snub of her sister made Gigi feel bad rather than victorious, like it might have before. She wanted to bring up something deep, something that would anchor them. "Are you sad?" Gigi asked. "About Rebecca's wedding?"

"Not sad," Gus said. "Just bummed."

Gigi wasn't really sure what the difference was.

"You could try calling her more," Gigi said, thinking that would be nice for Rebecca, and for Gus too. "I know she loves you."

Gus stopped fiddling with the sailing equipment and sat down next to Gigi at the back of the boat. Gigi liked how it felt having him so close.

"How do you know that?" Gus asked.

"Because it's impossible for a daughter not to love her dad. No matter how hard we try sometimes." She smiled.

Gus wrinkled his nose like he'd breathed in pollen. "I just feel like I've messed up a lot."

Gigi hadn't seen this side of her dad in a very long time, if ever. It would be easy to pile on, call him out for all the ways he'd let them down in the past. But instead of wanting to punish him for his wrongs, she found herself wanting to make him feel all right.

"It's called being human," Gigi said. "And for the record, if I ever get married, I'll ask you to walk me down the aisle. But I probably won't. I don't really believe in the institution of marriage."

That wasn't really true, though. She just didn't believe she'd find someone she'd actually feel confident committing to. Someone she wasn't worried she'd outgrow, or who would outgrow her. The idea of promising to call someone on the phone felt daunting, let alone the idea of promising to be someone's partner for life.

"Same," Gus said, dropping an arm on Gigi's shoulder, leaving it there like it wasn't an accident. "And no guy would ever be good enough for you anyway."

Gigi was glad her bangs were hiding her eyes. They were bleary from the sting of the wind, nothing else. "Very true."

Gigi caught herself whistling as she pattered down the stairs later that week. It wasn't one of those annoyingly chipper whistles, but it was a whistle nonetheless. Not the kind of sound she typically made, particularly before 9:00 a.m. She'd taken to waking up earlier now that Gus was back. There was more to do: bike rides and cliff jumping, sailing and swimming. The routines of family life had returned with alarming ease.

Eloise making Gus his morning coffee, then taking it back into the bedroom (they had abandoned the pretense of the couch after Gigi had called them out on it). Bike rides around the island, stopping at Sunset Rock for a family selfie. Gus standing behind Eloise, his hands on her waist as she cooked. Movie nights on the couch rewatching the original *Batman* and *The Princess Bride*.

It wasn't like Gigi was suddenly thinking her parents were going to get back together or that Gus was really here for good. She just thought it seemed healthier than before. Like both her mom and dad had done some growing up. Maybe it helped that Gigi was better behaved too, slower to lash out. She liked to think she might be playing a positive role in the family dynamic. Without Rebecca here she was stepping up to the plate.

It was the most in sync Gigi had ever seen her parents. The chemistry between them wasn't new or giddy like it was with Clyde and Eloise, but something more tested, more textured.

I'm not predicting a reunion or anything, but I'm just saying it feels different this time, Gigi texted Rebecca last night.

I'll believe it when I see it, Rebecca had replied.

The house was empty this morning. Eloise and Gus were likely out for a morning walk. Gigi raided the homemade cinnamon rolls in the bread basket. Eloise had been whipping up all the special-occasion treats like they were everyday staples.

The side door creaked open. Eloise came in from the front porch, two mugs in hand. She was still wearing her nightgown. Gigi knew right away that something was wrong. There was a rawness about her. Her breathing was too loud.

"What happened?" Gigi asked. She set down the cinnamon roll.

Eloise didn't say anything. She didn't need to.

Gigi already knew. "He's gone, isn't he?" she said, the kind of hunch too good to be a guess.

Eloise nodded. She wasn't crying, wasn't shaking. An eerie calm hung about her like a rain cloud had been wrung dry and all that remained were wisps of fog.

"I hate him," Gigi said, body quaking. She hated herself more, the way she'd let herself be duped. She should have known by now that unreliability was the only thing she could rely on her dad for. "I hate him so much."

Eloise began loading the mugs in the dishwasher, spacing them carefully so they wouldn't clank against each other. "Blame me," she said. "I'm the one who told him to go."

Chapter 41

Eloise

Eloise had wanted to believe that Gus had changed. Of course she had.

Especially with how close Georgiana and Gus were getting again, out sailing and swimming every afternoon when Eloise returned from work. But the definition of insanity was doing the same thing over and over and expecting a different outcome. And this time, at least, Eloise refused to be insane.

Maybe it was Georgiana's bluntness getting to her, or the reference point of Clyde, or just the sirens of her own anxiety, but she'd pushed Gus for an answer last night. It was after they'd made love (quietly, so Georgiana wouldn't hear) but before they'd turned off the bedside lamp.

"What're your plans?" she'd asked, her head nestled into his shoulder. "For the future?"

"Thought I'd stay here longer."

"How much longer?" Maybe progress was like that, asking one hard question and then waiting for an answer, not rushing to fill the silence or give him an out. Outside, an owl hooted from the nearest birch.

"I haven't really thought that far ahead," Gus said. "Just taking it one day at a time."

Eloise felt herself clench. "I'd like to know your plans. By morning, I want an answer."

Gus massaged Eloise's neck. The touch wasn't as soothing as it usually was. Something had changed, and it wasn't her husband.

"Why so pushy?" he'd asked.

"I just think it's reasonable. To know where this is going."

"But that's not how you and me are. We never really *know*, do we?"

"That's the issue."

She'd slept beside him feeling lonely, more so than on the nights when it was just her in bed.

This morning she asked him again. "Have you decided?" she'd probed, sitting up on the pillows, arranging them around her for support. She was proud of herself for sticking with her resolve. In the past, mornings were when she relented.

"Decided what?" Gus said groggily.

"If you're moving back for good."

He stifled a yawn. "That's a big decision for this early in the morning."

"Or this late in life," Eloise said.

The answer came in how Gus stumbled around it.

"I think you should go," Eloise heard herself say. It was her own voice, but she had the sensation she had borrowed it from somewhere, loaned it at a high interest rate.

She got out of bed, put on her most modest nightgown. Something had cracked inside her. It had started cracking long ago but finally reached the threshold where the fissure became a full-blown fracture. All his old habits scrunching up and unfolding like an out-of-tune accordion. The way he could never give her a plan, never commit to anything other than his own caprice.

Everything she'd been holding in for years, she released. Not in venom, not in malice. Just in truth.

"I don't want to live like this any longer, Gus," she said. "I can't be your placeholder."

He told her that she wasn't his placeholder. That he loved her so much. That he'd never loved a woman half as much as he loved her.

"Then let me go," Eloise said. "Please."

"You really mean it?"

"I do," she said, the vow taking on a new meaning.

He hardened then, moping around the room, packing up his back-pack. "We both know you're going to call me when you're lonely."

Eloise had done this more times than she wanted to admit. She knew she wouldn't anymore. That was what a breaking point was. Leveraging momentum from a thousand weaker moments to create one big push of strength. Enough to get you through, enough to make you new.

She pulled the divorce papers from the desk drawer where they'd been collecting dust. Wordlessly, she handed them to Gus with a pen. He didn't read them over; he'd known what they said for years. He just signed them, scrawling his chicken-scratch signature.

"Happy now?"

Eloise put the papers back in the envelope. "Thank you."

"Tell Gigi to call me," Gus said, slinging his backpack over his shoulder.

"Don't you want to say goodbye yourself?"

Gus did not, which riled Eloise more than all the rest of it.

"She deserves an explanation," Eloise said. "You owe her that."

"*You* owe her that. Gigi understands me better than you ever have. She'll get it."

He shoved bare feet into his shoes. Eloise thought about Clyde and how he always wore two pairs of socks. There was a metaphor there for how he tended to overdo things rather than underdo them. It was a good way to live, a great way to love. Tomorrow she would go and see him. Tomorrow she would tell him how she felt.

Perhaps he would give her another chance. Perhaps not.

Before Gus left, Eloise brewed a pot of coffee and poured them each a mug and they sat on the front porch, the morning air stagnant. She sipped hers slowly; Gus chugged his.

Gus stood up and gave her a scruffy kiss on the cheek. She breathed him in one last time before he took off down the drive and disappeared beyond the rise of the hill.

Eloise sat on the porch for a while, counting breaths, counting clouds, counting whitecaps.

We're okay, Mackinac seemed to be saying to her. *We're okay.*

Movements came from inside the house. It was Georgiana, awake with a bounce in her step. Eloise felt a new level of loss. It was one thing to come to terms with Gus breaking her own heart. It was another when he mangled her daughters' hearts too.

Chapter 42

Alice

A lice hadn't meant to snoop.

It was just that when she let herself into Thistle Dew to solicit help with the crossword, she heard voices out back on the screened porch. And what was she supposed to do? Walk away and pretend she hadn't heard?

"The marriage thing took me aback, I'll admit," Clyde was saying. "I may not have the most scrupulous conscience, but that's one line I try not to cross."

Alice figured she should dart out of the house but didn't want to draw more attention to herself. She stayed quiet in the kitchen, tucking herself behind the refrigerator.

It had been quite the couple of weeks. Alice had found herself hoping this might be the time Gus stayed on the island for good. He had made mistakes, and big ones, but people could change. Forgiveness was important.

Not only did Eloise still love Gus, but they were still married! What a shock that had been. Though, selfishly, Alice was rather happy about it. It made her feel better about keeping a secret of her own.

And it gave her more reason to think Eloise and Gus might get back together once and for all. It was better for Eloise to be with her husband and the father of their children than with someone new and unpredictable. Gus was unpredictable too, but his unpredictability was predictable, which held its own sort of comfort.

But Eloise had been the one to tell Gus to leave this time. Alice felt disoriented by it all, and Clyde's thick accent wasn't helping.

"It's my fault," Eloise said to Clyde. "But the divorce is in motion. Gus signed the papers before he went. I can finally move on. *We* can finally move on. If you'll have me back."

Alice had heard that Europeans weren't emotional. But Clyde was positively gooey, all that sniffing and gulping. It was excessive.

"I'm just not sure I can get so invested again knowing I leave in a few short weeks," Clyde said. "I know I was the one saying let's stay in the moment, but the last couple of weeks showed me how much I care about you. I love you, bonny Lou."

Alice flinched, both at Clyde's confession and at the way the ice gave a rumble in the freezer. She felt exposed and took another step back into the shadows.

"I care for you, Clyde," Eloise said, and Alice hoped this was a lead-in to the letdown. "There's just a lot going on. I can't say anything more definitive right now."

"I understand," Clyde said. "Though may I ask, is that because you're not sure how you feel, or because you don't want to sound crazy?"

"Because I don't want to sound crazy," Eloise said. "Just yesterday I was with Gus and now here I am with you. I don't want people to think I'm having a midlife crisis."

"Who cares what it looks like?" Clyde said. "What does it feel like?"

It took a moment for Eloise to reply. "Love," she finally said. "It feels like love."

Alice couldn't believe what she was hearing. "I suppose we could try long-distance," Eloise went on. "Maybe even split our time, go back and forth."

"You'd come to Scotland?"

There was a pause as Eloise seemed to be considering it. Alice was sure she would decline. Eloise thought Traverse City was too far away, let alone Scotland.

"Sure I would," Eloise said. "If I had a local tour guide."

Alice blinked away her shock.

"It would be an honor," Clyde said.

Silence followed. Alice suspected they were kissing. She peeked out but couldn't see anything and didn't want to risk moving closer.

"So what do I call you?" Eloise asked. "My boyfriend? I don't really like that word. Too adolescent."

"I'd rather you called me your fiancé," Clyde said. "At my age, I'm not looking to be in an intercontinental relationship unless it's with my future wife."

Alice leaned her head against the refrigerator wall. What was he doing putting such foolish ideas in Eloise's head? At least she could count on Eloise to bring him to his senses.

"You have a ring," Eloise was saying. "Clyde, you have a ring!"

"That I do," he said. "Figured my chances were low, but when I heard Gus had left, I took the next ferry to the mainland and went shopping over there to avoid gossip. I'm all in, Eloise. For the rest of our lives, I'm yours if you'll take me."

Alice waited for Eloise to say no. Surely she was going to say no.

"I'll take you," Eloise said. "On Mackinac and in Scotland, I'll take you."

"What about on Neptune's moon?" Clyde asked.

"Even there."

Alice hoped her hearing aids were giving out on her. It was all very hasty, very rash.

"I don't know how I'm going to tell the girls," Eloise said.

"They already know," Clyde said. "I talked to Gigi last night. We FaceTimed Rebecca."

Alice grew very still. If David were here, surely Clyde would have asked him. Alice was all for tradition, but if the daughters were going to be consulted, the mother should be too. It was only fair.

"I knocked on your mother's door but she wasn't home," Clyde went on, as if hearing Alice's thoughts. "So I figured we'd tell her together. It all happened rather impulsively."

At least he admitted it, Alice thought.

"Not that the decision is impulsive," he clarified. "I've known since the moment I met you, I really have."

"Better that I tell my mother myself," Eloise said. "I'm not sure she'll approve."

Alice felt hurt and very misunderstood. She should leave now, exit quietly through the side door and let Eloise come to her in her own time, on her own terms.

Just then, she saw a penny at her feet, lying there on the tile of the kitchen floor. She picked it up, gave it a rub. Was David here with her? It felt less like a love note and more like a lecture. It wasn't Alice's job to tell Eloise how to live her life or where to live it or who to live it with. It wasn't her job to vet Eloise's suitors or warn her away from an engagement. Maybe it had been, back when Eloise was fresh out of high school. But not now, when Eloise had two grown daughters herself.

Alice had always assumed that letting go of motherly control would get easier as she got older, but it was proving the opposite. Now that habits had been formed over so many years and Alice's life was so entwined with her daughter's, it was even harder to release the grip, to accept that Eloise's path might be diverging from her own.

Alice wanted to make her daughter proud with how she responded. She wanted to make David proud. And more than anything, she wanted to make herself proud.

"I do approve, actually," Alice said, walking out onto the porch, feeling like the heroine in one of her favorite dramas, the kind of thing she watched now that David wasn't around to put sports on the TV every night. "So long as you don't kidnap my daughter and take her to Scotland full-time."

"Mother," Eloise said, standing up. "I'm so sorry."

"Why?" Alice said, her own eyes damp as she looped her daughter for a hug. "You found love a second time. That's nothing to be sorry about."

The words didn't feel as difficult to say as Alice anticipated. They came out quite naturally, as if she had been preparing for this moment for a very long time. Which she supposed in some ways she had been. There was nothing more instinctive for a mother than to love her daughter unconditionally. Except perhaps to protect her daughter, which was really just a manifestation of that same love, though sometimes distorted.

It became clear to Alice as she watched Eloise and Clyde basking in their happiness that Eloise wasn't some fragile, weak thing. She didn't need to be protected against making the wrong decision. She needed to be trusted in making the right one.

They toasted with a bottle of champagne that Clyde had brought along (he seemed very prepared for someone who thought he was going to be turned down, Alice noted).

He and Eloise looked cartoonishly blissful. It made Alice ache for David and also think, accidentally, of Liam. Their first kiss up by the cannon at British Landing when Alice was only fourteen. The way the whole world felt like it was imploding and exploding and Alice had never wanted it to stop. But when you're that young, love doesn't last. If it doesn't blow up on you, you find a way to blow *it* up. Which Alice had done, spectacularly so.

She didn't regret any of it. It led her to David, to Eloise and Penelope, to her grandchildren. But in another life, she would be curious to see where that fork may have taken her. The fork where her seventeen-year-old self apologized to Liam about their fight—what it had been about, she honestly couldn't remember—instead of seeking solace in David's arms. It was foolish to think that way, but it was liberating too, looking back on the past without being consumed by guilt or pain, longing or regret. Just appreciating it for what it was, where it led.

"What do you think Dad would say?" Eloise asked.

Alice thumbed the penny she'd found in the kitchen. She tried to be content with it, tried not to hope that someday David might give a sign even clearer than stray coins.

A loud sound came from just outside the porch. It was the generator turning on, buzzing to life.

"That's odd," Eloise said. "The generator already did its weekly test yesterday. Why is it going off on a Wednesday?"

Alice checked her watch. She couldn't believe it. It was 3:03 p.m. Goose bumps peppered her skin. David had always been a few minutes late.

She didn't feel she deserved such a gift from David, given how she'd betrayed him. But she received it nonetheless.

"Your father would be so happy," Alice said to Eloise. Her voice cracked. She was newly aware of how the broken bits were what let the light in, let the love in. She took Eloise's hand and admired the elegant amethyst ring, how it seemed to release the sunlight rather than catch it. "He *is* happy. We both are."

The generator gave a loud shudder, then turned off.

Chapter 43

Lillian

News of the engagement of Eloise Jenkins and Clyde MacDougal spread like the wildfire during Mackinac Island's great drought of 1987.

Some said he'd recited a ten-page poem during the proposal in the Grand Hotel ballroom. Others were insistent he'd taken Eloise on a carriage ride to Arch Rock, then dropped to his knee with a five-carat diamond, or a vintage sapphire, depending on who told it. Patricia Doud was running around town telling everyone Clyde had wooed Eloise with a home-cooked meal (with groceries from Doud's, coincidentally enough) before popping the question. Josephine May had a similar story, but with May's turtle fudge as the centerpiece.

Lillian heard more about it from Trina during a long shift at the Pink Pony.

"Eloise Jenkins is getting married before my own daughter," Trina fumed in the kitchen. "It's a sad summer, that's what it is."

Trina was disconsolate about Lillian's breakup with James, which had formally taken place earlier that week. After Lillian had told Gigi what was going on, it felt ridiculous to keep up the farce any longer. James had agreed.

"What did you do?" had been Trina's first question when Lillian broke the news. "I thought we had fixed everything."

As if that was all Lillian was—a problem to be fixed, a single woman in need of a husbandly solution.

"It just wasn't right," Lillian said. "We both knew it."

"You think I waited for everything to be perfect before I married your father?" Trina had replied. "But we got married, made it work. That's what you do."

"No." Lillian unleashed pent-up lip from her teenage days. "That's what you do."

Lillian should be making her way back to Chicago. She still had her lease. She could find another job. But she had promised herself that she wouldn't leave until she'd talked to her parents.

The island was stickier than the Pink Pony's toffee pudding. Lillian sweated through her restaurant uniform, her tennis outfits, her satin pajamas. August had arrived, the busiest tourist month, making July look like the warm-up act. The Pink Pony was packed, hour-long waits and well-coiffed heiresses leaving two-hundred-dollar tips after multiple rum runners.

It was something to console Lillian's parents. Business was booming, even if their once-promising daughter had turned out to be a sore disappointment.

Gigi's reaction—or lack of reaction, really—to Lillian's news had boosted her spirits. Perhaps Gigi was right and Lillian had been building it all up in her head too much, overestimating how much of a disaster it was going to be.

Lillian needed to give her parents a fair shot. Well, her mother, at least. She would start with Trina and then perhaps together they could talk to Lillian's father.

───────~───────

"Why do we have to go out for ice cream when we already have some in the freezer?" Trina asked Lillian the next day as they walked from the Pink Pony to Sadie's.

Things had cooled down just a little, in both emotions and temperature. They were enjoying a break at the restaurant between when the lunch rush finished and the seniors started coming in for the early bird special.

"Gigi and Eloise wanted to get together," Lillian said. "They invited us."

Trina looked suspicious. "You and Gigi don't get along. And surely you know Eloise and I have never been close. I've always been on the outside of their little foursome, even though Kitty moved to the island after we did."

"Maybe it doesn't always have to be like that," Lillian said. "Gigi's grown up a lot."

Gigi had helped her plan this ice cream outing as a way to keep Lillian accountable. They'd agreed that Lillian would have the conversation with Trina right before meeting up with Gigi and Eloise. Then, even though Trina would be upset, she'd care about her own reputation enough to hold it together in public and let the initial fury pass before confronting Lillian privately.

"Do I have her to blame for the fact that you've seemed to regress in maturity this summer?" Trina asked.

"Mom." Lillian felt the cut of the comment. "Do you really think I'm that bad?"

"Of course I don't. I'm just confused. Everything you said you wanted out of life: the big job, the husband, the family. It seems like you're throwing it all away. And for what?"

"For freedom," Lillian said.

"Please," Trina said. "You had the privilege of growing up in America." She gestured to the cozy Main Street scene: the flags, the families, the friendliness. "Don't talk to me about freedom."

"I don't mean that kind of freedom. I'm very lucky that way. What you and Dad have given me, and given up for me, is incredible." She hoped her mother knew how much she meant it.

"Then what kind of freedom do you mean?"

"Freedom to love who I want to love."

"And who exactly do you want to love?"

"Women." The word didn't stick to Lillian's tongue, didn't ask for more time. It was as ready to be out as she was. "That's it. That's everything."

She meant it both ways. That she had nothing more to say, and also that this truth was all-encompassing. That if she couldn't do that, she would always be performing, always be changing herself to fit someone else's template, always be tucking into the shade of the pines rather than standing boldly in sunlight.

Trina stopped walking. She asked Lillian to repeat herself. Lillian did, then waited. Her mother asked if this was the reason the wedding was called off.

Lillian said yes, that she had nearly gone through with it but just couldn't in the end.

"You still could have gone through with it," Trina said. Lillian felt her stomach fall, though there was already a lightness in having the secret out of her. "Many people do."

Lillian tried to prepare a reply. Her air supply felt low.

"But if that is really how you feel," Trina continued, "then I am glad you did not."

Lillian looked up, hoping she hadn't misheard.

"Do not misunderstand me," Trina said, an intensity in her dark eyes. "I am not glad about this. It will make your life harder; it is sure to."

"Not so much." Lillian was thrilled to feel concern coming her way rather than condemnation. "Times have changed. I'll have a good life, Mom. A great life. And I want you in it."

"What is that supposed to mean?" Trina said harshly. "Why wouldn't I be in my own daughter's life? My only child's life?"

Lillian had never been so elated to see her mother indignant. "I just thought . . ."

"You think too much; you always have," Trina said.

Lillian felt very shaky. She sat down on the curb to rest for a moment.

"Get up." Trina frowned down at Lillian. "It's dirty down there."

Trina reached out a hand. Lillian took it as she got to her feet, holding on a few seconds too long.

They kept on toward Sadie's. Lillian had never seen Mackinac so beautiful. The charm of the horses, the cheer of the tourists. The island had a new expansiveness to it. Lillian's heart was brimming with all the love she'd been prepared to lose so that she might not lose herself. The love she'd gotten to keep after all, so it doubled up within her, overflowing.

Perhaps she should have had this conversation many months ago, many years ago. But she had still been figuring it all out. She wouldn't have been able to express her truth before she was standing in it so firmly. And Trina might not have responded as she had, respected her as she had, if Lillian had been wavering herself. As much angst as it had brought, there was beauty in the timing, silver in the lining.

They found Gigi and Eloise waiting for them on a bench outside Sadie's. Gigi had two massive ice cream cones in hand and Eloise held two double-scoop cups. As they greeted each other, Gigi gave Lillian an inquisitive look. *How did it go?* her green eyes asked.

Lillian gave a subtle thumbs-up. Gigi smiled at her so widely that Lillian was nearly knocked over by the brute force of it, the true north of it. Resurrecting their friendship from the dead had not been on her summer bingo card.

"One lilac ice cream for you," Gigi said, handing a cone to Lillian. "I had them dig into their reserves in the back."

"And I got you Moose Tracks, Trina," Eloise said, somewhat tentatively. "I noticed you buying it at Doud's before, so I figured it was a safe bet."

"Thank you." Trina accepted the ice cream and congratulated Eloise on her engagement. Gigi was telling the story of how Clyde had asked for her blessing when a cyclist sped by, careening to a stop

in front of Sadie's. Mayor Camille Welsh dismounted. She was carrying a stack of what appeared to be campaign flyers.

"Look what we have here!" Camille said, spotting their foursome.
"A most magnificent display of neighborly relations."

"What's that supposed to mean?" Gigi asked, sensing something
sinister beneath the saccharine greeting.

The mayor seemed to be smiling but her face wasn't moving much,
whether from the Botox or lack of genuine emotion, it was hard to
tell. "Well, with the long rivalry you two girls have had, and then
the ongoing competition over the doctor," Camille said to Lillian and
Gigi. "It's mighty good of you to put on such conciliatory faces."

Lillian expected Gigi to come up with an acerbic retort, but it was
Trina who spoke first.

"Enough, Camille," Trina said. "Stop trying to tear them apart.
Like you're trying to tear this town apart."

Lillian felt a swelling of pride. Her mother, who had tried so hard
to assimilate to this town, was now standing up against its leader.

"Trina," Camille said disapprovingly. "You would do well to remember the tax cut I'm giving small businesses."

"You mean the same tax cut you've been promising the last two
decades? You expect us to believe that if we elect you again, *this* will
be the term that you actually bring about real change?"

"I've done everything in my power," Camille said, huffing haugh-
tily. "You must understand, a mayor isn't a dictatorship. I can't just
wave my hands and fix all the problems."

"You could try harder, though," Gigi interjected. "Rather than just
turning your position into your own personal vanity project."

"I don't know what's gotten into you ladies today," Camille said.
"But I'm going to carry on with my campaigning and hope that by the
time I see you next, you'll better embody our Mackinac ethos."

With that, Camille taped not one but three of the "Re-elect Mayor
Camille Welsh for Mackinac Island" flyers to the door of Sadie's. The
flyer featured no policy stances, just a glamorous full-body shot. Lillian

was nearly certain it was generated by artificial intelligence, so different did it look from the actual Camille.

"Nice photo," Gigi said. "Looks nearly as fake as your promises."

Camille ignored her as she got back on her bike and pedaled away.

"She's vile," Eloise said when it was just the four of them again.

"Someone needs to run against her this November," Trina said. "So far she's unopposed."

"Have you ever considered it, Trina?" Eloise said. "You'd be great. A small business owner with a real pulse on our local economy."

Lillian could tell her mother was flattered. "I appreciate that, but it has no appeal to me," Trina said. "Too much chaos."

"I'm with you on that," Eloise said.

The word *chaos* made Lillian think of Gigi. "Remember how you always said you were going to be mayor when you grew up?" Lillian said to Gigi. Young Gigi always used to bring it up when something didn't go her way. *"When I'm mayor, I'm going to change that!"* had been her refrain.

"Yeah, back when I thought local government could actually make a difference. How naive."

"What if it wasn't naive, though?" Lillian said. "What if you actually ran against Camille?"

Lillian liked the idea more with every passing second. It was abrupt and unusual, sure, but in many ways it was tailor-made for Gigi.

"That's ridiculous," Gigi said, though her eyes sparked. "It would be herding a bunch of spineless sheep. I'd have no patience for it."

"That's why the island needs you," Lillian said. "You'd break the political gridlock and actually get stuff done."

"Forget it. I'm the opposite of qualified."

"Ah, yes, Camille is much more competent. My mistake." Lillian saw how her comment riled Gigi, how the wheels were turning in her head.

There was no need to push her on it now. She'd let it settle, let it simmer. Today had already been eventful enough.

"So, Trina and Lillian," Eloise said. "Are you getting some good mother-daughter time this summer?"

Lillian glanced at Trina. They shared a look that felt like a starting point.

"Yes," Trina said, offering Lillian a spoonful of her ice cream to try. "We really are."

Chapter 44

Gigi

The fact that her mother was engaged hadn't sunk in yet.

Maybe because Gigi had been genuinely unsure what Eloise's answer would be or because it had all happened so quickly. Gigi was pleased, at least, that Clyde had consulted her first.

"You can ask her," Gigi told him when he'd come to talk to her while Eloise was out at euchre. "But I put the odds at thirty percent she'll say yes."

She thought this might deter him, but he appeared bolstered. "Thirty percent?" he said. "You're saying I've got a decent chance, then!"

They'd gotten Rebecca on the phone. She'd been more diligent with her questioning: Did Clyde think it was too soon? (At their age, he said, they knew what they wanted and weren't keen on wasting time.) Where did they plan to live? (Mackinac half the year, Scotland the other half.) What was it about Eloise that made him so sure it was the right fit long term? (He rattled off an excessively long list, most of it amorphous qualities about the feeling that stirred deep in his soul when he looked into her eyes, but there were some practical compatibilities too.) Rebecca wanted to know, too, if he saw any conflicts in their faith. (He didn't; he believed in God in the sense of universal oneness; Eloise had said before that she wouldn't push Christianity, just needed him to respect it.)

By the time the call wrapped, both girls had decided he might as well shoot his shot. Given the way Gus had left without saying good-bye, Gigi was in no place to defend him.

Gus had texted her a few days ago. Sorry I couldn't stay longer. Give me a call and we'll plan a visit out here!

Gigi wasn't sure where *here* was. She hadn't replied yet. She liked holding the cards, or at least the illusion of it.

Gus's arrival on the island—and then his departure—had helped Gigi see some flaws in the stories she'd been telling herself about him. And flaws in the stories she'd been telling about herself. Like how if she stayed on the move and traveled all over and avoided Mackinac, she would be more loved by the father whose footsteps she still kept trying to follow in.

But love wasn't won by traveling or auditioning or inventing extreme scenarios to test your parents. It wasn't won by anything at all. Love was only ever given, only ever gifted. And as for freedom, well, that didn't come from moving from city to city or relationship to relationship. Freedom came from standing in one place, holding your ground and showing up exactly as you were.

Lillian had helped her see that. Gigi was proud of her old yet new friend. She hoped she would avoid wrecking their friendship a second time. The odds seemed good, better at least than the thirty percent she'd given Clyde, and he'd managed to prevail.

Now, days after the proposal, Eloise was still drifting around the house in an ethereal daze.

"Am I the only one who ever cleans up around here?" Gigi said, affecting annoyance when she found Eloise's dirty mug on the coffee table.

"I'm sorry, I could've sworn I already cleared it," Eloise said. She twirled her new ring.

"You're allowed to have engagement brain. But only for a week. Then standard chores and mother-daughter infighting is set to resume its regular programming."

"Lillian was right, you know," Eloise said. "You'd make a very good mayor."

"No, I wouldn't," Gigi said. But the idea was growing on her. After years of being a tiny fish in a big pond, she found something tempting about being a big fish in a tiny pond. "Besides, it would mean living here full-time."

"Well, it might be nice to have someone to watch the house while I'm in Scotland," Eloise said. "Or I'm sure we could find you an apartment in town."

"I'm not running for mayor," Gigi said. Eloise's smile turned up. "Why are you giving me that look?"

"I'm not giving you any look," Eloise protested.

But Gigi could read her mother's expressions better than she'd been able to at the start of summer, and she was clearly skeptical of Gigi's denial. Gigi didn't mind. It was nice to know she thought she could do it.

"I heard rumblings that Dr. Kentwood might be staying beyond summer, you know," Eloise said. "Deirdre is trying to persuade Fred to retire and have Dr. Kentwood take over the medical practice."

The news stirred something in Gigi. "Why are you telling me that?"

"I just thought you might be curious," Eloise said innocently. "Given you like to meddle in other people's business." She grinned.

"Right," Gigi said. "*I'm* the one who meddles."

"You did meddle with Clyde."

"Only to get back at you for meddling with James. And I wouldn't complain. You got a fiancé out of it."

"Yes," Eloise said happily. "I suppose I did."

"Are you changing your name?" Gigi wanted to know. "To Mac-Dougal?"

"I haven't decided yet. Maybe I'll go back to my maiden name or take Clyde's. It might feel strange being married to Clyde while having my ex-husband's name."

"It's not just your ex-husband's name," Gigi said. "It's mine too."

Though Gigi had long judged Eloise for continuing to go by Jenkins, deep down she was glad they still shared a name.

So much about her mother she seemed to have taken for granted: her presence, her name, her location, her love. Gigi was trying not to do that anymore, or at least do it a little less.

"I'll give it some thought," Eloise said. Then a shadow fell over her face. "Do you think it sounds crazy? That I'll be living half the year in Scotland?"

"I think it sounds amazing. Maybe I could go with you." Gigi said it lightly, disguising how much she'd actually been thinking about it. She didn't want Eloise to think she was trying to glom on as a third wheel.

Eloise looked longingly out the kitchen window, onto the open land and lakes she'd called home her whole life. "I just don't know how I can leave Mackinac."

"She'll be okay," Gigi said, patting her mother's shoulder. "She's tough like us."

Chapter 45

Mackinac

Mackinac was pleased that the Jenkins girls were giving her so much thought.

It would have been easy for her to be forgotten amid all of the excitement, but she felt the loyalty of her citizens, even reluctant ones like Gigi.

Speaking of Gigi, she was the one on whom Mackinac now set her sights. With Eloise's engagement in order and Lillian's parents coming around, it was time to focus on helping Gigi find her own happy story.

It wasn't a love story that Mackinac was scheming for her. It was a career move, something that would give Gigi the purpose she'd been lacking. And yes, it would benefit the island too. (She did admit to a selfish streak, but felt this plan was truly for the greater good. Perhaps it was how Eloise had felt when she'd set up Gigi and James.)

Mackinac wanted Gigi Jenkins as her mayor.

She was the kind of leader the island needed. Someone bold and decisive who would usher in a new era. The island was not threatened by change. She had always been somewhat of a rebel herself. The prospect of transformation excited her. Things had been getting stale for a while now.

The island had tried to set up the ideal conditions to entice Gigi to put her name in the hat.

Eloise was heading off to Scotland with that delightful Clyde and needed a house sitter. Camille was being her usual insufferable self. Lillian was reminding Gigi that the mayor dream had always been in her. And Gus was helping show Gigi that constantly moving sometimes meant never really knowing yourself, making Gigi more open to deepening the roots she already had here.

Mackinac tried to think what else it would take to convince Gigi that she was perfect for the role.

Perhaps there was something to be done with Dr. Kentwood. Eloise's instinct to set them up had been right, but the timing was wrong. It might be different now, with how Gigi had softened over the summer. And James was much less shy now that he'd gotten into the rhythm of the island, the rhymes of her people. If there was a reason for James to stay on Mackinac beyond summer, perhaps Gigi would be more inclined to as well. Yes, that might be leverage worth exploring, though Mackinac was wary to rely on it too heavily. Gigi was on a self-growth journey, and Mackinac didn't want a man to mess anything up (they certainly had a habit of doing that, the island had learned).

Something subtler, more internal, would have to persuade Gigi to run for mayor. A dream that might wake her up in the night. Or perhaps a flash of clarity as she bicycled past the Grand Hotel stables. Rather than pinching her nose, this time Gigi would breathe in the aroma, realizing that no matter where she went, no place would ever belong to her more than this one.

The horses . . . That gave Mackinac one more idea.

But tonight she would have to usher in a striking sunset and hope for the best. Like Eloise, the island could meddle, but she could not change minds. Gigi would have to do that herself.

Chapter 46

Gigi

A few days after the engagement, Gigi went down to the beach at British Landing for a late-afternoon suntan.

She was napping, deep in a recurring dream where she was riding a motorcycle. She was always strapped to the back with a guy whose face she couldn't see. She thought it was her dad, but the dream never let her take off his helmet to verify. This time, though, she didn't have her arms around a man. She was the driver, the sole rider. She had a police escort too, on horseback. It was clear Gigi was a very important figure, though before she could find out why, a voice stirred her awake.

"Gigi?"

Groggily, she lifted her head. She could feel sand still smeared to her cheeks. Some had dribbled into her mouth too; she seemed to have slept with it half open.

It was James. He was standing there shirtless in a bathing suit. It was an abrupt, though not unpleasant, sight to wake up to. Gigi found herself squinting, whether from the sun or the shine of his abs, it was hard to discern.

This was the first Gigi had really seen of James since finding out the nature of his relationship with Lillian. She'd wanted to talk to him, but there had been so much commotion with Eloise's engagement. Besides, James could reach out. If he wasn't with Lillian and still wasn't trying to get to know her, Gigi figured there was little point in putting in effort herself.

"What's wrong?" Gigi asked. "Is my mom okay?" She never used to worry like this—that was Rebecca's job—but she couldn't help it now.

"Everything's fine." James was smiling. His gray eyes were calm but not cool. "I got off work early today. Eloise said I might find you here."

That was when Gigi noticed the dandelions. A big bundle of them, all different shapes and sizes. He was holding them like a bouquet.

"I picked these on the way here," James said, handing them to her. "I couldn't help but see your dandelion tattoo on our first date. I wasn't trying to look." He blushed. It softened his strong cheekbones.

Gigi hoped she wasn't still sleeping. She much preferred this to the dream she'd been having, police escort and all.

Sitting up straighter, Gigi took off her sunglasses to look James in the eye. She didn't think her mom would have put him up to this, but there were other suspects. "Is Lillian behind this?"

James's face colored further. "No. I mean, sort of."

Gigi's hopes dropped. She was annoyed at herself for thinking he might have come here of his own volition.

"All Lillian did was tell me to stop being a coward about it and tell you how I feel," James said. "So I guess I have her to thank. Or blame, if this blows up in my face."

Gigi wanted to ask him what he meant. But all she said was, "You picked me weeds?"

She sniffed the dandelions. They smelled like her childhood: the sunny days, and the stormy ones too. How beautiful and strange it was to breathe in the good and the bad of her past and not try to sneeze it out. She just exhaled slowly.

"Dandelions aren't weeds," James said. "They're flowers. At least that's what my mom used to say."

Gigi felt a warmth spreading within. This was what she had always seen in them too. "Your mom sounds like a very wise woman."

"She was." James's expression snagged on the sunlight. "We lost her when I was in college."

"Shit." Gigi felt like an idiot for not knowing this huge piece of information about him. "I'm sorry. I had no idea."

"I don't tell many people," James said.

It made Gigi feel good that he trusted her, though she didn't feel she'd earned it yet.

"She had cancer when I was a kid. Beat it twice. That's when I decided I wanted to be a doctor."

James sat down and joined her in the sand. Gigi extended her beach towel for him to sit on with her.

"It came back a third time. Three years ago, when I was in residency. She couldn't quite kick it that time," he went on. "Felt like I lost my dad too. It's taken him a while to recover. Both of us, I guess."

His voice was tender but not fragile. He kept his gaze out on the horizon, where the sky was squeezing the last juice out of the lemony sun.

It explained something about James—the way his edges were so carefully tied, as if he were aware that everything might unravel at any moment.

"Is that why you came to Mackinac for the summer?" Gigi recalled how James had told her a little of his story on their first date. But that was all it had been, one small slice. She wanted the whole thing. "To get away from all that?"

"I thought of it more as a respite," James said. Gigi related strongly. "I needed a break. I was overworking myself as a distraction so I wouldn't have to actually process how I felt about losing my mom."

"Processing emotions is overrated," Gigi said to lighten the mood. "I prefer to project them onto other people."

James laughed, and Gigi felt like she'd won a thousand dollars. He was letting his guard down.

"I thought slowing down might be what I needed," he said.

"And was it?" Gigi asked. "What you needed?"

"And more. Though in a town so small, I felt tempted to hide a little."

Gigi made a sympathetic face. "I know the feeling."

"I was always the shy kid growing up," James said. "The one who was scared to raise my hand in class even when I knew the answer. And that's what I've been doing this summer. I'm sorry if I came off as rude."

Gigi felt elated. Her intuition had been correct. James *had* liked her all along. She just had next to no experience with shy guys, so she didn't know how to read him. The extroverted, smooth-talking charmers who fizzled out faster than a Diet Coke were her usual type. But it was time for something new. Something deeper, something steadier.

"Well, I'm sorry if I came off as too hot," Gigi said.

They both laughed at that, the sounds layered like music on top of the lake.

"How about a swim?" James suggested.

Gigi agreed. She set down her bouquet of dandelions on her towel. Tugging it farther up on the shore, she made sure there was no chance of it getting washed away in the waves. This was her new favorite bouquet, surpassing the expensive one from Clyde.

"Race you to the water," Gigi said, feeling like a little kid again, yet a full-blown adult too. The best of both worlds. She started bolting toward the water. James was on her heels. He was faster, but she was craftier.

"My ankle!" she yelped as he overtook her. Mere inches from the water's edge, he stopped in his tracks and came back to check on her.

Gigi took advantage of his momentum shift. She bolted into the lake, sealing her victory.

"No fair," James complained good-naturedly. "That's cheating."

"It's my island. I get to make the rules." Gigi felt a surge of affection for Mackinac as she said it. "You haven't learned my tricks yet."

They were standing in the lake, the water up to their waists. The sand felt spongy beneath Gigi's feet.

"I hope I'll get the chance to," James said.

Something about the earnest way he said it made Gigi think about what Eloise had mentioned.

"There are rumors you might be taking over the medical clinic from Fred. Is there any truth to them?" She let the question hang there like a limp sail, trying not to care if it caught wind.

Seagulls squawked to fill the beat of silence.

"He did ask me," James said. "But I declined."

Gigi told herself she didn't have a right to feel let down by this, but the disappointment flooded anyway. "Right," she said. "I figured it was just gossip."

"It's so much responsibility being the only doctor on the island," James went on.

"But you're good at responsibility." Gigi's instinct was to persuade him to take the job. And rather than fight that instinct or fear that it would make her seem like she cared too much, she followed it to see where it would take her. "Just think about how you saved my life from those pistachios."

James grinned. He looked so good without his doctor's coat on. Just his bronze skin free to breathe in the late summer air.

"And Mackinac is pretty far from my dad. He's back in Detroit," James elaborated. "We're trying to rebuild our relationship since things got rocky when Mom died."

Gigi nodded. She thought about her dad and realized how much she wanted to tell James about her own jagged past.

"I know your dad stopped by the island this summer," James said. "He actually came into the clinic. Said his knee was hurting, but it seemed fine to me. I got the sense he'd heard some rumors about us and was scoping me out."

This news was the last thing Gigi had expected. Did Gus have a protective father instinct after all? She loved the thought of it, the feel of it. Especially with how abruptly he'd left this summer. This felt like evidence that he did care about her, even if he would never really change. "He did?"

James nodded. He looked like he was going to ask more about her dad but seemed reluctant, like there was a wall blocking his movement toward her. It was the same wall Gigi felt, the one reminding both of them that there was little point in going too deep because it was all coming to an end regardless.

"Can I ask you why it matters to you if I take over the clinic?" James's tone wasn't aggressive, just curious. "You're leaving after Labor Day, aren't you?"

"That's the plan." Gigi's headache mounted again as it often did when she thought about how much she still had to figure out.

James took half a step toward her, and she took half a step toward him. One whole step divided the two, yet multiplied too.

"I wish I could get to know you more," James told her. "I wish we had more time."

They stood there in the lake, wading in deeper. Usually Gigi sprinted in and out of the water, scared away by the cold. But she had no desire to run out now. The water had had time to warm by this point in the season. The air had too.

James was looking impossibly handsome. His wet hair slicked back, his svelte body standing tall. They were just about the same height. Their eyes locked, though it felt more like an unlocking. A release of her past judgments about James, and those about herself too.

He stepped toward her again. They were nearly touching. She could feel his breath warm on her face. His eyes weren't just gray but also speckled with earthy brown. His eyelashes were black and thick. Everything was a little blurred this close.

Gigi thought he might kiss her. She hoped he might kiss her. But he didn't, just tucked her bangs behind her ears so they were out of her eyes.

"Maybe we could give us a try?" James said. His mouth was inches from hers. He was asking for the green light to close the gap.

Gigi was so close to saying yes. She was so close to throwing caution to the wind and plunging in. But there was a steady sort of stirring deep within. The kind of nudge she usually ignored but now found herself valuing more.

She took a step back. "I don't think so. I can't believe I'm saying this, but I'm not looking for a fling."

"I'm not either," James said quickly.

"But we're both leaving in a couple weeks. That's the literal definition of a fling."

James's thick brows pulled together. "Can't we create a new definition?"

Gigi wanted to keep things clear and organized. Maybe it was Eloise or Rebecca wearing off on her, or maybe she'd just found that ambiguity and anarchy were more fun in theory than in practice.

She wanted more of James, but she didn't want to complicate things with romance. Not at this stage, not in these circumstances. She'd been reflecting more on her long list of exes and even her very brief fling with Ronny, and that wasn't what she was looking for anymore.

"How about we expand the definition of friendship?" Gigi suggested instead.

James looked open to this. "Under this expanded definition, can friends kiss?" he asked innocently, though mischief sparked in his eyes.

"They cannot," Gigi said. It was a test of her willpower.

"Can they hold hands?"

"Also no. But," Gigi went on grandly, "they can link arms."

She demonstrated. There in the water, she looped her arm through his. His touch felt foreign yet dependable too. Not like a home she'd ever had, but like one she might yet build.

"How very intimate," James said.

He was teasing, but there was a truth in his words too. There was something old-fashioned and tender about linking arms rather than skipping straight to making out or jumping in bed. More emphasis on eye contact and emotions and energy rather than just a commoditized version of physical touch, which Gigi had gotten used to. She didn't have her usual desire to cut the intimacy by saying something snarky or cracking a joke. She just stood her ground in the lake and looked James straight in the eye.

"May I assume that eye contact is safe?" James asked.

"I wouldn't say it's safe," Gigi clarified. She felt the temptation in every twinkle of his eye. "But it is permitted, yes."

"Thank you for such a detailed overview." James took a step back, as if trying to dutifully keep his distance. "With these terms, I accept our friendship."

Gigi held out her hand. He shook it.

"You really are cut out to be mayor," James said.

Gigi fought a smile. "Did Lillian tell you that? Because it's not true."

"Too bad. You'd be incredible."

The vote of confidence meant more to Gigi than she let on.

They looked out at the horizon, all corals and cotton tonight. The sunset had the ease of something that happens every day, yet the flair of something very rare. She realized how glad she was that she hadn't managed to stay away from Mackinac this summer.

"Do you actually think I could make a difference?" she asked. There it was, her greatest fear rebirthed as a strand of hope. "On this island, I mean."

James considered it, then found his answer. "I think you already have."

Gigi squeezed James's forearm rather than his hand so she wouldn't be breaching their contract. She was more interested in creating rules than breaking them these days. But she felt the meaning of their touch just the same.

"You have too, Dr. Kentwood," she said. "You have too."

He grinned at that, and Gigi marveled how she had ever found his smile cold. Probably because it had been a mirror then, just as it was a mirror now. Not projecting the past or refracting the future, just reflecting the present and all its unexpected light.

———⟫———

"Will you be my campaign manager?" Gigi asked Rebecca over the phone a couple days later. From the front porch, she waved to Nonni, who was zooming by in the golf cart, off to pickleball. Liam was not with her.

"Campaign manager for what?" Rebecca said. "What else did I miss?"

"I'm running for mayor," Gigi announced. "To oust tyrant Camille."

"Mayor of *Mackinac Island*?" Rebecca seemed convinced this was one of Gigi's pranks.

It took significant explaining before Rebecca began to believe her. Gigi didn't blame her. She still found it hard to wrap her head around. The idea of running had felt like a whim at first but was turning into something much sturdier. In some ways it felt like she'd been zigzagging toward this moment all her life.

"You're sure you're not just doing this for the entertainment factor?" Rebecca said. "You actually want to be mayor and have to deal with the public all the time?"

"I want to be the face of a new generation on the island," Gigi said. "And tell people what to do without actually having much responsibility. Mayor is the perfect fit, really."

"Well, we'll need to mobilize quickly," Rebecca said, coming around to it. "It's August already and the election is in November." Gigi could hear her flipping through her calendar. "An eighty-day push."

Gigi relished the way Rebecca said *we*. It made her feel like part of a team. They had always been a team, she supposed; she'd just been reluctant about accepting it, scared that being close to someone more conventional would wear off on her, make her lose her edge. She understood now that relationships didn't work like that. A softer reference point just made her corners look sharper.

"I only need two hundred votes to win. It's kind of a joke," Gigi said. "I looked up the results from last time. It's not like I have that many doors to knock on."

"No, but we'll need to clarify your messaging," Rebecca said. "What you stand for, what's going to get people out to the polls."

"I stand for kicking out the old regime," Gigi said. "I stand for change and action and making everyone feel like they can live here and shine here, no matter if you're a college dropout or an Ivy League grad or queer or liberal or conservative or Christian or Buddhist or Jewish or Muslim or a vegan or a carnivore or a tarot card reader or have blue fucking hair."

Gigi couldn't remember the last time something had lit her up like this. She waited for Rebecca to pick apart her words, say she had to tame it down.

"That's not a bad start," Rebecca said. "I'm taking notes now. We'll leave out the f-bombs, but it's good to let your passion come through. People want authenticity."

Gigi hoped this might be true but wasn't sure based on Camille's tenure.

"The challenge will be how you inspire the people who want change without alienating the ones who don't," Rebecca went on.

"If they don't want change, I can't help them. Camille can have those voters."

"Remember the demographics of the island, and particularly those who actually vote. They're older, more conservative. You can't disenfranchise the base."

"I'm not going to become some political puppet," Gigi said. "If I go down, I'll go down in style."

Mayor was a nonpartisan position on Mackinac, so she didn't have to pick a party. She was very glad about this. Political parties were a scam if she'd ever seen one, putting people into boxes and stripping out all original thinking.

"The more I think about it," Rebecca said, still typing up her notes, the *click, click* of the keyboard audible through the airwaves, "the more I realize how you're made for this job."

"I get to be the boss without working my way up the ladder," Gigi said. "I just have to emotionally manipulate people into voting for me."

"I don't think politicians call it emotional manipulation. I think they call it inspiring their constituents."

"This is why you're my campaign manager. Adding value from day one."

"The timing is good," Rebecca prattled on excitedly. "Since I decided not to apply for grad schools this year, this gives me a good project to focus on."

Gigi probed more about why Rebecca wasn't pursuing grad school after all. She didn't like the idea that her talented sister was sitting home all day alone. She told Rebecca as much.

"Well, I'm not technically alone," Rebecca said.

"Sadie doesn't count," Gigi said, though she did love that little pup.

"Not just Sadie . . ." Rebecca trailed off. "If I tell you something, will you promise not to tell anyone? Especially Mom?"

Was Rebecca about to confess an affair? Gigi was riveted. "I promise."

"You have a new title coming your way," Rebecca said. "In addition to mayor."

"Enough with the riddles. Spit it out."

"Aunt," Rebecca said. "You're going to be Aunt Gigi."

Gigi felt the thrill in her spine. "You're pregnant?"

"Shhh," Rebecca said. "You're the only one who knows other than Tom."

This touched Gigi deeply. So she had beaten out Maggie the Maid of Honor in the end. "Why are you keeping it a secret?"

"It's still early. Things could go wrong."

"Or they could go right," Gigi said, like she had at the beginning of Eloise and Clyde's relationship. And she'd been correct about that; the proposal was proof.

"I don't want to get my hopes up and then have them come crashing down."

"Then you'll never feel anything at all. You'll always be in the middle. Where's the fun in that? Go to the top and if you fall, we'll be here for you. That's what family's for, right?"

There was a silence, a sniffle. "I'm sorry I didn't ask you to be my maid of honor," Rebecca said.

"It's fine," Gigi said. "I would've complained about it anyway. And I would've given a messy, drunken speech and distracted from your big day."

"Still . . . if I could do it over, it would be you."

It was gratifying to hear this, more so than Gigi had expected. "You've done enough for me over the years. Coming to find me after I ran away, giving me money when I've needed it. I know I haven't thanked you very well."

A long pause followed. Rebecca seemed rather emotional today, though that could just be the pregnancy.

"You can throw me a baby shower to make up for it. Come up with a creative theme. But first we're going to get you elected mayor."

Gigi thought that sounded good. "When are you going to tell Mom about the baby?"

She'd started calling Eloise *Mom* again. She wasn't so worried anymore about Eloise micromanaging her. In many ways, Gigi could see how she'd tried to control her mother too—judging her for how she dressed (too conservative), how she dated (not enough), how she worked (a boring job). The irony was rich, Gigi could see now. And though she had called her mother *Eloise* to remind herself that she was an adult now, calling her *Mom* again actually made her feel more mature, like she didn't need to trick herself into believing she was a grown-up; it was just the natural state of things.

"At the three-month mark," Rebecca said. "Mid-September."

"I like that it's our secret for now," Gigi said. "Just between sisters."

"What's one of yours?" Rebecca asked. "A secret?"

"I've tried drugs. Psychedelics, crazy shit."

"That's not a secret."

Gigi thought harder. She decided Rebecca could be trusted with a bigger one. "I think I sort-of-maybe-hypothetically-but-not-hypothetically-accidentally-yet-intentionally might like James." She rushed the words together, but Rebecca seemed to catch every one.

"I knew it!" Rebecca whooped. "Mom is never going to let you live this down. You know that, right?"

"I'm aware." Gigi told Rebecca about the backstory with Lillian and how James had brought those dandelions to the lake. "There was almost a moment between us, but I told him I just wanted to be friends."

Rebecca groaned.

"He's leaving at the end of the summer," Gigi explained. "I don't want to repeat my past mistakes."

"Nothing about James is a repeat of any guy you've ever dated."

"Well, he's still leaving," Gigi said. "That's a similarity."

"Maybe he'd stay if you asked him," Rebecca said. "Sometimes people just need to know someone wants them around."

"Are we talking about James or you? Because if you're asking, then yes, I want you to move back to the island, Rebecca. It's terrible having to be the responsible daughter all the time."

Rebecca sounded pleased. "We're actually starting to bond with our neighbors here. But Mackinac is in our five-year plan. Tom is on board."

"He's really not so bad, that Todd." Gigi said it with a grin, misnaming him the way their mom used to.

"Ha-ha," Rebecca said. "He's been in a much better mood since I stopped trying to force him to eat all these exotic dinners. He finally sat me down and told me I was trying to make him into someone more interesting than he was. And that he was a simple man and liked plain food but he felt like he was letting me down when he didn't rave about my experimental cooking. So now we do chicken and salad and tacos."

"That's the trick to a happy life, isn't it?" Gigi said. "Letting go of how we think people should be, how we think *we* should be, and embracing what is."

"Who's the philosophical one now? I can't wait for the voters to see all the different sides to you. You're going to demolish Camille. Everyone likes an underdog."

"I wouldn't call myself the underdog," Gigi said, though she certainly would be. "But yeah, it's going to be a landslide victory. One for the ages."

Chapter 47

Eloise

"G igi and my mother are throwing an engagement party, aren't they?" Eloise asked Deirdre as they laid out place settings in Deirdre's nautical-themed dining room.

Deirdre had shifted this week's euchre night and requested Eloise come early and help her get ready. Gigi had gone through Eloise's closet and complimented one of her more fitted floral frocks, casually mentioning it might be a nice night to wear it. It was all very suspect.

"Don't ask questions I can't answer." Deirdre poured herself a glass of white.

"I don't like surprises," Eloise said. "Everyone knows that."

Not that she was actually upset. She was so over the moon that it would take more than thrusting her into the center of attention to bring her back to earth.

"Maybe you don't know what you like," Deirdre said. "Take Clyde, for example. He's been the biggest curveball of your life."

It was true. The way he'd burst onto the scene, turning everything upside down and tipping it right side up. How he made her feel safe and comfortable while also electrified and excited to explore the world. The way she'd answered yes with such a sureness in her chest, the kind of thing she thought she'd never feel again.

She'd told herself that Gus was the safer choice, staying invested in the person who already held her heart. But she saw now how expecting something old to change was actually riskier than trusting something new to grow. Maybe Eloise should have learned this long ago. Maybe it was all God's plan and she was right where she was supposed to be.

"I'm out of wine," Deirdre lamented. "Fred drinks too much, goes against his own doctor recommendations," she said, though she was on her second glass. "Could we swing by yours for a bottle or two? I don't feel like trekking all the way to Doud's."

Eloise lifted her brows. "Very subtle."

"Just go with it, please," Deidre said. "Your daughter will have my head if she thinks I spilled the beans."

Linking arms, they set out to Thistle Dew. There was just the foreshadowing of fall in the air. It usually made Eloise sad, summer coming to a close. Now, for the first time since she'd planned on going off to college all those years ago, the end of summer signified the start of something.

"I'm going to miss you," Deirdre said.

"Just promise not to shut me out like you did when you got to college," Eloise said, thinking back to that time and how Deirdre hadn't wanted much to do with Eloise after she'd decided to stay on the island and marry Gus. She'd only gotten a couple of letters that whole first year Deirdre was away. "Long-distance friendship didn't suit us."

"No." Deirdre frowned. "It didn't."

"This will be different, though," Eloise said. "I'll still be here April through September every year. You hardly see me in the winter anyway. We're always bundled up inside."

Spending half the year in Scotland had not been on Eloise's radar screen. But it had scratched her old itch to get out and see the world. Only this time she'd be doing it with her husband by her side. And Mackinac would still very much be her home. She would be there for her mother, and her daughters too, wherever they ended up. "Think of it as an extended holiday," Clyde had said, so irresistibly that

Eloise had decided there wasn't a good enough reason to veto, especially once she'd talked to the church and they'd agreed she could do her bookkeeping job remotely.

"What I mean is I'll miss *this*," Deirdre said. "Having you all to myself." Their footsteps synced. Eloise wasn't sure if she'd learned to shorten her stride to match Deirdre's or if Deirdre had lengthened her stride to match Eloise's. It didn't really matter. What mattered was that they were in step.

"I've had to share you with Fred for decades and we've done just fine," Eloise pointed out.

Deidre's expression knotted. "I have a confession."

Eloise tensed, assuming the worst. Divorce, cancer, or the news that Fred was transitioning into a Democrat. "What is it?"

Deirdre looked conflicted, like she had a few things she might say.

"I'm jealous of you and Clyde," she said. "I'm happy for you, I am, but I'm jealous. What you two have is so romantic and fun, and sometimes I hate it, I just hate it. I'm a terrible person, a complete abomination." She turned away from Eloise, extricating herself.

"If you're a terrible person, then I am too. I've been envious of you and Fred many times. I still am, to be honest."

Deirdre blinked. "Me and Fred? You're jealous of *us*?"

"Absolutely," Eloise said. "You're each other's best friends. You're there through thick and thin. You don't have to stress about what you wear to date night or worry about going through a sickness alone. You two have commitment, the real thing. I think that might have been part of the reason I was hanging on to Gus for so long. I wanted what you two had and I just couldn't accept that I wouldn't get that. My forever person, the one I could look back with at the end and reflect on sixty years of marriage with."

Deirdre took Eloise's arm again. "Fred *is* there for me, I suppose. Even when I diagnose myself with new illnesses three times a day and complain about how we never make love while also shutting down any attempt he makes to initiate it. He's a marvel, really. I'll bake him a chocolate cake tomorrow, diabetes be darned."

Clyde approached them on the path. He'd been invited over for euchre tonight at Deirdre's so he could take notes for his novel.

He was wearing the same pinstripe suit from their first date but a new fedora. Eloise greeted him with a kiss.

Deirdre asked if he might help them carry wine back from Eloise's. He readily agreed, winking at Eloise. They'd discussed their suspicions of a party. Alice had played pickleball with Clyde yesterday and hinted that a man should always have a freshly shaven face, that you never knew who you might run into.

"I only have two bottles of pinot," Eloise said. "We hardly need an army to transport them."

"Jesus will help us multiply it. Now, just remember, she was mine first," Deidre said, ceremoniously passing Eloise off from her arm to Clyde's.

"Wouldn't dare forget it," Clyde said. "I've already named the best friend character in my next book after you."

Deirdre clapped at the news and kicked her shoes together like Dorothy in her ruby slippers. "I'm going to be immortalized," she proclaimed. And then, "Make her thin. A size two."

"I do love you islanders," Clyde said to Eloise as Deirdre bustled on ahead. "Such complex characters and sweeter than fudge."

Eloise relished the solidness of him, right here, right beside her, no expiration date. "*We* islanders certainly are. And you're one of us now."

When they reached Thistle Dew, shapes were shuffling on the front porch from behind the Adirondack chairs.

"Don't forget to act surprised," Clyde whispered.

"I don't have to pretend," Eloise replied. "I'm genuinely astounded by the way this summer has unfolded."

"Good astounded?"

"Better than good," Eloise said. "So much better."

It was Georgiana who jumped out first, a second or two before everyone else. "Surprise!" she yelled. It was just like her to steal the show at someone else's surprise party. Eloise wouldn't have had it any other way. She dropped Clyde's hand and wrapped her daughter in a hug.

"Thank you for this," Eloise said in Georgiana's ear.

"It was all Nonni. I just bossed everyone around. It's good practice for mayor. You'll mail in your vote from Scotland, won't you?"

"That's all your dear old mother is to you?" Eloise said. "A vote?"

"Don't take it personally."

"Of course not. And I wouldn't miss voting for you for the world. It's not every day that your daughter who's denounced her hometown decides she wants to move back and govern the entire island."

"I'm prone to extremes," Georgiana said. "What can I say?"

"Say you'll be my co–maid of honor. Along with Rebecca."

That was when Rebecca popped out. She'd been hiding inside for one more surprise. Eloise embraced both daughters at once. Nothing felt lacking today. They were a small family, but a whole one. Not broken, but balanced.

"Rebecca is married, so she'll be matron of honor," Georgiana said. "I'll be your only maid of honor."

"Fair enough," Rebecca said with a grin. "Gigi, you know James keeps staring at you, right?"

Eloise glanced over her shoulder. Sure enough, Dr. Kentwood did seem to be looking Georgiana's way. Eloise sensed something between them. He had shown up at the door the other day looking like a man on a mission. When Eloise had asked Georgiana about it that evening, she'd divulged more than expected. The story started with Lillian and ended with how Georgiana had gone swimming with James but told him she didn't want something short term. Eloise was proud of her daughter for knowing her worth. She was proud of herself too. She must have started doing some things better to make Georgiana want to open up to her like that.

"We're just friends," Georgiana said now. But her face glimmered.

"I've heard that one before." Rebecca nodded toward Eloise, who laughed at herself.

"We Jenkins ladies are rather irresistible this summer, aren't we?" Eloise said. In the background, she overheard Clyde telling the neighbors about their first date and how he fell "socks first" for her when he saw her in the Grand Hotel lobby. "And Wood ladies," she added quickly.

"I'm still Jenkins by blood," Rebecca said.

Eloise felt how much she'd been craving this reassurance. That even as her girls went off and had their own lives, their own families, their bond would be unbreakable.

"We've always been irresistible," Georgiana said. "This is just the summer the world woke up to it."

"Maybe it's the summer we woke up to it ourselves," Eloise said.

"That too," Georgiana said. "So will you finally admit I'm a good matchmaker?"

"I've never said you weren't. I'll be thanking you forever for this."

"You can thank me via campaign donation. I'm fundraising."

Georgiana kissed Eloise's cheek, then Rebecca's, and dashed off into the crowd to deliver her mayoral pitch to anyone who would listen, and especially those who wouldn't.

"That's my girl," Eloise said, watching her go.

"*Our* girl," Rebecca amended.

"Yes." Eloise's island bones felt Mackinac herself joining in, also wanting to claim Georgiana as her own, not to cage her, but to care for her. "Our girl."

"We're doing this," Clyde said to Eloise as the guests occupied themselves with cornhole, bratwursts, and speculation about the wedding.

There was much debate over whether the governor would attend and use the event to position Mackinac as a leader in foreign relations, what with the groom's international status.

Clyde didn't wrap his arm around Eloise's waist the way Gus used to. He stroked her back instead, gentle calligraphy motions like he was writing her a note.

"You bet we are." She kissed him on the lips.

Clyde beamed. "I thought you didn't like PDA."

"I didn't think I did either," Eloise said. "But turns out there's a lot I never knew about myself. In meeting you, I've met me too."

"You can't say poetic phrases like that and not agree to cowrite a book with me," Clyde said.

Eloise felt the pride of it, being tapped for something so grand. All the potential she'd never reached, now back on the table.

"Maybe someday. I'd say we have enough to focus on right now." Eloise looked around at the party, all her family and neighbors celebrating them. She still couldn't believe it.

She noted how Liam Townsend had his gaze on her mother, though Alice had her back turned away from him. Eloise wondered if there might be a speck of truth in what Georgiana had said, that perhaps Liam might want more. Was it possible Alice did too? Everything felt on the table after the summer Eloise had just had. She would broach the topic with her mother soon.

Notably absent was Camille Welsh, who had been invited but declined due to "mayoral duties." Eloise guessed it was code for scrambling and stressing now that Georgiana had officially announced her entrance into the race earlier today. It would take more than some photoshopped flyers for Camille to compete with Eloise's force-of-nature daughter.

Eloise was a proud mother. And she was more than that. She was an ex-wife, a title that had come with more peace than pain. And she was now a fiancée, as absurd as that was. She loved how elegant it sounded, how optimistic it felt.

"I came to Mackinac Island for a book," Clyde said. "And I'm returning with a bride."

"A very productive business trip, I'd say."

Eloise still had no idea how she was going to leave her beloved island behind for half the year. She loved how cozy Mackinac was in winter, all draped in snow. And be away from her mother and friends for so long, and Georgiana too, now that she was staying. It was a thought she stowed away, something to revisit later once the celebrations quieted down.

For now, she let herself get swept up in it—the mystery, the mastery, the mythical. She kissed him once more, longer this time. The crowd roared.

Chapter 48

Gigi

At the beginning of summer, Eloise and Clyde had been strangers. Now they were life partners.

The difference a few months could make was astonishing.

The same went for Gigi and Eloise. Gigi was at an engagement party for her mother and had baked a carrot cake from scratch for the occasion. If someone had told her this would happen when she was on the ferry ride back to Mackinac in June, she would have denounced it as ludicrous.

And yet, despite the rapid changes, the pace had felt unhurried. One of the mysteries of island time.

Gigi watched as Eloise and Clyde waltzed together under the back porch lights that Clyde had climbed up on a ladder to replace. (Gigi had to admit it was nice to have a man around to help her mom with those things, as stereotypically gender normative as it felt.) Music sifted out from speakers Gigi herself had set up.

Half the island was packed into the backyard of Thistle Dew, soaking in the late-summer evening. Fireflies blinked, lighting up the scene like lanterns.

Gigi and Rebecca were getting a few minutes to themselves, sitting around the small bonfire.

It was the first time Eloise had permitted the firepit to be used in many years. There were three pitchers of water and a hose next to it, but still, it felt like progress. A sign Eloise wasn't so scared anymore of things burning down.

Tom had a work conference, but Rebecca had driven the three hours herself, her longest drive ever. Gigi was a proud sister.

"I'm sorry I ever judged you for cooking," Gigi said as they ate her carrot cake. It hadn't risen much, but she'd slathered it in many inches of cream cheese frosting to mask the blunder. "It's actually very rewarding."

Rebecca grinned. "You're telling me that being a woman who enjoys the kitchen isn't a flagrant denunciation of female empowerment, but is actually an embodiment of what true feminism should be, the freedom for every woman to make her own choice?"

Gigi was impressed. "You sure you don't want to do a PhD? That was pretty good."

"Maybe down the line, but I'm very happy being your campaign manager for now. Your mayor announcement is going viral."

They both checked their phones. Gigi's short video was making the rounds online. Seven hundred thousand views and counting. It had only posted eight hours ago. She'd filmed it at the Grand Hotel stables, with the horses behind her. The social media world seemed riveted by this peculiar horse-and-buggy island and the young woman who was trying to run the town she'd once run away from.

"You edited and posted the video," Gigi said. "I just rambled and ranted like I do best."

"Team effort." Rebecca grinned. "No cold feet now that you've announced it to the world?"

"Warm feet," Gigi said, toes curled up by the bonfire. "Very warm."

Rebecca excused herself to check on the food supply and see if anything needed refilling.

Gigi spotted Lillian making the rounds to say her goodbyes. She was headed back to Chicago tomorrow. There seemed to be a few whispers and stares, but between the astonishment at Eloise Jenkins getting *married* and Georgiana Jenkins running for *mayor*, the news cycle seemed to have hurried past Lillian's own updates. Gigi took this relative disinterest as a good sign that Mackinac might be ready for a new era of leadership.

Lillian came over and joined Gigi at the bonfire for their good-bye. Gigi was roasting a marshmallow, patiently waiting for it to turn golden brown.

"I thought you liked your marshmallows burned to a crisp." Lillian sat down next to her. She smelled like lilacs. It mixed well with the bonfire smoke.

"Not anymore. Charcoal doesn't taste as good as it used to."

Lillian put a marshmallow on a roasting stick and positioned it next to Gigi's, in the same pocket of embers that was protected from the flames. "I'm glad we got this summer together."

"Me too. But it's good you're leaving," Gigi said, though she was sad to see Lillian go. They had just started getting close again. "Before the tide sucks you back in like it did to me."

"The tide didn't suck you in," Lillian said. "You sucked the tide in."

Gigi liked that. She thought again about how she'd been a bad friend for all those years. It didn't seem like Lillian held that against her, but Gigi still held it against herself.

"I'm sorry for how I acted when we were younger," Gigi said. "Shutting you out overnight and everything. That was the summer my dad came back—well, one of the summers. And I got my period and had all those teenage insecurities. I'm not trying to make excuses. I'm trying to apologize." She kept her eyes on the embers.

"You don't need to apologize," Lillian said.

"I do, though." Gigi wanted to clear space for the future. Not by avoiding the past, but by acknowledging it. "I never should've pushed you away." Gigi lifted her eyes to meet Lillian's.

"Then don't do it again," Lillian said.

"I promise," Gigi said. Promises didn't feel as flimsy as they used to. This one at least felt strong.

"If you ever want to come stay with me in Chicago, there's plenty of room in my apartment. I'd be happy to have the company."

Gigi sensed Lillian's nerves and excitement at what her life would be like on the other side of tomorrow's ferry ride.

"I might take you up on that if I lose the election." Gigi took her marshmallow from the fire and ate it whole. "No way I can live on an island that's literally voted me off."

"You're not going to lose," Lillian said. "And if you do, the islanders don't deserve you anyway."

Gigi grinned. "That's true."

From her pocket, Lillian withdrew a string of beads. Gigi recognized it right away. It was the old friendship bracelet she'd made with Lillian all those years ago. The colors had faded but the elastic seemed strong as ever.

Lillian dropped it into Gigi's hand, the one that wasn't sticky with marshmallow. "Keep it. A little souvenir from summer."

Gigi couldn't believe Lillian still had it. She had thrown hers out long ago. Wriggling her wrist into it, Gigi put it on. "Still fits."

"Good," Lillian said. "Now go talk to James. He can't take his eyes off you."

Gigi hugged Lillian, then hopped over to do just that.

———— ≈ ————

"I thought you said those mayor rumors weren't true," James said as Gigi approached him by the dessert table. She was happy to see he was eating a slice of her cake.

Dressed in beige linen to fit the English tea party theme (Nonni lumped England and Scotland together), he looked like a model hired by a magazine doing a spread on island chic summertime style. If he had dressed like *this* for their first date, Gigi might not have been able to deny her mother's matchmaking prowess so readily.

"All my patients could talk about today was your campaign launch video," James went on. "They say it's gone viral."

"It has, thanks to Rebecca," Gigi said. Sharing the credit made her feel bigger rather than smaller. The sensation was a strange one, though good. "This is just the start."

James asked what changed Gigi's mind. She told him how she craved having an outsized impact in a small town rather than an undersized impact—or none at all—in a big one. James said he related, that this was what he liked about being a doctor on the island too.

What Gigi didn't say was how much his words meant to her—about the impact she had already made—but that was just as well. It was too sappy for friendship territory.

"Are you excited to get back to Detroit?" Gigi asked.

They had been texting a little since their lake swim but hadn't seen each other again.

"Not really," James said. "Especially now that I know you're staying on Mackinac."

"At least through the election," Gigi said. "Then we'll see."

She thought about what Rebecca said about how sometimes people needed to know they were wanted.

"Have you thought of doing a trial run to see how you'd like taking over the clinic? Fred could take an extended vacation but still help out here and there."

She liked the prospect of having more time with James to explore if there might be something there. Something beyond end-of-summer emotions that were always a little inflated.

"I actually have thought about it," James said slowly. "But I think I'd still feel guilty being far away from my dad. He's all by himself. I want to make more of an effort to be there for him."

"Maybe he could come visit for the fall," Gigi said. "The foliage is really something. And you could reevaluate how it's going sometime before winter sets in. November 11, for example."

Chapter 49

Lillian

Free fudge flights at May's Candy Shop. Bootscooters line dancing on Market Street. A fudge treasure hunt put on by the tourism bureau and a "guess the flavor" contest at Murdick's. Day-trippers clad in fanny packs with melted chocolate dribbling from their chins.

The Mackinac Island Fudge Festival was kicking off. It was all too much for Lillian. She was ready for Chicago again. She didn't have a new job lined up, but she wanted to get back to her apartment and see what it felt like now that it was just hers. She wanted to catch up with her friends and hopefully with Alex too. She wanted to feel the urban buzz and walk along the Great Lakes from their southern shores rather than their northern ones. She wanted to find out what it felt like to live in the city now that her identity didn't feel so split.

Lillian said goodbye to her parents at the Pink Pony the morning after Eloise's engagement party.

"Can't you stay one more day?" her dad asked. "We're short on staff again."

Lillian wavered. It meant a lot that her dad was asking her to stay, even if it was in his own gruff way. Trina stepped in and said she'd better go before the swell of crowds from the festival worsened. "Call me when you're back in the city," Trina said. "Maybe I could visit for a long weekend this fall."

Lillian was glad that Trina seemed to want in on Lillian's life. There was no promise on how things would evolve, but she was leaving the island with as much hope as she was fudge (she had a bulging tote bag of Mackinac sweets to dole out to her friends).

Lillian patted her father's shoulder in goodbye, hugged her mother, then made her way to the ferry, Birkenstocks skidding across the dock.

She settled into a seat on the bottom deck of the boat, leaning her head against the smeared window, and stared out at the island as it grew smaller and smaller, moated by blue once more. The Mackinac Bridge hung like a paper chain, the kind of thing Lillian had made in elementary school that her parents still kept, tucked away in a neatly organized closet.

A chatty tourist sat next to her, a frizzy-haired woman with a young girl. "Was this your first time on the island?" the woman wanted to know.

Lillian told her no, that she'd grown up on Mackinac.

The woman was enthralled. "How lucky you are! What an idyllic childhood that must have been."

"It sort of was," Lillian said. "And sort of wasn't."

"What do you think of that young lady running for mayor?" the woman asked. "Ginny Johnson, is it? She's gone viral overnight, hasn't she?"

"Gigi Jenkins," Lillian said, the name skipping off her lips. "We grew up together."

Again, the woman was rapt. "Do you think she'd actually be a competent leader? Or is she all smoke and mirrors?"

"I know she'll be great." Lillian felt their farewell hug still on her body like a promise that what was lost might be found again.

"Well, she certainly has charisma, I'll give her that," the woman said. "Seems a bit *much*, though, if I'm being honest."

"Oh, she is," Lillian said, not sure if she was talking about Gigi or about Mackinac or even about her own reflection staring back at her in the smudged ferry boat window. Not sure if the distinction even mattered anymore, or if the lack of partition was more important, the undrawing of boundaries, the letting go of labels. "That's why I love her."

Chapter 50

Alice

G eorgiana was a natural on the campaign stage, there was no denying it.

It shouldn't have surprised Alice, given how her granddaughter's entire life had been an exercise in tossing out inflammatory statements and watching them detonate. The difference now was that there was a real purpose behind them.

One of those purposes was to dethrone Camille once and for all.

It served her right, what with how she'd treated Liam. Running over his heart with the tires of that ridiculously fancy bicycle of hers. Swapping him out for a new man Camille was parading all around town.

Though Alice wasn't sure she herself was treating Liam much better, with the cold shoulder she'd been giving him since he tried to push the boundaries on their friendship.

They said hello at church and played pickleball a couple times, but he had started asking Maureen Slack to be his partner instead. Maureen was a widow and very pretty, fifteen years their junior. It infuriated Alice, not that she could do anything about it. She was the one who had pushed him away.

"That's my granddaughter," Alice told spectators as Georgiana gave an impromptu stump speech on the steps of City Hall.

It was the second day of the Fudge Festival. Georgiana had captured a large audience. Many people were holding up their phones to record the speech, or at least that was what Alice supposed they were doing. She felt protective over her granddaughter's privacy, though she figured she shouldn't, given how many videos Georgiana herself posted online each day. Alice had never believed in the internet but found herself too curious to stay away now. Just yesterday she'd let Georgiana make her one of those social media accounts so she could follow along. It was all very foreign, but exciting too.

"She's a natural, isn't she?" Eloise said. "She's got the audience in the palm of her hand."

"A true performer," Clyde admired from Eloise's side. "She's an artist at her core."

"I suppose she is."

Georgiana was pitching for campaign donations, passing around one of Clyde's hats as a collection bucket. Even fudgies, with no personal investment in the island, were stuffing the hat with bills.

"I ran away from this island when I was eighteen," Georgiana said, her voice projecting far and wide. "And now I'm back to fix the problems that made me want to leave in the first place. I'm an insider in blood, an outsider in perspective." The crowd went wild.

"We'll start an organic community garden!" Gigi went on. "And take our seniors out dancing! And make electric scooters legal! And put in a dispensary on Main Street!"

Alice wasn't sure whether to cover her ears or clap harder. She did a little of both.

Georgiana could get carried away, that was true, but she would be fair and kind and advocate for this community the way no one else would.

"What did you think?" Georgiana asked, approaching Alice and Eloise afterward. Her eyes were blazing, energy coursing. Alice wanted to borrow it, bottle it.

"Captivating," Alice said. "Absolutely captivating. Your pop would be so proud."

"The governor had better watch out," Eloise said, hugging Georgiana. The movements between them had relaxed over the summer, and Alice was glad to see it. "You'll be taking that job soon enough."

"Why stop there?" Clyde said. "Georgiana for president."

"I'll be the first one without a high school diploma," Georgiana said happily.

Dr. Kentwood appeared at Gigi's side. "It's sorcery, what you do," he said. "Everyone was entranced."

Georgiana insisted they were just friends, but Alice had her doubts. Either way, she was glad to see her granddaughter getting out of her own way to give a good person a good chance, whether for friendship or something more.

"Were *you* entranced?" Gigi asked.

"Guilty as charged." Dr. Kentwood really was a charmer, but without any of the ego that typically came with it.

"Good," Gigi said. "I'm channeling spirits from the witches who were drowned in the lagoon."

Alice could never tell if Georgiana was joking when she said things like this. She prayed she was.

"Twelve thousand dollars in online donations plus three hundred forty-three dollars in cash," Georgiana said, tallying everything up. "Dinner's on me."

"You do realize my job is to manage budgets, don't you?" Eloise said. "And watch for fraud?"

"That's only half your job. The other half is being my adoring mother who oversees all of my flaws because you created me and love me eternally."

"How did I get so lucky?" Eloise said dryly. She mussed Georgiana's hair. The strawberry roots were growing out, the bleach fading. The natural coloring suited Georgiana far better.

"Meet back at the house in an hour," Eloise told Georgiana. "There's something we want to show you. It's from your dad."

Alice smiled. She was excited about this one. She'd been with Eloise when Gus had called about it. She'd heard the cordiality in their voices, the careful peace. Gus still wasn't pulling his weight when it came to being there for the girls. But this gift, it was a big one.

"I don't want Dad's money," Georgiana said. "I'm making it on my own."

"It's not money," Eloise said. "Come back to Thistle Dew after you're finished signing autographs."

"Might be a few hours," Georgiana joked as she and James walked off together.

Clyde stepped aside to talk to a fudgie who was telling a ghost story about the fort.

"They look good together," Alice observed, watching Georgiana and James.

"They *are* good together," Eloise said. "I knew they would be."

"I did too." Alice had been the one to butter up James with flattering stories of Georgiana before their first date. Some of the stories had been embellished, if not fabricated altogether, but that was beside the point.

"I just wish James was staying past summer," Eloise said. "I don't want to see Georgiana get hurt."

"I know the feeling." Alice still wasn't sure how Eloise was going to manage splitting time between Mackinac and Scotland. She was someone who loved to feel deeply rooted. But Alice didn't think it was her place to say anything. She was trying harder not to meddle. Besides, it would be good for Eloise to get out and see the world, though half the year abroad did feel extreme.

"I really feel like we've gotten Georgiana back this summer," Eloise said, her complexion bright and rosy.

"I don't know if we got her back. I think we just realized she never actually left."

"How are you always so wise, Mother?"

Alice was not *always* so wise, of course, but Eloise didn't need to know all the dirt. "There have to be some perks of aging to outweigh the failing eyesight and incontinence," was all she said.

"You're getting better with each passing year," Eloise said, "Liam Townsend clearly thinks so."

Alice felt her body quiver. "Liam Townsend is an old friend. Nothing more and nothing less."

They made their way down Market Street for the Fudge Festival Art Walk. The galleries and shops had their doors flung open, canvases spilling onto the sidewalk.

"I don't want you not pursuing someone because of me," Eloise said. "If Gigi can support me being with someone new when her dad is still alive, I should certainly be able to handle you being with someone other than Dad. It's been seven years now."

Alice wondered if Eloise would still feel this way if she knew about the affair. She doubted it.

"No one could ever replace your father," Alice said.

"I know that. But what I'm learning is that letting new people in is more about addition than subtraction."

Leave it to Eloise to make everything a math problem.

"There's nothing between Mr. Townsend and me," Alice said, feeling parts of herself splinter as she said it. "But I appreciate your approval, hypothetically speaking."

Chapter 51

Gigi

A creamy Norwegian Fjord was grazing in the front yard of Thistle Dew. Majestic and tall, she stood like a queen. Her tail swooshed playfully, swatting gnats and flies, or maybe just dancing along to a self-made melody.

"Who's this?" Gigi asked when she got home.

"It's your present from Dad," Eloise said. "He said a mayor needs a horse, that a bicycle won't do."

Gigi stared, trying to take it all in. "What's the catch?"

"No catch," Eloise said. "I think it's his way of trying to say sorry."

"Sorry for walking out on us in the first place or for leaving this summer without telling me goodbye?" Gigi asked.

"Your guess is as good as mine."

Gigi let the resentment pass, or at least budge.

Her dad might find a way to use it against her if she kept the horse. Tell her that she owed him, maybe even ask for money down the line to square up. But he also might hold it against her if she didn't keep the horse. He could say she was trying to be difficult and couldn't accept a simple apology. Either way, this horse was going to come with strings attached. She might as well keep the horse along with the strings.

"I'll call you Noelle," she said to the horse, stroking her mane, dropping kisses like confetti. "Because it feels like Santa came in summer."

"You should give your dad a call," Eloise said. "Thank him."

"I will later. I want to take Noelle for a ride first."

Gigi hopped on the saddle and went to fetch James and Willow.

———— ≈ ————

They trotted side by side through secluded stretches of the lakeshore trail. Though the track was circular, it felt open-ended to Gigi, the way nothing had in a long, long time.

"Now you can give me riding lessons," James said. "I need them."

"Just in time for you to leave." Gigi was trying not to sound sad.

"I wanted to talk to you about that," James said. "But I didn't want to distract from your campaigning."

"Distract me all you want." She found she was having a hard time trying not to flirt.

"Dr. Moore and I agreed to do a trial run this fall," James said. "He'll scale back and I'll stay on. We'll see how it goes and I'll decide if I want to formally take over the clinic after that."

Today felt eerily good, what with how her campaign speech had gone and then the horse from her dad and now this. She wanted to trust the happiness but found she could only test it. Like having a tiny nibble of pie to see if it had pistachio before taking a real bite.

"You're serious?" Gigi said.

"I know you said you didn't want to make any decisions until November," James said. "But I would like to propose we move up the date in light of this new information."

Gigi wanted to agree with him straightaway. But there was a reason she had decided to wait, and she was going to stick to it. It would take more than a handsome doctor on horseback for her to slide back into past patterns. Though she was awfully tempted.

"I'll consider your request," she said, grinning over at him. "And get back to you soon."

———— ≈ ————

Gigi left a voicemail for her dad later that day.

He texted back while Gigi was brushing Noelle, ensuring her coat was free of fleas.

Might not have gotten you that pony for your 10th b-day
but hope this makes up for it . . . and for everything.

It wasn't an apology, but it was as close as he was going to come. Gigi was inclined to accept it. Keeping score of rights and wrongs felt too rigid these days.

"Thanks, Mom," she said to Eloise when she finally came inside, reeking of horse.

"There's nothing to thank me for," Eloise said, taking out a fresh tray of peanut brittle.

"Except the free rent, food, and laundry all summer. And for setting me up with a guy who turned out to be pretty great after all."

Eloise's face folded like origami. "Well, yes, I suppose there's that."

She didn't even scold Gigi for diving into the peanut brittle before it had cooled. She just broke off a piece herself.

When Gigi pattered up the stairs to the loft that night, her twin bed felt much bigger than it had when she'd first arrived for summer. Like she could straighten her legs and kick and not even touch the edge.

Chapter 52

Rebecca

"There were sounds coming from Mom's bedroom this morning, Rebecca," Gigi said, just about gagging over the phone. "Sounds I'll need to rehire my therapist to forget."

Rebecca found this rather alarming as well, but she couldn't help but be a little impressed. "Isn't it inspiring to know that passion can come at any age?"

"No, I would not say that listening to our mother get railed by her fiancé is *inspiring*. Now that they're engaged, she finds it appropriate for Clyde to stay over. As if he doesn't have an entire suite at the Grand that they can shack up in. But she says she likes seeing him integrated into her everyday life, whatever that means."

"She really has loosened up this summer." Rebecca wondered if things would have happened this way if she were still on the island. She had a sense that her mother had benefited from some space from her. It didn't hurt her as much as she'd expected it to. She, too, was valuing a little distance.

"Mom told me that when I'm engaged, I can share a room with my partner," Gigi went on. "Rather than saying I have to be married, like she always used to. She's probably just changing the rules because she realizes it'll never happen."

"Never say never," Rebecca said. "Things sound like they're getting pretty good with James."

"We're just friends," Gigi clarified quickly. "I've told you."

"I thought things might've changed now that he's staying."

"Nothing's changed." A beat passed. "I do want to give it a try with him," Gigi went on. "I'm just scared."

"Since when have you let that hold you back? The best thing about you is how you go for what you want."

"But I don't usually want things this badly. The mayor position, James . . ."

Rebecca appreciated the way her sister seemed to be taking things more seriously without losing her spunk. "It'll work out," she said, knowing better than to push too far. "So tell me about this horse Dad got you." She couldn't remember the last time he had even sent Rebecca a birthday card.

"It was just a gift for my campaign," Gigi said, downplaying it, though Rebecca couldn't help but feel it was more than that, that it was cold, hard proof that Gus chose Gigi as his favorite daughter. A prior version of Rebecca would have held this against Gigi, but now she only felt inclined to hold it against her dad. Not like a weapon, but a boundary. He would need to try harder if he decided he wanted back into her life.

"But we can share Noelle when you visit," Gigi went on. "You deserve her more than I do for all the work you're doing to launch me to global stardom. I just give good speeches; you're the one who makes me go viral."

"I do have a knack for it," Rebecca said, enjoying the newfound purpose Gigi's campaign had given her.

From the comfort of her couch, Rebecca edited clips of Gigi's campaign rallies. In a matter of weeks, she had turned her sister into one of the most recognizable names in local politics. Rebecca's best idea had been to include the link for donations in every video. Total funding for the campaign was now over one hundred thousand dollars. The figure made Rebecca stagger.

"I'll use the money we've raised to rent a house on the island," Gigi said. "My very own mayor's mansion."

"Unfortunately, campaign finance laws don't work like that," Rebecca said. "But we could put the fundraising money toward a local TV and radio push."

"Old media is dead," Gigi said. "I want to keep making viral videos for social. Cause a real scene."

"I think you've already done that," Rebecca said. "You've brought more attention to Mackinac than anything since the governor's attempted kidnapping."

"Soon we'll have surpassed that news story too. Has your campaign manager paycheck arrived?"

"It's a volunteer position," Rebecca said. "I'm under no illusions."

"Who would I be if I exploited my sister now that I'm loaded? I'm paying you a salary. It's well within the rules. I researched it, or at least I had Mom research it. Go check the mail."

Rebecca slipped on her loafers and walked out onto the driveway. It was a muggy August day. Kaley, the wife next door, was outside watering the flower beds. Rebecca braced herself for an icy interaction, but Kaley smiled and flagged her down.

Rebecca told Gigi she'd call her right back.

"I just wanted to apologize," Kaley said. Her voice had a Southern drawl, and her hair hung in perfect ringlets. "I realize we haven't been the most neighborly since you've moved in. Caught up in our own little world, I suppose."

"That's all right," Rebecca said. "We're still acclimating. I'm from a very small town, so Traverse City has been a little overwhelming."

"I get that," Kaley said. "I grew up in rural Georgia. How 'bout you?"

"Mackinac Island," Rebecca said. "Up north."

"I've seen that place on social media!" Kaley exclaimed. "Videos of that spitfire of a gal running for mayor have been going viral."

"That's my sister," Rebecca said, feeling more proud than embarrassed, which was quite the change.

Kaley nearly sprang out from the flower beds. "Well, how about that. We'll have to visit the island one of these days. And what're you and your husband up to this Friday? We're hosting a little end-of-summer gathering. You'll come, won't you?"

Rebecca tried to play it cool, though she was doing cartwheels inside. "That sounds great. What can I bring?"

"Just some ghost stories to share around the bonfire."

"Can do," Rebecca said. "Mackinac has a lot of those."

Feeling oodles lighter, she went back inside and opened two envelopes she'd retrieved from the mail.

The first was from Clyde, a handwritten card.

You don't need to think of me as your father, of course. But I might not be able to keep from thinking of you as my daughter. I love you, Rebecca. Thank you for sharing your mother with me.

Rebecca reread the card three times, tearing up—whether from the pregnancy or the poignancy, she wasn't sure. All she knew was a growing family was a good thing. She would never turn down love from someone who thought of her as his daughter. Tacking the card on the refrigerator, she couldn't wait to show it to Tom when he got home.

The second envelope was from Gigi. It held a check for five thousand dollars. "It's too much money," she told Gigi when she called back.

"You've earned it," Gigi said, and Rebecca felt a rush of independence at having her own income stream, separate from Tom's. "Use it to furnish the nursery. Nothing pink, though. I'm still recovering from all the bubblegum and Barbie programming from childhood."

Rebecca smirked. "Tom and I will pick the colors," she said. "You can pick the name."

"You're not serious," Gigi said.

"Dead serious. Neither of us wants the responsibility of our child not liking their name and blaming us. They can hold it against their crazy aunt Gigi instead."

Gigi was delighted. "I'll find the perfect name," she assured her. "Just watch."

"We do retain veto power, though." Rebecca lifted the blinds in the house so the neighbors weren't blocked anymore. "I'm going to get back to work on these campaign videos. Keep up the momentum."

"I liked that filter you put on me last time," Gigi said. "My skin looked like it was glowing."

"I didn't use a filter. You're just naturally radiant. Couldn't be because you're in love, could it?"

"Of course not," Gigi snapped. "It's because I'm stepping into my own as a nearly thirty-year-old woman assuming a leadership position over an entire island."

"Right." Rebecca smiled and patted her stomach. "My mistake."

Chapter 53

Deidre

"I guess sometimes the cliché is true and you do *just know*," Eloise said to Deirdre one late-August evening.

They were setting up for euchre, waiting on Kitty and Paula.

"Like with my parents, and now with Clyde and me. With Gus, there was always some uncertainty, even from the start."

Deirdre fluffed a pillow and rearranged the cheese platter. She was trying not to intervene, but the secret was tapping on her chest.

"Every marriage has its own set of challenges," Deidre said. "For example, how Fred keeps telling me he's going to retire but doesn't. Though, good news, he agreed to test out the transition this fall with Dr. Kentwood, bless his soul."

"I did hear something about that," Eloise said coyly.

Deirdre could tell Eloise was trying not to say too much about Georgiana's "friendship" with Dr. Kentwood. It was a disappointing regression this summer. They used to have such fun analyzing Georgiana's every move. Part of the joy, after all, of having a daughter was getting to gossip. Many mothers weren't so lucky.

"I never really understood how my dad knew he was going to marry my mom within a few weeks of meeting her," Eloise said. "But it makes more sense now."

Deirdre poured herself a brandy. It wasn't healthy, Deirdre thought, to go into an engagement with such an idealistic view. Especially when Eloise and Clyde didn't know each other that well.

"That's all very nice," Deirdre said. "But like I said, all marriages have their challenges."

"What's that supposed to mean?" Eloise said. "Deirdre, do you have concerns about Clyde and me?"

"It's not that," Deirdre said, treading cautiously. "I've just never heard you wanting to move off the island before. You love Mackinac more than life itself."

"Love requires compromises," Eloise said, though Deirdre detected a waver. "And it'll be my chance to stretch out of my comfort zone and see the world."

"It certainly sounds exciting." Deirdre felt that she would enjoy Scotland a lot more than Eloise, who would likely be holed up with books and crosswords and quilts.

Deirdre decided she would let the secret drop. But if Eloise brought up her parents' marriage one more time, she simply wouldn't be able to hold it in any longer.

"We're thinking a summer wedding on the island next June," Eloise went on, thumbing her engagement ring. "I won't wear a proper wedding dress—that would look silly at my age. I think I'll wear a sundress, probably with a nice shawl, though maybe I'll live on the edge and go without. Georgiana's gotten me to be more daring about my shoulders." She laughed breezily. Deirdre noted enviously how this summer had aged Eloise in reverse. "And I'll borrow my mother's wedding pearls for good luck."

Deirdre was beside herself. "For good luck," Deirdre said. "That's a very nice thought."

She topped off her brandy and fanned her blouse. The heat of summer had broken, but she felt very sweaty.

"Deirdre, what's going on?" Eloise said. "You're acting strange. If you don't approve of my engagement, just say it. Please. I value your opinion. I know you only ever want what's best for me."

Deirdre did not think that was entirely true in the past, but it was true now. She really did want to see Eloise happy with Clyde. It helped her believe in second chances. Not that she was thinking of leaving Fred, of course not. But there was another area of life where she would like another chance . . .

She tossed those thoughts aside. That secret was hers and hers alone. But the one she was bringing up now—well, that one belonged to Alice. Deirdre didn't really have any right to it. But Eloise deserved to know the truth.

"It's not any concern I have about Clyde," Deirdre said. "It's just that I don't want you idealizing anyone's marriage too much when you're about to embark on your own."

"Whose marriage am I idealizing?"

"Your parents'."

Eloise was as defensive as Deirdre had expected. "My parents had a beautiful marriage."

"They did. A long, beautiful marriage. But not a perfect one."

"Well, no marriage is perfect," Eloise said. "But theirs was as close as it could come. Such fidelity, such commitment."

Deirdre sat on the couch, steadied herself. "There's something I need to tell you, Eloise." She felt awful and nervous.

"Deirdre, what's going on?"

She sat on the couch beside Eloise and took her best friend's hands in her own. Eloise's skin wasn't quite as soft as Deirdre's. Deirdre wanted to credit her expensive hand lotion, though she suspected that having a husband around to help with all the everyday labor was more likely to credit. She felt for Eloise and how she had done so much of life alone. She didn't want anyone to leave her friend again. If revealing this information might help remove Eloise's blinders, might help avoid another divorce, then so be it.

"As you know, my uncle is Liam Townsend," Deidre said.

"That's right. And I know my mother probably slept with him before marrying my father."

"It's not just that . . ." Deirdre almost stopped herself, but she carried on out of a sense of duty that she hoped wasn't misplaced. "My uncle told me about a time in the early eighties, when your parents were married, when the feelings were reciprocated."

She watched Eloise's face tense, her posture pinch. "Go on," Eloise said.

Chapter 54

Eloise

Eloise felt like she was going to pass out in Deirdre's living room. Everything was spinning, and not in the romantic way she'd felt since the engagement. This was the kind of spinning that tipped things over, knocked them down.

In a haze, she marched over to Alice's house, the cabin her father had built log by log all those years ago.

"Is it true?" Eloise asked, letting herself in. Alice was sitting at the table, snacking on carrots while squinting down at a pile of bills. "You slept with Liam while you were married to Dad?"

At the way Alice's head fell into her hands, Eloise's fears were confirmed.

Turning on her heels, she bolted out of the house as quickly as she could.

"Eloise," she heard her mother call out after her. "Please let me explain."

But Eloise didn't want explanations. She didn't want to listen. She wanted to yell, to shriek.

With all the fluctuations over the years—Gus coming in and out, Georgiana rebelling, Rebecca getting married and moving away—Eloise's parents had been the one steady fixture. Not just how they loved her, but how they loved each other. It gave Eloise a model of something she hadn't been able to build for herself but still knew existed, knew was possible.

Now suddenly she wasn't so sure.

Chapter 55

Alice

A lice should have suspected Deirdre knew.

She'd trusted Liam never to breathe a word about their affair, but if anyone could pry out information, it was Deirdre Moore.

Deidre had been jealous of Eloise ever since they were kids. She'd always been looking for something to hold over her. And now she'd found it.

But Alice wasn't going to wither. She wasn't going to be made to feel like some despicable person. She had paid her penance privately for long enough. And she had truly been a devoted wife to David in the years that followed, all the way up to his death.

"How dare you." Alice confronted Deidre the next morning when she ran into her on her walk to the cemetery. She couldn't help but note that Eloise wasn't with her, despite how she and Deidre walked together every morning. Perhaps Eloise was icing her out as well. "How dare you spill information that's not yours to share."

"I wasn't trying to cause a family rift," Deidre said. "I was worried about how Eloise kept putting your marriage on a pedestal. I was trying to show her that relationships are nuanced, that's all."

"Very big of you," Alice said. "Where would this island be without Deirdre Moore here to point out the nuance of it all?"

"I'm sorry, Alice," Deirdre said. "I really am." She looked very tired, not her usual put-together self.

"You will be. You'll lose Eloise's friendship from this, just watch. This whole thing will backfire in your face."

Deirdre winced like Alice had thrown a punch. It didn't make Alice feel as good as she'd hoped.

"You have such a beautiful family," Deirdre said meekly. "Nothing can take that away."

"Except that it can," Alice said. "I lost David too young, I'm losing Eloise to Scotland, and who knows where my granddaughters will end up. And I've lost Liam too, because I still feel that damn guilt every time I so much as make eye contact with him."

Saying it all out loud made Alice realize this had been building up over the years, and especially over this summer. And now that her secret was out, it was all coming to the surface, stirring up the waves she'd tried to tame. She was in her late seventies, the prime of life well behind her, and she was headed into her final chapter all alone.

"And we lost our daughter," Alice carried on, unable to stop up the dam now that it had blown open. "We lost little Penelope."

This was the wound that hadn't closed at all, even though the grave had so very long ago. Somehow every hurt always traced back to this one.

Deirdre offered Alice a tissue. Alice accepted it reluctantly, dabbing her eyes and her nose.

"I know how you feel," Deirdre said.

"No." Alice's anger boiled. The audacity of Deirdre to even pretend. "You don't."

"Well, of course I don't know *exactly*." Deirdre dropped into silence, then reared up from it suddenly. "But I lost my daughter too."

Alice had no idea what Deirdre meant. Deidre had only had boys as far as Alice knew. But she could feel Deidre's emotions radiating off of her, not heat waves, but hurt waves. This was not the type of pain someone feigned for pity. It was very real, very deep, very dark.

"Please don't tell Eloise," Deirdre said.

And before Alice knew what was happening, the two women were holding each other as they cried out similar parts of different hearts.

Chapter 56

Deidre

Deirdre didn't know what had come over her to spill her final secret—the biggest of them all—to Alice of all people.

She would like to put it down to the guilt she felt over how Eloise had taken the news about the affair, but she knew it was more than that.

The secret had been weighing on Deirdre for so long. Her mother and aunt had been the only ones who knew, and they were both dead now. Deirde had never even told the baby's father, not that he deserved it, that sweet-talking cheat.

For a while now, the secret had been begging to be shared, and with someone who might understand. And although Alice and Deirdre had lost their daughters very differently—one to death, one to adoption—an intimate connection had been made between them.

Though it should have been Fred she talked with first.

Many times Deirdre had meant to tell him about how she'd gotten pregnant the fall of her freshman year and gone away to her aunt's house in Iowa and put the baby girl up for adoption and then returned to college the next school year like nothing happened.

But she hadn't wanted Fred to see her differently or judge her for her checkered past. So she had decided to wait until their marriage was on solid footing before revealing the news. Then that time had come and gone and suddenly it felt like she had passed the point of no return. To tell him so many decades into their marriage would be to admit she had been keeping it from him all these years.

But she would have to tell him now. She couldn't have Alice knowing about her daughter and not her own husband.

Deidre hoped Fred would understand, hoped he could see how this was tied to everything. Why she was always talking about needing antidepressants and sleep meds. Why she wanted Fred to retire and spend more time with her so she didn't have to be alone with her thoughts.

Why she always got so triggered when Eloise talked up her girls. Why she always had a drink in her hand because that at least numbed the pain, though only for a moment. Why she was terrified of getting older because it might mean dying without ever getting to know her daughter.

Deirdre finished the loop of the walk she usually did with Eloise. Being alone with her thoughts wasn't quite as terrible today.

Deirdre had been so scared to share her secret. She had figured it would mean losing the intimacy of the one thing she had between her and Baby Lilac. But to her surprise, Deirdre found herself feeling closer to her daughter than ever before. Like telling someone else about her made Deirdre more of a mother.

She passed Camille, who was going door-to-door on her bicycle.

"Deirdre!" she said, approaching. "You're looking wonderful today."

Deirdre said a curt good morning. Like the other ladies, she was not very fond of the current mayor.

"Can I count on your vote this November?" Camille asked with a big, white smile. She handed Deirdre a new flyer, debuting the slogan "Preserve Mackinac's History." It was quite the contrast to Gigi's mantra: "Move Mackinac Forward."

Camille respected the convention of this island, the tradition. As exciting as Georgiana's campaign was, Deirdre could never vote for her. She was far too progressive, far too disruptive.

The island ladies judged Camille for her cosmetic work and her big hair and big boobs. She was very tacky, very fake. A Dolly Parton knockoff.

But Deirdre wondered how much of what people said about Camille might be a caricature. And though Deidre had long preferred caricatures to real people, she found herself changing her tune.

It took a lot to devote yourself to a town for as long as she had. Camille could go too far sometimes, but who didn't? And like everyone on this island, Camille Welsh was somebody's daughter.

"You've got my vote," Deirdre told her. "But don't tell anyone I told you that."

Camille gave a big smile and zipped her lips. "Your secret is safe with me."

Chapter 57

Eloise

Sunlight sloshing in, casting golden discs on the quilted bedspread. The scent of freshly baked pastries wafting up from the kitchens below. A breeze, nearly autumnal, fanning through the cracked widow. Clyde's hands massaging the base of her neck, ironing out the knots.

The Betty Ford suite in the Grand Hotel was starting to feel like Eloise's second home.

"Why couldn't this summer last forever?" Eloise said. The Fudge Festival was over. September was here and Clyde was leaving in just a few days. She would be joining him in October, giving herself a buffer to pack and plan.

The high season seemed to be toppling off a cliff. The news of her mother's affair had brought an abrupt end to the summer warmth.

The initial emotion may have passed, but the aftershocks kept coming. Eloise hadn't yet had a real conversation with Alice about it. She wasn't ready. She was focused on trying to make the most of these last days with Clyde. Hold on to her engagement bliss, make the bubble stretch a bit longer. Though it was proving difficult.

"Scarcity is what gives things meaning, isn't it?" Clyde said, wrapping Eloise in his arms. Her stomach still fluttered when he touched her. This sensation of being a teenager in love . . . How had it happened? How long could it stay? The rest of their lives, Clyde told her. It could stay that long.

Eloise's body was alert, pricked by pleasure. Some parts of sex got better with age. Less critiquing her flaws, less pressure to fake the orgasm. Not that faking anything was a concern right now . . . Clyde knew her body inside and out. She couldn't bear the thought of being away from him. Her trip to Scotland was still six weeks away.

"The time will fly by," Clyde said when Eloise voiced her concerns about being apart for so long. "Soon enough I'll make a proper Scotswoman out of you."

Eloise lifted a smile but couldn't hold it. Scotland felt so impossibly far away. Everything felt a little shaky, especially with the news she'd just learned. She didn't know if she could keep her family together an ocean away.

"It'll be okay, bonny Lou," Clyde said, tracing circles around her hip bones. "We have each other."

Eloise wanted to believe that their back-and-forth plan would be as simple in practice as it looked on paper. "Is that enough, though?"

"Of course it is," Clyde said. "Love conquers all. It's the truest aphorism of them all."

"But what if it's just that, an aphorism?" Eloise said. "A pithy cliché because the truth is too complicated?"

She thought of her parents. The visual didn't bring its usual reassurance, just more questions. Had her dad ever suspected? If he had known, would he have forgiven Alice?

Yes, Eloise felt. *He would have*. Still, it was just guesswork. She would never truly know.

Clyde got up and brought back a glass of water for Eloise. She took a sip, but it didn't change the parched feeling in her throat.

"I can't go," she heard herself say. "I can't leave the island. Not for six months of the year. It's too much. And I know you can't leave Scotland. It's where your audience knows you; it's where your home is."

"Let's see how it goes after you visit," Clyde said. "We'll take it one step at a time."

Eloise was committed to Clyde. She had the ring to prove it, and the travel itinerary too. So why did the walls feel like they were closing in on her?

She walked to the window, opened it wider, and took a breath of fresh air.

It wasn't just her fears that were flaring. Her hopes were too—hopes of cheering Georgiana on as she ran for mayor, hopes of getting more time with her mother while Alice was still healthy, hopes of visiting Rebecca in Traverse City and being there if and when their family expanded.

"I can't go," Eloise said again, looking out at the island unfolding before her in all its humble glory. "I'm sorry, Clyde. It's just not right for me."

He stood with her at the window, arms wrapped around her like a seat belt.

Eloise turned to face him head-on. "My family is my world. This island is too," she said, feeling the depth of a lifetime love, one so sturdy it had never let her down. "I just can't go, Clyde. I can't live away half the year and I can't ask you to come here full-time. We'd both be giving up too much."

"I don't see it as giving up things," Clyde said. "I see it as gaining."

"So you'd move here?" Eloise asked. "Permanently?"

Silence handed over the answer the way words never would.

The amethyst ring felt like it was cutting off the circulation in Eloise's finger. She took it off, held it in her hands for a moment, committing to memory the shape of it, the shine. "We can keep the door open," she said. "Reevaluate after some time apart."

Clyde sat down on the edge of the four-poster bed, his hands in his silver hair. "I don't think so." His voice was low and clunky. "I need to move on with you or move on from you. There's no in-between, not with us."

Eloise knew this was true, but her body still rejected it. She passed the ring back to Clyde. Reluctantly, he put it in his pocket.

"This summer," Clyde said, dabbing at his cornflower eyes. "This summer was perfect. Exactly where we were both supposed to be. I really thought our love was the one to last forever, but maybe that's what my books are for. To immortalize the things that don't stick. The lives I'll never get to live."

It was so poetic that Eloise felt tempted, just for a moment, to say she would go to Scotland after all. But her mind was set, as was her heart. "I feel like I've led you on."

"You're listening to your intuition," he said. "I have to respect that, even if I don't like the direction it's pointing."

"You can make me the villain in your novel," Eloise said. She put on the oversized robe from the hotel room closet, attempting to cover up all she'd bared to this man. "I deserve it."

"It would be an insult to my creativity to distort your personhood like that."

Eloise sat down next to him on the bedspread. "Why do you always say the perfect thing?"

"I'm good at endings," he said sadly. "I've written a lot of them. This one, though. It's different."

They held each other a long time, swayed in the suite to a song that wasn't playing, the echoes of the one they might have danced to at their wedding.

"How about one more carriage ride around the island?" Clyde said. Even in his aching state, Eloise found him enchanting. "End things on a high note?"

Eloise didn't know what that was like, having a proper goodbye, one with crisp lines. She wanted to find out.

"I'd like that," she said and went into the bathroom to get dressed. Just for today, she wanted to pretend she still had her Prince Charming. She wanted to pretend she wasn't the type of person to rip apart a fairy tale and tear it to shreds.

Chapter 58

Gigi

W hat do you mean the engagement is off?" Gigi shrieked when Eloise delivered the news that evening.

Gigi couldn't accept it. She wouldn't.

Dinner simmered on the stove. Pluto was lurking, eyes peeled for scraps. Outside, a summer thunderstorm brewed, thunder clapping.

Gigi had been caught out in the rain while on a trail ride with Noelle. Her breeches were splattered with mud; she'd been planning to shower before dinner. Those plans were now derailed, along with everything else.

"You can't just end things because you're scared," Gigi said.

This was her mother's fault. Just when she'd thought Eloise had actually changed for the better . . . here she was, back to her risk-averse, self-sabotaging habits.

"It's not because I'm scared."

Eloise added homegrown basil to the marinara sauce, carrying on as if nothing was wrong, nothing was broken. When that was all it was—wrong and broken and terrible.

"It's because I know what I want, and it's being on Mackinac year-round with you and Nonni," Eloise went on.

The way Eloise said Nonni's name was tense. Gigi knew something was going on between them but wasn't privy to the details. She figured Nonni might be encouraging Eloise to go to Scotland, to take the risk, and her mother was resisting.

"I might not even be here," Gigi said. "If I lose the election, I'll be on the first ferry out."

Gigi wasn't sure if she meant it, but she liked having the option. There were a lot of moving variables right now, but her mother's broken engagement was not supposed to be one of them.

"You're going to win," Eloise said. "But either way, I want to be closer to Rebecca. I can't be a good daughter or a good mother from Scotland. It's absurd."

"Rebecca and I are grown women," Gigi said. "And Nonni wouldn't want you giving this up because of her."

"I'm doing it for me. Why does everyone have such a hard time accepting that?"

Gigi held the image of Eloise and Clyde dancing at the engagement party. She refused to drop it. "Because we know how you feel about Clyde. It's meant to be."

"I love him," Eloise said simply. "But I love other things more. Other people more." She looked pointedly at Gigi.

Gigi felt the pressure behind her tear ducts, the tingling in her nose. "You're quitting," she accused. "You're quitting on him and you're quitting on yourself."

"This isn't your breakup, Georgiana," Eloise said. "It's mine."

Gigi had the sensation that her mother was stealing something that wasn't Gigi's to lose. But the loss still came.

"You're right," Gigi said. "It's not my breakup; I was just the one to set you two up. I was just starting to think I'd get to have Clyde in my life as a man I could count on to be there for me because my own dad isn't."

Gigi was getting hysterical and she didn't care. It felt like the rug had been ripped out from under her own happily-ever-after.

"Your father loves you very much. He'll always be there if you really need him."

"Just like he's always been there for you?"

Perhaps Gigi would have had more sympathy if her mother were sobbing or yelling or showing any evidence of distress at all. Instead, she spoke of the broken engagement so calmly, so candidly.

The emotion was falling entirely on Gigi to express. And express it she did, kicking the refrigerator so hard that she might need James to x-ray her toes later.

"I thought I'd fixed it," Gigi said. "I *had* fixed it. I found the perfect guy for you. He's obsessed with you, asked you to marry him, and now you're throwing it all away."

Eloise turned off the stove, strained the pasta over the sink. "I'll forever be grateful for meeting him. He showed me I can love again."

"And that you can lose again, apparently," Gigi added.

Eloise wiped Gigi's snot with the sleeve of her own cardigan. "It'll be okay. I promise."

"That's what you said when Dad left." Gigi remembered those nights so clearly. Her eight-year-old self climbing in bed with her mother because neither of them could sleep. Hiccupping and coughing and spitting—anything but breathing. Eloise patting her back, telling her to picture a water wheel moving in a smooth, circular motion, the breath moving over the top of the wheel, water splashing on the way down, then a pause at the bottom of the wheel for the exhale. "*Everything will be okay,*" Eloise had said so many times.

"And I was right about that, wasn't I?" Eloise said now.

"Love is a hoax," Gigi said. "One giant hoax." The lie of it and the truth of it entangled like vines, strangling the tree she had just started to trust.

"It's not a hoax." Eloise fixed their bowls of pasta. "And you want to know the very best thing to come from all of this?"

"I don't care."

But Eloise carried on anyway. "The best thing is that I have a daughter who loves me so much that she would try to find someone for me." It was the first time she looked close to crying.

"I only set you up with Clyde as payback," Gigi said. "There was no good intent in it at all."

No matter what Eloise would say, Gigi was determined to disagree. She wanted to reinstate every inch of the distance between them that they'd begun closing this summer.

"Maybe that was true at the start," Eloise said. "But I saw how you made an effort with him, how you were rooting for us. I know it wasn't easy, especially with everything with your dad, but you put me first—you did."

"No, I put myself first. I didn't just want Clyde for you. I wanted him for me too."

She thought about how comfortable she'd gotten with going over to the Grand Hotel, using the facilities and charging smoothies and fries to Clyde's tab. It wasn't about the money or the luxury. It was about the feeling of having something that was always open.

But now here it was, closed again.

"I'm sorry." Eloise's seafoam eyes were squinting. "Georgiana, I'm so sorry. I just can't go through with it."

Outside, lightning flashed. Thunder trailed. Gigi suddenly felt very tired. "Okay. I hope you don't regret it."

"Please shower before you sit down at the table," Eloise said. "You're covered in mud."

"Of all the things to worry about, mud on the chairs is really at the top of your list?"

"If we stop caring about the little things, we stop caring about the big things too." Eloise's shoulders were held high and straight, like she knew that if she let them drop even a notch, they would fall all the way down.

"Fine." Gigi loped off to shower, glad for a reason to wet her face so her tears would blend in better.

Chapter 59

Alice

Alice was clipping grocery coupons and watching *Jeopardy* that night when Eloise entered through the creaky side door. Her movements were distressed, her energy distended.

The boxy TV made a staticky sound as Alice turned it off.

"I'm sorry," Alice said, praying Eloise might take at least one of her hundred apologies. "I never meant to hurt your father. Or you. Or anyone."

"We'll talk about it later," Eloise said. "The engagement is off."

Alice leapt up from the couch so fast that her hip twinged. "What did he do? What did that foreigner do to my girl?" She would go after that Clyde with David's old shotgun if she had to.

"It was me. I did it."

Eloise explained what happened, which is to say she didn't explain very much at all.

"This isn't because of me, is it?" Alice asked. She prayed she wouldn't have to blame herself for another of Eloise's failed relationships. "Because I made you question my commitment to your father? Or because you're worried about leaving me to fend for myself? I'm all right on my own, I really am."

Alice meant it. Some days she felt overwhelmed by it all, as she had the day she and Deirdre had collapsed in each other's arms. But on the whole, she felt more capable on her own than she ever had. It was nice knowing Georgiana would be sticking around, at least a little longer. Liam, too, if she really needed something.

"It's not because of you," Eloise said.

Alice wasn't convinced. She didn't want to hold her daughter back.

"What if you and Clyde just carry on dating for a while?" Alice suggested. "Take the pressure off."

Alice went to the kitchen and cut into the homemade apple crisp she'd stress-baked earlier today. She gave Eloise the bigger piece and served it à la mode with vanilla ice cream.

"Clyde says you're either moving forward or backward," Eloise said.

"Such extremes." Alice wished she hadn't given her blessing quite so readily. "Have you been in touch with Gus? Since the engagement?"

"I left him a voicemail. He texted back to say congratulations."

Alice knew it wasn't her place to pry. She pried anyway. "I know your father and I always liked Gus," she said, testing out how it would be to bring up David.

Eloise seemed open to hearing, so Alice kept going.

"We were so excited to see you two together that we overlooked some things, condoned his behavior. I should've given him a talking-to back when he first left. Your father should have too." It felt wrong to critique David when he wasn't here to defend himself, especially in light of recent disclosures, but she felt he would agree with her.

"That wasn't your job."

"Of course it was," Alice said. "My biggest job in life—my only job, really—is to protect my daughter. And now my granddaughters. And I feel like I let you down by not doing more when Gus left. When he wronged you. He really wronged you, Eloise."

"I know that," Eloise said, and she seemed glad to hear the words, to hold them as validation. "But the divorce is final, and we're both moving forward. My decision with Clyde is unrelated." Eloise set down her fork, her appetite seemingly retreating. "I have to trust my gut on this."

"As long as I'm not the one who ruined it," Alice said, and she felt the multiple meanings of her words. She didn't want to be the one who ruined Eloise and Clyde's relationship, nor the one between Eloise and Alice.

"As Georgiana says, 'Mom, maybe not everything is about you.'"

They were able to share a laugh, however short, and it meant more to Alice than she could express. "You've raised two wonderful girls," she told Eloise. "You're a good mother, Eloise."

Eloise hugged her bare shoulders. She wasn't wearing cardigans as often these days, whether because of the summer heat or a new preference to show off her very nice shoulders, Alice wasn't sure.

"I don't always feel that way," Eloise said. "Georgiana isn't taking the news of Clyde and me well. I feel like no matter what I do, I let her down."

Alice could empathize. "But you're sure of your decision?"

Eloise nodded. "I am."

It was nice at least to see Eloise so decisive. "Well, one thing your father used to say was if it's not a hell yes, it's a hell no."

Alice thought back to walking down the aisle of the Little Stone Church with David, how she'd felt like she was floating, how every molecule in her being had been so sure he was the one to walk through life with, to draw her last breath beside. And yet she had gone on to be unfaithful, and then David died, precluding their plans of exiting this world together. Even when you were so absolutely sure, things could still go wrong. But she supposed that not having that kind of faith in the beginning would make for some very bleak times when things inevitably got tough. Being sure about something wasn't a guarantee, but it was still a helpful prerequisite.

"Have you talked to Deirdre recently?" Alice asked gently.

Alice hadn't talked with Deirdre for very long after their surprise cry together that morning. All Deirdre said was that she'd had a daughter long ago and put her up for adoption. Deidre wanted to tell

Eloise herself. Alice understood. She felt kinder now toward Deirdre, who had always seemed to have a chip on her shoulder.

It was understandable to act that way when the chip was something as big as a daughter.

"This is delicious," Eloise said, complimenting the crisp. "One of your best."

"Is that your way of saying you might forgive me?"

"It's my way of saying that I think we'll get there," Eloise said.

Alice felt instantly lighter. There was something so cleansing about the release of a secret, especially one that had burrowed as deeply as this one.

They still had things to talk through, to work through, but Alice knew they would get there.

"Needs a bit more spice," Alice said. She added an extra dash of cinnamon. "Hard to believe it's apple season already."

———≈———

Georgiana came over the next evening to watch *Jeopardy*.

"So tell me, Nonni," Georgiana said. "What's been going on between you and Mom? I know things are weird."

"Just some mother-daughter stuff," Alice said vaguely. She was relieved Eloise had agreed that the girls did not need to know about the affair.

"Is Mom upset you're dating Liam?" Georgiana guessed.

Alice fussed with the afghan, made sure it was properly covering Georgiana's shins and toes. "I'm not dating him."

"Well, you should go for it if you want to," Georgiana said. "Not like you have to commit to him for fifty years at your age." She grinned.

Alice couldn't help but chuckle.

"We all just want you to be happy," Georgiana said. "I'm sure Pop would want that too."

"I *am* happy." Alice turned up the volume on the TV just a little so Georgiana might take the hint to drop the topic.

"Well, will you at least think about what I said? About giving Liam a chance? He's clearly obsessed with you. Believe me, I know the look."

Alice found this assessment quite encouraging before she remembered she wasn't supposed to think like that. "Since when did granddaughters start lecturing their grandmothers about love?"

"Since their grandmothers started becoming hot commodities on the dating market, that's when."

Alice shook her head, amused. "I've missed you."

"I saw you this morning for pickleball." They had clobbered Camille and that Yooper boyfriend of hers. A satisfying win indeed.

"Before this summer, I mean," Alice said. "In the years you were away."

Georgiana looked sheepish. "I should've kept in touch better. Especially after Pop died."

"I didn't mean it like that," Alice said, though she absorbed the words like bath salts. "It's just good to have you back. For now, at least. I know mayor is only a two-year term. It's probably not forever."

"Well, nothing's forever, right?"

"Very true. Except this island. She's eternal."

"Hopefully our ghosts can haunt it together," Georgiana said. "How fun would that be?"

It felt almost irreverent, but Alice couldn't help but giggle. "Yes," she said. "How fun."

Chapter 60

Deidre

Deirdre was glad she and Eloise were back in the routine of their morning walks. But now she was going to upset things again.

"I'm not the person you think I am," Deirdre told Eloise one morning.

"You're frightening me, Deirdre," Eloise said. "There are only so many surprises I can take in one summer."

Deirdre drew a long breath. She still hadn't told Fred. Eloise, she'd decided, would be the next to know.

"Remember when I didn't do a good job at keeping in touch that first year of college?" Deirdre said.

"Of course I do," Eloise said. "I figured you were upset I was marrying Gus instead of going to college myself."

"I wasn't upset. I mean, sure, I probably was a little. But that wasn't the main reason." Deidre hesitated only for a moment. "I was having a baby."

Eloise stopped in her tracks. "Deirdre. What are you talking about?"

They sat down on a bench along the shoreline. With thick cloud cover, the water was dark and moody today. Deirdre wondered how many secrets the Great Lakes held. She could hide so much.

"Nolan Plunkett," Deirdre went on. "My freshman-year boyfriend. He convinced me to sleep with him, promised me I wouldn't get pregnant. I did, the first time. I told my mom but no one else, not even Nolan. My mom didn't want me coming back to the island, of course—can you imagine the scandal?—so she shipped me off to live with my great-aunt Carol in Iowa. She was good to me, God rest her soul. Let me stay, came with me to the hospital, helped me with the adoption paperwork."

Eloise took Deirdre's hand and held on to it. It felt good to tell Eloise, even better than she'd expected. Deidre kept going.

"It was a girl. Baby Lilac, I called her, since she was born in mid-June. Peak lilac season. Not that many lilacs were blooming in Iowa so late in the season, but I was homesick."

Deirdre could still see the bundle of cloth in the hospital room. She'd been bleary from the pain medicine, but the sight had cut sharply. "My biggest regret to this day is that I didn't ask to hold Lilac in my arms before they took her away. I don't even know what color eyes she has. My own daughter."

Deirdre winced. She'd thought it would be too hard to get even a glimpse of what she was going to miss. But over the years she'd realized it was much better to get to feel the love and then lose it, rather than never feeling it at all.

"Deirdre," Eloise said gently. "Why have you never told me this? You know I would've been there for you, don't you?"

"I know that," Deirdre said, and she did. "It just felt so good, or at least less bad, being the only one who knew about my daughter. Like I was the only one who got to love her." She paused. "I know it sounds ridiculous. She must have people now who love her. She probably doesn't ever think about her birth mother."

This was the part that got Deirdre. She could handle driving herself crazy wondering about her daughter, but she could not handle the thought of her daughter not driving herself crazy thinking about her.

But no one had ever tried to track her down, not once. Deirdre even picked up every sales call, every solicitation, just in case. She listened to every wisp of gossip on the off-chance something came her way. Nothing had in thirty-six years.

"I just can't believe I didn't know," Eloise said.

"No one knows. Not even Fred. Except I did accidentally tell your mother." Deirdre briefly filled her in.

There was a break in the clouds. The sun split through, the rays fragmenting like prisms. Deirdre didn't believe in signs, but she gobbled this one up.

"You're going to look for her, aren't you?" Eloise said.

Deirdre nodded. It was why she wasn't crumpled over right now. She felt a new sense of purpose. An old sense of purpose, really, since it had been born the same day as her daughter. But a new sense of moving from imagination to action to make it happen.

Her daughter had always felt real, yet not real too. Separate from her daily life and far away. Now, since she'd told Alice and then Eloise, something had shifted. Her daughter felt integrated into her island life. Within reach.

"I want to," Deirdre said.

"You're sure about this?" Eloise said. "It might not go as you're expecting."

Deirdre knew that. But she had to try. She had to get answers, even if they weren't the ones she wanted.

"It's the surest I've ever been about anything. Tied perhaps with knowing I picked the right person to be my best friend."

Eloise had stuck by her and loved her every step of the way. Deirdre may have been dealt a tough hand in some things, but her friendship with Eloise . . . that was one stroke of luck she'd never deserved.

"Well, you didn't really pick me, did you?" Eloise said. "Our parents forced us together from the cradle."

"A match made in heaven."

"A match made in Mackinac."

"Same thing."

"All right," Eloise said. "I'm going to help you find her. Baby Lilac, here we come."

Deirdre buried her head in her best friend's shoulder. She didn't cry, just shook.

As she lifted her head, the clouds were shifting. All the splintered rays from the sun once again became one.

———————≈———————

A crowd gathered at the dock the next day to send off Clyde on the 8:45 a.m. ferry. Deirdre arrived early.

She had gotten the best night's sleep she'd had in many years.

Eloise had been there for her, and now it was important for her to be there for Eloise.

The breakup had caused quite a lot of drama among the islanders. Deirdre wasn't going to stir the drama like a batch of molten fudge; she had better things to do these days. But she still had to help oversee Clyde's departure, just in case anything went wrong.

Eloise had spread the word that she didn't want anyone picking sides, that she and Clyde were still good friends, but Deirdre felt that some level of division was necessary. Healthy, even. If you could be so delightfully civil with the person you were breaking up with, what was the point of ending things, really?

Naturally, sides had formed anyway (Mackinac was not a place where you passed up a reason to be petty). Just about everyone was Team Eloise except Camille and her city commissioners. It irked Deirdre enough to make her wonder if she had been too hasty in pledging her vote. Camille presented Clyde with a Mackinac Island plaque, something large and heavy that he'd never get through airport security.

Clyde was in good spirits, thanking everyone for welcoming him in, doling out hugs and trinkets he'd collected over the course of the summer: ties with miniature stallions and sailboats, peanut butter jars repurposed into shell-collecting vases, vials of sand from British Landing. Deirdre could only detect his pain in the way he didn't look straight at Eloise.

The ferry horn belted, announcing last call for boarding.

Clyde and Eloise came face-to-face. "What's fer ye won't go past ye," he said softly, whatever that meant.

Their last hug was tender and melancholy, but it held gratitude too. Or maybe Deirdre was just relieved that her best friend wasn't abandoning her.

"It all feels like a fever dream, doesn't it?" Deirdre asked Eloise. "Clyde arriving, courting you, getting engaged . . . now saying goodbye. An old classic film on double speed."

"It was a dream, all right." Eloise was poised as usual, but there was a suppleness to her that hadn't been there at the beginning of summer. "One I'll remember for the rest of my life."

"Until the dementia strikes," Deirdre said, trying to shake a laugh out of Eloise. "We need to eat more fish oil."

Deidre had fresh enthusiasm for fish oil and exercise and anything that would keep her healthy. She wanted to be in the best condition possible if and when she met her daughter. Which all depended, of course, on whether she could track down Baby Lilac, and then whether she even wanted any relationship with Deidre. But she had told Fred right after Eloise, and he hadn't just been understanding; he'd been genuinely excited. "I always wanted a daughter," he said. "I just felt bad ever mentioning that to you since we had sons." Deirdre kissed him on the spot, and they had a most unexpected night of lovemaking (after which Deirdre conked out and snoozed a full eight hours).

Dr. Kentwood joined the farewell party, and there was definitely something simmering between him and Georgiana. They could hardly take their eyes off each other. Georgiana hadn't stayed over with Dr. Kentwood in the guesthouse yet—at least Deirdre didn't think so— but she would keep an eye out through the window (she still hadn't asked Fred to fix the guesthouse blinds).

"At least you got a boyfriend out of this summer," Deirdre said to Georgiana after Dr. Kentwood had headed off to work.

"He's not my boyfriend," Georgiana said. "And either way, I got a lot more than that this summer. I got a friend." She slung an arm around Eloise's shoulder.

Eloise returned the hug. The two of them stood there like Lorelai and Rory in a *Gilmore Girls* episode.

Deirdre was triggered by such a blatant display of affection. It made her think not just of her daughter but also of her sons, who had been icing her out, telling her she was overstepping her demands on family time. If she heard the term *boundaries* one more time . . .

"Parents and children can't be friends," Deidre reminded. "You've always said so yourself, Eloise."

"I've reconsidered my stance." Eloise was no longer looking at the ferry, just her daughter. "When you're both adults, you can be great friends."

Deirdre tried to smile as she watched Eloise and Gigi interact, but she felt it again, bubbling in her stomach, ready to boil.

The envy . . . it was back. Except this time it came with a thin coating of hope.

Chapter 61

Rebecca

Eloise's broken engagement had cracked over Rebecca's head like a dinner plate.

The fancy kind of plates she and Tom had been gifted for their wedding and hadn't used yet because Rebecca was scared to break them. But sometimes it didn't do any good to wait to use good things. Sometimes you should use them right away, before they broke themselves.

Rebecca didn't express her disappointment as vocally as Gigi, nor with as much volatility, but it was a blow, especially when she'd pored over Clyde's books and let herself think he might become something of a father figure. It now felt like wasted time, for both herself and her mother. Since the breakup, she'd spent hours on the phone with Eloise and with Gigi. Their reasonings for why the engagement failed didn't totally match up, but the outcome was the same: Clyde was gone, and they were hurting.

"I need to think of something to cheer up my mom," Rebecca told Tom over a Moroccan fish dinner the day Clyde had purportedly left Mackinac. "Gigi too."

"Why don't we tell your mom about the baby?" Tom suggested.

"It's still not quite three months yet," Rebecca said. But she decided Tom was right, so she FaceTimed Eloise from the beach the next afternoon, a fresh collection of Petoskey stones drying on her towel.

"I nearly committed to moving to Scotland with a *grandchild* on the way?" Eloise yelped. "How could you have let me? My intuition was telling me to stay, I could feel it. And here it is, the proof in the pudding."

Eloise babbled on with joy and then put Nonni on the phone so Rebecca could share the news twice over. "I thought you looked a little fuller when you came over the Fourth," Nonni said. "Didn't I say that, Eloise?"

When Rebecca explained that she wasn't even three months along, Nonni hastily said she only meant that Rebecca was "a little rounder in the face, only because of how wide you were smiling."

"Something could still happen with the pregnancy," Rebecca cautioned. "It's still early."

"Either way, you're carrying a baby," Nonni said. "I love my Penelope so much even though we never got to take her home from the hospital. Your pop felt that way too. Whenever people asked how many children we had, we said two. One heaven-side and one earth-side."

Rebecca hadn't thought about it this way. That whatever happened, no one could take away that she held this child inside of her today, that she had been for the past ten weeks. This baby was always going to be hers.

In the background, Gigi was boasting about how she already knew the news, how Rebecca had told her first. "I'm getting to name the baby too," Gigi said.

There was too much excitement for anyone to find much critique in this, though Rebecca knew they would later.

"Tom and I are coming to Mackinac for a fall weekend soon," Rebecca said. "Apple cider and donuts and all that. We're bringing our friends."

Next-door neighbor Kaley and her husband were coming. Rebecca's maid of honor, Maggie, and her husband were coming too, flying up from North Carolina. She was excited to get them all together, to blend the different chapters of her life.

"But don't be pushy about having us move back," Rebecca went on. "We're very happy in Traverse City."

It wasn't even a stretch to say that these days.

Kaley's endorsement seemed to have done the trick, and Rebecca and Tom found themselves at the center of the neighborhood social scene. That, combined with a writing workshop Rebecca had started going to every Wednesday at the local library, had helped cure her ennui. She was still terrified of having people judge her writing, but she no longer found that a good enough reason not to write. Reading Clyde's books had stoked her own literary ambitions. She didn't need to be in a PhD program, though maybe she would enroll in one down the line. She could start writing now and see where it led. Tom joined the class when he could, too, and they had turned over a new creative stone in their marriage.

"I won't ask Mr. Townsend to take you around and show you houses," Eloise promised.

Nonni made a strange grunting sound. Rebecca had long suspected something might be going on between her grandmother and Liam.

"Though if you want to buy, you might want to do it soon," Gigi said. "Real estate is about to skyrocket under my leadership."

"Like I told Gigi," Rebecca said with a smile, "moving back is in our five-year plan."

"Five years!" Eloise exclaimed as if Rebecca had said five hundred.

"Eloise," Nonni chided.

Eloise quickly put her hands over her mouth. "Sorry, sorry, not my place. It's so nice to see you thriving."

And she sounded like she really meant it.

"Does your dad know?" Eloise went on. "About the baby?"

Rebecca noted how she said *your dad*, not *Dad*, like she usually did.

A layer of distance inserted, a signal that the divorce papers carried some weight. "Do you really think I would tell him before you?"

Eloise looked gratified. "Tell him when you're ready. He'll be thrilled."

"He'll probably spiral into an existential crisis about how old he's getting and disappear to Bali," Rebecca said. "You don't have to defend him, you know."

"I'm not defending *him*," Eloise said. "I just want my girls to get what you both deserve from that relationship. You only get one father."

"Almost got two," Gigi said. "If you hadn't vetoed Clyde."

Gigi could smile, showing how far she'd already come. It was good that she had the election to pour herself into. It seemed to be electrifying her the way that unsavory relationships and illegal substances used to.

"Dad has my number," Rebecca said. "He can call if he wants to know about my life."

It was a big shift for her. Boundaries drawn, in sand, not stone, but they were boundaries nonetheless. There was some sadness as the distance set in, but Rebecca reflected on how the distance had already been there. She was just acknowledging it now, respecting it. She would always give her dad the chance to close it if he wanted to.

Eloise and Nonni began rattling through the long list of baby things they had hoarded for this very day (strollers and onesies, toys and picture books, car seats and diapers). "I think I've still got some freeze-dried formula in the basement," Nonni said.

"Yeah, I'm sure that's still good," Gigi said dryly. "Okay, are you ready to hear the baby's name?" She didn't wait for Rebecca to reply, just blurted it out. "Jenkins! That's the name!"

There was a beat of silence.

Eloise pinched her face.

"Jenkins isn't a first name," Nonni said.

"Who says it can't be?" Gigi said.

Rebecca's first reaction was to roll her eyes, tell Gigi to please take this assignment more seriously. But the longer the name sank in, the more Rebecca liked it. If it was a girl, she could go by Jenny.

Tom was a fan too, when she told him that evening on the way to their writing workshop. "Jenkins is an ideal name for a pro athlete!" he said. "Or an artist," he added quickly.

"Or an artist," Rebecca agreed happily.

Your "Jenkins" proposal has officially been approved, Rebecca texted Gigi.

I knew you'd find a way to get back at me for changing my name when I got married.

This is it, Gigi replied. This is my retribution.

Chapter 62

Gigi

Am I making a morning person out of you, Gigi Jenkins?" James asked.

It was the third day in a row that she was out riding with him at sunrise. This as much as anything showed her that try as she might to deny it, her feelings for James were not of the friendship variety.

"I'm not just getting up for you," Gigi said. "I have a packed agenda these days. The election is only sixty-eight days away, as Rebecca reminded me on yesterday's strategy call."

Gigi liked starting her day with James and Noelle and Willow. She liked trotting around the lakeshore path with them before the island woke up. She liked the way the fresh air lined her lungs.

And rather than sleeping the day away, waking up early gave her a new sense of accomplishment. Gigi was campaigning, meeting with community leaders, and recording her videos. Yesterday she even had coffee with Principal Reid, who had led the school since Gigi had been a student. Though Gigi had been sweating going into it—What must he think of her? And why did she still care?—it had been surprisingly pleasant and productive. It seemed most people were as ready to move on as she was.

"I'm honored that you're making time to give me horseback riding lessons," James told Gigi as Willow and Noelle kept pace beside each other. "Especially with how much of a public figure you've become."

Gigi continued to rack up social media stardom, and the perks were more than political.

The Main Street shops were sending boxes and boxes of freebies to Thistle Dew in hopes Gigi would post about them. And as a thank-you for the positive PR from the viral campaign video that Gigi filmed at their stables, the Grand Hotel had gifted Gigi a free stall for Noelle. Gigi had negotiated a second stall for Willow, so both horses had gotten to upgrade from Fred and Deirdre's barn. They would be wintering downstate, but they had a few more weeks before saying goodbye for the off-season.

"You're a quick learner," Gigi said, noting how much more easily James held the reins now, not the tight grip of before. "You're nearly skilled enough for that outfit you wore to our first date. You know, the nineteenth-century polo player one?"

"How could I forget?" James said. "You hated me that day."

"I never hated you. I just buried my positive emotions under negative ones. It's a party trick I've been doing my whole life."

Gigi had known this for a while, but this was the first time she had actually voiced it to anyone. She felt quite mature, not in a boring way, but in a brave one.

"Maybe we can break the habit?" James said.

"I think I already have. I've been very nice to you recently, haven't I?"

"You have been. Very nice."

The way he said it implied he might be hoping for something a little more than *nice* one of these days.

Gigi still hadn't answered him about whether they could move beyond friendship. It continued to be the elephant in the room. With both of them staying, there was no longer a good reason for them not to be together. James had put himself out there. Now it was Gigi's turn.

Beyond the fear of messing up their friendship, something else was holding her back. The fear that James might feel stuck or trapped on the island, and during a fight—because fights *would* happen if they were dating—he'd fling it on her that he'd given up a big job in a big city to be here in this isolated town with nothing to do.

"You're not just staying on the island because of me, right?" she asked James now.

James glanced over at her. "What if I said yes?"

Gigi felt a thrill, but fear too. "It's too much pressure. We haven't even ever kissed."

"We *almost* kissed," James said. "In the lake."

Her body heat shot up at the memory, though it was still cool and dewy this morning. "But we didn't."

"You can relax," James said. "I'm not staying just because of you." He told her how he loved the islanders, how he'd bonded with his patients, how he didn't want to go back to the pace of big-city life where everything felt impersonal and he had to commute half an hour to work on a busy highway. "But yes, you were *a* factor. One of several."

"One of several," Gigi repeated. She appreciated his transparency. Still, she found herself wanting him to say she was one of one. She realized she was asking for the impossible, especially when she hadn't validated James much herself. It was a no-win game. She wanted to have her fudge and eat it too.

"Was that the wrong answer?" James said. "I'm not a mind reader, Gigi."

"They didn't teach you that in medical school?" Gigi quipped.

"Neuroscience and psychology, yes. The inner workings of a woman's brain, no. That would've taken an extra ten years of schooling at least."

Gigi felt her smile slip on and her fears slide off. She was glad they were out riding. There was something about moving and having their eyes on the path ahead that made it easier to have deep conversations. And Noelle had such a steadying presence.

She couldn't expect James to know exactly how she felt. She couldn't expect him to be her knight in shining armor (despite the uncanny resemblance as he rode horseback) and do all the work for her.

It was time for Gigi to step up and break the damsel-in-distress cliché, shatter the glass slipper and turn its shards into glitter.

"I've thought about your proposal. I mean, not *proposal* proposal," Gigi said, flustered. "But the suggestion to amend our friendship rules. And I agree with you," she went on. "I think we should be more than friends."

She kept her gaze straight ahead as she said it, but she stole a glance right after.

James was smiling ear to ear. "Do you, now?" he said. "And what might the details of 'more than friends' be, exactly?"

Gigi resisted the tug to back down from her feelings, back away from her body. "I think you should be my boyfriend."

"Oh?" James seemed more than interested. "But as you pointed out, we haven't kissed yet. What if I'm not a good kisser?"

"You'll be a good kisser."

"Why don't you test it out first?" James said. "So you don't have buyer's remorse."

She loved how James could give her a hard time. He had so much more zest to him than Gigi had first thought.

"I can't kiss you right now. I'm in the saddle." As she said it, she felt the metaphor of her words. How she was back in the saddle on this island, holding the reins of her own horse, her own life.

"Race you to the stable then," James said. He tugged at Willow and they took off in a tear.

"Hey!" Gigi called, feeling her own trick used against her.

It made her even more confident in her choice of a man. Here was someone she still got to race with, still got to explore with. But instead of running away, this time Gigi was running toward.

Toward the man who showed her that consistency wasn't the antithesis of excitement but rather the underpinning of it.

Toward the stables where she'd had her first job mucking stalls and now visited every day to brush out her horse and film videos to help her land her next job, a bigger one than she'd ever had.

And toward herself, especially the parts she'd tried to drown in the Great Lakes when she'd left this island as a teenager. The parts she'd deemed small or ordinary, when really, they were just that, parts. Pieces that had floated in the water like driftwood, waiting for her all this time.

Gigi brought Noelle to a full gallop, egging her on affectionately. They closed the gap on James and passed him on the home stretch. Gigi whooped, the wind blowing through her partially grown-out hair, all her grounded hopes back in the air.

———— ≈ ————

"I'm only staying over with James tonight because I have my meeting with small business owners at the Pink Pony tomorrow morning," Gigi told Eloise one evening a couple weeks later as they ambled along the lakeshore, taking turns holding the flashlight that lit their way. "And his place is closer, so it just makes sense, practically speaking."

It had become their routine, an evening walk after cooking together. They were bundled in fleeces and headbands, late September having descended with a blustery chill. The tourists had largely cleared out and the trees were shedding too, amber leaves nearing their peak, oranges and reds just around the corner. The sun set earlier now, swaddling the island in a dark and silky cocoon that would only thicken come winter.

"Right, because 'practical' has always been the top adjective to describe you," Eloise noted.

"Exactly," Gigi dished back. "I'm glad you understand."

"I just want to make sure you're not rushing things," Eloise cautioned.

"Says the woman who got engaged to someone after two months," Gigi said. "Sorry. Too soon."

"It's a fair rebuttal."

The crescendo of heartbreak had dipped into something mellower, something malleable. Eloise seemed just about back to her old self, though some differences remained. She was quicker to laugh and poke fun at herself, less rigid in her schedule. She had emptied out Gus's side of the closet completely, down to the tattered golf tees and ragged handkerchiefs he'd left. Freeing up space, that was what Gigi saw her mom doing these days. Gigi tried to take credit for the progress whenever she could, then shoved it back in Eloise's face whenever her mom tried to hand it over in earnest.

"You're not a teenager anymore," Eloise said. "You can make your own decisions. Lord knows you'll be leading this whole island soon enough."

"Let the Jenkins dynasty begin."

The leaves crunched under their feet. Gigi was borrowing a pair of Eloise's walking shoes. The laces were tightly tied. Gigi no longer just slipped shoes on and off.

"I'm glad it's going so well with James," Eloise said. "But I don't want you thinking you'll be letting me down if it doesn't work out."

"This might come as a shock," Gigi said, "but letting my parents down has never been my highest concern."

"Really?" Eloise deadpanned. "I never knew."

"Did you actually think James and I would be good together when you set us up? Or were you just trying to get our summer off to a rocky start?"

Earlier in the day Gigi had noticed her tan lines fading, her skin reverting to its natural pasty tinge. She didn't mind. The next season felt exciting in more ways than one.

"I didn't think you and James would become anything serious," Eloise said. "I just hoped he might show you that other types of men existed, beyond just the . . ." She trailed off, searching for the words.

"Typical assholes I went for?" Gigi finished for her.

"I don't care for the phrase, but that's the gist of it."

"You didn't think I was emotionally mature enough to appreciate James."

"That's not what I said."

"Well, it's true. I wasn't," Gigi said. "But I've grown a lot since the start of summer. I'm pretty much perfect now." She wagged her tongue.

"Like mother like daughter, right?" Eloise said.

"Absolutely. We Jenkins girls are as good as they come."

"Which is why I've decided to keep the name," Eloise said. With the divorce underway, she'd been talking about reverting to Klein, her maiden name. "After all, how would all your fans know I was your mother if we had different last names?"

"I'm glad to hear it," Gigi said, and she meant it. "Though you might prefer some anonymity once the paparazzi start knocking."

"I fielded a call today from a national reporter. They found our home phone number; no surprise given how the government tracks our every move. But my cell phone is safe, for now at least."

"Going back to the topic of names," Gigi said. "I've decided to run as Georgiana Jenkins, not Gigi. Only because it looks more professional on the ballot."

That was partly it, but it was more than that. She wanted all the letters, all the layers, to play a role in how she led. And *Georgiana* made her feel a little closer to Queen of the Grand Hotel, the regal leader she'd once envisioned.

"Is that so?" Eloise said. "So I can go back to calling you Georgiana?"

"You've only called me Gigi a couple of times."

"Well, it's hard to change a habit after so many years."

"I guess it is." Gigi thought about James and how it was hard to change her relationship habits. Hard not to let her sarcastic defenses take over, hard not to give in to her avoidant tendencies. And yet loving James (if she could call it that—she thought so, but would wait a bit longer to say it) was also the easiest thing she had ever done.

It was a paradox Gigi didn't care to square, reveling in the circular nature of it all.

What she knew was that she wasn't just attracted to the commitment of her relationship with James or to the commitment of being mayor for at least a two-year term because they were a novelty. She wanted both of these things because they felt mature, not in a dull way, but in a sturdy one.

It felt like she was unlearning everything just to get back to who she'd been before, when she'd come into this world. Before her parents had divorced or she'd run away from the island or gotten all those jobs and boyfriends she didn't care about. Before all the pain, shame, and programming had taken over.

It turned out that deep down, commitment was her default state after all.

"It doesn't really matter what you call me," Gigi said.

She used to care so much. When it felt like life was spinning out of control, her own name had been the only thing she could control. She was glad to move beyond that, above it. "I'm still keeping my social media handles as @GigiJenkins4Mayor. The character count with Georgiana is too long."

"Well, I must say, you've built quite a movement, Georgiana," Eloise said.

"Yeah, my so-called friends from LA have popped up again since I've gone viral. Funny how after ignoring me all summer they're suddenly texting and posting old photos of us now that I'm a somebody."

"You've always been a somebody," Eloise said.

Lake Huron shone through the darkness, reflecting the first specks of starlight. Its waves lapped up on the rocky shore like lullabies.

"Do you believe me now when I say that you don't have to leave Mackinac to have a big life?" Eloise carried on.

It felt like Eloise had been waiting awhile to find a way to slide that one in. Gigi wasn't even annoyed. She did love how it felt to reach so many people—both near and far—from this little island perch. And it wasn't just the scale of it but the soul too. There was a depth to her work Gigi hadn't felt before.

"I believe you," Gigi said, and she did. "The data points for my videos are pretty compelling."

"I'm proud of you. I really am."

Gigi slurped up the words like the last of summer's lemonade.

"There's nothing to be proud of yet," Gigi told Eloise. "I haven't won the election. Perhaps Camille's smear campaign will take me out."

Deirdre had reported that Camille was designing yet another round of flyers featuring photos of the news articles from Gigi's high school runaway. "Vote for Camille, Not the Convict" was apparently the new tagline.

Gigi hadn't unleashed any attacks of her own. Calm felt better than conflict these days. Not that Gigi was backing down; she was just trying to take the high road where she could. It led to better views anyway. Like up to Arch Rock, where she and Eloise were walking now.

"No one is dragging my daughter's name through the mud," Eloise said. "Or they'll have me to answer to."

Gigi looked over at her mother. Her rolled-back shoulders, as if she'd been trained to hold a heavy load. Her elegant profile that cut like a cliffside. The hardness in the lines around her mouth, yet the softness in the ones around her eyes.

Gigi thought about how Eloise had nearly gone off to college as a teenager. How she had nearly left for Scotland last month. Eloise never made it seem like she regretted her choice to stay, never insinuated that she had settled. Maybe Gigi was projecting, but she thought there might be some unfilled ambition wafting from Eloise, cool and brisk like a northern breeze.

It gave Gigi an idea.

"Maybe we can write a short story collection about this someday." She liked what Clyde had suggested about leveraging Gigi's bursts of creative energy for short stories, or "vignettes" as Lillian called them. The prospect felt much less daunting than a novel. She also liked not feeling reliant on Clyde or anyone else to tell the story of this island. They could pick up a pen and write it themselves.

"About what?" Eloise asked. "Your campaign?"

"Not just that. About us. About this summer. About this island."

"I'm not sure our lives are exciting enough for a story."

Gigi recalled Clyde's words and said, "There's no such thing as a boring story, only boring writing."

She didn't cite Clyde. It might make her mom sad to think about him. Besides, Gigi liked taking the credit. She had evolved in some ways but not in others.

"I'm no good at writing," Eloise said. "I'm a numbers person."

"Discomfort is how we grow."

"It's not by hijacking private planes and running away to Florida?" Eloise said with a wry smile.

Gigi was glad they could joke about it now. But she felt newly awful for all the old trouble she'd gotten into, the things she'd put her mom through. "I don't know if I ever said sorry for all that."

"No." A beat thumped between them. "You didn't."

Gigi looped her arm through Eloise's. "I'm sorry," she said. "Or I'm sorry I took Xander along, at least. He was such a spoiled brat."

"That's quite the apology."

"Thanks. I learned from Dad."

"Be nice," Eloise said, though Gigi could tell she was trying very hard to hold in a smirk.

"Really, though," Gigi went on. She gave Eloise's arm a squeeze. "I messed up. If I had a daughter who acted how I did, I'm not sure I'd ever let her back in my house."

"I think you'll feel differently if you're ever a mother," Eloise said. "Not that I'm pressuring you. I have one grandchild on the way and that's plenty."

Gigi appreciated the words. "We'll see. I have enough to focus on for the moment. But about what you said about mothers always letting daughters back in the house . . . Any chance we can extend the free-rent thing until Election Day?"

She didn't want to breach campaign finance rules and use her donations for rent. Besides, she had grown quite fond of living with Eloise and their little routines after they both finished work. Cooking dinner together, cleaning up, watching a movie (they were on a string of political documentaries for Gigi to gain inspiration, and Gigi had to admit her mother's commentary was brilliantly brutal).

"You sure are the negotiator," Eloise said, and Gigi detected a smidge of pride. "I'll make a daily list of chores for you to help with. I'll be needing more help now that Clyde's not here to fix things and all that."

Eloise didn't say it bitterly or sadly. Just matter-of-factly, which was how Gigi knew her mom was bouncing back.

"I'll be your handyman," Gigi said happily. "Thank you for letting me stay."

Eloise linked her arm through Gigi's. "Thank you for wanting to."

"So about this book we're going to write," Gigi said. "Rebecca has started that creative writing class. She could help us."

This seemed to intrigue Eloise, who always loved anything that brought the family together.

"And maybe Lillian could write some chapters too," Gigi said. They'd been texting and catching up on the phone too. Lillian seemed to be thriving back in Chicago, with a new job that gave her time to have a social life and even write some music.

"Maybe Deirdre could too," Eloise said. "She'd have fun casting herself as a villain."

"What should the title be?" Gigi said, unable to keep from zipping ahead to the end. "Something simple and classic—*Summer on Mackinac Island?*"

"It would need to be something easier for outsiders to pronounce."

"True, we need to appeal to the masses. I can post the book on my socials and we'll sell out in the first week, guaranteed. We can do a global book tour. Maybe stop in Scotland!"

Gigi couldn't help but hope that Clyde might come back around at the right time, though Eloise seemed to have her closure.

Eloise didn't respond to that, just offered up a title suggestion. "*Summer on Turtle Island*, perhaps?"

"That would be good, except it's cultural appropriation of an indigenous name," Gigi said, referring to how the Native Americans had named Mackinac "Big Turtle."

"Oops."

Gigi was glad Eloise didn't fight it.

They kept thinking. "How about *Summer on Lilac Island*?" Eloise proposed. "Since the lilacs are so central to summertime here."

"Yes," Gigi said, loving it on the spot. It was more refined, more modest than her usual taste, but for a family book about the island, it was just right.

"We can call Rebecca tomorrow to start planning," Gigi said. "Maybe Nonni wants to write some sections too."

"Let's take one thing at a time," Eloise said, though she was smiling.

Gigi wondered what her angsty high school self would think of this scene—she and her mother talking about writing a book together as they walked each other home.

Chapter 63

Rebecca

Rebecca was arranging pumpkins on the front steps to decorate the house for a harvest-themed dinner party with the neighbors when her phone rang. She set down the pumpkins and checked who was calling.

It was her dad. She'd recently changed him in her phone from *Dad* to *Gus* to try to lessen the emotional attachment.

"Hello?" she said, as if she didn't have caller ID.

"Rebecca." It sounded strange to hear him call her by her full name. He always used to shorten it to Bec or Becca Bean. "It's your old man."

"Oh," she said. "Hi, Dad."

She counted to three on her inhale and six on her exhale to calm her nervous system.

"I heard about the baby," Gus said. "Gigi told me."

Rebecca had told Gigi she was able to share the news.

"And Gigi says she picked out the name Jenkins?"

It felt like an intimate piece of information for him to know. "We're leaning toward that, yes."

"So Jenkins isn't dying off, even though I didn't have any boys to carry it on."

Rebecca didn't think he meant it as a dig that she and Gigi were daughters, but she couldn't be sure.

"Girls can carry names on too," Rebecca said. "Like Gigi is with her mayoral campaign."

"She says you're the one making those videos. All my biker buds have seen them. They say I must be one proud dad."

"Gigi is something," Rebecca said.

"Both of you are. I'm glad you got your mother's brains. Hopefully I don't pass down any of my traits to my grandkid." He said it lightly, but Rebecca could feel his own type of hurt.

"I hope they have a few of your genes," she said, finding that she still wanted to make her dad feel better.

Rebecca could hear his smile as he said, "So when can I come see this kid?"

"The due date isn't until March 28." Rebecca prepared herself for him to say he would be busy then, that he had some trip he couldn't miss or that he would play it by ear.

But without missing a beat, he said, "Great. I'll plan to come for a couple weeks to help out." Then he added, more tentatively, "If you want me."

Rebecca thought about saying no. She thought about saying he hadn't yet earned the right to be back in her life. But this was him trying to be there for her as much as he was capable of. Rebecca could accept him as he was or keep wishing for a version of her dad that didn't exist. The boundaries could stay, but the locks could loosen.

"That would be very nice," Rebecca said.

Having a relationship with him felt especially important in light of losing Clyde. Gus was Rebecca's father. And she wasn't even guaranteed to always have him. Life was fragile. She felt that truth more tenderly than ever in pregnancy.

"Great." He sounded excited. "I'll start scouting flights now."

Rebecca knew there was a decent chance he would bail. She knew his plans and promises still couldn't be trusted. But she felt secure enough in her life right now—with Tom, with her mother and sister, with a baby of her own—that she knew she could hold up even if he let her down.

And she wasn't going to assume that he would. She was going to try to have no assumptions at all. Easier in theory than in practice, but she would do her best. Her baby deserved that.

"And, Becca Bean?" Gus said.

Rebecca felt the coziness of the old nickname.

"I hope you weren't offended I didn't get you a horse too. I didn't want you feeling any more pressure to come back to Mackinac. I figure you get enough of that from your mom."

"That's okay," Rebecca said, treasuring the apology even as she winced at the dig. "I wasn't offended."

After the call, Rebecca sat down on the front steps to let herself process it. She held her belly with both hands. A dandelion was growing up through the cracks in the concrete. Rebecca blew on the seeds and watched them scatter. She didn't wish on anything today, not because she was scared it wouldn't come true, but because she knew it already had.

Chapter 64

Alice

Y ou're my most valuable campaign asset," Georgiana said to Alice
as they went knocking on doors one September afternoon.

Autumn had always been her favorite season, before the affair.
Afterward, though, the foliage made her feel guilty, like it was tinged
with the scarlet of her sin. But this year she found herself looking forward to autumn again. Like Georgiana's campaign slogan said, it was
time to move forward.

"I'm just one person," Alice said. "You get millions of views on
those videos of yours." The scale was hard to comprehend.

Alice had made a cameo in one of the videos.

She had been reluctant for privacy concerns, but she'd been seeing all the free things Georgiana kept getting for her videos and she
wanted in. The government already had everyone's data anyway.
Alice figured she might as well put her face on the internet and get
some freebies out of it.

It had worked. The video with Alice was a hit. They'd filmed it on
the pickleball court. Not only had she gotten three brand-new pastel
pickleball dresses donated by the Pink Pony gift shop, but thousands,
maybe millions of people online were calling her "America's Grandmother." She loved it, how regal it felt, how formal.

When Georgiana was born, Alice had wanted to go by Grandmother Alice. David, on the other hand, chose Pop. Alice thought it
sounded ridiculous, like the Rice Krispies character. But he had the last

laugh because Georgiana quickly learned Pop, whereas Grandmother Alice proved trickier. "Nonni!" Georgiana would call out from her crib, drool spilling, dimpled legs dancing. "Nonni!" And who could resist that? Certainly not Alice, and the name had stuck.

But it was gratifying in a way she hadn't expected to have so many people calling her America's Grandmother. It was vain to get caught up in the opinion of strangers, but still. Alice was thrilled by it all, especially how it was strengthening her bond with her granddaughters.

"You're helping me win over a key demographic," Georgiana said.

"And which demographic might that be?" Alice said. "The old folks?"

"The esteemed elders of the island," Gigi corrected.

"Look who's gotten all politically correct," Alice teased.

They reached the next stop on their route. A gingerbread A-frame tucked back off the road, shrouded in maples that were just beginning to turn. This was where Liam lived.

"I'll let you do this one by yourself," Georgiana said.

Before Alice could protest, Georgiana was speed-walking away.

It was ridiculous how nervous Alice felt. She was a grown woman (an overgrown woman by many standards). She should have no problem walking up to his red front door and having a simple conversation. But she inched down the driveway and stood bashfully on the front steps, wondering if she should ring the bell or walk away.

The door opened before she had made her decision.

Liam was standing there in a flannel shirt and a cautious smile.

"Alice," Liam said. "I saw you walking up."

It was a nice trait about him, that he was the type of person to open the door before you even rang, but Alice wished he might have given her another minute to prepare.

Over the past weeks, they had carried on being cordial but nothing more. She missed his presence terribly. Josephine May was not nearly as good of a pickleball partner. They were second to last in the fall league. And it wasn't just that. There was no one else who made her laugh, made her think, even made her want to twirl again like Liam did. The way she'd longed to dance with him to Frank Sinatra at Eloise's engagement party . . . It had been excruciating.

"Liam," Alice greeted. "I'm campaigning for Georgiana."

"So I've seen," Liam said. "You're famous now, Alice Klein."

He was the only one who still called her that. She had been Alice Klein for so long. But something about having her youthful identity stirred up . . . She didn't hate it.

"Too famous for me these days, I presume," he said. He had a smile on his face, but the twinkle was gone from his eye.

It pulled at Alice's heart. "Liam," she said. "I owe you an apology."

Liam waved a gracious hand, as if tossing it aside. "It's okay, Alice. We wanted different things. I don't fault you for not feeling the way I did."

Alice bristled at the past tense. She hoped it wasn't too late.

"That's not what I wanted to apologize for," she said. "I wanted to apologize for still holding what happened in 1982 against you. It was my choice as much as yours. But I never really let it go."

"It was a big thing to let go," Liam said kindly. "Again, I don't fault you."

"But that's not all." Alice felt a rush similar to the one she'd felt when she crashed Clyde's proposal. It was freeing to speak her mind, to let it all out there without worrying about the gossip or the consequences. Perhaps Georgiana had helped her with that this summer. "I'm sorry because I haven't been truthful about how I feel. I was so happy with David, truly."

Liam nodded bravely. He looked resigned to hear a rejection in yet another form. But Alice felt stronger and clearer now that Eloise knew about the affair. The secret was no longer searing. She had confessed to her daughter, to her late husband, to God. Rather than trying to edit past chapters, it was time to turn the page and start afresh.

"And your friendship over the years has meant so much. But as we've spent more time together, my feelings have changed. They have deepened." She took a breath, filling her lungs from the bottom up. "I am seventy-seven years old," Alice said, feeling the age of it, and the youth of it too. "And I believe I am falling back in love with you, Liam Townsend."

Liam stood there, blank in the face. But the shock didn't last long. He lit up with the glow of a teenage boy. Or perhaps the glow of a nearly eighty-year-old man, because who was to say that young people had a claim to love?

"Alice," Liam said, taking her hands in his and giving them a squeeze. "I know for you it has not always been me. That's okay. That has been your path. But for me, it has always been you. Always."

"You were with Camille for quite a while." Alice couldn't help but bring it up.

"And she left me because I couldn't commit," Liam said.

In spite of herself, Alice felt a jab of sympathy for Camille. She really wasn't that terrible; she just wasn't right for Liam. And certainly not right for mayor.

"You showed me so early in life how love could feel," Liam went on. "And I refused to ever settle for less."

"I just hope you're not building me up too much. I'm really quite ordinary."

"Says America's Grandmother. You have a light about you, Alice. Everyone can see it. And even if a time comes when no one can see it, I still will."

"So long as your eyes work," Alice joked. "Let's keep eating as many carrots as we can."

Liam broke into a grin that didn't feel like yesterday or tomorrow; it just felt like right now.

"Would you like to come inside for some now?" he said. "I was just about to have a snack."

"I suppose Georgiana can manage without me for the last few houses," Alice said, and she followed him inside.

Chapter 65

Gigi

"You're the perfect mascot for Mackinac," Gigi gushed to Noelle later that week.

She was brushing her out in the stables before a campaign rally later that afternoon. Willow was snacking on hay in the stall next door. They liked grazing in the grassy pasture together, munching on dandelions, sneezing out the seeds.

Through bonding with her horse, Gigi also felt like she was bonding with her dad. She hadn't fully psychoanalyzed that yet, but she texted her dad a selfie of her and Noelle now.

Gus was three in a row for the newly instated Sunday calls with Gigi and Rebecca. It wasn't much, but it wasn't nothing. Taking it week by week seemed to be working.

Gigi dropped kisses on the white star between Noelle's eyes. "We're going to be a power couple, you and me."

Noelle nuzzled close, her huge, tickly tongue slobbering over Gigi's face. *We already are*, Gigi felt Noelle saying. *We already are.*

"Should I be worried?" a voice asked. James was standing in the doorway, grinning with his hands stashed in his white doctor's coat. It was his lunch break. "I was under the impression that I was the other half to your power couple."

"It's stiff competition," Gigi said. "Get in line."

"I can fight," James joked.

Gigi greeted him with a kiss. It was long and slow, the kind of thing that made her feel like she was floating on a raft on a hot sunny day.

During their initial kiss in this barn three weeks ago and again today, Gigi was aware not only of what she was thinking about (taking that doctor's coat off him, having privacy at his place) but also what she wasn't.

She wasn't thinking about any of the people she'd kissed before, except in a vague sense of wanting to thank all thirty-four exes (Ronny had not been important enough to earn a spot on the list). They might not have been spectacular (and she could admit she wasn't perfect herself), but they had led her here, to this. Her thirty-fifth. And yet somehow, her first.

"I know you have a campaign rally to prep for," James said, reluctantly breaking apart. "I don't want to be a distraction."

"Relationships aren't distractions. They're propellants."

Gigi was reminded of playing dolls with Rebecca when they were younger. Her lively little sister used to invent happy endings for their dolls, back before Gus's absence sucked the optimism from her imagination.

This summer felt like getting that type of optimism back. For Gigi, for Rebecca, for Eloise. And maybe Alice too, who had certainly seemed to enjoy her campaign stop at Liam Townsend's house.

"Careful there," James said, wearing an amused smile. "You sound dangerously close to a character in one of those corny rom-coms you love to hate."

"Kissing my family-approved boyfriend in a horse barn in my tiny Midwest hometown definitely fits the trope," Gigi said. "But the heroines in those movies don't run for political office. They work at bakeries or Christmas tree farms."

"And they fall for lame guys who make them give up their big dreams to raise six kids on said farm," James said. "You, on the other hand, chose a guy who finds your ambition and unpredictability sexy as hell."

"Is that so?" Gigi said, feeling triumphant. She'd never been called ambitious before, though she'd always felt it, in an unconventional sort of way. She had never before had a guy embrace all of her, though that could have been because she had never before shown all of herself, or even known all of herself. "It's a good thing I'm a skilled multitasker. I can govern an island of five hundred residents while also having time for my boyfriend-slash-doctor."

"And if you're overexerting yourself, I'll be happy to give you a complimentary checkup," James offered. "A full-body exam, just to make sure you're adequately coping with the stress."

The temperature in the barn seemed to rise twenty degrees. "I need to go shower before my rally," Gigi said. "Just because I have to change outfits, not because I'm hot and sweaty picturing that."

"You're not wearing this?" he said, giving Gigi an appreciative once-over, from boots to breeches to ranch jacket. "It would show you're in touch with Mackinac's equestrian charm."

"Might not be a bad idea," Gigi said. "Noelle is more popular than me. Her videos get more views."

"You'd better watch out. She might be the dark horse in the election."

"Ha-ha."

"Never underestimate the power of a poorly executed dad joke to defuse the tension in a doctor's office," James said. "But in all seriousness, there was a dog elected mayor of a town in California."

"That's California for you," Gigi said, then gargled a laugh as she realized how much like her mom she sounded. "If Noelle or Willow edges me out, I'll take it gracefully. But no human is beating me, you can bet on that."

"I'm betting on you every time, Georgiana," James said.

"Good." Gigi loved how supportive he was. "Because I'm betting on you too. To be voted Michigan's Most Fragrant Doctor." Gigi pointed down at James's black oxfords, smeared with manure.

James swore under his breath. "You're trying not to laugh, aren't you?"

"Very hard." The corners of her mouth rippled.

"Your self-restraint is admirable. And if I'm already going to have to change my clothes . . ." James took another step toward her, a roguish glint in his eyes.

Gigi pinned him playfully against the barn's solid cedar wall and kissed him. Her body curled into him, wanting more.

"Don't tell on us," Gigi said to the horses. "We don't want the media catching hold of this one."

"Let them talk." James's hands were in her hair, a tangling and an unknotting all at once. "We've been through worse."

It was true. James had endured losing his mom and working himself half to death in the aftermath. He'd clawed out from grief through his own willpower, and when that wasn't enough, he'd quit the city grind and moved to Mackinac for the summer, and now longer. He'd dared to start over in a little island town, choosing peace over prestige and healing over hustling.

And Gigi, she'd been through her fair share too. So hell-bent on freeing herself from childhood traumas that she'd shut out the only people who'd ever really cared about her, stringing together deliberately shallow relationships with friends and lovers, cities and jobs. Villainizing everyone because at least playing victim was something consistent, something she excelled at.

Gigi and James were at the age where old people called them young and really young people called them old. They hadn't figured out life, but they'd figured out that they wanted to figure it out together. Their shoes and boots might be covered in muck and straw and sand, but here they were, still standing.

"All press is good press, right?" Gigi said, and instead of pulling James's mouth into hers again, she rested her cheek against his, feeling the rise and fall of their breath. She envisioned it moving through a water wheel, generating energy, like her mom used to tell her to do when she had a hard time sleeping after Gus first left all those years ago.

"Everything will be okay," her mom had said. It had taken Gigi twenty years to believe it, but she was starting to now.

She thanked the God who probably didn't exist—but might—that despite her best efforts to mess things up, she'd accidentally ended up exactly where she was supposed to be. In this single moment, at least.

As for tomorrow, or anything beyond Election Day . . . well, that was still up in the island air.

Chapter 66

Eloise

J ames is walking up the driveway," Eloise said later that week, looking out the front window at Thistle Dew. There were no longer
curtains to peer through. Eloise now kept them gathered to the side,
letting the sunlight trickle in as it pleased. "He's with someone."

"That'll be James's dad." Georgiana hopped down the steps from
the loft, dressed in faded Levi's and an oversized sweater.

Eloise lit a pumpkin candle.

She'd started to loosen up about the no-candles rule. She no longer
fretted so much that Georgiana would forget to blow them out and
burn the house down. And Eloise did love the scent of autumn.

She was so glad to still be on Mackinac.

It had been hard to tell in the moment if it was intuition or fear
that had kept her from going with Clyde, but now she felt confident it
was the former. Not just because of having a grandchild on the way,
though that was certainly something. She also felt it in her nervous
system.

Intuition is the answer that comes when you slow down your breath.
Fear is the answer that comes when you speed it up.

Eloise had written these words in an old, blank journal she'd found
on her bedroom bookshelf. The idea of writing a book was growing on her, especially with the girls so excited about it. Rebecca had
started organizing weekly family calls to create an outline. They were
currently in the "pre-draft ideation phase," as she called it.

They would see where it went, but Eloise had a good feeling. A good *intuition*.

She and Clyde had agreed to monthly emails. She had just received her first one but was waiting until tonight to read it. A bedtime story of sorts.

"His dad's name is Brian," Georgiana elaborated now as she raised her eyebrows at Eloise's candle. "James got him an apartment on Main Street for the next couple months. They're trying to do that whole father-son bonding thing. Things got rough when James's mom died."

Eloise hoped Gus might be figuring out that whole "father-daughter thing." Georgiana had started using a calendar, and Eloise had seen a yellow heart drawn around *4pm call with Dad*. Eloise was wary Gus would let them down again. He did seem to be trying, though whether he could sustain it remained to be seen. For now, the girls seemed cautiously optimistic, and Eloise would take their lead.

"And that's all very nice, but I didn't cook enough chili for extra guests," Eloise said to Georgiana now.

Having James around had started to feel like such a regular occurrence that Eloise now put him in the friends and family category, no longer bringing out the nicest place settings for him. It was rarefied air. None of Georgiana's past boyfriends had made this cut.

"I'll cook up some more veggies and pasta," Georgiana offered. "We'll make it work."

There was something a little too generous about the way she said it. Eloise's alarm bells chimed.

Thinking back, Eloise recalled some passing comments Georgiana had made about James's dad—that he was a widow, involved in his church, and loved his morning walks. Little things like that.

Eloise sized up her daughter. "Georgiana," she warned. "Don't tell me this is a setup."

"Of course not." Georgiana averted her eyes. "I just want you to meet my boyfriend's family. Is that a crime around here?"

"No, but you have that twinkle, like you're up to something."

"I'm just caught up in the glow of my feelings. Go ahead and rub it in."

"Rub what in?"

Gigi fiddled with the Petoskey stone necklace Eloise had crafted for her as a congratulations for launching her campaign. "How you just may have found me the love of my life."

Eloise felt it, the flush of accomplishment, the relief that Georgiana hadn't ended up with a yoga instructor in Australia after all. There were times it had felt like a very close call.

"I thought I was the great love of your life," Eloise teased.

"Well, obviously," Georgiana said, and she hardly even sounded sarcastic. "But I mean romantically speaking."

"What can I say? Sometimes mothers really do know best."

"Sometimes," Georgiana conceded. "And other times daughters do. I might've struck out with Clyde, but I'm not giving up yet. And just as a forewarning," she went on, before opening the door, "there's a nonzero chance that James's dad *might* think it's a double date."

Eloise felt her breath catch like bicycle chains changing gears. "And where might he have gotten that idea?"

"Not sure." Georgiana shrugged innocently. "Definitely not the conversation I had with him yesterday when I told him all about you and that he'd be the luckiest man on the planet to have a chance with you."

Eloise tried to scrounge up some anger. She couldn't, though exasperation stuck. "I thought we'd decided to stay out of each other's love lives."

"Had we?" Georgiana said, feigning forgetfulness. "Just promise you and Brian won't tie the knot before James and I do. Otherwise I'd be dating my stepbrother, and that isn't really a news story I want to bring to the island."

The landline rang. It would be Deirdre, reporting on James's father and his backstory. Or Alice with an update on her latest outing with Mr. Townsend. Eloise would catch up with them later. She ignored the phone and stood in front of the fireplace mantel, now free of all photos of Gus, except the one of the four of them that she'd moved out from her bedroom.

In the mirror hanging over the mantel, she pinched her cheeks for color and reapplied lip balm. She didn't feel so plain anymore. Clyde had seen something radiant in her and reflected it back. Maybe that was the purpose of her relationship with him—of every relationship, really. To help your partner see themselves a bit more clearly, a bit more beautifully, so that even when you weren't there anymore, the other person still felt the affirmations, held them as truth.

"Ready?" Georgiana asked.

Eloise's heart gave a jolt. The kind of thing she thought she'd lost when she'd given up Gus and then Clyde. But it was still here, still beating despite its beatings. She could do this. *They* could do this. "As ready as I'll ever be."

With Eloise standing just behind her, Georgiana opened the front door and welcomed James and his (very handsome) father into their home.

"Brian," Georgiana said, lips curling like a devil, like an angel, like a daughter. "I'd like you to meet my mother."

Chapter 67

Mackinac

The island looked happily on her work over the high season.

She had accomplished one of the more difficult tasks in her history. Not making Gigi and Eloise fall in love; that part was easy enough. The real triumph was in bringing them back to each other.

Mackinac was shifting seasons now, losing her touristy performance art. Everything was being stripped back. But the island wasn't worried that Gigi and Eloise's newfound bond would cool without the summer sun. Some things were powerful enough that they could heat icy streets in a Northern Michigan winter, dissolve the clouds that would shroud the island until springtime. Mother-daughter love was one of those things.

Mackinac put on a particularly powerful sunset one October night, the skies and lakes painted a vivid vermillion. There was nothing so special about this night that warranted extra attention. It was the mundanity of it that was so captivating. The way the locals' routines were setting the scene for the quiet months ahead.

Gigi and James, astride Noelle and Willow, galloped along the perimeter of the island, talking about Gigi's mayoral platform, the initiatives she would focus on first should she win. "The school has agreed to plant an organic garden," Gigi said. "We'll partner with the Pink Pony to create a signature dish with the produce. It'll make school less boring for the kids and teach them about sustainability. Plus, it'll show islanders that vegetarian food can actually taste good and they don't have to eat meat eight days a week. I've already talked with the Tongs about it too, and they like it."

"My girlfriend continues to amaze me," James said from atop Willow's saddle.

"Says the guy who resurrected someone from cardiac arrest today."

"It was simple CPR. Nothing impressive."

James's once-bare office looked homier now. On the wall was a beautiful framed photo of James and his mom. Gigi had surprised him with it on what would have been his mom's sixtieth birthday, and they had scattered dandelion seeds in her honor.

Eloise and Alice were doing a crossword at Alice's kitchen table, sipping chamomile tea. Alice had finally stopped brewing coffee for David and started boiling tea for herself, though in no way did that mean she had stopped holding him close. Alice was telling Eloise how she had found two pennies in the garden, that she had taken them as signs from David. "I felt like it was his blessing," Alice said. "For pursuing my relationship with Liam."

Eloise was listening, but her mind kept drifting toward James's father, Brian, with whom she'd frequently been getting coffees at the Lucky Bean, just to help him settle into island life, of course. Eloise had also received her second of the monthly emails from Clyde, in which he told her he was "fedora deep" in his manuscript. He also revealed who the book would be dedicated to: Bonny Lou. She didn't know yet how that made her feel. There would be time to sift through things later, decide what to keep and what to toss, what was gained and what was lost. For now, she was soaking up every minute of the Mackinac autumn and drinking more salted caramel lattes than she ever had before.

Off the coast, Rebecca and Tom were driving their new minivan up from Traverse City for a weekend of fall festivities. Rebecca was in her second trimester now. The baby had just started to kick—quite forcefully—which made Rebecca more confident that everything was coming along all right.

Kaley and Brody, their next-door neighbors, as well as Rebecca's college friend Maggie and her husband, Mike, were piled in the back of the van. A merging of old friends and new ones.

"I've heard all about the ghosts," Maggie said.

"Bring on the paranormal activity," Kaley added.

"Just to warn you, Mackinac is a place where the real-life people are more interesting than the phantoms," Rebecca said.

"Rebecca is writing a book about the island," Tom said proudly.

"My whole family is writing it together," Rebecca clarified. "All the women, at least. A couple of friends too."

Inside their bedroom with the newly fixed blinds fully drawn, Deirdre and Fred were cuddled up close, drafting a letter to Deirdre's daughter. After much searching, they had located her contact information. Deirdre couldn't believe it. There was no such thing as false hope; Fred had been right about that. And no matter how it went, she and Fred were in this together. She pulled him under the sheets with her. It was amazing how much more energy she had for romance now that the secret wasn't clogging so much space in her heart.

The Main Street shops were closed for the night but not yet the season. Street sweepers cleared out trash and horse muck, brooms swooshing. Seasonal workers, the stragglers who were procrastinating their inevitable return to the real world, gathered around a beach bonfire, taking bets on whether Gigi Jenkins was more likely to become president of the United States or the star of a reality TV show. "Probably both," they agreed, noting how it wouldn't be the first time in American history. They'd all gotten her autograph, determined their fortune would come from reselling it one day.

The Pink Pony no longer had a wait for tables, but a lively crowd persisted—locals who were again venturing downtown now that it wasn't corked with tourists. Trina Tong stepped outside to answer a call from Lillian. They talked mostly of the restaurant and Lillian's new job at an environmental law firm that helped protect the Great Lakes. "I'm making enough money to support you and Dad," she told

Trina. "I can pay off the mortgage; you can retire." Trina was touched by the offer but rebuffed it immediately. "I like to work," Trina told her daughter. "It's who I am." Lillian knew better than to bring it up again.

Camille Welsh was relaxing in the outdoor jacuzzi of the Pink Pony, sipping a Mackinac mule as she hosted one of her hot tub town halls. Her legs were sore from the hundred-mile bicycle charity ride she'd recently completed. The plan had been for her to give her donations to an animal shelter on the island, but she had found a loophole to divert the funds to her mayoral campaign instead. She needed it, given how Georgiana was surging with that darned social media. China was probably capturing the data and spying on the island this very moment. Still, Camille was counting on the loyalty of the old-timers to get her reelected. After all, *change* was still a four-letter word on Mackinac.

The Grand Hotel sat on its perch, already missing the summer crowds, particularly the boisterous author who at this moment was sitting up in the middle of the Scottish night, penning the first draft of the story that would feature Mackinac as its main character. It was fortunate that the breakup had not thwarted Clyde's plans. On the contrary, he seemed more inspired than ever to showcase the island, or so were the reports from the ghosts, who had intel from their Scottish counterparts. The ghosts on the Mackinac side also relayed that Clyde's book would not be the only book published about their dear island. There were reports that another book was being drafted. It was hard to trace down the author, as the pen seemed to switch hands quite often, but the ghosts were on the case.

The governor's mansion stood empty at the brink of the shore, with a "Georgiana Jenkins for Mayor" sign in the perfectly manicured yard. Before flying out for the summer, the governor had come down from her perch on the top of the cliff and attended one of Gigi's rallies, even posing for a selfie that nearly broke the internet. Rumor had it that the prior governor's son, Alexander Vanderhosen III (yes, to this day he insisted that the roman numerals be used in every article about him), had donated to Gigi's campaign. Maybe because he believed in her candidacy, maybe because he wanted to dissuade her from going public with her side of the story.

Gus Jenkins was not on the island, but his presence lingered like a low-hanging fog that never quite burned off. He would be back for Election Day to cast his vote for Gigi (he was still registered to vote locally). Eloise had told Gus she'd be glad to have him join them for dinner but that he'd have to find another place to stay. He'd faltered at that, only letting it drop when he saw Eloise wasn't going to change her mind.

More permanent in his departure was Officer Ronny, who was headed for his next rotation in the Upper Peninsula and taking very little with him except a stack of phone numbers. The most frequent prayer heard inside the Little Stone Church these days was that Ronny wouldn't be staffed on the island ever again. Never had the congregation been so united on an issue.

Kitty and Paula were on the north side of the island, squeezed onto the same electric scooter, out for a joy ride.

"Georgiana's got my vote if she makes these legal!" Kitty hooted as she drove.

Paula held on tightly. "Who needs them to be legal? It'll just clog up the roads. I like keeping it underground."

"Good point," Kitty said, and they disappeared into the night.

A certain Liam Townsend could be found bent over his underwear drawer, pulling out a ring box he had kept hidden there for so long. He had first bought it at age seventeen for his high school sweetheart, before she'd left him for that smooth-talking David, who'd swooped in from downstate. The diamond might need a bit of a polish, but it was still in good shape. Liam had known quality even back then. His joints weren't fit for kneeling, but he'd find the right way to ask. Hide it in a pickleball, maybe, or inside a roll of pennies. Alice loved pennies; frugality was one of her qualities that might drive him crazy if they spent every day together. He'd like the chance to find out.

Earlier in the day, Lillian updated Gigi on recent life events. She told Gigi how she was heading to a Chicago recording studio after a rewarding day at work. Lillian was working on her debut single, an indie pop ballad about the latest woman she'd accidentally fallen in love with: herself. It was called "For Lillian." "I'm not sure if that makes me egotistical or emotionally healthy," Lillian said. "Probably both," Gigi said, and they shared a giggle.

Noelle, Willow, and the other horses in the Grand Hotel stable were munching on hay bales, tails swatting the last of the fleas that hadn't yet been zapped by the frosts. There was a heightened buzz in the barn, the animals sensing that they'd soon be moving downstate for the off-season. They would miss it here. Nowhere else were they the stars of the show, doted on day and night, never competing with cars or trucks for attention like they had to at their winter residences.

Mackinac released a long breath. The waves lapped and the trees shook, dropping leaves as mementos of the past season. The island could rest now. Her work was done. For now, at least. There was always next year. She never stopped with her machinations, never ceased with her scheming.

That, after all, was the magic of Mackinac Island.

Acknowledgments

Thank you to everyone who helped bring this book to life.

This is my third published novel and my first to be classified in the women's fiction genre. The journey has been both challenging and deeply rewarding, and I'm grateful to have had an incredible team with me along the way.

To my literary agent, Emma Parry: Thank you for believing in my vision, challenging me to elevate my writing, and securing my best book deal yet. Your guidance, wisdom, and confidence in my potential have been invaluable.

To Amanda Bostic at Harper Muse, for seeing my writing as something bigger than just romance and helping me break out of the rom-com box into women's fiction. I'm thrilled and honored to be part of the Muse family.

To my editor, Kimberly Carlton, for asking such insightful questions, identifying gaps and opportunities, and helping me shape what I feel is my strongest work yet. You encouraged me to bring out the depth and heart of this story in ways I couldn't have achieved alone, and it was a joy to work together.

To my copyeditor, Julie Breihan, for meticulously combing through this manuscript time and time again. Your skillful eye and attention to detail ensured that every word shines.

To the entire team at Harper Muse, for treating the book with such care and dedication. I'm grateful for the support you've given to launch this book into the world.

To the inner voice that never lets me give up, even during those years of hearing "no" while working a corporate job and dreaming of becoming an author. You kept me relentlessly focused on making this dream a reality.

To God, for blessing me with the creativity, courage, and resilience to share my work with the world.

To my family, for your unwavering love and support. A special thank-you to my mom and grandmother, who inspired me to write a multigenerational story and explore different perspectives.

To my friends, especially Alyssa and Addison, to whom this book is dedicated. Thank you for visiting Mackinac Island with me when the idea for this story first blossomed. Your encouragement and enthusiasm have been such a gift.

To the island of Mackinac and her people, for your charm, kindness, and endless inspiration. You are a magnificent muse.

And to Declan, for helping me fly while keeping my feet firmly on the ground—a paradox I will be reveling in forever.

Discussion Questions

1. Mackinac Island is more than just a backdrop—it shapes the characters' journeys. In what ways does the island's unique culture, history, and quirks influence the story and its themes?

2. Gigi and Eloise's relationship evolves from fraught to supportive as they transition into friends and confidantes. How do the events of the summer—particularly the matchmaking scheme—facilitate this shift? Do you think they would have reached this level of understanding without it?

3. The book explores Gigi's mother wound, but the father wound is also significant. How do these wounds intersect for Gigi, and what did you think of her healing journey with both her parents?

4. Have you and your mother (or another family member) ever played matchmaker for each other? If so, how did it compare to Gigi and Eloise's experience?

5. Among the women featured in the book—including Mackinac Island herself—which did you connect with the most and why? Whose character arc felt the most personally fulfilling to you?

6. Lillian's presence plays a key role in Gigi's arc. How does her character contribute to Gigi's growth? In what ways is the summer back on the island equally transformative for Lillian?

7. The novel touches on themes of unity across generations, urban vs. rural divides, and even political differences. Why do you think Mackinac Island is the ideal setting for a story with these themes? Which theme felt the most powerful to you?

8. Gigi resists James for much of the story. What do you think drives her resistance, and how does their relationship ultimately help Gigi evolve? What lessons does this romance bring to the broader themes of the novel?

9. Even though Eloise and Clyde aren't together at the end of the novel, their connection plays a significant role in Eloise's healing. What do you think Clyde represents for Eloise, and how does their relationship help her grow?

10. The novel's ending leaves room for imagination. What do you envision happens to the cast of characters after the final chapter? Do you think Gigi will become mayor and stay on the island?

11. If there were to be a sequel, whose story would you most want to follow? What aspects of Mackinac Island or its residents would you love to see explored further?

About the Author

LINDSAY MACMILLAN is an author, speaker, and creative entrepreneur. A Dartmouth graduate and four-time TEDx speaker, she left her role as a vice president at Goldman Sachs to follow her passion for writing. This is her third published book and her debut women's fiction novel.

———— ≈ ————

Visit her online at lindsaymacmillancreative.com